Other Novels by Mildred Walker
Available in Bison Books Editions

THE CURLEW'S CRY

DR. NORTON'S WIFE

FIREWEED

IF A LION COULD TALK

LIGHT FROM ARCTURUS

THE QUARRY

THE SOUTHWEST CORNER

UNLESS THE WIND TURNS

WINTER WHEAT

Mildred Walker

THE BREWERS' BIG HORSES

Introduction to the Bison Books Edition
by David Budbill

UNIVERSITY OF NEBRASKA PRESS
LINCOLN AND LONDON

∞ The paper in this book meets the minimum requirements of American National Standard for Information Sciences—Permanence of Paper for Printed Library Materials, ANSI Z39.48-1984.

First Bison Books printing: 1996
Most recent printing indicated by the last digit below:
10 9 8 7 6 5 4 3 2 1

Library of Congress Cataloging-in-Publication Data
Walker, Mildred, 1905–
The brewers' big horses / Mildred Walker; introduction to the Bison Books edition by David Budbill.
p. cm.
ISBN 0-8032-9786-6 (pa: alk. paper)
I. Title.
PS3545.A524B7 1996
813′.52—dc20
96-31427 CIP

Reprinted from the original 1940 edition by Harcourt, Brace and Company, New York.

To

M. R. S.

who is intolerant only
of knaves and intolerance

INTRODUCTION

David Budbill

I wonder if fiction writers still sit around and talk about who will write the great American novel. I suppose they don't. This is a time of small dreams, diminished ambitions, a jaded age. No epics for us. But if somewhere they still do, then the answer to the question must be that nobody ever will because so many already have. And Mildred Walker's *The Brewers' Big Horses* must be one of them. In order to write a "great" novel you've got to go after something big, something great, and in *The Brewers' Big Horses* Mildred Walker does. In her usual modest, self-effacing, ladylike way Walker tackles the great themes and conflicts that still swirl around the question of what it means to be an American.

Set in the late nineteenth century in Armitage City, a middle-sized city in Michigan built on the treacherous logging industry and on the backs of the French Canadians who worked in the woods, on the rivers, and in the mills, the novel begins wrapped in the sedate elegance through which the upper classes float.

> When the spring drive was on, the west side of Armitage City, where the crocuses were just starting through the wide green lawns, turned a deaf ear. If the ladies at the last meeting of the Winter Club heard the dull drumming of the logs through their reading of *The Merchant of Venice* they kept their minds on culture. Most of the wealth behind those big houses on the west side had come from just such pitch-covered logs of white pine ridden down the river by the swearing lumberjacks, but the ladies of the first families knew precious little about the sources of their luxuries.

Thus Mildred Walker articulates the essentials of class awareness and conflict that will remain at the heart of her story and to this day remain at the heart of our American story.

From the very beginning the world in Armitage City is divided into the west side and the east side, into the upper classes and the lower classes. At the age of nine Sara Bolster takes a ride on a beer wagon. She smells the sweaty driver, the sweaty horses, the beer. Right away the world is divided into the sensuous, earthy lower classes and their peasant ways and the withdrawn, orderly, proper, cool, and aloof manners of the upper crust. Sara's mother's name is, for heavens sake, Corona.

From the beginning Sara is in conflict with these upper-class ways; she is a tomboy; her father, in fact, calls her the boy in a family of daughters. Sara is a sometimes reckless, sometimes impudent young woman intent on following her own path, which she does no matter what kind of hot water it lands her in and it lands her in plenty. She is, it is clear from the beginning, a nascent feminist.

Paul, Sara's childhood friend and would-be boyfriend, says to Sara one day, "Girls are lucky; they don't have to think of doing anything useful." To which Sara frowns and says, "I do wish I were a man." Shortly after that, Sara says to her mother, "Mama, why can't I do something? I'm eighteen and I'm sick of being around home and sewing and making leather things for the church bazaar. I could be a secretary or—or *something*."

At the age of twenty-one Sara gets a job, to the consternation of her family, as a reporter on the local paper, the *Courier*, where she not only hears, much to her delight, the tough talk of hardened and cynical newspapermen but egalitarian talk as well. While the upper crust attends to the establishment culture of the day, in the city room at the *Courier* they are reading Walt Whitman and discussing the pros and cons of the labor strike for a ten-hour day. For someone who is supposed to be a society girl, it's fast company and a different world, and Sara loves, absolutely revels in, the difference. Her fascination does not go unnoticed. At one point, Little Rollo, tough guy and journeyman editor, who becomes her School-Of-Hard-Knocks writing teacher, observes that "the fair virgin hath a listening ear."

Sara is ready then to meet and fall in love with the "foreigner" William Henkel, a young doctor in town and the son of the founder and owner of Henkel's brewery. If Sara's family was upset by her newspaper job, they are now horrified that she has taken up with one of "the foreign element" and a brewer's son to boot! On Sara's first visit to the brewery William says something about the architecture of the brewery building itself that sums up everything Margaret Walker is trying to tell us about the difference between the upper and the lower classes. William says, "When I grow tired of the false pomposity of some of the buildings on Main Street I come down and look at the brewery. It's just what it is; no false front, no ornamentation; as German-looking as the beer we make."

Later, after they are married, Walker lets William make the same point again, this time with food. William and Sarah are about to entertain some of Sara's stuffy family friends with a dinner party, fussy food. William says to Sara, "Sorry, Liebchen, but I don't like course dinners with a wine for every course and port afterwards. They leave me with a headache and there's no . . . joy in them. We all go solemnly through our paces; there's no spontaneity." William prefers, as we find out later, hash, hard bread, and beer, and a lot of talk and laughter.

With Sara's marriage to William she enters this other world, the "foreign element," these brewers of . . . beer! When the WCTU (The Women's Christian Temperance Union) attacks the Henkel brewery, Sara understands for the first time what it is like to be on the other side, the outside:

> All her life she had belonged to one of the leading families of Armitage, representative of all that was best in culture and tradition in the city. It was a new experience to be connected now with a business that a whole group of people felt was detrimental. She had never encountered hostility until today. She held her head under the sailor hat a little higher as she crossed the street. . . .

Sara's independence of spirit, her daring, her feminism have gotten her in trouble. It is interesting to read a story written more than fifty years ago and set more than a hundred years ago in which the heroine struggles with the same issues that so many women struggle with today.

The book becomes at this point the story of how this strong-willed woman with an indomitable spirit and an iron will deals with the plethora of troubles and public disapproval that await her. Don't worry that I've given away too much of the plot; this is only the beginning. This novel has enough action, twists, and turns in the story line to fill half a dozen novels. To accommodate it, Mildred Walker needs a heroine of epic proportions, for she is out to write an epic.

Readers should attend to the epigraphs that writers choose for their books. Writers mean to tell their readers something with them. *The Brewers' Big Horses* is divided into three parts; each part begins with a quotation from Homer's *Odyssey* in which the proud and powerful horses leap forward at dawn and course through the day until darkness falls. These horses represent energy and life and the will to power that inform this novel; they also represent so much power that once it is out of control the potential for destructiveness is overwhelming, a heartbreaking fact Sara must face again and again.

In other words, what Mildred Walker is after here is something big, epical, and the quotations—from an epic poem that stands in the European tradition as one of the definitions of the epic—are Walker's way of letting us know what her intentions are for this novel. Mildred Walker will have nothing to do with small dreams or diminished ambitions. She, like Homer, intends to tell a great tale, the story of her country, a story of energy, power, and life, and a woman's will to possess those things. But this is an American epic and made even more American by the mundanity of the situation, for this is an epic centered around something as lowly and ordinary as beer.

This story is also about "the romance of America," as William Henkel puts it. The young William Henkel tells Sara's father that he and Sara could be happy in spite of the differences in their backgrounds because of "the romance of America"—the idea that neither class nor background nor ethnic group nor race should matter, but that human love and goodness, hard work, honesty, and good humor should unite us all. To which one of Sara's upper-class sisters says, "Fiddlesticks!"

The Brewers' Big Horses begins in 1882 and ends in 1918; Walker has some territory to cover and she does it with great mastery, because she knows how to use what, for lack of a better phrase, I'll call the Tempo of Plot. She knows how to move her story along, how to accelerate the action when economy demands, then slow it down and make it move so slowly that we can observe the minutest details. At these times she gives the reader a feeling of great, luxurious space within which the story can amble, as if no one, least of all the author, were in any hurry to press on with what happens next. Then just as suddenly as things slowed down the story leaps forward again, vaulting over years while Walker sketches in only the broadest outline.

At the end of the book the tempo becomes so fast, the events tumbling upon each other with such hectic alacrity, we have trouble keeping up and we are as breathless as her characters as they plunge through the twists and turns of their lives. It's as if we were little children and Walker were yanking all of us, characters and readers alike, down the street toward the end to which we must for some reason hurry. The rush of events seems so surprising, sudden, and intense, that the book ends abruptly, unexpectedly. As the plot tumbles over itself to conclude itself, there is no finality. So many possibilities for the lives of the characters have opened up that the end has become only another beginning.

In *The Brewers' Big Horses* we again get to enjoy Mildred Walker's wonderful metaphorical abilities. She is a novelist, not a poet, and therefore has more on her mind than metaphor—she must attend to character, setting, plot—but although she uses metaphors sparingly, the ones used have the explosive, illuminating brilliance of fireworks. For example, as the men and women watch and applaud the floats in the Fourth of July parade, Walker says, "The men's hands made a bare sharp sound; the women's hands were muted by their gloves and sounded more like book covers flopped closed again and again." Or after Sara's husband dies and Sara sits wondering what happens next, Walker says of Sara's future, "Life stretched ahead as empty as William's closet." Two categorically different kinds of metaphors, both equally interesting.

There are metaphors here likening a brewery to a bakery and the brewing process to the movements of a symphony. There is, by the way, a plethora of detail about the process of making beer; beer drinkers and home brewers alike are going to love this book.

One other stylistic matter: Mildred Walker completely avoids irony and irony's extreme sister, sarcasm, which surely are the two tyrannies of contemporary literature, the modern style. This is an earnest and quietly impassioned writer with not even a drop of our contemporary obsession which, it seems to me, must place her suddenly in the avant-garde.

In *The Brewers' Big Horses* Mildred Walker—like her protagonist Sara, between whom one suspects there is a deep autobiographical connection—challenges established and establishment views on everything from the rights of laborers, to the arrogance of the upper classes, to the misuses of art, literature, music, clothing, and food—"culture"—to create an elite, to bigoted attitudes toward "the foreign element," to the narrow-minded attitudes of prohibitionists, jingoistic warmongers, the WCTU, and turn-of-the-century evangelist and charlatan, Billy Sunday.

Walker takes on these themes with the same boldness and daring her heroine does. Readers, if they are not careful, might miss this since it is easy to mistake Walker's modesty, her quiet good manners, for smallness, something foreign to Mildred Walker. The novel for Walker is clearly a place to articulate and think about the deepest and most important questions that a culture and a group of people have to ask.

Perhaps most illustrative of Walker's bold daring is that at the heart of *The Brewers' Big Horses* is a warm-hearted, enthusiastic, and loving portrait of German Americans. Not necessarily bold or especially daring in itself until you learn that this book was first published in 1940, a scant year before we entered World War Two. Mildred Walker is a self-conscious and deliberate writer and it could not have been a mistake that she flew in the face of the growing anti-German sentiment and at the same time refused to be jingoistic in any way, but instead sings the praises of "the foreign element" and also articulates a mother's fear of war. One wonders if her portraits of the myopically narrow-minded WCTU and Billy Sunday's evangelism aren't Mildred Walker's way of talking about all kinds of intolerance and demagoguery.

Walker, in this historical context, demonstrates a wonderful kind of guts, chutzpah, a recklessness in the face of establishment opinion. Behind Walker's quiet modesty hides an audacious and committed writer intent on doing what she is called to do in a time when following her own path could land her in a whole lot of trouble, just as such a path did for her heroine Sara.

I have concentrated on the social and political aspects of this story—the daring nature of a tale of a woman's will to energy and power—yet *The Brewers' Big Horses* is equally a sweet and gentle story of human relationships. At the risk of calling down upon my head the wrath of the Harpies, I want to say that this is, in addition to everything else, a story told by a woman with a woman's sensibilities. Mildred Walker has here, as she has in all of her work, an unerring eye for the subtle delicacies and nuances of relationships, how people feel in unspoken ways about each other. No one surpasses Mildred Walker at revealing the unspoken in human interaction.

Again and again at critical junctures where Sara must make a difficult and irrevocable decision, Sara does so with determination and will, yet immediately afterward we see her plunge into paroxysms of self-doubt. Her self-critical agonies over how her decision will affect her children, for example, are touching and real. Would a male writer have included these sections?

And the ways in which Sara and her childhood friend, Paul, both become more and more like their fathers as they grow older, yet also forge new and different lives by avoiding some of the traps into which their fathers fell is a story within this story steeped in deep psychological observation and importance.

In addition to her feminist sensibilities and deep psychological observations, Mildred Walker is a romantic writer. There are passages here about clothing and food and furnishings that Sara might have written for the society page of the *Courier*. *The Brewers' Big Horses* is, at times, a "ladies' romance," yet all this romance rushes out of a radical, dare I say revolutionary, heart.

The Brewers' Big Horses has a cinematic quality, almost as if it were already a screenplay. There are vivid, shifting scenes that move with the swiftness of a filmmaker's jump cuts. It's a period piece with plenty of opportunity for a great variety of costumes and sets illustrating both the upper-class west side of town and the lower-class east side; there are loggers and drunks, prostitutes and arrogant snoots, brewery workers, immigrants, and simple, hard-working stiffs. There are men and women and those magnificent brewers' big horses and action galore. In other words, why doesn't some woman producer/director/actress discover this book and find in it and in Sarah Bolster Henkel an epical, feminist heroine for our time? This novel is a movie just waiting to be made.

Finally, *The Brewers' Big Horses* is an enormously entertaining novel. It is, as the blurbers say, "a page turner . . . a great read." Prost!

PART ONE

Day-break: and the rosy-tinted fingers of dawn crept up the sky.

Now it is time to harness the long-maned, proud-tailed horses.

THE ODYSSEY OF HOMER
BK. III
Translation by T. E. Shaw

I 1882

THERE was more room to breathe outdoors. In the tall house back of her a hushed atmosphere spread like heavy carpeting over the rooms. All yesterday and all last night there had been an air of waiting. Even the clock's face in the hall seemed anxious as though it held back its stroke. Dr. Barnes had come and gone as though he were living here. Sara had sat on the landing of the stairs most of the morning, watching the silent panels of her mother's bedroom door. Just before the long hand of the clock joined the short hand at twelve she had escaped from the house. When the baby was born Dorothea would come and tell her.

If she walked back and forth across the terrace ten times perhaps it would happen. It must be a boy; Papa was counting on a son. He had always said that she was his son and Sara had liked that, but now if the baby were a boy everything would be different. It would be queer, though, not to have to try to be Papa's boy any more.

Sara started across the terrace the eleventh time. She passed the corner of the porch and the summerhouse and the lilac bush and came to the hedge between their grounds and the Sevrances'. She turned around stiffly as Uncle Tracy did—Uncle Tracy who had been in the Civil War. Nothing on earth would make her stir from her post of guard. Perhaps she would hear the baby cry even before Dorothea came to tell her. That was the first thing that babies did, Emma Carthugh said. Emma had younger brothers and sisters and knew all about babies. Sara had only older sisters.

The terrace in front of the Bolsters' home sloped down a hundred and fifty feet to the avenue. Not a dandelion or a blade of plantain marred its smooth green weave; the heavy clover gave it a self-figure like a fancy afghan.

Sara started counting the carriages that passed, but the intervals between were too long. She gave up walking back and forth and sat on the base of the sundial, leaning her chin on her hand. It would be nice to have a baby brother. He would be younger than she by seven years. But he would be nearer her age than Belle or Anne or Dorothea. Belle and Anne were both married and Dor was grown up. The baby would sleep in the nursery with her for a while, and she could play with him early in the morning when the rest of the house was asleep.

Noise along the avenue jerked her head up instantly; a jingling of horses' bridles, the sound of an enormous clop-clop of hoofs, the heavier rolling thunder of big wheels.

Sara ran down the terrace and stood beside the black hitching-post, swinging around it by the iron ring. The dray was drawn by four horses. The barrels on top brushed the branches of the big elms. The driver had red cheeks and a big black mustache. He held the reins of the horses proudly, like the picture in the library of Apollo driving the sun across the sky. He waved his big whip so the tassel at the end quivered up in the trees and came to rest as lightly as a fly on the front horse. His straw cuffs made him look very fancy.

Sara watched the dray, held by the colors and the size and the power of the horses. The first horses had red tassels hanging down from their bridles and their tails were braided with ribbons. All the silver parts of their harness shone as brightly as the silver teapot. She looked at the forest of gray and white legs, some lifting up, some coming down. They were the largest horses she had ever seen. They were beautiful. The front horse on her side rolled his eyes; white foam oozed from his soft, full lips. Sara hugged the hitching-post as they came close to the curb. She was only as high as the floor of the wagon; the big barrels towered above her like a wall.

On the crosspiece that ran along the side of the dray she spelled out the name JOHN HENKEL BREWING CO.

The driver saw her and laughed. He wiped his straw-cuffed arm across his mouth and waved. His black mustache was like the tassels on the horses' bridles. He called out to her in German and pulled the horses up. He was stopping. He had to lean way back, and his shoulders showed wet when the shirt stretched tight across.

"Wie geht's! You like John Henkel's new team, eh?"

Sara drew the curl at the end of her braid tight across her cheek and chewed it between her teeth in an agony of shyness. The man's shirt was open on his chest way down to the belt and showed his heavy underwear beneath. Black hair as thick and black as a puppy's cropped out above the shirt.

"Very much," Sara Bolster stammered out.

"You want a ride?" He grinned down at her.

She wanted it more than anything else. She looked quickly back at the gray cupola of the house.

The terrible man set the wooden brake. He was climbing down now. She slipped a little back of the hitching-post. The man smelled queerly. He lifted her up, her blue dress against his shirt. Her hair caught on his straw cuffs and pulled.

She knew she shouldn't go; she tried to shake her head, to say no, but he was so big, so quick. He set her on the seat beside him. She was higher up than the swing would go—as high, anyway. The smell from the barrels behind her was strong here. It was still a little sour but almost pleasant. It was almost a good smell. He had stopped just under the trees and it was cooler up here. The horses' backs were so broad! Their ears were laid back as though to hear what was happening back of them.

"My name is Sara Bolster," she said breathlessly.

The man laughed. "Sara, eh? Me, I'm Charlie Freehahn."

He didn't seem to know her father as everyone in Armitage City did.

"Round the block?" he said in a voice that asked no questions. It was as though he said, "Round the world."

"The nigh horse's name is Thor, an' the far one, Donner. 'N that one with the all-white mane's Minna and the gray's Star; got a star right in his forehead." Charlie Freehahn pointed out each horse with the tip of the long whip.

The horses were trotting. They made a splendid sound. Their tassels blew out from their bridles. The leaves of the trees swished against the barrels. It was far better than the swing, better even than a merry-go-round. She wished the girls could see her, or Paul. He would stop boasting then about seeing the races at Saratoga. Even this hot day the hair blew back from her face, they were going so fast.

Charlie Freehahn looked down at her and laughed. He waved his hand in a fine gesture of hilarity.

"Hi-y-ih!"

Sara squealed too. She had never in her life had so much fun.

"Were these horses ever in the races?" she shouted to him over the rumble of the wagon and the jingle of the harness.

"Races?" Charlie Freehahn laughed as though he would never stop. "Mit little thin jumpy horses? Nein." He frowned down at her so darkly she wondered if she had hurt his feelings. "Race horses is afraid from these horses. You know how much a race horse weighs?"

She shook her head, keeping her eyes on Mr. Freehahn's ever-changing face. He gathered his lips together judiciously. "Say nine hunderd pound, an' these!" His whole expression changed. His cheeks rounded and the high part under his eyes shone with perspiration and pride. "Twenty-two hunderd pound Donner weighs!"

"My!" Sara said. "I'll tell Paul that. He thinks racing horses are wonderful."

Charlie Freehahn disposed of racers with an airy gesture of his thumb across his palm. "They'll be getting the policemans out after me if I don't get you back quick." He pulled hard on the reins. The horses' necks arched just like Apollo's horses in the picture. He set the brake and climbed down. He picked her up as though she weighed nothing and swung her down by the hitching-post.

She was surprised to be back home. She had a swift impression again of the smell of Mr. Freehahn's clothes and his breath as he lifted her. "Thank you ever so much," she said quickly, remembering her manners. "I had a very nice time."

"You won't ever look scared again when you see handsome horses like these, will you, eh?"

"But I wasn't really," she assured him solemnly.

He laughed and pinched her cheek. She watched him climb up over the wheel and lift the whip, and she stood by the hitching-post until the jingle of the harness and the rumbling of the wheels had merged again into one sound. Then she raced back up across the lawn so full of her experience she had to tell someone about it; not Mama—Mama might mind her riding on a dray. Papa wouldn't, though. He would call her his boy.

She went in through the summer kitchen. Mary was slicing ham in thin pink slivers that fell over the knife onto a curled heap. Mary held the knife in mid-air. The inside of her hand was pink like the ham, but the back of the hand was almost black, like her face.

"Where have you been, Miss, running off on some wild-goose chase with a brother being born right under your own roof!"

"Mary, have I really?" Sara rushed across to Mary and hugged her, jumping up and down until Mary's skinny body was joggled up and down, too. "Can I go and see him now?"

"You set here and wait and I'll see. I just took your father's best port into the library for the doctor. An' I give 'em the damask napkins an' the crystal glasses. It's time your father had a son so's you could learn to be a lady like your sisters."

Sara washed her hands at the sink and ate a slice of ham. Then she pushed the swing door softly open.

She had a brother! Mama and Papa would be so happy. When she was twenty he would be . . . twenty take away seven makes . . . she stopped in the shadowy dining room to think it out. There was a thin coating of dust on the corner of the mahogany sideboard and she wrote the sum with her finger . . . thirteen! He would be named Winthrop Bolster, after Papa, of course.

"My brother, Winthrop," she said in the hall. The library door was open. She could see Papa and Dr. Barnes sitting by the table sipping from the crystal glasses. They were talking politics, she could tell. She stood still just beyond the threshold and admired her father as she always did. He was so handsome. He looked like pictures of "Great Men." Once she asked Mama if Papa was great, too. And Mama had said with that tone of voice that settled everything:

"Your father is a gentleman, Sara; that is greatness in itself." It was a satisfaction to her.

She would like to run in and climb on Papa's knee and have him tell her about the baby, but with Dr. Barnes there she hesitated. Mama was strict about interrupting grownups.

Mary came downstairs with a queer, unjoyful look on her face.

"Can I, Mary, can I go up and see him?"

"Hush, child." Mary brushed her aside and crossed the hall to the library. "Excuse me, sir." She went in and pulled the roll door closed after her.

Sara curled her finger around the oak leaf carved on the newel post. Mary had looked almost scared. She had never seen Mary scared before.

The door was rolled back so hard it banged into the wall. Dr. Barnes came across the hall without seeming to see Sara and ran up the stairs. Papa went after him. Sara had never seen Papa move so fast. Mary stood in the hall looking after them, her brown face twisted.

"What happened, Mary?"

But Mary ran out of the hall with her apron over her head.

Sara opened the front door and closed it solemnly behind her. It was dusk now, but it was not soft with shadows and the smell of the syringa and wet grass the way it was sometimes. It was empty and sad. For a while she had had a brother. And now he was dead. It wasn't hardly worth being born at all. She had never even seen him alive.

Papa had taken her in to see him. He was so tiny and cunning lying in the bassinet. It was hard to believe he was dead. How could Mama stand it?

But worst of all had been Dr. Barnes' face when he came out of Mama's room. He didn't speak to anyone. She had watched him climb into his buggy and drive away. Mary had come in from the dining room and shaken her head.

"He's the same as a murderer!" Mary had said.

"But, Mary, how could he have let the baby bleed to death?" She couldn't understand.

"He didn't tie the cord right. When I went in I see the ugly red spot on his wrapper and I looked!" Mary rolled her eyes. "And me takin' him the oldest port in the house!"

Just before supper Mama had called them all in; she looked little in the big bed. She held Papa's hand.

"What happened was an accident. Dr. Barnes brought you all into the world and he would gladly cut off his hand to bring this baby back to life . . ." Mama's voice had trembled. She had to wait a minute before she could go on. "If this were known it would only hurt him and . . ." she had stopped again as though she couldn't make the words . . . "it wouldn't bring back the baby."

Sara remembered now how still the room was. Papa's breathing had sounded loud. Belle sat on the other side of the bed. She was the oldest. Anne was standing by the fireplace. Dorothea was crying softly. Sara always thought of them as her grown-up sisters, but right then they had seemed like little girls, too.

"No one knows anything about it except ourselves. No one will ever know. The baby was born dead." Mama's voice didn't tremble any more.

Sara climbed up into the mulberry tree, but even being so high up didn't ease the ache. The sky had lost all its color except a little bluish tint far off. It was like the color of the baby's skin. She had touched the baby's hand, and thinking of it now made her knot her fingers in the pocket of her jacket.

Winthrop, they would have named him, Papa said, just as she had thought: Winthrop Bolster. Sara looked out through the branches across the lawn to the road and heard Papa's voice saying the name.

There was Derrick's buggy. Derrick was Belle's husband. Sara liked him. He had been out the valley on business and was coming back late. He was whistling.

Sara watched him throw his reins carelessly around the whipstock and step out. He didn't know yet about the baby. It seemed too bad that he would be as sad as the rest of them in a few minutes.

It was a long time back to this morning when she had gone for a ride on the big brewery wagon.

Then she remembered; she would still have to take the place of a son for Papa.

2 1884

SARA had the distinct feeling as she came into the dining room that Mama had glanced suddenly across at Papa and they had stopped talking about something.

"Excuse me, Mama, for being late," she murmured, and squeezed into her chair without pulling it back. The chairs were so heavy it was hard to pull them up again. Mama nodded without seeming to think very much about it.

When Mary brought in her bowl of cereal, Sara frowned, seeing that the steaming porridge came above the bird's tail on the side. Sometimes the level was only under his wing. She watched the thick cream branch out like the Nile, leaving little gray deltas of the soft soil. The brown sugar scattering down from her spoon made it look even more like Egypt. She began to eat rapidly to get to the hot cakes and sausage.

The sun came in through the bow window across the green leaves of the plants and clung to every glittering edge on the table: the rims of the glass goblets, the silver butter dish, the tall casters, even on Papa's diamond stickpin in the black knot of his cravat. Mary came in with a plate of fresh pancakes and a platter of sausages. Sara knew beforehand just how they would taste.

"Sara, your sister Belle is coming home to live," Mama said quite calmly.

Sara cut the morsel of cake on her plate in two because Mama was watching.

"You mean to live here all the time?"

Mama nodded. "And we are delighted to have her home; it will be such a joy."

But Belle's house was beautiful. It was built new for her when she was married and had a rounded bow window with glass that rounded. And Belle had a carriage of her own and a handsome black horse. And Derrick was so jolly.

"Will Derrick come too?" she asked.

"No," Mama said. "Belle will come alone."

There was some note in Mama's voice that told more than her words. Sara speared the left-over piece of wheat cake that had no sausage to go with it daintily on her fork and put it in her mouth. It was so small it had scarcely any taste at all. Papa was looking at her.

"Sara, I think it is best for you to know that Belle has been bitterly unhappy. Mr. VanRansom has done certain things that cannot be forgiven or overlooked. Belle will live with us now. That is all that needs to be said about it."

Papa folded his napkin and pulled it through the heavy silver ring that was mounted on a silver standard, and sat a moment looking across the table at Mama and at Dorothea and Sara. A little smile showed above his gray beard.

"It will be nice to have three of our girls home again for a little while," he said, and nodding to Mama he went out to the hall.

"The carpenters will start today on the new wing for Belle and we shall have the rest of the downstairs decorated at the same time," Mama said briskly. "I'm sure that Belle will be much happier than she has been for a long time."

Sara thought back. Belle had never seemed unhappy. She thought of her driving in her new carriage that Derrick gave her for Christmas. When people were bitterly unhappy they grew thin and pale in fairy tales. Belle was even a little bit plump.

"And, of course," Mama said, looking at Sara, "if anyone *should* stoop to discussing the matter with my little girl, she will say politely, 'I really don't know.' "

"Yes, Mama," Sara said.

Mama opened the top of the silver coffeepot and, tilting her head a little for the steam, looked in to see how much was left. The steam made her face flushed. Then she poured herself another cup. How pretty Mama was with her face so pink, Sara thought.

When the kitchen door to the pantry creaked, Dorothea glanced significantly at Mama.

"There's nothing we have said, Dorothea, that Mary or anyone else cannot hear."

A moment before there had been a secretive feeling in the dining room like the inside of the coffeepot; now it was gone. Mama smiled. "We're all through, Mary." Sara stored the news about Derrick and Belle away in her mind to think of later. What things couldn't Derrick be forgiven for?

But that morning everything seemed to happen at once. Mr. Albee, the carpenter, drove up with a wagonload of lumber. And men began to dig for the new cellar hole. Sara ranged up and down in an ecstasy of excitement. The dull sound of the shovels, the thud of the dirt, the carpenter going through the house, talking to Mama, made even dusting the music room exciting.

Mama and Dor and Papa kept remembering when the house was built and Papa teased Mama about her storeroom that had to be added afterwards because the pantry wasn't nearly big enough. "Mama's wart" Papa always called the storeroom. But all their remembering was before Sara's time and made her feel, as she often did, separated from the rest of the family.

By afternoon the cellar hole for the new wing reached out to the weeping willow tree. It looked like a cave, only, of course, it was all open and not secret at all.

Paul Sevrance came over and they played follow the leader in and out across the new lumber. When they were tired they sat down between the willow and the lilac bush, where it was cool. Paul rolled over on his stomach. Sara pulled her legs up under her chin and tucked her skirts around them.

"Are you glad Belle's coming home to live?" he asked.

"Of course," Sara said.

"Is she getting a divorce?"

Sara was startled. A divorce was a terrible thing. She wasn't very sure about it. "I don't know," she admitted with a little embarrassment.

"You don't! What did your mother say about it?"

Sara hesitated. "Just that Belle was coming home to live and that she's going to have an apartment of her own; that's why they're building on the new wing."

"I guess Mr. VanRansom is a pretty gay dog," Paul said, chewing a twig from the hedge. His voice had a sharp, knowing sound.

"Why is he a gay dog?" Sara asked after a moment. She wasn't looking at Paul but at a heart-shaped lilac leaf, stroking the veins on the wrong side with one finger. She had never noticed before how shiny green the top side of the lilac leaf was and how cloudy green underneath.

"Well, you wouldn't know, being a girl and three years younger."

Sara eyed him sharply, ready to fly at him, but, for once, his voice sounded merely matter-of-fact. His expression was innocent.

"A gay dog is . . . well, being gay, like Mr. VanRansom is; you know, driving a spanking horse and the way he always looks so dressed up . . . and he is handsome," Paul floundered.

"But I think that's the way to be. Belle is handsome too, only you call a woman beautiful instead of handsome. Go on!"

"That's all. I've got to go home, anyway."

But Sara sat still. She held the lilac leaf against her mouth and sucked it in with her breath. When she blew it out the soft brown fringes of her bangs moved out from her forehead. The leaf fluttered down to the ground. Her eyes returned to Paul.

"Go on, Paul Sevrance. You know what we swore."

Paul scowled. "That was a silly oath," Paul said pompously. "We made it really about the deserted house we pretended was a deep mystery. I couldn't tell you everything I found out. Girls don't know the same things." He looked away from Sara.

Sara narrowed her eyes, pursed her lips and tilted her head back a little so that her chin pointed out. "An oath is an oath, Paul Sevrance! You know very well we didn't just make it about the deserted house. We said we'd tell each other anything important we knew."

Paul stood up. "Well, a gay dog is just an expression, like calling someone a foxy-quiller. Oh, bother, I came over here to tell you something really important and now you're mad. I'm going to K.M.A. Father told me this morning!"

"Oh, Paul!" The little girl's face changed instantly. "Kingston Military Academy! And you'll wear one of those uniforms!"

Paul reddened. He smiled a little sheepishly. "It isn't the

uniform so much, but this school here is babyish compared to K.M.A."

"Coming, Mary!" Sara called quickly when she saw Mary at the side door. She started off, chanting impishly, "Somebody I know will be a gay dog or a foxy-quiller when he gets his uniform on!" Then she ran into the house without looking back.

When she started up the stairs from the lower hall she heard Mama talking to Mr. Albee.

"We don't want to hurry you too much, but Mrs. VanRansom wants her apartment as soon as possible. She plans to leave the Woodbridge Avenue house by the end of the month." The house that had been Belle and Derrick's became coldly "the Woodbridge Avenue house."

Then Mama saw her. "Sara, why don't you run down to Belle's and tell her how happy you are that she is coming home to live?" Mama always made the things she wanted you to do into a question.

"Well . . . it's eight blocks down to Woodbridge," Sara answered cautiously. But she would go, of course.

Belle's house looked just the same. It was the largest on the block and had three lots. The iron fence with the little gold balls on every other scallop ran way around the corner. It was a pity Belle was leaving all this. Belle's new wing would only have three rooms. Sara felt suddenly shy about seeing Belle.

"Mrs. VanRansom is out," Hannah told her. "Won't you come in and wait for her?"

Hannah bustled back to the kitchen, and Sara was left to wander through the downstairs rooms. The curtains and portières were down; that gave the house a queer look. All this furniture wouldn't go in the new wing. But maybe Derrick wanted some of it. Where would Derrick live?

Sara went quietly up the stairs to get Belle's jewel box that played six tunes when the top was up. As she started to open the door to Belle's room, Hannah's voice came clearly up the back stairs.

"Well, Mr. VanRansom's a handsome man and free with his money an' all, but when a man takes to going with a professional no lady could stand it! It's known all over town. And Mrs. VanRansom's a lady!" Hannah rattled her pots and pans and whatever else she said was covered over by the noise. Sara closed Belle's door again.

"A professional!" Was that what Papa had meant that couldn't be forgiven? Why was it known all over town? She wanted to be out of the house. She couldn't wait for Belle. The house was changed. She looked at the wide upstairs hall; the sun made a fence on the carpet with the shadow of the balustrade. The doorknobs shone, but there was something unpleasant about it all. She felt trembly inside and her legs were as shaky when she went down the stairs as though she had been walking on the log jam in the river.

She couldn't ask Mama about a professional; she was sure Mama wouldn't tell her. And Dor and Anne would only act more grown-up than Mama. There was only Paul. Paul could find out anything. She could make him tell her. She would think of some way. Perhaps that was what Paul had really meant when he said Derrick was a gay dog!

Sara walked so fast back along Woodbridge Avenue that the plaited ruffle on the bottom of her pinafore kicked out like a fan. The small face under the bang was dour. It was because she was the youngest and so much the youngest, she reflected, that they only told her part things.

She was looking down at the planks of the sidewalk in her preoccupation, taking care not to step on a crack:

If you step on a crack,
You'll break your Mother's back!

"Well, well, what a serious face on my favorite sister!"

Sara's head jerked up. Before she had time to think, she was smiling at Derrick. He always made her smile. Then she remembered what Papa had said: that Derrick had done things that could never be forgiven. Her face sobered. Her eyes fell to the little gold charm that dangled on his watch chain.

"I'll walk part way with you." Derrick took her arm in that grown-up way that she loved, or she had until now. She held her arm as far inside her sleeve as she could. She must say something. "Where've you been, my pretty maid?" Derrick asked.

"To see Belle, but she wasn't there. I don't think I can walk any more with you; I . . . I'm awfully sorry." Sara looked down the street under the green hanging elms. The afternoon was peculiarly still. Derrick VanRansom was still. She felt he was hurt. She stole a little glance at him.

"That's right, Sara. I forgot that I'm an outcast. Even the VanRansoms don't care for me. Well, your sister is a beautiful and a virtuous woman. I love her, Sara, even though I have made her unhappy. But, Sara, don't you grow up thinking there is only your kind of people in the world: the Bolsters and the VanRansoms. That's the trouble with our side of town."

His voice was so quiet, so pleasant, Sara's eyes found his face. Everything must be all right, after all. She wanted to ask him to be good. Maybe he could be forgiven. He was so much fun at the big family dinners. And he said he loved Belle.

"But your sister's heart won't be broken. She has her name and her virtue and her culture clubs!" Derrick's voice was no longer pleasant. Sara remembered that she shouldn't be talking to him at all. She pulled her arm away from his.

"I beg your pardon, Sara." Derrick stepped away and bowed elaborately, mockingly. "How old are you, Sara?"

"Nine," Sara told him. She was mixed up in her own mind. Her eyes were troubled.

"You may be the most beautiful of the Bolster girls, yet, Sara. Good afternoon." He bowed again and went on.

Sara stood watching him. When he passed the Wakefields' where the syringa spilled over the wall, he broke off a little piece and arranged it in his buttonhole. He turned and saw her watching him. He waved. Sara wanted to wave back, but she knew she shouldn't. Then, suddenly, she lifted her hand, but Derrick had already turned around, so he didn't see her. She wouldn't tell anyone at home about meeting him.

After dinner Sara left the others, walking around the cellar hole of the new wing, and slipped over to the hedge that separated Paul's garden from theirs. She climbed the beech tree and whistled. Paul said she could whistle as well as any boy. Then she remembered that Derrick had teased her once, telling her that

A whistling girl and a crowing hen
Always come to some bad end.

Perhaps Paul wasn't there. She whistled again, then she slid through the hedge and crossed the lawn to the Sevrances' front porch. Mr. Sevrance had imported two peacocks for his garden, but this evening they were standing sulkily on the iron bench and their feathers looked dull, all folded up.

She had to stretch to reach the door-knocker. Bailey opened the door. Bailey was the Sevrances' butler. Sara looked at him closely, wondering why the girls wanted to have a butler.

"Won't you come in and sit down, Miss? I'll call Mr. Paul," Bailey said solemnly.

Then Mr. Sevrance came out from the dining room.

"Well, little lady, so you came to call for Paul!" Mr. Sevrance was tall and rounded in front. His face was always red and he was shiny-bald on top of his head. "Aren't you going to give me a kiss?" He stooped down and Sara kissed him. She didn't like it, but it seemed simpler to kiss him and have it over with. When Mr. Sevrance bent down she saw Paul standing in the doorway. He was frowning. "Paul, you're a lucky young rascal to have this young lady calling for you. I'm ashamed of you that you didn't call for her!" Mr. Sevrance's laugh filled the hall. Sara felt she should smile, but Paul didn't.

"H'lo," he said.

"Good evening, Sara." Mrs. Sevrance came out into the hall. She was a small, plain woman with a low voice.

"Can you come out?" Sara asked inelegantly.

"I guess so," Paul answered.

"Here, here, that's no way to talk to a young lady!" Hiram Sevrance scolded. "Well, run along, run along. Give my compliments to your parents, Sara."

As they went out Sara saw Mr. Sevrance going up the oak stairway where the bust of Napoleon stood in the niche along the wall. Mrs. Sevrance was following him.

Once outside the house, Sara went straight to the point. "Paul, do you know what a professional is?"

"I can figure it out," Paul said slowly.

"What is it?"

"Say, you're too busy trying to know everything."

Sara seemed not to hear. "You might as well tell me or else . . ." She paused dramatically. It was hard to think of something that would awe him. She could feel Paul waiting. "Or else I'll hold my head on the tracks until the train gets to the signal light, and if I get killed it'll be your fault," she finished triumphantly. It was the most dangerous feat she could think of. They had often held their heads on the rails until the train reached the bend, but even Paul had never held his head any longer than that. That Paul should mind her doing anything so risky she took for granted. She gloried in Paul's slow expression of admiration. He whistled.

"Well, are you going to tell me?"

"I might show you."

"Show me a professional?"

Paul nodded. "You can't ever tell I took you there, though!"

"Of course not," Sara agreed promptly. "Now?"

They walked the length of Park Avenue without speaking. Sara was intent on her aim; Paul was uncomfortable.

"I ought to let you lay your head on the rails if you're so brave," he muttered.

"All right." Sara began to hum a maddening little tune that suggested her superiority.

They crossed the Racine Street bridge and turned down past the Brooks House. Sara had never been downtown after dinner on foot before. She looked at the carriages for hire lined up along the river side of the hotel. A little proudly she brought out the twenty-five-cent piece Mama had given her for picking all the currants.

"Paul, I have a quarter; do you think we could take a cab? Or isn't it very far?"

"Sara, you're a caution!" Paul said. "Here, give it to me."

Business was very slow in the early summer evening. The

elderly cab driver took off his derby hat, smoothing his hair thoughtfully.

"You're the Sevrance boy, ain't you?" He got down and opened the carriage door for Sara. But Paul was more uncomfortable now that the driver knew who he was. "Where to, sir?" the driver asked with a slow smile.

"Why, just, just for a drive down around Diamond Street and the lower end of Water Street." Perspiration broke out on Paul's forehead.

"Lots of prettier places to drive than that way," the driver said, not offering to move.

His mind quickened by desperation, Paul thought of a credible reason for driving through the disreputable section of town. "We want to see the river all the way through the town . . . as far as you can take us on the money," he added hastily.

A little hesitantly, the driver picked up his reins and chirruped to the horses.

It was growing darker. The lights in the Brooks House lighted up the chairs set out on the sidewalk. The Water Street trolley hid all the other sounds in its high screech. The other carriages seemed to roll noiselessly on their wheels. It was hotter down here and the smell of the river mixed with the smell from the saloons along the street.

Paul saw a look of distaste on Sara's face. "You wanted to come down here!" he reminded her.

"I do want to," Sara answered stoutly. "I like it, all but the smell, and you get used to it after a while." It was hard, she thought, to think of Derrick having anything to do with this part of town. He always looked so spick-and-span. Then she forgot about Derrick.

The doors of a saloon just ahead of them swung back violently. A thin woman in black was propelled through the doorway by a portly man whose white hair was combed slick across a round red head. The children had a moment's delighted gaze at the interior of "Dick's Place": little lights on dark wood, a big mirror with bottles on the shelves beside the mirror, the gleam of a brass rod below the counter and men crowding around the door. A loud roar of laughter came out to the street. It was so exciting to see back of the swinging doors that Sara gave a little bounce on the carriage seat.

"Sara, that's Mrs. Whitcomb!" Paul whispered. Mrs. Whitcomb was someone they both knew; someone who lived just around the corner on Maple Street. She was Rupert Whitcomb's mother! Paul felt uneasy knowing her. Five other women came out after her and, all at once, they knelt together on the pavement in front of Dick's Place, and Mrs. Whitcomb began to pray in a sing-song voice that carried above other sounds.

"Whistling Jehoshaphat! Those women'll stop at nothing," the cab driver exclaimed. He had stopped the horse now and was sitting with his whip across his knees, missing no least detail.

"She's praying, Paul, for that fat man," Sara whispered. Paul felt his neck grow hot. He glanced at Sara. She looked as cool as you please. Girls didn't ever get embarrassed. He doubted if they had as much feeling as a boy had.

The discomfited saloonkeeper vanished behind the swinging doors. There were loud voices and laughing, then all Paul and Sara could see were the trouser bottoms and boots beneath the half doors. Two of the women took Mrs. Whitcomb's arm and they went down the street, a close and virtuous bevy.

"That's them women that go right in an' try to make a man take the pledge never to touch a drop when that's what he makes his money in!" The driver snorted. He pulled impatiently on the reins.

"Sara, look! See up in that window? That's a professional!" Paul whispered, pinching her arm. He had felt grown-up and important, knowing things girls didn't know. But now he knew that he shouldn't have brought Sara down here. What if Sara asked him questions! What would he say? There was a limit to his knowledge too.

But Sara was busy looking, staring up at the lace-curtained windows above Dick's Place and the grocery warehouse. The windows were open to the sultry summer evening. A woman sat by one of the windows. There was bright color on her cheeks that you could see even from the street. Her hair was frizzed in a bang. Just the top of her blue dress showed.

"All along there, that's where they live!" Paul muttered. He had never had a good look at the places before.

Sara looked across the street at the old houses. There were stores on the first floors of some of them, and in one of the doorways a woman, not any older than Belle or Dor, Sara decided, sat crocheting.

"She's making lace," Sara said.

Paul was relieved. Sara was just a child, he decided.

The driver turned at the corner back up town. He pointed with his whip-end. "You should see this street in the spring when the Red Sash Brigade's in. Then there's something doing!"

"I'll bet," Paul said. "He means the lumberjacks," he explained to Sara.

"I know that!" Sara retorted indignantly.

"The seamy side of life, eh! Do your Pas and Mas know you're out?" The driver chuckled without waiting for an answer. Paul and Sara made no answer. Paul reddened and plunged his hands into the two high pockets of his double-breasted coat. His fingers closed on a ten-cent piece in the left-hand pocket, the coin his father had given him. He fished it out and showed it to Sara.

In a voice as like his father's as he could make it he said to the cab driver, "I find we have thirty-five cents." He wanted to say "my good man" the way his father did, but his tongue refused. "So you can take us a little farther, can't you?"

"Well," said the driver, half turning toward them in the back, "I should say that would take you just about across the drawbridge."

Sara sat back. That was five whole squares.

The tollbridge to the west side was up. It always looked funny no matter how many times she saw it, Sara thought. She wondered whether she could hang on if she should be right in the middle when the bridge started up. A dirty tugboat glided by slowly. The lights on its deck threw spots of shiny dark on the surface of the river, like water spots on a dry floor. A wagon drew up along one side with a heavy, lumbering creak.

On the other side of the cab came the lighter sound of a carriage. It came to a stop with a flourish, just at the gate. The light on the tollgate post fell directly on the seat. Sara leaned forward. Then she nudged Paul.

Paul was already looking at the occupants of the carriage. Derrick VanRansom sat on the side next to them. He was driving Belle's carriage, the shining black buggy with yellow spokes to the wheels, and beside him was a woman in a light dress and a wide-brimmed hat with a plume on it. She was laughing at Derrick.

Both children were silent, watching. Paul sat back stiffly in the seat for fear Derrick might notice him, but Derrick was taken up with his companion. Sara's mouth hung slightly open, she was watching so intently. The woman *was* pretty.

The bell on the bridge rang busily. The bridge creaked back into place. Derrick's buggy was the first one over the bridge.

"Paul, do you think she was?"

Paul nodded. "A professional? Of course, I know it." Then, since he had said so much, he continued. "That's what all the trouble's about and why Belle's coming home to live."

The little girl's face was troubled under the lamplight. "But, Paul, she didn't look like . . . those others. She was prettier."

"Yes, but I think she is. They both looked as though they were having a good time, didn't they?" Paul asked slowly.

"Well," the driver stopped his horse on the other side of the bridge, "that's about three times as much as anybody ever got for thirty-five cents, but business was kinda slow. Hop out."

"You might say thank you," Paul suggested as they walked toward their own homes.

"Oh, I do, Paul, and I'll tell you the very first important thing I know."

"And you'll never tell where we went?"

"No, silly."

Sara approached her house carefully to locate the family first. When she found they were all in the music room listening to Dor and Anne sing while Belle played, she went up the back stairs to her room. She undressed quickly and climbed into bed. They hadn't noticed she was gone. Then she heard the chime clock strike the hour. It was only eight o'clock, after all.

3 1887

THERE were pegs along the mahogany baseboards of the drawing room and the music room and the sitting room. From them little strings tied the canvas that covered the red velvet carpets. It made a slithery sound, a little like water lapping against the shore, when you slid across it. But there was nothing like it for dancing. The canvas had to be stretched taut. Only Hingham and Lowery from Detroit knew how to do it.

The mahogany stair rail was twined with green and the new bow window at one end of the drawing room was banked with green. There were tall white candles in high iron brackets on either side of the bow window and a white satin cushion lay on the floor between them.

Sara stood in the doorway, all ready dressed in the pale pink organdie. Everywhere else in the house people were busy, but these rooms stood empty. Almost a churchly hush filled them. She touched the new wallpaper with one careful finger-tip. There was an embossed figure on it that was like felt standing out from the satin ground. The woodwork was newly painted; new lace curtains fell from under the carved valances in stiffly transparent folds. Tonight was the peak of the months of preparation: Dor's wedding. The house was as handsomely decorated as the new houses on Jefferson Avenue in Detroit, Mr. Hingham had told Mama, and Sara remembered it proudly.

"Well," Papa had said, "we probably won't have it redecorated again until Sara's wedding."

That seemed terribly far off, Sara thought, looking into the long pier glass. Dor was twenty-two; Sara was twelve. Twelve from twenty-two is ten years. The mirror that was ready to reflect the bridal party as they stood before the improvised altar gave back the picture of a slender little girl staring at herself with critical eyes. Slight shadows under the eyes deepened their blueness. The firmly formed jaw had already lost its childlike curve. But Sara was not looking at her face but at the ruffles of the pale pink organdie.

It came lower in the neck than any other dress she had ever had, she thought with satisfaction. She pulled the round neck a little lower, thinking how unpleasant it would be to have your neck turn into a tunnel between two hills like old Mrs. Higbee's; and Mrs. Higbee's skin was wrinkled and powder lay in the wrinkles. Sara hadn't been able to help seeing when Mrs. Higbee sat on her feet on the floor turning the hem of her skirt.

Sara laid her hands around her waist, stretching the fingers to try to make them touch. Suddenly, she dropped her head back so her brown hair touched her back and began a noiseless jig. Her hair thumped up and down and her skirts spread as wide as the hoops Mama used to wear.

"Sara, you are a hoyden! I've been looking to see if you needed help dressing, and here you are!" Belle stood watching her. By some subtle process Belle had seemed older since she came home. She seemed to have moved into Mama's and Papa's group. Sara saw her family now in layers: Papa and Mama and Belle on the first plane, the girls on the second, and then herself. Sara left off jigging and smoothed her dress.

"You look lovely, Belle." Sara fingered the topaz intaglio that caught the real lace at Belle's throat. The figure of a dancer was cut so deeply into the stone that even the fingers of one tiny hand were clear. "You haven't worn this for ever so long!"

"No, Derrick gave it to me for a wedding gift," Belle answered.

"Oh." It had come to be a habit to drop the whole subject at any mention of Belle's marriage.

"It seems too pretty not to wear. . . ." Belle's voice trailed off into silence. Then she said briskly, "I'm going up to help Dor. You better save your jig until the dance begins. People will be coming right away."

Sara wandered out through the house. In the pantry the strange caterer from Detroit was laying the tiny boxes of wedding cake on a tray, each one tied with white ribbon, each with Dor's new initials in silver. Over on a table were plates of iced cakes that would be passed.

"Do you like weddings, young lady?" the strange caterer asked. His voice was patronizing, as though he were speaking to a child. Sara raised her eyelids slowly and answered judiciously,

"Some weddings."

But when the caterer had gone back to the kitchen Sara edged nearer to the trays of new cakes to inspect them more closely. There was one with a tiny pink daisy. There were other pink daisies on other little cakes, but none so perfect.

The guests were already coming. Sara could hear them going up the stairs, laughing and talking; the almost steady jingle of the doorbell, the cautious tuning of instruments from the music room. The orchestra must have come. There was a rattle of dishes in the pantry.

Sara hesitated; drawn back to the other rooms, drawn, too, by the little white iced cake with the perfect daisy. She heard Papa's voice in the dining room giving orders about the punch. She didn't want the cake to eat, but neither did she want it to be eaten by just anyone. She reached out and took the cake with the pink daisy. She held it hidden in the loop of her blue taffeta sash as she came through the dining room.

She saw the Bishop talking to Papa. The Bishop had come especially by train, just for the wedding. The orchestra was playing softly in the corner of the music room. There were the Lowerys and the Carthughs and the Ingalls . . . all the people she had always known.

"How do you do," Sara said to Mrs. Ingalls.

"Well, well, I thought this was the bride for a moment!" Mr. Healey said teasingly, turning her around.

Sara passed on through the room to the potted palms placed along the stairs, and standing close to one deposited the little cake carefully behind the stalky trunk of the plant. Then she saw Belle beckoning to her from the stairs.

"Sara, when I raise my finger like this you walk downstairs and the musicians will know it's time to begin the wedding march."

Sara felt very important. She stood in the doorway of Dor's room. Mrs. Higbee was straightening the folds of the satin wedding dress. Belle tied a narrow velvet ribbon just under Anne's chin and others under her own and Sara's.

Mrs. Higbee nodded approval. "That's it, a note of black, that's the French way."

"All the happiness in the world, darling," Mama said, kissing Dor. There were tears in Mama's eyes, but she was smiling and Dor was smiling, and Anne and Belle.

"Ah, Mrs. Bolster, you should be happy with such beautiful daughters," Mrs. Higbee said. The Bolster girls glanced in Dor's big mirror and, meeting each other's eyes there, laughed.

"Here are your flowers, Sara; now walk very slowly in time to the music and hold your head up," Belle whispered in the hallway.

The music began so softly at first, so smoothly, it didn't seem as though anybody made it. Sara glanced at the people standing at the foot of the stairs and in the doorways and along the wall of the drawing room. She knew them all, but now with the music playing they were altered. No smile of recognition touched her lips as she walked, carrying in one arm the basket of pink roses. She felt proud. She was one of the beautiful Bolster girls. And the house was beautiful and the music swelled joyously.

George Crawford and Chauncey Baker came from the library and walked toward the end of the drawing room. George had a brilliant future as a lawyer, Papa said.

It was funny how long the drawing room seemed. Just in front of Mrs. Carthugh Sara's ankle wobbled. She flushed ever so slightly. Then she came to the Bishop and turned to one side as they had practiced it.

Sara wondered while the Bishop spoke the words of the service what it would be like to be married. Some day she would wear the same dress and veil and stand right there. She would marry Paul, probably. She wondered where Paul was. The Bishop was praying; she couldn't look now.

"I think the dance is more fun than the wedding," Emma Carthugh said. "Except the supper, maybe. How soon will the supper be?"

"At ten o'clock," Sara told her, wondering now if she

should have stood in the receiving line after all. She had begged Mama not to make her. But now she watched her family at the end of the room, feeling again so separate from them, so much the youngest. There was Paul! He and his mother were going down the receiving line now.

Paul was very handsome in his new uniform. The dark blue braid on the lighter blue flannel was sweet. She would like a dress in those colors, Sara thought, trying not to admit that what she would really like was to be a boy wearing a uniform from K.M.A.

He was looking for her. She whistled, a very little whistle that sailed across the room under cover of the waltz music. Paul saw her. He had to walk way around the end of the library to avoid the dancers. He looked so grown-up, she wished she hadn't whistled.

"Hello. I thought you'd be in the receiving line."

"I didn't want to be," Sara said a little crossly.

Paul bowed as the cadets at K.M.A. were taught to bow. "May I have the pleasure?" Sara scowled. He *was* grown-up.

"Oh, Paul, stop it. I think you've gotten too silly and affected for any use!" she stormed at him, her eyes as bright and clear as glass.

"Affected! What about you? You're awfully fussed up in that. I bet you don't do all the things you used to do!" he teased.

"I do too. I slid down the roof of Green's salt shed last week and went up to my waist in the sawdust!"

"Paul, I see you found Sara," Mama said, coming up to them. "We're going to have supper now. I've put you young people at the table in Belle's parlor. Sara, you help the others find their places, will you, dear? There's Emma Carthugh over there."

As Sara started after Emma, Paul murmured, "Been holding your head on the railroad track any lately, Sara?"

To Sara it sounded like a taunt. "After supper's over, I'll show you, Paul Sevrance! When the 12:30 flyer comes through . . . or will you be in bed then?" She swung away with the pink ruffles swishing. She would show him. Military school had made him hateful, unbearable. . . .

"Aren't you going to change your dress?" Paul asked when Sara met him at the side of the porch, her red winter coat, trimmed with beaver, on over the pink organdie, the organdie showing a full ruffle beneath it.

"No," said Sara grimly. They went down the walk in silence. The snow-covered planks had a coating of ice. Sara slid along on the ice as though she had runners beneath her feet. Now that she had started, the feat loomed up bigger than she had thought. It was so late at night, and it was winter. Her fear made her more angry. Paul ran and slid along just behind her.

"You don't waste any time getting there!"

Sara was mollified for a minute and took Paul's arm going down the bank. With one accord they avoided the road to the station. Dor and George were leaving on the flyer for their wedding trip. Sara and Paul had slipped out of the house when the guests were crowding around the hall to see Dor throw her bouquet from the top of the stairs.

The station below them looked small at night, outlined by the gaslights along the platform and the dim lights inside. The whistle of the train was mournful, coming through the night.

"If they run over me, it'll spoil Dor's going away," Sara remarked sadly. She had forgotten Paul. She was living it all out. Everyone would run out from the station and crowd around the engineer as he carried her in with her head gone. She would look lovely in the pink organdie, anyway.

They could see the round light in the front of the train now. It shed a cruel beam on the piles of logs along the river. Then it would be hidden again around the bend before it came down the straight track. Sara's teeth were chattering. She stumbled over the icy rail and Paul grabbed her arm.

"Don't do it, Sara; I'll believe you can do it." Paul's tone was conciliatory. He was frightened. Sara made no answer. She would do anything she set out to do. Hadn't she made him take her down in the red-light district that time?

The train whistle came again, relentless, final. A second later, laughter floated out from the station platform. Perhaps that was Dor, Sara thought.

"You sure you can get off in time, Sara?" Paul whispered. There was no need to whisper except that he was too frightened to speak out loud.

"Maybe," Sara answered. She was almost crying now. She sniffed desperately and rubbed her arm across her nose inelegantly. This was the exact place, ten yards from the signal light. She knelt on the ground and laid her head against the rail. She could feel the thundering of the train through the live steel of the rail. The rail was so cold her hair stuck to it. The train was hidden now behind the curve.

"Sara, get off there, quick. You'll be killed!" Paul pulled her arm. She kicked out with her foot, striking him in the stomach so that he doubled up for a second.

"You didn't think I'd do it; well, I will. Get away!"

The train came into view. The beam of light searching out the dark lit up the two children beyond the signal light with stark clarity. The train whistle screamed out, leaving the throat of the night raw with its clamor. Its mournful, eerie note was gone. It was terror, imperative, frantic, hopeless.

"Sara, quick!" Paul tugged at her, not minding the flying feet. Sara's face was white, her eyes wide and colorless in the bright glare. She could see the number of the engine beneath the light. She read it in a long unhurried moment. She saw the face of the engineer staring out of his window in fright. She could almost feel the heat through the cold and smell the cindery smell that made her car-sick when she was on the train. Almost! Another little bit and she could jump.

Paul jerked her off the rail with such force they rolled down the slight embankment of the railroad bed as the train came to a grinding stop beyond the iron signal light.

"Quick! They'll catch us!" Paul whispered. He was holding Sara tight behind an alder bush. "Are you all right, Sara?"

Sara nodded and started creeping along the embankment in the snow. They saw the engineer get out of the train. People from the station were coming out to see what was wrong.

"Looked like a girl!"

"They was a couple of kids," the engineer said; then a string of oaths worthy of a boss lumberjack on a Water Street binge came out to the children as they scrambled up the bank behind the last car of the train. Paul went first. Sara took his hand gladly, letting him help her up the slippery bank. The fear had gone now leaving her only excited. She gave a high, short laugh.

"Did I do it, Paul?"

"You're a damned little idiot, Sara Bolster."

Sara smiled complacently at his back. "You swore, Paul," she said sweetly.

Under the street light on the Boulevard Sara looked herself over. The organdie dress was only a little wet from the snow. She tried to stamp the snow from her dancing slippers.

"Here!" Paul knelt down and wiped them off with his handkerchief. Sara held out one foot at a time. He looked up at her with admiration in his face that was still a little pale from fright.

"Sara, I don't see how you dared do it!" he said solemnly.

"Why, Paul!" Unabashed pleasure stood out on her face. Then she laughed. "I was scared," she admitted generously. "We better hurry home before they find we're gone."

Washing the Royal Worcester cups and plates, the filigree sandwich tray, the gold-leaf cake plate, or the Bohemian glass and crystal goblets was a sacred rite to Mrs. Bolster.

"Just leave them in the pantry," Mrs. Bolster always said to Mary or the caterer. "The girls and I will wash them later." Mrs. Bolster had no patience with those housewives whose treasured china and glass were broken by careless servants. "A lady always takes care of her things," she used to say to the girls.

So now, after the orchestra had gone and the last carriage rolled away and Winthrop Bolster had turned the big silver key in the lock of the front door, Mrs. Bolster and the girls washed and polished the fine china and glassware at the big round table in the dining room.

The rite had a certain beauty of its own. The candles in the wall sconces were still burning, even though the crystal chandelier over the table was lighted. Mrs. Bolster sat at her usual place at the table, a pan of suds in front of her. When she lifted her hands to put a dish in the rinse pan, the suds clung to her hands like diamonds. There were special heavy-weight linen towels, marked C.C.B. for drying the best china and glass.

"I thought she looked as happy as a lark," Mr. Bolster said. He sat down to smoke a last cigar with Anne's husband while Mama and the girls were busy. It was a pleasant time to talk over the evening.

"Didn't the house look lovely!" Belle exclaimed.

"I drove the Carthughs home and stopped in at the livery stable to have a shoe looked at," Roger said. He held the cigar his father-in-law had just given him under his nose appreciatively. "Richards told me they had an accident at the drawbridge today. One of the Henkel brewery wagons was waiting there and the horses started up too soon. One of them caught his leg in the crack."

"Mercy! Was his leg broken?" Mrs. Bolster set the goblet gently in the rinse pan, listening to Roger's answer.

"Yes, they had to shoot him, but the driver said he'd have to wait for their stable boss. Richards said it was rare: this big German arrived and gave the driver a regular dressing down for not holding the horses. Then he shot the horse and looked as cut up over it as though he had shot his best friend!"

"Well, I suppose one of those big Clydesdale horses is worth a good deal," Mr. Bolster remarked. "Henkel is coming to be a person of considerable wealth and influence on the east side in the German section. I was surprised to see that he was elected to the town council last year. But he's really quite a gentleman in his way."

"Papa, he's an immigrant!" Anne said, polishing one of the delicate crystal goblets with meticulous care.

Sara stood beside Mama, forgetting for a moment to wipe the pearl-handled knife in her hands. Her eyes were clouded under the brown bang. It was the Henkels' Brewing Company wagon that had come by that day when she was waiting for Winthrop to be born. The driver had stopped and lifted her up on the high wagon for a ride. She remembered how beautiful the big horses were; they were brand new, the driver said. She hoped it wasn't one of those horses that had to be shot.

Belle hung the fragile-handled cups on the hooks in the tall cupboard. "Wasn't that a dreadful prank of those children! They got right in front of the tracks until the train was almost on them," Belle said. "I'm thankful they weren't killed on Dor's going-away night."

Mama shook her head at the thought. Then she said, "George looked proud, didn't he?" Mama's mind was never busied long away from her family's affairs. "There! We're all through. Sara, you must sleep in the morning. It's nearly two." Mama's velvet skirt fell in gracious folds as she stood up. "I saw you and Paul together, dear. He's a manly boy."

Sara went up to bed obediently. She had bent over the silver cases when Belle talked about the children on the track. No one had seen her face. She was halfway up the stairs when she remembered the little white cake with the perfect daisy on it and came back downstairs to get it. It was still there behind the swarthy trunk of the potted palm. She would eat it just before she got in bed.

But the cake was tasteless, just as she had feared. She ate all around the flower, leaving it on a little round plaque of white icing. She was half minded to save it on her dresser, it was so pretty. Then she popped it into her mouth instead.

4 1891

WHEN the spring drive was on, the west side of Armitage City, where the crocuses were just starting through the wide green lawns, turned a deaf ear. If the ladies at the last meeting of the Winter Club heard the dull drumming of the logs through their reading of *The Merchant of Venice* they kept their minds on culture. Most of the wealth behind those big houses on the west side had come from just such pitch-covered logs of white pine ridden down the river by the swearing lumberjacks, but the ladies of the first families knew precious little about the sources of their luxuries. Most of them did not drive out in their phaetons when news went round that the Red Sash Brigade was in, tearing up the white-pine planks of the sidewalk with their calks, stampeding like cattle to Moll's or Kate's on Water Street, only stopping to have a drink in every saloon along the way.

The drive when the river was choked with logs was merely a sign of the season. Mrs. Bolster and her daughters had by then usually had their heavy carpets taken out and beaten and the stiff lace curtains in the upstairs rooms "done up" and rehung. Vague stories of the drive and the antics of the lumberjacks trickled to them through their menfolk or the headlines in the *Courier*, such astonishing morsels as that every windowpane on the coaches that took the lumberjacks out from the Baker Street station was smashed or that there had been a fight in front of Little Ike's clothing store and one man was killed. But the lumberjacks seldom came up as far as Park Avenue, and unless you climbed up to the square cupola on top of the house you need not even be aware of the excitement on the water front.

But Sara, home for vacation from Madame LaVerne's Select School for Young Ladies in Detroit, knew the drive was coming down the river. She had seen the coaches with the broken windows standing in the Baker Street station the minute before she had seen Papa and Belle waiting on the platform to meet her, and the carriage with Brown sitting on the box. And from the train windows she had caught glimpses of the river with the logs coming down. She had been sitting beside Mademoiselle Beaujean, who chaperoned her on the train. Mademoiselle was improving the time by French conversation.

"Voulez-vous que j'abaisse la jalousie, Mademoiselle Sara?" Mademoiselle Beaujean asked, nodding toward the bright sun coming through the dirty windowpane of the coach.

But Sara, looking through the dirt on the windowpane at the river, gave a sudden unladylike bounce on the plush seat.

"Mademoiselle!" the short French woman protested, clutching quickly for the paper-backed novel sliding off her knee.

"The drive . . . oh, Mademoiselle, the drive's coming down while I'm home. Look!"

Mademoiselle Beaujean stared, uncomprehending, at the logs floating on the water, at the stubby fronts of the buildings along the river and the big docks.

"When the logs come down from the woods is the most exciting time in the world, Mademoiselle. And there are so many lumberjacks in town they tear up the plank sidewalks and smash up things and everything."

"The sidewalks!"

"Yes, with the spikes on their boots. And Paul has seen some wonderful fights they've had right out on the street!"

"Mademoiselle!" the little French woman murmured again. "Quel horreur!" What terrible things this young girl knew. Yet her neat little hands in their fine kid gloves and her nicely tailored jacket and perky little hat were clearly the expensive clothes of a jeune fille bien élevé.

The train steamed into the station beside the coach with the broken panes, and Mademoiselle handed over her charge to the dignified gentleman with graying hair, whom Mademoiselle Sara introduced quite prettily as "mon père, M'sieu Bolster, Mademoiselle, et ma sœur, Madame VanRansom."

As Sara rode home in the carriage behind Brown, she glanced at the embankment, remembering that winter night three, no, four years ago; she had been only twelve then, when she had laid her head on the track till the train reached the signal light.

"Is Paul home?" she asked Belle.

Belle laughed teasingly. "Why, Sara, I believe you are growing up. No, he's gone to New York for his holidays."

"Oh, I just wondered." But she was disappointed.

There was a family dinner to celebrate Sara's homecoming, just as Sara knew there would be. The flavor of it was in the house when Mama opened the door.

"Mama! Madame sent her regards to you, Mama."

"And what did she say about my youngest daughter?" Mama held her away from her to ask.

"That she was pleased with me, but that I was impetuous, but, Mama . . ."

Mama stopped Sara's words with a kiss, patting her reprovingly on the shoulder. "We'll talk about that later, Sara."

"Anne!" Sara ran up the stairs to meet Anne, trying not to notice Anne's condition, but being excited by it all the same. Anne was going to have a baby. Roger came down the stairs behind Anne.

"Well, Sara, you're nearly a young lady!" It was pleasant to have Roger think her more grown-up.

"Sara, baby!" Dor called from the dining room, making her feel the youngest of them all again. Dor was wearing her hair a new way.

"I haven't seen Mary." Sara rushed out through the dining room and the pantry to find her, more lean and black than ever. "Mary, did you make méringues for dessert?"

But dinner was long. By dessert she was no longer as hungry as she had thought she would be for the méringues. She was sleepy after the long train ride.

"Sara, do you sit that way at Madame LaVerne's?" Mama asked reproachfully. Sara straightened in her seat. Here at home she forgot that she was sixteen and fell quiet, watching with bright eyes each member of her family.

"The Briggs are all going to Europe this spring," Anne said.

Mama sighed gently. "I always hoped you girls could go abroad before you were tied down by too many responsibilities, but Papa says it's out of the question this year."

"Hiram Sevrance is going to pay for every acre he cut!" Papa was talking to Roger and George. Sara stared at his usually calm face. His eyes flashed. His jaw came out strongly and his lips lay firmly against each other.

"He expects to," George said with a short laugh. "As long

as he didn't get away with it, at least. He figures he's no worse off than if he'd had to buy a hundred and sixty acres at a dollar and a quarter an acre in the first place."

"There's the little matter of the dishonor," Papa said gravely.

"Not very many people will think any the worse of him for it. Old man Blodgett never paid for all his timber land. People'll just think he's smart. Why, the round forty is a standing joke!"

Sara watched Papa carving another slice of beef from the big roast. He laid the horn-handled knife on the table, resting the blade on the cut-glass rest.

"As long as I am head of the Government Land Office I shall prosecute any theft of land even if it is committed by my neighbor." Papa's voice was low but it had an edge as sharp as the carving knife. He was talking about Paul's father! Sara realized slowly.

"Of course he'll claim not to know anything about it. He'll say his loggers just went ahead," Roger remarked with a shrug.

"Hiram Sevrance will know that I know. . . ." How hard Papa's eyes could look, Sara thought.

Mama frowned across the table. "Winthrop, at the table I do think . . ."

"Quite right, my dear," Papa agreed, and the stern expression on his face was replaced again by his usual one of kindliness.

After dinner Belle sat down at the piano and played for them. Suddenly she thundered on the bass keys.

"That's like the logs this morning when I went across the Water Street bridge," she laughed.

"Papa, may I go down to see the drive tomorrow?" Sara whispered softly in Mr. Bolster's ear. "Please, Papa."

Mr. Bolster smiled. "Still more boy than girl even after Madame LaVerne's, aren't you, Sara? You come down to the Land Office tomorrow morning and you can see the river from my window."

But that wasn't quite the same as standing along the river. She had watched it from Papa's office before. And why didn't Mama and the girls want to see it?

The Land Office fronted on Water Street. It had been a landmark from the beginning of Armitage City. The hatrack in the entry had held straw hats, the slouch felts of the war period, silk toppers, white beavers. Sometimes the wearer of a straw hat on his first visit returned in the next decade in a white beaver hat. The umbrella stand beside it had embraced hickory sticks, peaveys, and gold-headed canes.

Racks along one side of the room held ledgers already yellow-leaved and breathing a musty odor. Great maps hung on the wall. The long window at the rear looked on the river, and from one or the other, or both, there blew into the dun-colored office a sense of space, a feeling of adventure. The scuffed black oilcloth covering of the long map table might have been the green felt of a gaming table; such large fortunes had been won across its surface.

To Sara the Land Office was as familiar as their own house. She was allowed to go down for Papa on foot and alone, but she must go straight and not stop on the way and "cross over, remember, Sara," which meant when passing the Gaiety and the Bijou, two objectionable entertainment houses that stood on opposite sides of the street though separated from each other by several blocks. No lady would sanction their presence by walking past them on the same side of the street. But Sara always stood still, squinting a little to see the pictures of the dancing ladies on the posters.

Sara pressed down the latch of the big double door. The UNITED STATES printed on one door and the seal of the United States on the other always thrilled her.

"Good morning, Mr. Dell." Sara spoke to the clerk in her most grown-up manner. "May I see Papa?" The way Mr. Dell bowed to her pleased her. Mr. Dell used to give her peppermint drops from his coat pocket, but this morning he stood up as she came in, quite as though she were Belle or Anne.

"Well, Miss Sara, you've surely grown up. Just have a chair; your father's busy."

Sara walked over to the window at the back that looked on the river.

"The logs have stopped, Mr. Dell! Why, it's a jam!"

Instead of lying docilely, side by side, as they had yesterday when Sara came in on the train, the logs were piled up like the sticks in a beaver pile, water dripping from their shining bark. Below the logs where the water ran clear the river looked too still and narrow to carry such a load. The lumberjacks were running across the logs, thrusting in their peaveys to loosen a log here and there. The whole wide mass of logs heaved a little. A creaking sound came in through the window, no louder than the squeaking of leather boots rubbed together. The slate-gray river teemed with color. The men's curses were only a faint sound up here in the Land Office.

"It's backing up all right. I been watchin' it all forenoon," Mr. Dell said, lively interest in his mild eyes. "See, the water's up above the docks now."

"Look at that man run across the logs, Mr. Dell!" Sara watched breathlessly as a lumberjack ran over the logs as though they were as firm as the Baker Street bridge.

"Lord A-mighty!" Mr. Dell's yell and Sara's little scream

brought Mr. Bolster out of the inner office. Mr. Sevrance followed him.

A red-shirted body had been tossed clear above the logs. It disappeared under the rush of the jam. Everywhere lumberjacks were running for the bank. The whole mass was loose. The river was no longer still. The drumming of the logs was on again, but its roar was a menacing growl. Sara watched the place where the red-shirted body had disappeared, searching the river farther down, but there was no space in the onrush of the logs.

"He was the one that loosed the jam. I seen him get the key log; then they started too fast."

"Must've slipped," Mr. Sevrance said briskly. "How do you do, Sara."

"How do you do, Mr. Sevrance." But Sara's smile was fleeting. Her gaze went back to the window.

"Good-by, Bolster, you have my check," she heard Mr. Sevrance say stiffly. "If you change your mind . . ."

"Good day, Sevrance. I'll make my money my own way!" Papa interrupted him.

The room was so quiet as he left that Sara looked up to see Papa standing back of her, watching the swift floating logs, almost as though he didn't see them.

On the way home, Papa stopped three times to collect rents. Sara liked sitting in the carriage. When he came back from the large house on Chestnut Street he shook his head.

"We can't force people when they haven't got it, Sara, can we?"

Sara didn't answer. She always sat still when Papa talked to her like this, as though he were thinking aloud, but she wondered.

As they reached the house Papa said, "Sara, I wouldn't mention to your mother that you saw the man drowned. It would disturb her."

"No, Papa," Sara answered. Mama and the girls always missed everything exciting.

5 1893

WHEN Sara came home the third spring vacation from Madame LaVerne's Select School for Young Ladies she brought her trunks with her. One sentence in Papa's letter bothered her: "At the present time, daughter, circumstances are such that it will not be convenient to continue your schooling. I have written Madame LaVerne to this effect. After all, there is only one more term and you are eighteen."

"Inconvenient" had an unpleasant sound that Sara considered as she rode home on the train. "Circumstances are such" stayed in her mind as she drove up from the station in the buggy beside Papa.

"Where's Brown?" she asked.

"He's driving a delivery wagon for a grocery store," Papa said. It was queer to think of the big barn without Brown living above it. "I hope, my dear, that you won't mind not finishing the term," Papa added.

"Oh, no," Sara answered quickly. "It will be lovely to be at home." But she did mind. Madame LaVerne was going to take some of the girls to see the World's Fair after school was over.

The house was just the same. Mama came rustling down the front stairs. Belle hurried across the hall from her apartment, and Mary was in the kitchen, just as always. She heard all about the girls; Anne's husband was sick in bed now, Mama said. And little Roger was not strong. Dor and George had put off building their own home, after all. Business was so uncertain. Dor was expecting a baby. Soon Sara felt she had hardly been away.

At dinner Sara looked out through the dining-room windows.

"Why, there's a fence on this side of the beech tree!"

"Yes," Mama said quickly. "Papa sold Mr. Sevrance twenty feet on that side because he wanted it for a croquet ground and we really have more ground than we need."

Sara thought about the fence. She followed Belle into her room. "Belle, why did Papa sell the Sevrances that land? That gives them the beech tree."

"Papa has had some financial troubles lately, Puss; so many of his tenants can't pay him. You're eighteen, Sara, you might as well understand these things, but don't say anything to Mama. It worries her."

"Oh," Sara said slowly.

"Don't feel badly, Puss. You wouldn't want Papa to be like Mr. Sevrance. He's willing to make money any way he can, in ways Papa wouldn't stoop to."

Sara looked pensive. There seemed to be so many things her family didn't do because they were Bolsters.

"Don't look so solemn, Puss. Here!" Belle went over to the piano and played little tinkling notes while she sang:

On a tree by a river a little tom-tit
Sang "Willow, titwillow, titwillow!"
And I said to him, "Dicky-bird, why do you sit
Singing Willow, titwillow, titwillow?
Is it weakness of intellect, birdie?" I cried,
"Or a rather tough worm in your little inside?"

With a shake of his poor little head he replied,
"O Willow, titwillow, titwillow!"

Sara laughed. Things couldn't be so bad as she thought.

Belle swung around on the piano stool. "If *The Mikado* comes to Armitage next winter you must go to see it. Did you know I'm having a party for you Tuesday night? We'll have all your old friends who are in town. Mama thought you were old enough to have a supper party now that you're through school."

Sara stood in her own room before the big bureau and tried turning under the hair that until now had hung loosely over her shoulders. If she kept the ribbon around her head, just above the bang, Mama wouldn't mind. Her hair did look well that way. It made her face more oval. She leaned closer to the mirror and wondered if Derrick would think her beautiful if he should see her now. Quick color rushed into her face at her own conceit. She picked up the embroidery she had been doing at Madame LaVerne's and hurried downstairs to sew with the girls in a kind of self-imposed penance.

The girls always came over in the afternoons and brought their work.

"Now I have all my girls together," Mama said, a small satisfied smile around her lips. "Sara, it's time you learned to do fine mending. A lady should always know how to mend beautifully."

At first it was pleasant to sit by the window in the long sitting room. Sara slyly pulled her skirt down as far as it would go and every now and then reached up to feel the soft roll of hair. The napkin she was mending was deceitful. It was soft and cool at first and then it changed. The softness became a hot, crumpled mass. The self-pattern of ferns was too shadowy when she worked over it a while, and the raveled threads she was working with were too short. She was tired of sitting still. When she was through she would run across the avenue and go down by the river. There might be swallows along the mud banks by now. Her thimble was hot on her finger. She took it off and tried sewing without it.

"How does Roger feel today?" Mama asked.

A worried pucker showed in Anne's forehead when she spoke of Roger. "Oh, his cough is better, I think, since Dr. Barnes ordered port for him every day. But the baby bothers him and he doesn't sleep well. He wakes up at night wringing wet."

"With spring coming on he'll feel stronger," Mama said cheerily.

"There!" Sara held up the napkin with a bright drop of blood on it. "I've stuck my finger! I hate sewing anyway."

The girls laughed at her, but Mama's face was serious.

"Sara, I should regret having you such a hoyden that you couldn't sew nicely."

"Paul Sevrance is coming up the walk!" Belle reported from the west window. Dor and Anne exchanged glances.

Sara jumbled her sewing things into her bag and rushed to the door.

"Hello, Paul," Sara said as she had been saying every vacation.

"Hello, Sara," Paul answered, grinning. They both laughed for no reason at all, taking stock of each other. Paul was twenty-one and a senior at Harvard.

"You look so different! Oh, Paul, it's your mustache!" Sara laughed.

"What about you? You've done something to your hair."

Sara felt the soft roll cautiously.

"Father gave me a new horse; I came over to take you riding."

"How wonderful, Paul! I'll get my hat and coat." Then, remembering, she said quickly, "Won't you come in and speak to Mama and the girls?"

"Mama, Paul has a new horse. May I go riding with him?" Sara asked eagerly.

Mama hesitated. "You're driving alone, Paul?"

"Yes," Paul said, "but the horse is perfectly safe."

"Well," Mrs. Bolster said slowly, looking from Sara's eager face to Paul's, "don't be gone more than an hour. Sara, put on your warm jacket; it's very windy."

Sara settled herself in the seat with a sigh. "Oh, I hate to sew. You came at just the right minute."

"Only because you hate to sew?" Paul asked, grinning.

Sara turned indignantly. "Just because you've been to college you don't have to make fancy speeches."

Paul laughed and pulled up the reins. "I thought you were all grown up now."

"Well, I'm not at all," Sara answered promptly with sudden distaste for maturity. "What's the mare's name?"

"I thought I'd name her Sara," Paul answered.

"Paul, I'll get right out now!"

"Names are free. I happen to like the name of Sara."

Sara sat stiffly, trying not to laugh, her eyes on the shining coat of the chestnut mare.

"We'll drive up Webster's hill and I'll let Sara out a little."

The sound of the mare's hoofs was lost on the cedar blocks, but the wheels made a light, swift whirring sound. The wind blew against Sara's face. Paul flourished the whip so that it whistled in the air. The chestnut mare laid back one ear, switched her tail and stepped out.

"She's a beauty, Paul," Sara said.

"Oh, you mean Sara!" Paul laughed at Sara's heightened color. "Look, the gates are still open; let's tease old Weaver and rush them," Paul said as they came to the tollbridge.

"You can't; he's coming out for the toll."

"Watch me!" Paul said.

The tollgate keeper shuffled out of his house. Paul pulled on the reins and touched the horse smartly with the whip. The horse sprang forward so suddenly that Sara's head bobbed back. They whirled past the tollgate window and across the bridge.

"Hey, you!" the tollgate keeper yelled.

"Oh, Paul, we shouldn't." But Paul laughed.

"Why not; we've paid enough toll to build a bridge of our own. Remember the time we drove in a cab the length of Water Street?" Paul asked.

Sara flushed suddenly and pulled off a tiny thread from the seam of her glove. She felt Paul looking at her. She sat up a little straighter in unconscious imitation of Madame LaVerne at tea. In a voice a little more formal than her own she said:

"That was when we were children. Did you know I'm not going back to school?"

"Girls are lucky; they don't have to think of doing anything useful. You'll be going to parties and doing what you want to this spring while I'm slaving away." Then before Sara could retort indignantly he said, "I want to go to Germany next year to finish. Father won't say I can yet, but I think he'll give in."

"You'd come back with an Imperial and a walking stick and everything; oh, Paul!" Sara laughed, seeing him.

"I do wish I were a man," she said, frowning.

"I don't." Paul tried to take her hand, but Sara reached quickly in her pocket for a handkerchief and stared out across the city.

They were up a little from the valley. The town lay below them in an irregular circle with the river running through it and streaming out beyond like a gathering string. Only the chestnut trees had buds; the maples and beeches and elms were bare. The lumber mills along the river held up black stacks, the water tank stood out above the roofs of the houses, and over on Pomona Street Henkel's brewery reared its stolid German outlines in nice contrast to the fancy cupolas of the big houses on the bayou.

"Look, Paul, isn't that a fire?"

Above the only sawmill on the west side, almost midway between the docks on the river and the fancy cupolas of Park Drive, a cloud of yellow-black smoke belched out into the sky. Almost simultaneously came the fire bell tolling the number of the ward.

"Holy old Mackinaw! It's the old Wheelock Lumber Mill." Paul reined in the horse. "There's an awful wind blowing for a fire."

From the station house across Racine Street clanged the fire engine, and thundering after it, the hook-and-ladder wagon.

"That's from Number Four," Paul said. The smell of smoke reached up to the hill. The sky was covered over by the yellowish black film. "It's a whopper!"

Again the deep bell tolled the ward number. The frantic alarm bell of another firetruck beat out its terror in time to the rapid course of the firehorses down Water Street.

"They're calling them all out. It's in our ward."

"Oh, Paul, let's get home quick!"

✦

At the Racine Street bridge they were stopped by a guard. "No carriages can go through. The fire's spreading; you don't want to go over there now!"

Before Paul knew it, Sara had jumped down from the carriage and was racing past the man standing guard.

"Here, hold this horse," Paul told the astonished guard. "Here's a dollar for you." He ran after Sara.

Once, Paul pulled her up on the lawn as a fire engine clanged past. Now and then a burning piece of wood or cinders rode by on the wind. They passed a street where every house seemed on fire. They heard the screams of horses trapped in a barn and smelled the burned flesh. A woman ran toward them away from the fire. "The whole west side's going!" she called to them.

"I knew it," Sara said when they reached Park Avenue. The street was blocked with fire engines. The hook-and-ladder truck was drawn up on the terrace. The first two houses in the block were furiously burning ruins.

Sara gazed in horror at the roof of the Healeys' house that stood next to theirs. It seemed shingled with fire. She saw the Healeys standing by piles of household goods.

The locust trees were blowing in the wind. They were blowing toward their house. She had always loved the swish of the wind in the locust trees.

The firechief stood in the driveway, bawling out orders through his big trumpet. Sara scarcely heard him, but she heard the water falling on the locust trees.

"They've given up trying to save the Healeys' house," she heard Paul say. She pushed through the crowd. She felt a quick rush of joy when she saw their house. It hadn't caught yet, but it was wood. Its gray clapboard sides were already blistered from the heat. The great plate-glass windows were monstrous squares of red. It looked strangely somber after all the burning houses they had seen. Sara stood still, looking at their house as though she had never seen it before.

"Come on, Sara; don't stand there!" Paul yelled impatiently.

A big bundle of clothes tied in a quilt came flying down to the ground from the second-story window. Belle leaned out after it. As though she had known Sara and Paul would be there she called out, "Take it way over on the lawn, Sara, where Mama is."

Paul took one side and she took the other. They were running now. There was Mama, and Dor was holding little Roger.

"Mama, it hasn't caught yet!" Sara called out.

Mama shook her head. "Quick, Sara, we must get some of the china and silver out."

They went back and forth, walking carefully with their loads, running back. She and Paul carried out the rosewood chest with the brass clasps and corners. Mama carried out the family Bible that held the record of all their births and Winthrop's death. It didn't seem queer to find strangers helping, going through the rooms. Two men carried out a bureau and dropped it with such a thud at the foot of the front steps that the top drawer spilled out, disgorging its contents in the driveway. Sara ran by, noticing Mama's black satin bag with the silver top, and a black taffeta petticoat in the jumble of things. A bracelet had rolled across the road; it had a lock of hair braided in it. Sara stopped to pick it up and slipped it on her wrist.

Paul came down the steps, carrying a big gold-framed painting of Sara's grandmother.

Sara only glanced at the picture. She was running back into the house.

"Get all the clothes you can, Sara. If the house goes we

won't have anything to wear," Belle called. Sara pulled dresses off the hangers, her red coat with the beaver trimming. . . .

They could hear the sound of water in the attic above. It sounded like a heavy rain. It couldn't be anything more. But the smoke, thick, suffocating smoke came from somewhere, from the other houses. Theirs wouldn't burn.

"Everybody out of here!" a fireman yelled.

Sara ran down the stairs, behind Belle, her hand passing swiftly over the polished stair rail in a caress. Mary scuttled out of the music room, panting under the burden of the Rogers' group she carried in her arms.

They stood across the lawn and watched. Mama caught her breath as a burning piece of wood from the Healeys' house blew onto their own roof, before their very eyes. The fire was in the top of the locust trees. White ropes of water spiraled over the locust trees, hissing against the flames, trimming the trees like strings of popcorn. The spindles of the railing on the little balcony of the cupola had caught. A spiral of water moved up to the cupola; it straightened into a lance, striking at the flames. But the flames had caught the blinds on the cupola window.

"The barn's caught!" someone shouted. The barn that was so big and clean and smelled of horses and leather and grain. Flames darted out around the corner of the roof from the back. Mary was moaning in a half sing-song to herself:

"Lord help us . . . God's son, Jesus, stop the fire . . . oh, Lord help us!"

"Why, where's Papa?" Sara asked.

"He had to see about some land out the valley. He'll see the smoke but he won't ever get here before the house is all gone." Mama's voice sounded queerly; she hid her face against Belle's shoulder. Dor and Anne stood with their arms around each other. Mary had thrown her apron over her head. But Sara stood apart from the others, watching, seeing every detail: the roses in the hall carpet, the chandelier above the landing. The flames were climbing up the stairs.

Paul Sevrance came home for Thanksgiving with the first bicycle seen in Armitage City. He taught Sara how to ride it within the safe confines of the back drive.

"Let me ride it down to Anne's, Paul."

"You'd kill yourself. If you get it going too fast you won't be able to stop it."

"I can manage it." Sara sat a little insecurely on the high seat, her full skirt billowing around her like a pincushion. She grasped the handlebars and pedaled slowly around to the front of the house.

"Walk it down to the avenue," Paul called out.

But Sara pointed the wheel down the drive, between the big white-washed stones that lined it. The hill seemed to seize the wheels. They turned so fast the thin wire spokes merged into silver disks. The pedals carried her feet around for her. Out on Park Avenue the wheel gathered speed. She wouldn't have stopped for anything. Faster and faster under the bare elms and chestnut trees. This was like sailing. People stopped to watch her, but she couldn't take her hand from the handlebars to wave. She heard Paul cheering her on.

She wasn't afraid. It was as easy as pie. When she came to their house—Anne's house, that is—she would just turn up on the lawn and the steep bank would slow the bicycle so she could jump off. It was more wonderful than riding horse-back.

She passed the black iron hitching-post with the horse's head on it and the horse-block with BOLSTER carved in the front of it. Every time she went by she almost expected to see their house still standing. But it wasn't.

The wind had changed only in time to save the Sevrances' house, the Sevrances, who could afford to build themselves a new mansion so easily, while the Bolsters couldn't even keep the land where their house had stood, Sara thought bitterly. If Papa only hadn't lost the Land Office appointment just then, too!

Almost against her will she looked back over the slope of their old lawn. The old cellar hole had been filled in, and the burned trees had been cut down and cleared away.

"That's one thing about Hiram Sevrance, whatever belongs to him he takes care of," Mama said.

"I suppose he thinks he needs more land for his peacocks!" Belle had said, sniffing.

It was hateful having Mr. Sevrance buy their lots. Mama said never to mention it in front of Papa; Papa felt it so. It was nice of Paul not to say anything about owning them, either. Sara's eyes were shaded by her felt sailor; they were shaded, too, by her thoughts.

They had lived with the girls since the fire. That was in March; seven, no . . . eight months. Mama and Papa were at Anne's because Roger was so sick; no one said that he was dying, though everyone knew it. She and Belle were at Dor's. It was hard for Dor to have them there with the new baby. Sara pedaled faster. She didn't care where they lived, only she hoped they could be settled soon.

Park Avenue leveled out now. The pedals still carried Sara's feet around without effort, but the wheels went more slowly. She began to pump the pedals.

She turned too sharply for Anne's walk and crashed into the big snowball bush. She picked herself up hurriedly and smoothed down her skirts. With her handkerchief she polished a little scratch on the bright enamel of the wheel. Paul must think she had made a perfect ride.

She could still feel the wind in her ears as she went into the house. The house had to be kept warm for Roger, but it seemed hot and stuffy after whirling down Park Avenue in the cold air. Her face stung from the wind. She couldn't wait to tell Paul she had made it. Maybe he'd leave the bicycle here while he was away at school.

She heard Mama and Papa talking in the back parlor.

"You see, Corona, Mr. Atkinson wants me to raise some money and come in with him to start the bicycle factory here. He talks about some sort of a horseless carriage, too, but I don't take much stock in that. I am convinced, however, that in five years everyone will be riding one of these bicycles. It seems like a great opportunity."

Sara stood outside the door listening. Papa sounded as though he were making a speech.

"Well, if you think best, Winthrop, but isn't that the Atkinson who married some German girl and they live over on the east side?" Mama asked irrelevantly.

"Atkinson is an able man and a successful manufacturer," Papa said with dignity. "I don't know anything about his wife. But you see, Corona, the trouble is that the fire has about wiped me out. It's going to be difficult even to keep up the taxes on my present properties now that I no longer have the revenue from the Land Office appointment. If I join Atkinson in his venture it will be necessary to make a drastic cut in our living expenses. We can't quarter ourselves on the girls indefinitely and I thought for a while, at least . . ."

"What, Winthrop?"

"Well, we could live in that house I own over on the east side. It's large enough and . . ."

"Winthrop, you can't be serious!" Unbelief was in Mama's voice. "My home means everything to me and I know what it means to my girls. Think of Sara! She'll be having friends in and going to parties, and Belle . . ."

"Well . . ." Papa's voice drooped. He sounded disappointed. Sara couldn't stand to have him hurt. She burst into the room.

"Oh, Mama, I've just been riding Paul's new bicycle. It's the most glorious thing I've ever done. I was going upstairs and I'm sorry, but I heard you talking about a bicycle business and I knew you'd want to hear about my ride." Sara's words came out with a rush.

"You see, Corona, it's bound to succeed!" Mr. Bolster's thin lips smiled.

"Sara, you might have been killed! Go quickly and tidy yourself. Hiram Sevrance lets Paul have everything he wants."

"But, Mama, you don't know what it's like. And I wouldn't mind living on the east side at all. Please . . ."

"Sara, your Father and I must decide these things as we see best. You've torn your stocking."

Sara looked down at the white flesh of her ankle showing through the stocking. She glanced at Papa. He seemed busy with his own thoughts. On the desk in front of him was a paper with columns of figures on it.

"Hurry, Sara," Mama said gently but firmly.

"Mama, why can't I do something? I'm eighteen and I'm sick of being around home and sewing and making leather things for the church bazaar. I could be a secretary or—or *something*."

"There happen to be certain things that my daughters never have done and I hope never will do. You're raising your voice and I know poor Roger is trying to sleep," Mama said.

Sara left the room, but she stood shamelessly in the hall listening.

"Madame LaVerne wrote me that Sara was impetuous." Mama sounded as though she were amused. "But don't you see from what she just said, Winthrop, how much she needs the proper environment these next few years?"

Papa's answer was not audible.

"I know that we must get settled soon, Winthrop. I talked to Mrs. Higgins yesterday at church. She said they had thought of selling their house, but they would be willing to rent to us."

"Yes, Mrs. Higgins called to see me this morning about it." Papa's voice sounded tired. "The rent is pretty high, Corona."

"But, Winthrop, if it were *my* home I wouldn't want to rent it for any less. I know we'd feel at home there; why, I used to go there as a girl." Mama's voice sounded sweetly reasonable.

"Of course, Corona, but it will be expensive to run in addition to the high rent."

"And then, Winthrop, you'll have time now to write your history of Armitage City, and the Higgins' house has a library with a view toward the river that would be a splendid place to work," Mama said, as though she hadn't heard.

Why didn't Papa say he didn't want to do it? He must be just sitting there, looking at those figures. Couldn't Mama see?

"Winthrop, you know what I want most is your happiness and that of the girls. I suppose we could move over to the east side, but it would mean changing our whole way of living . . . " Mama went on dubiously.

"No, Corona, I wouldn't think of it." Papa's voice sounded as though he were sighing. "You're right, my dear. Some things are a good deal more important than money."

Sara ran upstairs, the sound of the wind in her ears displaced by the tired sound of Papa's voice. Why couldn't they change their way of living? Why couldn't she find a position? She was eighteen. All the satisfaction of being the first girl to ride a bicycle in Armitage was gone.

6

WITHIN a month the Bolsters were established in the Higgins' house. It was so much like their own, they nearly forgot that it was rented. Roger's death precipitated their moving. Mama felt that Anne needed to be in a different house and with her own family.

Winthrop Bolster moved his big walnut desk from the inner room of the Land Office into the Higgins' library. He moved his big bookcase and the calfskin-bound books he had used to read during a lull at the Land Office. Close to his desk were his old favorites: Gibbon's *Decline and Fall of the Roman Empire, A Pioneer History of Michigan,* two volumes of Macaulay, and a copy of Shakespeare with the inscription on the flyleaf: "To Winthrop Bolster from his wife, Corona Colton Bolster, as a pledge of her undying affection." There was the ledger in which he was writing the history of Armitage City in his fine copper-plate hand. And there, by some subtle process of transplantation, even without the maps, was the atmosphere of the Land Office.

Corona Bolster often looked in the open door as she went by, smiling contentedly to see him. He had said no more about the bicycle factory. She had seen in the news that Mr. Atkinson had taken in someone with a German name as a partner, one of his wife's relatives, doubtless.

"I'm so thankful we're so nicely settled before the holidays, aren't you, Winthrop?" she called in from the hall.

Mr. Bolster did not always listen closely to the chatter of his wife and daughters. "What was that, my dear?" he asked; then realizing he had heard, "Very thankful," and retired again into his own thoughts, against which the contented chirping of his wife was only a faraway tinkle.

"I invited the Griffiths for dinner tonight, Winthrop, and Dor and George. You know we bought box tickets for Modjeska in *The Merchant of Venice*."

"Just a family party," Corona Bolster said, greeting the Griffiths at the door that evening. "Of course we're not entertaining any, but it does Anne good to see old friends."

"How comfortable you are here!" Mrs. Griffith exclaimed. "This furniture isn't unlike yours, is it?"

Mama smiled. "Well, Jessie, don't you think that people with the same background usually have about the same taste? Emma Higgins and my mother grew up together."

"How Sara has grown, Winthrop!" Mr. Griffith said. "How old are you now, young lady?"

"Eighteen," Sara smiled.

"Well, we'll be printing your wedding picture in the *Courier* one of these days!" he said teasingly. Mr. Griffith was editor of the evening newspaper.

"Not for a long time, Mr. Griffith," Sara insisted, but she glanced in the hall mirror on her way in to dinner. She felt as old as the girls tonight in her long red faille, made over from Anne's.

The dinner satisfied even Mrs. Bolster. The turkey was brown yet juicy, the chestnut stuffing both rich and light, but after the consommé, turbot, and squab, the appetites were dulled a trifle. The sauterne was better than the food for its very tartness. The Roman punch freshened the palate like cold water on the face.

Sara, sitting between Mr. Griffith on one side and Anne on the other, listened politely, but she was impatient for dinner to be over. There hadn't been a play in Armitage City for ever so long and Paul would be there. He was bringing his roommate home for the holidays.

"We need a Board of Trade here to bring in new business. The city can't survive always on lumber," George declared emphatically.

"More industries like Hans Bocksch's soap factory, you mean, George?" Mr. Bolster asked sarcastically. "The smell of the soap would drive anyone away for six blocks around."

"Oh, these industries all have their distinctive fragrance. I own a piece of land over on the east side and I'll tell you the smell from Henkel's brewery is enough to make you think you're actually drinking beer. I'm not sure it couldn't intoxicate you." Even the ladies joined in the laughter at Mr. Griffith's wit.

Then, at last, the women were going upstairs to put on their wraps. Winthrop Bolster passed his fine Havana cigars from the carved box in the library. His sharply etched nostrils twitched, breathing in the faint aroma as he opened the box. He lighted his cigar with satisfaction. He must stop in and ask Beecham to order him some more tomorrow.

Sara knew when Paul came in, pushing back the green curtains in the box across the theater. This year she pretended not to see him, only glancing in his direction after the play had begun and the theater was dark.

At the intermission Paul came over to their box with John Seabury, his roommate. They were much alike with their curled mustaches and their big club pins on their vests. Sara looked at them coolly. Belle and Dor talked to them more than she did.

"It's no wonder that Paul can't see the girls around Boston, at all, Miss Bolster. I understand now."

Sara felt the quick color spring into her face and neck. It was very pleasant to have two young men bowing over her in the box at a play.

Then the little bell rang and she forgot everything but the black eyes burning out of that pale face on the stage. She felt for Belle's opera glasses without taking her own eyes from the stage. How beautiful Madame Modjeska was! When her voice deepened it sent little shivers down Sara's spine.

The quality of mercy is not strain'd,
It droppeth as the gentle rain from heaven
Upon the place beneath.

Sara leaned a little closer to the railing of the box.

When the curtains fell on the third act and the lights were turned up all over the Opera House, Sara's eyes were shining.

"Wasn't it the most beautiful thing you ever saw, Mr. Griffith?" Sara said, turning to Mr. Griffith, who sat in the chair back of her.

"An excellent performance, indeed!" Mr. Griffith remarked ponderously. "I hope my young cub of a society reporter does a proper job on it in the *Courier;* I can't see him here. He has a way of . . ." The last of Mr. Griffith's remarks was lost in an apologetic cough.

"Oh, Mr. Griffith, I could write it up for you." Sara's eyes were bright in their eagerness.

"Why, Sara, I didn't know you had any such leaning! I don't know what your mother would say to such an idea."

But Mrs. Bolster was talking with Mrs. Griffith. Both

ladies were bowing and smiling at the occupants of other boxes.

"You see more strange faces every time you stir out," Mrs. Griffith remarked, looking over the railing on the audience below. "Fifteen years ago, there were the families on the bayou and Chestnut Avenue and lower Park, and the foreigners and all that element stayed on the other side of the river."

Belle leaned nearer to Mrs. Griffith. "I meant to tell Mother this afternoon that Sadie Pyle announced her engagement to that young Irishman who is head of the new Plate Glass Company."

Both ladies raised their eyebrows.

"I have been fortunate with my girls, after all," Mrs. Bolster said.

After the last act Madame Modjeska took several curtain calls, then the curtain fell again a little more swiftly, thudding to the floor with a note of finality. The occupants of the boxes rose, putting on their wraps, praising the famous actress and the performance in well-bred murmurs.

"Remarkable emotional range!" Mr. Griffith declared, falling into one of the clichés often used by his reporter.

But a new burst of applause came from the upper gallery. People were stamping on the floor, sending a faint powder of dust down on the occupants of the boxes. Those in the rear on the ground floor took it up, and standing, some with their wraps on, applauded until their hands were red.

A deep voice called out in German: "Wundervoll, Frau Modjeska, bravo! . . ."

"Hoch!" another voice called far back in the gallery.

"Really, that is going a little far," someone in the adjoining box said indignantly.

"Their enthusiasm is getting out of bounds, I think,"

Judge Rand said to Mr. Bolster across the dividing rail of their boxes.

But the curtain rose again. Madame Modjeska appeared in smiling good humor. She waved to the boisterous top gallery and threw a kiss to them. The gallery went wild. No one moved from his place. The curtain rose and fell a dozen times. And as it fell finally and the lights were turned on full in the theater, a deep German voice called out: "Danke, gnädige Frau!"

The orchestra struck up. Laughter and voices rose beneath it. And in the dressing room back-stage Madame Modjeska was saying: "It was like a performance in Europe. American audiences are often so cold. I like this, how do you call it, Armitage City."

"We'll just drive Sara down past Modjeska's private car; they say it's worth seeing, Mrs. Bolster, and we'll bring her right back." Paul Sevrance was hard to refuse anything. He had grown to a full six feet two and his features had strengthened. He held his silk hat in one hand, and his opera cloak that was the latest style at Harvard was thrown over his arm.

"Madame Modjeska said she would receive us in her car after the performance. We wrote on a card that we sent in with the roses and asked her," Paul explained, a little proud of his finesse.

"Let them go, Mrs. Bolster. I can remember when I used to visit stage doors, myself!" Mr. Griffith chuckled.

"Mr. Griffith, I'm serious about wanting to write for your paper. I'm coming down to see you, tomorrow," Sara told him earnestly. She was gone before he could answer—laughing, down the narrow little hallway that ran back of the boxes, Paul's hand on her elbow.

"Quite a girl, Winthrop!" Mr. Griffith said.

"I think so," Mr. Bolster agreed. He was proud of all his girls. "But she's full of notions at her age. She asked her mother the other day if she didn't think she could be a secretary!" They smiled benevolently together.

"Remember the time we waited two hours at the stage door to see Lillian Russell, and then we didn't get to see her?" John Seabury asked Paul on the way down to the station.

"Yes, but we didn't know the ropes on this stage-door business then!" Paul rejoined.

"Is that one of your courses at Harvard?" Mary Healey inquired.

The boys laughed knowingly.

"You must have a very gay time at school!" Sara said.

"Pretty. . . . I've been looking forward all term to seeing you, though." Paul's voice sank to a murmur. Under the fur robe his hand found Sara's in her small beaver muff. He turned to look at her and his face, close to hers, sent a curious stir through her. She met his glance an instant.

"There it is, over on the siding!" Mary pointed out.

"Holy smokes! I wouldn't mind having a car like that to go back to school in," John Seabury said.

Madame Modjeska's palace car had a tiny salon. Hothouse flowers smothered any faintest train smell. Silk curtains shut out the forlorn ugliness of the Baker Street station and the eyes of the curious.

Madame Modjeska was sitting at one end of the salon talking in German to a young man beside her when the maid showed them into the passageway. She lifted her hands in a baffled little gesture and finished her sentence in French. When the young man answered her in French she laughed delightedly.

"Wait, we must greet these young Americans!" She came across the little salon and shook hands with them.

"I thank you for your flowers; they are beautiful! You must meet a friend of mine, Dr. Henkel. He told me all about America before I came over here. I played in Göttingen and the students at the University gave me a gay party. Dr. Henkel was studying there then. But, of course, you know him. It was so nice to know somebody already in Armitage City." She smiled across at him. "I like your native city, Dr. Henkel!"

Sara glanced from Madame Modjeska to the young man. A smile lit up his serious face. His stiff little bow was the only thing about him that had a foreign air. He seemed older than Paul or John and more at ease with Madame Modjeska, for all their talk of stage doors. She smiled as she met his eye and looked quickly back to Madame Modjeska.

Madame Modjeska signed their programs for them before they left.

"Who's the linguist of Armitage City, Paul?" John Seabury asked when they were back in the sleigh.

Paul laughed. "That was pretty cool, wasn't it? He's the son of a brewer here. John Henkel's beer! I'll see that you sample some. He's one of the foreigners from the east side."

"He's carrying a good fraternity pin on his vest just the same," John muttered.

"Madame Modjeska is a foreigner, too," Sara said thoughtfully. How strange it was: foreigners had always meant queerly dressed thick-looking women. Madame Modjeska was the most beautiful woman she had ever seen.

"She's really Polish," Mary Healey said.

"What do you suppose the Red Sash Brigade would think of Madame Modjeska's palace car at the Baker Street station, Sara?" Paul asked, laughing. "She'd have a shock, too, if they mistook her set-up!" John laughed with Paul but the girls were noticeably quiet.

The horses were trotting again, shaking the bells at every step. Paul reached his hand over to find Sara's.

"Penny for your thoughts?"

"Oh, nothing much. I'd like to travel and know great people and be able to speak other languages easily. I've never been anywhere, really. Wouldn't it be exciting?"

"You're exciting to me!"

Sara leaned her head back to watch the cold stars riding overhead.

7 JANUARY, 1894

SARA was taken aback by the dingy stairway leading to the editorial offices of the *Courier*. The yellow plaster walls above the molasses-colored wainscoting that climbed the stairs were streaked with gas soot. One of the metal treads on the stairs was loose. At the top of the stairs the walls of a square gloomy hall were broken by long doors. Through the open transoms came the continuous rumbling of the presses, against which the typewriters made only a light staccato clicking.

Sara straightened her hat and felt the little bow at the neck of her dress. A bright pink colored her cheeks.

She knocked at the door, but too lightly to be heard through the din of the machines. She opened the door. A long thin man with red hair sat tipped well back in his chair, his heels on the top of the big desk. The eyeshade he wore was cocked over the left ear. He chewed at a strong cigar.

"How do you do," Sara began.

"Howd'ye do," he muttered. "Ad department downstairs, first door on left." He indicated the direction with his thumb.

"Mr. Griffith is expecting me, or at least he knew I would be calling some time this week. I'm Miss Bolster, Miss Sara Bolster."

The stringy man pulled himself out of his chair.

"Pleased to meet you," he said, laying the cigar down on

a blue glass paperweight. "My name's Clancy, city editor," he said with a sheepish grin on his face. "I'll tell the boss, myself."

When the door closed behind him Sara gazed around the big room that smelled so strongly of smoke, a leaking radiator, the dry smell of the yellowed sheets of newspaper hanging from poles on the wall, and dust. She removed her glove from one hand and then replaced it. Someone was racing up the stairs, hitting his heels against the brass treads. A young man, not much older than Paul, hurried into the room, glanced quickly at her as though to take her all in at once, and took off his hat.

"Good morning! C'n I do anything for you?"

"No, thank you," Sara answered, smiling gravely.

The young man seated himself on the edge of the chair at the desk the red-headed man had left and started writing rapidly. She could hear his pencil across the room. He tore the page off the pad and seemed rather to slide than to walk across to the inner office door, colliding, as he opened it, with Mr. Clancy.

"Look what you're about, ye young spalpeen!" Clancy roared at him. He laid his two enormous bony hands on the younger man's slighter shoulders and moved him out of the way bodily.

"Please walk in, Miss Bolster," he said, still holding his victim.

Sara smiled at both of them. Clancy's face continued dour; between his arms the younger man's face smiled admiringly at her.

"Well, Sara!" Mr. Griffith pushed back his chair. "So you were really in earnest! Well, let's see. . . ." Mr. Griffith strained the spring on his swivel chair to the utmost as he leaned back and ruffled the back of his hair with one hand.

"I don't know, now; there might be a place for you. Miss Alma's getting on; she runs the Housewife's Friend and Churches and Clubs and you have different, uh, connections from Rollo's . . . but what d'yer family say about this idea?"

Sara smiled faintly, a sweet-faced doll kind of a smile. "I haven't told them. I thought there was no reason for it unless I secured the position."

Mr. Griffith snorted so loudly he covered his mouth with his hand. He was a different person here from the person he was at dinner parties. The snort ended in a series of laughs. "Don't stir up trouble till you need to, eh? Smart girl!"

Sara flushed.

"Well, we don't pay very much. Why do you want to work? Your father's able to support you."

"I'm tired of staying home," Sara answered calmly.

Again the snort, more subdued this time.

"Well, I guess we could try you. Some of the Milwaukee and Detroit papers have female society reporters. I'll tell you, you know the new organ factory that's going up over on Calumet Street? You go over there and tell the man I sent you and write a story about it; anything that interests you."

"But," Sara began and closed her lips.

"We'll have you try out for a period of two weeks before I say for certain. You can do any society functions, and that don't mean just doings on the west side, either. My wife doesn't think anything happens worth putting in the paper, east of the Baker Street bridge, but I'll tell you the French Canadian ladies and the German ladies and the Irish ladies like to read about themselves in the paper, too, and it's their paper same as it is ours. I don't care whether the *Courier* is propped up on top of the range while a woman's stirring jelly or read in the drawing room."

"Of course not," Sara agreed promptly.

"And then a feature I've had in mind for some time is telling about the meetings of these clubs, who speaks, all that kind of thing. Suppose we start out with twelve dollars a week for the first two weeks, raised to fourteen if you're satisfactory?"

Sara's face glowed. "That would be fine!"

Mr. Griffith pumped her hand. He was a more emphatic person here than with Mrs. Griffith.

"But that means, young lady, that you've got to get here on time; eight a.m. sharp every morning; no indulging in strong spirits to point of excess, playing games for money or shirking the job, as I tell the boys when I hire 'em; much good does it do!" he told her with a wink of his eye so ponderous and complete that it made his round kindly face resemble an owl's.

Sara smiled and blushed again.

"And, mind! I don't want any crowd of swains hanging around the office in working hours." He threw open the door into the outer office and announced in a loud voice:

"Miss Bolster, meet the boys! Boys, this is our new star reporter!"

Clancy scowled and nodded. The young man whom Mr. Griffith introduced as "Campau, Barney for short," beamed on her and another young man, named Oldsworth, bowed abstractedly. The office boy and a thin, spinsterish-looking woman named Miss Alma completed the force.

"How do you do," Sara said in a small voice.

Sara waited until dinnertime to tell the family. She waited even until after the soup.

"I went in to see Mr. Griffith, today, Papa. He's going to let me work for him. If I'm satisfactory he'll pay me fourteen dollars a week. I went over to the new organ factory and wrote a story about it." Sara spoke very fast so she wouldn't be interrupted.

"What do you mean, Sara; as a reporter?" Papa was frowning.

"Sara!" Mama looked at her with a hurt expression in her eyes. "I can't understand how one of my girls couldn't be happy at home until she leaves to make a home of her own. Papa, you speak to Mr. Griffith."

Belle fingered the topaz pin at her neck. "Sara, I may as well tell you now; you were going to be asked to join the Winter Club. Mrs. Partlow thought you were a little young, but the others outvoted her."

"Sara, if it was the idea of working for money that attracted you, put that out of your mind. I think I'm still capable of providing for all my daughters," Papa said.

"I know that; and I am happy here, but I want to do something! This is going to be so interesting. You should see the red-haired Irishman that's the city editor. . . ."

"I dare say," Mama interposed. "Anne, have just a little piece of pound cake. You're not eating enough to keep a bird alive!"

The next morning the atmosphere at breakfast was strained. When Sara came home at night, everyone was pleasant. No one asked her about her work. Sara laid the fresh copy of the *Courier* on the table. On an inner sheet was the account she had written of the organ company. She wished it could have been more than three paragraphs long. No one made any move to read the paper.

At dinner, Belle said, "How would you like to go to Atlantic City after Christmas, Sara? Papa says perhaps you and I could go for a couple of weeks."

Sara hesitated. "I wouldn't like it at all. Mr. Griffith said

I did well with my article. I think I'm going to have the position permanently." She avoided Mama's hurt expression. She looked past Anne and Belle. When she had sufficient courage to glance at Papa she saw a slight smile above his white beard and felt reassured.

"I notice, Winthrop, that the front parlor is drafty around the long windows just as ours used to be," Mama said. They weren't going to discuss it any more. They didn't like it, but they wouldn't keep on about it. "A lady never argues," Mama always said. Sara had a warm sense of triumph.

And then before the two weeks were up, Sara was running up the long double flight of stairs, clicking the brass treads with her own small heels, without thinking how dingy the upper hall looked. She was calling Mr. Campau "Barney" and Mr. Oldsworth "little Rollo" and the tall, scowling Irishman "Clancy." She knew that Miss Alma had had a "devastating love affair" with a reporter who died of drink. She was no longer startled by the men working in their vests and shirtsleeves, nor did she even glance at the brown pottery cuspidors by the men's desks.

Already the little desk in the corner by the window had become uniquely hers. Her own red leather desk set was on the desk top, her own cut-glass ink bottle that she had bought in Healey's stationery store. In the top drawer were her personal belongings: a pile of small white linen handkerchiefs embroidered with an S, a large eraser, a dimunitive heart-shaped pincushion with pins, a box of peppermint wafers with which to ward off hunger, pads, pencils, pen points and the like, a dictionary, three letters from Paul, in order of their dates, and a copy of the first paper in which words of hers had ever appeared, unsigned, of course, but still hers: the account of the organ company, of which Mr. Griffith had

said, "Not bad, not bad at all." Clancy had scowled and said:
"You could tell a woman did it, any day."

Little Rollo read aloud from the article: " 'The marvel is that out of this intricate mechanism can come a single note as sweet and pure as a note on a violin. . . .' You know, that's not a bad sentence."

Barney, roused out of his extreme melancholia to say, "Too long; been mine, the boss'd have cut it."

The account of the organ was clipped together with shorter paragraphs reporting the arrival of "the C. Schyler-Bosworths from a two weeks' trip to New York City" or one announcing the "departure of Mrs. Josie Ahnfeld Goss to the metropolis of Detroit to visit her parents. Mrs. Goss will return to us in the early spring months." Sara had read them all over to herself until the names and even the words became blurred and only a cadence of her own creating remained like music in her head.

When Mary Healey or Beth Ingalls or the girls she had always known invited her to parties they still said, "I don't know whether you'll want to come, Sara; you'll be so late getting home"; or "I'm having dinner at six-thirty, Sara; can you get away in time?"

But of course she could come. She had even once changed her dress and shoes to the clothes she had brought that morning in a valise, in the dubious little lavatory that served the whole upper floor of the Flat Iron Building, doing her hair by the six-inch square of mirror that hung under the gas jet. When she came back into the office, little Rollo let out a loud whistle and even Barney's face was startled out of its usual gloomy cast.

"Cinderella steps out!" little Rollo said speculatively.

If Sara stayed overnight at Emma Carthugh's or Mary Healey's so they could talk the party all over and laugh again at the way Bert Hopkins was certainly crazy about Ginny More, she asked the maid to call her and crept out early enough to be at the office of the *Courier* on time.

She loved it. She loved having to be there at a certain time, and the list of assignments Clancy or sometimes Mr. Griffith left for her.

She sat very primly at her desk, in her high-necked blue mohair with only a piping of scarlet at her neck. Her pen moved busily across the page, but she was listening to Clancy and little Rollo and Barney talking. Miss Alma seldom talked to the men at all.

"Armitage City'll never grow," Barney declared in disgust. It's going downhill, now. It was built on white pine; now the white pine's gone. There's no future here. I'm going to get off a two-by-four little sheet like this and go down to Detroit."

"The thing I hate about this town is that it's so hypocritical. You couldn't find any more plain wickedness anywhere than down around lower Water Street. Anything you want: dope, drink, gambling, obliging ladies. Some of the worthy port-drinking deacons from the west side come down and have a fling and then go back and pretend they never knew such things existed."

If they aired their views sometimes for the delectation of the young girl in the corner they never looked her way while they were talking. But she sat demurely, gaining a liberal education.

"In Detroit, the first families don't think it's against a man to be born with a foreign name," Barney Campau muttered.

Sara listened. She did not look up from the paper under her hand that had on it, written over and over again like a copybook, a phrase of Barney's:

"The white pine's gone, the white pine's gone." She was

thinking, as she wrote, about the worthy deacons from the west side who went down to lower Water Street, about the time Paul showed her a professional, how Derrick had said: "There's more than just one kind of people."

"The white pine's gone." She wrote it diagonally this time and suddenly the words sank in. She looked up from her paper, across at little Rollo and Clancy.

"Do you mean there won't be any more log drives?" she asked.

Barney nodded solemnly. "You may have been born in a lumber town, Miss Bolster, but you won't die in one if you stay here. The end of our decade will see the lumber done."

"I loved the log drives," Sara said and then, a little embarrassed that she had shown she was listening, she crumpled the sheet of paper in front of her and threw it in the wire basket under her desk, and went out to report the meeting of the Century Club.

"The fair virgin hath the listening ear," little Rollo commented, letting the front legs of his chair down with a thump.

8

THE meeting was at the Newboldts'. The Century Club was an important organization. It and the Winter Club looked down from Olympian heights on all more recent culture and social clubs. The Century's membership exceeded sixty-five. It was possible to meet only in homes containing rooms of generous proportions.

Sara hurried up to the heavily curtained double doors. The last time she had been here was to attend May Newboldt's dance. It was funny to come with a notebook and pencil in her pocket. The Newboldts' butler opened the door quietly. The Newboldts had been the first family in Armitage City to have a butler. Theirs had been one of the first of the great fortunes amassed in the forests north of Armitage City.

It was all just as she knew it would be. The Century Club had met at their house, too. She could almost have reported it without attending. She smiled at Mrs. Healey and opened her notebook with a little conscious pride. She was partly hidden behind one of the wide oak pillars of the inglenook at the end of the library. Mrs. Newboldt was introducing the speaker. Sara leaned around to see him, but the post was in her way. She could see him when she stood up to go. She wrote the subject down and underlined it: "The Wanderjahr." She had trouble spelling it.

The speaker's voice was young. His words were carefully enunciated. They came smoothly. She wrote on her ruled pad in the manner of some of the other reports Mr. Griffith had given her to look over.

"The speaker of the afternoon possesses a pleasant voice and a clear manner of expression." She held her pencil still while she listened. The voice was strangely familiar.

"I suspect, that quite aside from acquiring knowledge in the seat of an older culture than our own, one important attraction of the Wanderjahr is that it puts off a little longer the selection of a pattern for life." There was a hint of laughter in the voice. Sara leaned as far to the left as she could without falling off her chair, but she could not see the speaker.

Now he was describing the town of Göttingen. Sara forgot to write. She could see the canal that crossed the town, dividing the Altstadt from the Neuestadt. The speaker pronounced the word as neatly as though he had brought his heels together. She saw the students loitering along the canal, the linden trees whose yellow leaves floated on the smooth water of the canal. He hadn't said that; she could see more than he said. She could see the narrow crooked streets leading up to the town hall, "built in the fourteenth century." "We have come a long way in this country, but we are still a little new, not properly aged, as my father would say of the beer he makes." There was again that hint of laughter in his voice. The rustle of the audience that filled the Newboldts' library and drawing room betokened the appreciation of such an incongruous simile. This was the young man she had met in Madame Modjeska's private car. Sara went back to the beginning of her notes, changing the words "the Speaker" to "Dr. Henkel."

"We can well afford to take the time to go to these richer,

older seats of learning and try to bring back something of their larger humanity, as well as the knowledge of their advances in science."

The applause at the end of the lecture was enthusiastic. The pleasant atmosphere of Culture and wide horizons seemed to envelop the audience. Mrs. Newboldt came over to Sara.

"Sara, my dear, I was so happy when Mr. Griffith said he was sending you to report the meeting. Excellent, didn't you think? It seems incredible that Dr. Henkel could be the son of John Henkel, the brewer. He's gone into practice here, you know." She dropped her voice to a whisper as she said these words. "You will want to meet him, won't you? Come with me."

For the first time, Sara saw the speaker. There was that same slightly foreign air when he bowed. How blond his hair was! He wore his mustache closer-cropped than Paul did. He seemed amused even while Mrs. Partlow was complimenting his speech.

"Dr. Henkel, this is Miss Bolster, who has surprised us all by becoming a reporter on the *Courier*—the society reporter, of course," she added as though that were not quite so bad.

Sara felt herself looked at keenly through his glasses.

"How do you do. I had no idea 'there was a chiel among us,' taking notes!" His eyes had a very definite twinkle. "We met, you know, that night at Madame Modjeska's."

Sara found herself coloring for no apparent reason. "Yes, I remember. I enjoyed your talk very much," she began, and then with an impetuous rush she added, "I should like to see that old town with the narrow crooked streets. You must have enjoyed living there."

"Yes, I did."

They continued to stand in front of Mrs. Newboldt's bust of Venus.

"I should like to show you some pictures I took of out-of-the-way places."

"I should love to see them," Sara answered simply.

"How could I bribe you to limit yourself to an announcement of my talk without any additional frills. This is not my line, you know. My sisters wanted me to do it."

"Oh, the *Courier* is above bribery, Dr. Henkel! If I didn't report your lecture in detail, Mr. Griffith would think I hadn't attended."

Someone came up to speak to him and Sara left. She didn't stay for the high tea that the butler was bringing in, though she took a quick survey of the tea tray because the feminine readers of the *Courier* would like to know what refreshments were served.

She walked all the way back to the Flat Iron Building. A kind of haze of a medieval town rested over the two-story buildings on Water Street. The elms and chestnut trees became linden trees. Why hadn't she said, "Won't you call and show them to us; my sisters . . ." That would have made it all right. "My sisters and I would so enjoy them." Now she might not see him for a long time. He was so different from anyone she knew. She ran up the stairs to the office.

"Well, how was it?" little Rollo called out. He was the only one in the office. "Two parts of culture mixed with five parts of sugar makes a dose the youngest child can take without choking."

At that moment little Rollo seemed rude and lazy. She had thought him romantic, perhaps a second Poe, before.

"It was wonderful, but I doubt if you would have understood it," she said witheringly, and sat down to write her account. She began by crossing out "Dr. Henkel possesses a pleasant voice and a clear manner of expression." It was too much like other reports. "Dr. Henkel," she began again, and then inserted the word "William." "Dr. William Henkel brings to the culture of our city a new viewpoint. He has recently returned from Göttingen, where he went to continue his medical studies, and has joined the ranks of the medical profession in Armitage City." What a nice twinkle he had when he looked at her, as though they had some special joke together that the Century Club didn't understand. He had remembered her. She bit the point of her lead pencil.

"If you swallow lead it makes you sick," little Rollo told her.

The first week of February was taken up at home with talk of a Valentine luncheon Belle was giving, but Sara was scarcely aware of that approaching occasion. In the office of the *Courier* there was excitement of a different kind. Even the temperance revival that had swept the town was shouldered aside into two columns because of the six-column spread given to the strike in the lumber mills. Mr. Griffith, himself, wrote editorials ridiculing the exorbitant demands of the workmen asking for a ten-hour day, recalling the heyday of the lumber industry when a man was willing to work fourteen to eighteen hours a day gladly. Times were changing indeed.

Sara had no part in the strike reporting, but she was caught up in the new tension of the office. There was no time for little Rollo or Barney or Clancy to sit and argue about the evils of the world.

The office was divided on the question. Little Rollo thought the strikers were right and vowed he would tell old windbag Griffith so. Barney was more gloomy than ever and quoted his favorite, Walt Whitman. Little Rollo whistled during his recital and Clancy went out slamming the door behind him, but Sara listened eagerly. She had never read poetry like this.

I think I could turn and live with animals, they're so placid and self-contain'd,
I stand and look at them long and long.

They do not sweat and whine about their condition,
They do not lie awake in the dark and weep for their sins,
They do not make me sick discussing their duty to God,
Not one is dissatisfied, not one is demented with the mania of owning things,
Not one kneels to another, nor to his kind that lived thousands of years ago,
Not one is respectable or unhappy over the whole earth.

Sara worried over which side was right. She discussed it at home until Mama looked disturbed. Mr. Bolster agreed heartily with Mr. Griffith's editorials and cut them out to keep on his desk.

It was later than usual one evening when she came down the stairs out on Water Street. The raw air blew off the river and lifted the loose dirt of the street along the walk. Sara buttoned her fur tippet and pulled down her hat. She always walked as far as the corner and waited there for the trolley car.

As she came out on the street, a young man stepped down from the carriage drawn along the curb, taking off his hat. Sara was startled. Then she recognized Dr. Henkel.

"Miss Bolster, I beg your pardon for seeking you out in so unconventional a way, but I wondered if I couldn't drive you home?"

Sara hesitated only an instant. "Thank you, Dr. Henkel, I would appreciate it. I'm late this evening."

"I thought so," the young man said as he helped her into the carriage. "I have waited before without presuming to ask you and it has usually been earlier than this."

There was the same curious indifference in his manner as to whether she knew that he had waited for her before as at the Century Club meeting when he had mentioned his father's beer, as though he took even himself with humor.

"After I had finished talking to the worthy members of the Century Club I looked around for you, but you had gone." He was looking at her as he spoke.

"Yes, I had to get back to the office."

"Isn't it rather unusual for a young lady like yourself to be a reporter?"

"My mother thinks it is. I like it," Sara said.

They rode in silence up to the tollgate. Sara stole a look at him as his face was turned toward the gatekeeper. He was older than she had thought; he must be twenty-six or seven, anyway. She liked his chamois-colored gloves, opened at the wrist and turned back; the way he held the reins. He managed the horse with hardly a word, more easily even than Paul.

"What a beautiful horse!" Sara said.

"Yes, the head of Father's stable at the brewery, Charlie Freehahn, bought her for me. I've only had her a week. I made my first professional call with her today."

"Oh, did she realize her errand?"

The young man smiled wryly. "I don't know. The patient died before we got there."

"What a shame!"

"Yes, it was. I was quite excited to have my first urgent call. I thought now I shall establish my reputation! I rehearsed what I was going to do all the way over and drove so fast the horse was in a lather. And then they opened the door and told me!" He caricatured himself in his recital.

Sara laughed. "If you'd arrived sooner?"

He shook his head. "A German woman, ninety-six years old. This was her year, you see. However, I had six patients today in my office and not all of them were friends of my sisters or owed my father money." Sara laughed with him.

"I live in the . . ." Sara began.

"I know." Dr. Henkel told her.

"Won't you come in?" she asked as he helped her out and went up to the door with her.

"Thank you, not this evening. But I should like to call sometime."

"Won't you come Sunday afternoon?" Sara said impulsively.

The matter of the strike had been erased so completely from her mind that she seemed to hear her father reading Mr. Griffith's editorial aloud at the dinner table from some level far above a mundane world of strikes.

A certain shyness fell upon Sara. She couldn't bring herself to mention young Dr. Henkel's call on the coming Sunday. Each evening when she came down the stairs of the Flat Iron Building she glanced quickly along the curb before walking up to the corner to wait for the trolley.

Friends often dropped in Sunday afternoons for tea. When Dr. Henkel came she would act just a shade surprised . . . but he might detect that, he was so very quick. She would tell Mama and the girls Sunday at dinner as though she had just remembered.

At dinner Sara said boldly, not quite looking at anyone, "Oh, I forgot to tell you, I asked Dr. Henkel to call this afternoon. He gave that splendid lecture at the Century Club, you know, Mama." She wondered if she were talking very fast.

"I had forgotten," Mama said. "Is he a friend of the Newboldts'?"

"I think he must be," Sara said vaguely.

"May Newboldt told me he really is very nice and quite intellectual," Belle said. "But the Century Club wish they hadn't had him now. The very next week Sadie Pyle Volkner proposed his sisters for membership. It seems they're quite cultivated in their way, but naturally . . ."

"Naturally," Mama agreed.

Sara felt her cheeks burning.

"It's a sign of the times," Mr. Bolster said. "I was noticing only the other day how many German and Irish names have crept into the city's rosters, names that represent considerable wealth, too."

Sara was glad when the meal was over and they went into the other room. Mrs. Bolster sat in her usual chair with Dorothy Elizabeth in her lap. Little Roger turned the pictures of the big album on the couch, but the others gathered around the piano.

"Let's begin with 'Drink to Me Only,' Belle," Mr. Bolster said.

Then Mama would ask for "Who Is Sylvia, What Is She?" Sunday afternoons always followed the same pattern.

Sara didn't sing. She played with the fastenings of the gold bangle that had been saved from the fire, and tipped her head so she could see in the mirror. She tucked in a curl of hair that had slipped out of the back comb.

Belle opened the Episcopal Hymnal that was always on the top of the square piano. "Here's Mama's favorite." Mama moved Dorothy Elizabeth gently in her arms in time to the music.

The King of Love my Shepherd is, Whose Goodness faileth never;
I nothing lack . . .

The front doorbell pierced through the music. There he was. Sara went swiftly to open the door.

"That's a lovely old hymn, don't let me interrupt," Dr. Henkel remarked after he had met them all. "I do wish you would sing another stanza."

"We always sing all the stanzas for Mama; it's her favorite hymn, Dr. Henkel," Belle said.

Sara only half heard the words. Her mouth was forming the words without her thinking of them.

And O what transport of delight
From thy pure chalice floweth!

Her eyes were on George's violin bow, but she could pick out Dr. Henkel's bass voice joining in. The music filled the room, pressing back the gray afternoon light at the curtained windows. Papa came back from the hall with the long brass lighter and lit the chandelier lights while they sang the last stanza. His head was tipped back as he turned the gas with the key of the lighter and then held the flame of the taper till it caught and the pictures in the glass globes came alive. Papa knew all the words and his heart was in them as he sang:

And so through all the length of days
Thy goodness faileth never.
Good Shepherd, may I sing thy praise
Within Thy House forever.

The lights touched with distinction the high forehead and lean face, the curling, iron-gray hair and white beard. Sara was proud, looking at him. She glanced quickly at Dr. Henkel, wanting him to see her father, too. But Dr. Henkel was looking at her. She met his eyes.

"Oh, that was fine!" he said warmly.

Papa stirred up the coal fire and they all drew up chairs. Papa and Dr. Henkel and George seemed naturally to sit at one end, smoking Papa's best cigars. Anne brought the tea tray in and put it on the little rosewood table in front of Mama.

The baby had fallen asleep, and Dor started to take her upstairs.

"Let me help, Dor," Sara said quickly.

"You like him, don't you, Puss?" Dor said when they were up in Belle's room.

"I think he's interesting, different from anyone I've known," Sara said indifferently, looking at herself in the mirror. "Do you like him?"

"Well, he seems like a gentleman; of course, he's really a foreigner. And he doesn't compare with Paul. I wouldn't think too seriously about him. Marriage is such an intimate thing, Sara; you both need to have the same, oh, the same background."

Sara watched Dor putting the baby to bed. "But, Dor, Derrick and Belle had the same background, really."

"But *Derrick*, Sara; he was fast. Belle never knew it when she married him. Look at Anne and Roger, how happy they were. They'd known each other's families all their lives."

"And three of Roger's family died of consumption," Sara said with brutal frankness.

Dor was shocked. "Why, Sara, no one could help that!"

"No, I was just thinking. Of course, Dr. Henkel hasn't asked me to marry him!" Sara said and went on downstairs without waiting for Dor, her cheeks bright with angry color.

From the doorway she saw them all. Dr. Henkel was shorter and a little heavier-built than Papa or George. He was not handsome, but he looked . . . she liked the way he looked.

"Once I was back there, it didn't seem entirely foreign to me," he was saying in answer to some question of Mama's. "Of course, my mother lived there until she was seventeen. My father left Germany when he was eighteen. He's almost forgotten that he ever lived any place but here," he laughed.

"He's done very well," Mr. Bolster said.

Did the family like him? What was Mama thinking, stirring her tea so slowly? Sara was unusually quiet. She got down the stereoscope that had used to be in Belle's library, for little Roger to look at, and passed the tiny hot biscuits and fruit cake again.

"You graduated from the State University, didn't you?" George was asking. "Of course, I am not acquainted with their curriculum, but at Harvard . . ." Sara bridled inwardly at the faint superiority implied in the remark. Papa had come from Harvard too, and Paul. No one at home thought much of the State University.

And then he was going. He was very courteous. He clicked his heels together when he bowed. They must certainly approve of his manners.

"Good-by, Dr. Henkel, I'm so glad you could come. Please come again," she had said more warmly to make up for the family.

"Ve Joimans!" George said humorously as she went back into the room. "Ve stick together!" Belle and Dor and Anne laughed.

Sara stood in the doorway. "I think you're horrid."

"Why, Sara," Mama remonstrated gently, "George is only joking; how touchy you are!"

Sara was glad to help carry out the tea things to cover her confusion.

That night in bed, Mrs. Bolster spoke her worries to her husband. "Winthrop, do you think that position of Sara's is a safe thing? She is acquiring such different ideas from the other girls. She speaks of a Mr. Clancy and a little Rollo, men at the office, and she seems rather interested in this young German doctor."

"I rather liked him," Mr. Bolster said, "but Sara isn't thinking of marriage yet, Corona. Don't worry yourself. Young Sevrance will be back in the spring. I had an idea they thought a good deal of each other at Christmastime."

Mrs. Bolster went to sleep happily. Hiram Sevrance would doubtless build a home for them on the lots he had bought from Papa.

9

THE first Sunday in March was as mild as April. Sara was going riding with young Dr. Henkel. She came downstairs all ready to go, just as George was tuning his violin and Belle playing chords at the piano.

"Sara, I don't like your going out. I always feel that Sunday is a home day," Mama said as she had said yesterday when Sara told her she was going.

"It's such a beautiful day, though, and I'm inside so much of the time at the office," Sara answered, a little importantly. She leaned on the piano beside Dor and sang, but all the time her eyes were on the piece of avenue she could see through the full lace curtains. She saw a horse and carriage pass at more than usual speed. That was his, but she went on singing at the piano until she heard steps on the porch and then the bell. This time she let Mary show him into the hall before she went to meet him.

"I feel guilty in taking you away from the singing," he said.

"Oh, no, it's so lovely; the mildest day we've had, isn't it?"

"Yes, it's like spring."

She was impatient now to be gone with him, while he

talked with Mama and Papa and the rest. She was glad when they started off down the avenue.

"It's good to be out," Sara said delightedly. "It feels like winter in the house so much longer than it is, don't you think?"

"I know what you mean. I think our houses are all too heavily furnished. I want to take you to my house this afternoon. My Mütterchen is afraid to have a breath of air in the house. She is proud that I am a doctor, but she doesn't quite believe all I tell her. I want you to meet her and my father and sisters."

Sara was startled to be going to his home but she said, "I shall like to meet them. You have no brothers?"

"Yes, one brother. He's away at the Wahl-Hennius Institute."

"Is that engineering?" Sara asked.

William Henkel laughed. "Not exactly. He did graduate in engineering at the University, but Wahl-Hennius is a school for brewmasters. Father is happy to have him going into the brewery. They both look on brewing as more of a science than medicine. I pleased my mother and sisters. Mother's people were all teachers or ministers or doctors in the old country. But the brewery means a great deal to my father."

"Of course," Sara said, not quite understanding. A brewery was something objectionable, like a soap factory.

"We'll go by the brewery on our way. It's an interesting place, almost like a piece of the old country."

"Last spring you were in Germany. Do you wish you could be there now?" Sara asked.

He shook his head. "I would rather be right here than any place in the world."

"I don't think I want to live in Armitage City always," Sara said slowly. "I want to go so many places."

"That's what I thought when I finished medical school. And last year in Göttingen I used to plan to settle in the East to practice; in Baltimore, I thought. But when I came back I realized that my father and mother and sisters had been counting so on my coming back here and they've given me everything I have; it doesn't seem too much to ask of a son, does it?"

"You're good about them," Sara said.

"One's parents . . ." he shrugged. "There!"

Ahead of them on the river side of the road stood the brewery. Sara had seen it before, but she had never really looked at it. It was a stolid brick building with notching along the top, built like an old castle or a fortress made of children's building blocks. Even from this distance there was a pungent sour smell. Sara sniffed.

"You can smell it." He smiled. "It's like nothing else."

Sara found herself accepting it because he did. "I like the door. It looks like the door to some old fortress."

He nodded. The wide wooden door fitted into an arched doorway of brick. It had iron studs at the joining of the wooden crosspieces.

"Let's walk down toward the river first." Between the brewery and the stables was a grassy meadow. The grass was the color of old hay. The stable was painted red. What would Mama and the girls think if they knew Dr. Henkel had brought her to walk around the stable of the brewery on a Sunday afternoon!

"Don't you like the weather vane up there?" Dr. Henkel took off his hat. Sara watched him as he stood looking up at the weather vane. The wind ruffled his hair and made him look more boyish.

"When I was younger I used to think it was the ship that brought my father from Germany in 'Forty-eight. It's rusty, but some day I'm going up there and clean it," he laughed.

"Did your father come right to Armitage City?"

"Oh, no. My grandfather cleared a homestead south of here. He had seven children. My father was the oldest. When he died in the cholera epidemic of 'Fifty-four my father gave over his share of the farm to his brother. Father took only a team of horses and drove up here to the booming lumber town of Armitage City. But I don't know why you should be interested."

"But I *am*. I've never heard about . . ." She stopped. She almost said "any immigrant before."

"Foreigners?" he smiled. "When I was in the little town where my father's people came from in Germany I realized how much courage it must have taken to go to a country where you would be a foreigner."

They were walking across the meadow to the bank of the river. The hard edge of winter was blunted a little: the angularity of the branches softened by the buds on the trees, the frozen ground thawed into a kinder line, even the clouds were thin over the blue of the sky.

"Father came into town with his wagon and his two hands and his honesty and made a living hauling anything: lumber, dirt, even garden truck. And all the time he saved his money so he could build the brewery."

The way Dr. Henkel talked about it made it seem important.

"And he's been so successful!" Sara said.

Dr. Henkel laughed gently. "Yes, and besides a son to carry on the business he has a son in a profession; to him that's part of his success. Look, I brought you down here to see the brewery with the afternoon sun on it. When I grow tired of the false pomposity of some of the buildings on Main Street I come down and look at the brewery. It's just what it is; no false front, no ornamentation; as German-looking as the beer we make. It has a kind of rightness about it. You must see the ivy growing up the side in the spring; and in the fall when it turns red."

Sara stared at the solid gray-stone building in front of her. Then she laughed delightedly. "I do see what you mean, Dr. Henkel. But I never would have seen it by myself."

"I hope you see a great many things with me," he said, smiling at her.

"Thank you," Sara said, startled a little by his tone of voice. "Tell me some more about your father," she added quickly.

"Well—the brewery has always seemed to me to be my father's dream, put into bricks and good beer. I like people who make their dreams live," he added as an afterthought.

"I do too," Sara said. Dr. Henkel talked of breweries in one breath and dreams in the next as though the one were as sensible as the other.

"I would take you in to see Charlie Freehahn and his horses. He's a great old character; but I promised my Mütterchen to bring you home for coffee. See that little white house inside the picket fence?" He pointed to a house across the road from the brewery. "That's where we live. I grew up there."

Sara looked curiously at the small white house, hardly more than a cottage. It was very neat. It had garden plots on either side of the walk up to the house. "It looks cosy," she said.

As she went up the steps, Sara thought she noticed a quick movement back of the heavy lace that curtained the small paned windows. He wanted her to meet his family, almost as if . . .

"This is my older sister, Marie," Dr. Henkel said.

"How do you do." Sara shook hands with the young woman at the door, sensing, instantly, something hostile in her pale face. She was a little fussily dressed in taffeta. Her hair was light and rolled into a pompadour. Her eyes were pale blue, her lashes and brows matched her hair. She couldn't be any older than Belle.

The hall was dark. Everything seemed carpeted or curtained or cushioned.

"And this is Ottilie." Sara was glad for Dr. Henkel's voice in the close dim hall.

"I'm glad to meet you," Ottilie said. She was not pretty, but there was a kind of distinction about her, what Belle would call an air. She was about Sara's age. Sara felt her eyes taking her all in at once; she was glad she had worn her blue dress.

"Is it you, Wilhelm?" a gentle voice called from the upper hall.

"Mütterchen, I want you to meet Miss Bolster." Dr. Henkel ran up the stairs like a boy, and came down with a frail-looking little woman who came only to his shoulder. There was a resemblance between the small tired face of the elderly woman and that of her son. But it vanished when she said in a strongly accented voice, to Sara:

"Herzlich Willkommen. . . ." She looked at her son in dismay. Dr. Henkel laughed and patted her hand.

"When my mother feels most deeply she speaks in German. Happy welcome, she is saying."

"Please kommen sie." Mrs. Henkel took Sara into the parlor on the left of the hall. The girls followed. Dr. Henkel went for his father.

Sara found herself sitting on the sofa by Mrs. Henkel. The girls sat in chairs facing them. Every place Sara looked in the room was filled with chairs, each with a hard-white crocheted tidy. The walls were covered with pictures. The windows had double lace curtains and between the two layers of lace stood potted plants.

"We had such a lovely ride out here. Dr. Henkel took me down by the brewery first," Sara said, trying to be natural.

The small erect figure in black silk beside her made a "tck" between her teeth. "Ach! to take you down there on Sunday." Marie looked genuinely pained.

"I imagine you had never seen a brewery before," Ottilie said. "It must have been a new experience." Her tone was low, but her eyes flashed as she said it.

Sara was uncomfortable. "I enjoyed it," she said, but she was glad when Dr. Henkel came back with his father.

"How do you do!" Mr. Henkel's voice seemed too hearty for the crowded room. His face was ruddy, his white hair and short gray beard bristled wirily. He was not so tall as his son, thick-set to the point of stoutness. He wore a vest with tiny blue and red flowers embroidered on it and a heavy gold chain looped from pocket to pocket. "It is mild out, like spring," Mr. Henkel said, sitting down in one of the big green upholstered chairs.

Mrs. Henkel nodded assent to what her husband said and looked at Sara for agreement.

"Yes, it was beautiful down by the river."

"I took her to see the brewery, Father," Dr. Henkel said.

Mr. Henkel's pleasure was apparent. He beamed at her. "But it is too small already. We need to build it bigger yet!" he told her, raising his square hands and his eyebrows at the same time. Ottilie rose and seemed to flash from the room as though indignant.

"Excuse me," Mrs. Henkel said, starting to rise.

"No, Mama, Ottilie and I will tend to everything," Marie insisted. Mrs. Henkel looked unreconciled to such an arrangement until her son said:

"Yes, Mütterchen, let the girls take care of it." Mrs. Henkel sat down again, reassured by her son's words. Sara noticed the piercings in the delicate lobes of her ears.

"The brewery looked big to me just as it is," Sara said, turning to Mr. Henkel, sensing that would please him.

"But it's a big growing business," Mr. Henkel told her. "And there are more Germans in Armitage City who know good beer. Did you show her the hops, Wilhelm?"

"We didn't go in," William answered.

"Ah! They are a new shipment; all the way from Bohemia we get them; the best hops we can get. You should smell them; they are fragrant like perfume. Isn't so, Mama?"

Mrs. Henkel nodded assent.

Sara looked across at Dr. Henkel. He was smiling affectionately at them and at her. She had a sense of unreality about sitting here in this red and green room, talking to the man whose name she had only read on the big wagons, JOHN HENKEL'S BREWING CO. She had not ever really connected young Dr. Henkel with that name or the brewery until now.

"We have eight double teams of horses already. Charlie Freehahn all the time says we need more! But I keep saying, 'Wait a while, Charlie.' "

"Is he a big man with a black mustache?" Sara asked with sudden excitement.

"Ja, a little gray," Mrs. Henkel nodded emphatically.

"I think he must be the one who took me for a ride when I was just a little girl, about seven. He was so proud of his new team."

"Do you really mean Charlie Freehahn took you for a

ride, on one of the drays, Miss Bolster?" Dr. Henkel asked.

"Yes. I was standing by our hitching post when he came by. I remember how big the horses were and that they had red tassels on their bridles. The horses were just new, he told me."

"Ja, they must have been Thor and Donner and Minna and Star," Mr. Henkel said.

"Can you remember them all by name?"

"They were the first pedigreed stock my father bought," Dr. Henkel explained. "They were Charlie's pride. When Star broke his leg at the drawbridge and Charlie had to shoot him, he felt as badly as though it were a human being."

"Clydesdales, they are," John Henkel put in.

"I remember; they were gray and white," Sara said.

"She has it right!" John Henkel looked at her with new interest. "Gray, and Minna was pure white like milk."

"I must take you to see Charlie," Dr. Henkel laughed.

The girls were busy fussing around the coffee table. Mr. Henkel was enjoying himself. His enjoyment spread to the others. Mrs. Henkel sat primly on the sofa. Now and then she touched her lips with a wisp of fine linen, but she listened eagerly to every remark of her husband or son, agreeing emphatically with a birdlike nod of her head, glancing at Sara with her small brown eyes. When the phone jangled out in the dining room, she jumped.

"Wilhelm, answer!" she said anxiously.

"Mother's afraid it's some seriously ill patient, Miss Bolster," Dr. Henkel explained as he left the room.

Mrs. Henkel swayed toward Sara on the couch and laid one small hand on hers. "He's a fine boy, Miss Bolster, isn't he, Papa?"

"Ja, he has a good education too; the best we could give him. Mama's side was all teachers and ministers in the old country. Me!" He dismissed himself with a generous gesture of his hands. "I am a brewer!"

"Dr. Henkel gave such an interesting talk at the Century Club," Sara said.

"Call him Wilhelm, mein Kind. He would like it so," Mrs. Henkel told her.

Sara smiled with a little heightened color. She found Marie holding the big coffeepot poised, watching her with cold eyes.

"How will you have your coffee, Miss Bolster?"

"Oh, with cream and sugar, please."

Dr. Henkel came back through the tasseled portières.

"Muss du gehen, Wilhelm?" Mrs. Henkel asked anxiously.

"Nein, Mütterchen. It was the apothecary. He doesn't yet quite understand my prescribing certain drugs he is not used to. It is his way of reproving me."

Mrs. Henkel looked worried. "You were right, Wilhelm?"

"Yes, meine Mütterchen, according to mine own lights."

"Mother!" Ottilie said indignantly. Dr. Henkel laughed gently at Sara.

"Ottilie, your confidence is heart-warming." His tone was teasing.

"Well, after you've studied in Europe!" Ottilie bridled.

"There's a line, meine Schwester, that goes,

> *How doth the fool that's been to Rome*
> *Exceed the fool that's stayed at home!*

Ottilie tried to frown at her brother and smiled instead. He was the center of the whole family, Sara thought.

The crumb cake was delicious. The coffee was fragrant and strong. Marie presided over the coffee table. Ottilie passed the cakes and refilled the cups.

"Ottilie paints," Mrs. Henkel said. "Ottilie, show Miss Bolster your Aquarellen."

Then only the color deepened in Ottilie's pale face.

"It's nothing that Miss Bolster would be interested in."

"Please, I would," Sara insisted.

Ottilie brought a big case of water colors and charcoal drawings. She was almost eager as she showed them.

"That's the drawbridge on Baker Street," Sara exclaimed, delighted, and Ottilie, who had been sullen before, melted into a smile. "Yes, I had to do it from memory and I didn't get it quite right there."

"You paint wonderfully," Sara said.

No one had noticed Mr. Henkel go out of the room. Now he came back with a slender-necked bottle, wrapped in a white napkin, on a tray with little glasses.

"Coffee ist all right, but among friends, a little wine is nicer yet. Dis ist some of Mama's wine."

Sara felt the girls' annoyance and saw the glance they cast at their brother. But nothing seemed to annoy him.

"Not from last year, John," Mrs. Henkel asked quickly. "Ach, ja. Year before last the grapes, I don' know, were besser," she explained to Sara.

Sara sipped the clear wine from her wineglass. The girls had relented and drank wine, too. Mrs. Henkel only touched her glass and put it down.

"It is not good for me," she explained to Sara, touching her lips with the bit of linen. "Look there." She nodded toward the opposite wall, where two old-fashioned, tinted photographs of two little boys hung on the wall. "Dis one, on dis side, ist Hans und de odder ist Wilhelm."

Sara looked at the little lad with long gold curls that fell over his white embroidered collar. She glanced at Dr. Henkel and met the twinkle in his eye.

"Ein schönes Kind," Mrs. Henkel murmured.

"Mütterchen!" her son murmured, looking at her reproachfully, "you mean, ein *Wunderkind!*" When he laughed he was a little like his father, Sara thought. Even the sisters laughed this time.

"I wish you would call me 'William'; I should like to call you 'Sara,' " Dr. Henkel said as he drove her home.

Sara was embarrassed. For an instant she wondered what Mama would say. She had not even thought of Dr. Henkel by his first name. But some sincerity in his voice took away her embarrassment.

"I will call you 'William.' " Her eyes met his.

"Thank you, Sara," he answered, looking as seriously back at her.

They drove a block in silence. Why had he taken her to his home? Surely his mother thought she meant more to him than . . . but her thoughts shied away from the idea.

"The air is so fresh after being in the house, isn't it?" he said. "You know that parlor of ours, so crowded with bric-a-brac and tidies that the girls haven't yet been able to persuade Mother to discard, is a symbol to me of my German background." He smiled gently. "It's a little stifling sometimes . . . like the blind affection that is always poured out on me because I'm the oldest son."

Sara was still. He knew how close and foreign the house had seemed to her. He understood. It was that way for him too. A sense of relief ran through her.

10

"WILLIAM has invited me to the concert of the University Glee Club," Sara said one morning at breakfast.

"William, Sara? Oh, you mean Dr. Henkel!" Belle laughed. Mrs. Bolster looked at Sara intently.

"Sara, I do think there is a nice line to be drawn between friendliness and familiarity."

"But I call Phil Briden and Bert Boyd and Paul Sevrance, all the boys I know, by their first names."

"That is quibbling, isn't it, dear?" Mrs. Bolster asked with a gentleness underlain with firmness.

Sara flushed. "I like him. He talks more interestingly than any other young man I know." She buttered her muffin precisely.

"I understand he is well spoken of by the doctors of the city," Mr. Bolster interposed with his usual mildness. "Mr. Yardley told me himself that when they left the hospital in Philadelphia the doctor told them there was a young Dr. Henkel that had been with him in Germany in Armitage now who could give them as good care as he could. They have been delighted with him."

"But the Yardleys' constitution is remarkable," Mrs. Bolster said. Mrs. Bolster prided himself on her knowledge of disease and doctors and could tell what family had a tendency for what disease for two generations back.

"His name has been put up for the Winter Club," Belle said. "Of course, his being a German will make some difference, but Clayton Forbes was in Germany with him."

"But still, Sara, I don't like your calling him by his first name," Mrs. Bolster said, coming back to the subject.

Sara finished her breakfast in silence. She was often grateful for having to hurry down to the office in the morning. It terminated so many dull or awkward conversations. She was putting on her hat in front of the big hatrack in the hall when Anne came out.

"Oh, Sara, could you leave out money for Mrs. Higbee? I wouldn't want to ask her to wait. Father doesn't have it just now . . ." Her voice trailed off into vagueness.

"Of course, Sis; up in my handkerchief box."

"Thank you, dear; good-by." Anne kissed her. Her dainty swiss morning gown breathed a fragrance of lilac. But some faint unpleasantness lingered in Sara's mind as she went. Anne's asking for money to help pay Mrs. Higbee, "Father doesn't have it just now." Some security of Sara's childhood tottered. At the corner she met the mail man and the discomfiting sense vanished. There was a letter from Paul. But she would keep it until she reached the office.

She propped the letter against her ink bottle and set to work on the first duties of the morning with firm will. It was not until Barney and little Rollo had gone out and Miss Alma was busy in the other office that Sara opened Paul's letter. She read it carefully from the scrawled address.

March 3, 1894
Gray's, Cambridge

Dear Sara,

This is just a line to tell you I shall be home on the eighth and am looking forward to seeing you. I have been doing a great deal of thinking this term, though what has been in my thoughts recently has perhaps always been there, and I have something to ask you that is more important to me than anything else in the world. Perhaps your heart will tell you.

May I take you to the Ingalls' dance on the 8th? You may as well say yes, because I'm taking you. I won't get in till that afternoon.

Until then,

Paul

Paul meant . . . what could he mean but one thing? She folded the note carefully and slipped it in its envelope. Then she put the envelope in her drawer under the pincushion and the box of rubber bands so that only the corner showed. When Mike, the boy who ran the copy back and forth, brought her the proof sheets to correct, he found her bent over the pad of paper on her desk. There was no sign of the inner turmoil of spirit. But when he had banged the door behind him again Sara did not turn at once to the inky printing on the proof sheet. Instead she took the letter out from under the pincushion and reread the scrawled words.

The week hurried by. Sara watched its passing in the changing date on the big calendar pad nailed to the wall back of Barney's desk. The numbers grew fatter each morning with anticipation. She would have forgotten Dr. Henkel's concert if she hadn't read the notice in the proof sheets of the *Courier*. She wished now that she hadn't said she would go.

"Mr. and Mrs. Hans Fichter announce the engagement of their daughter Emma Adeline to Mr. Peter Kopf . . ." Sara wrote and then sat idly ornamenting the initials of Emma Adeline. Perhaps she shouldn't accept invitations from Dr. Henkel. He was older than the boys she knew. His eyes had an intent way of looking at her. Until he smiled he was so serious. After all, she was just waiting for Paul to come back home. That is . . .

"Hard at it, I see!" Little Rollo came in, banging the door behind him. Sara looked up guiltily and fell to writing again.

When Dr. Henkel called for her, he looked as he had that night at Madame Modjeska's in his broadcloth cape and silk hat and white gloves. His blond hair shone under the hall light and his glasses twinkled. He bowed with his stiff little bow when he spoke to Mama and Papa.

Anne came running down the stairs just as they were leaving. "Oh, Dr. Henkel, could you just look at Roger? I tried to get Dr. Barnes but his wife says he's out in the country on a call. Roger's so frail and I can't get him to stop crying. He says he's going to die. I've even given him paregoric." Before, Anne had only spoken formally to Dr. Henkel and referred to him as "Sara's German."

"I should be glad to." Dr. Henkel laid off his cape and white gloves on the hatrack.

"Roger's always been a very nervous child, Dr. Henkel," Mrs. Bolster explained. "He was around his father so much and saw him die."

"How old is he?" Dr. Henkel asked.

"Four, but he's old for his age. I've had Anne keep him in a great deal because he is so frail. He can't stand cold at all. I'll go up with you." Mama had the manner of a general leading the army as she rustled toward them.

Dr. Henkel paused on the stair. "If you don't mind, I'd like to go up alone first."

"He's frightened of doctors!" Mama told him, shaking her head. Anne looked anxiously at Mama. They waited at the foot of the stairs, listening to the sound of Roger's crying. They heard the door closing. Then the crying seemed to stop. They could hear Dr. Henkel's deep voice and Roger's high one. A strange sound came down to them. Dr. Henkel was singing:

From a seven-story dwelling, they lowered him yelling,
The man with the sealskin pants. . . .

"I never would have let someone you knew nothing about walk right in like that," Mama said.

"But Roger's laughing!" Sara said.

"Do it again, please!" Roger's shrill little voice demanded.

"I'll sing you one more: 'Mush, mush, tra-la-la lady . . .' " Dr. Henkel sang gaily.

"He'll get the child so excited he won't sleep tonight!" Mama led the way upstairs.

Roger was sitting up in bed, laughing. Dr. Henkel was walking back and forth at the foot of the bed, gesturing in the manner of an opera singer. He stopped short when he saw Mrs. Bolster and Anne and Sara.

"These aren't my usual methods, Mrs. Bolster, but I had to improvise tonight," he smiled.

"Dr. Henkel, I'm afraid you don't understand how high-strung Roger is," Mrs. Bolster said firmly.

The little boy's laughter stopped instantly. Alarm showed in his eyes, accentuating their size and the shadows beneath them. "Is *he* a doctor? He just told me he was taking Aunt Sara to the concert and he'd show me what they'd sing." Roger burst into tears and buried his head in the pillow.

Dr. Henkel frowned. "Just leave him to me for a moment." He spoke peremptorily. Then he turned away from them to the little boy.

"Roger! I want you to stop crying and pull your covers way up around your neck so I can open this window to let new air in. And I'm going to turn down the light so you can see the night outside."

Roger stopped crying to watch the unusual performance. Dr. Henkel tucked the covers up around his neck. The clear air came into the room, carrying away the sweetish smell of paregoric.

"He always goes to sleep with the light on, Doctor, ever since his father died," Anne explained. Dr. Henkel seemed not to hear.

"If we turn it all the way out and raise the shades maybe you can see a star." Dr. Henkel turned out the light and threw one lace curtain recklessly over the mirror and caught the other behind a picture. The oblong of darkness outside the window grew less dark than the room; it took on its own shades and tones, darker where the tree was, lighter above the roof of the next house.

"I see a star, a teeny one!" Roger shouted.

"Where?" Dr. Henkel stooped down by the bed.

"There! Can't you see?" Roger laughed at Dr. Henkel's blindness. "There's another one!"

"Oh," Dr. Henkel said, "now I see. Well, star-gazer, Aunt Sara isn't going to hear any of the concert unless I go. Suppose I take her now so she can sing some of the songs for you tomorrow?"

"Will you come and see me tomorrow?"

Dr. Henkel hesitated. "I might, if I hear you went right to sleep."

"All right. Good night," Roger said after a minute, putting out a hand that looked too small and white in the dark room. He made no protest when they went.

"I certainly thank you, Dr. Henkel," Anne said in the hall as he was putting on his cape. "I was at my wits' end."

"What do you think he should have, Doctor?" Mrs. Bolster asked.

"Nothing!" Dr. Henkel answered shortly. "If you are

really asking my advice as a physician, I think he needs to get outdoors and play with other children and not hear himself discussed."

"You were wonderful!" Sara said as they drove away in the cab.

Dr. Henkel laughed. "Not at all. I hope I didn't make your mother as angry as she did me."

There was only one number left before the intermission.

"Would you like to go back and meet some of these boys? Their faculty adviser, Whalen, was a freshman when I was a senior."

"Will!" The first young man they met backstage threw his arm around William's shoulder. "Charlie, here's Will Henkel!"

Sara met them all. They seemed so glad to see him.

"I've heard how you used to sing 'The Man with the Sealskin Pants,'" one of the younger men said.

"Nobody has sung it as you do, Will," Charlie told him.

"Get him to sing it on the program, after the intermission. Come on, Will! We'll make an announcement: 'The eminent Dr. Henkel, after a successful tour of Europe—'" a young man with curly black hair and prominent sideburns was urging.

William shook his head, laughing. "It would ruin my practice! Who could take me seriously after that?"

"It'll bring down the house. Miss Bolster, did you ever hear him sing 'The Man with the Sealskin Pants'?"

"Yes, I have," Sara admitted, laughing. "It brought down the house that time, too."

"Come on, Will, sing with us then: Sing 'Maxwellton's Brae's.'"

"No, not tonight. I came to hear you." Dr. Henkel seemed

to have dropped off his usual reserved manner. He seemed as young as—as Paul.

"Appleby won the boxing championship this year, Will. You should have seen Will when he won the wrestling championship, Miss Bolster!" Whalen turned to her. "One hundred and forty pounds and every ounce iron."

Sara thought about Dr. Henkel when the second part of the concert had begun and the boys were singing softly, "There's a bank where the wild thyme grows." Dr. Henkel . . . William, was so studious-looking, she hadn't thought of him as singing and wrestling. She glanced at him quickly. He was different from anyone she had ever known.

"You know, now that you have agreed to call me William you don't call me at all," Dr. Henkel said to her at the door, "only with your eyes. Sometimes your eyes look as though they might say William."

Sara laughed. "Good night, William, I've enjoyed the concert greatly."

"Good night, Sara, I'm glad you did."

She liked to hear him say, "Sara"; he gave it a different intonation from anyone else's.

Thursday afternoon, the eighth, Sara was over on the east side, interviewing a Miss Emma Adeline Fichter on her coming wedding. Clarke Street was five blocks east of the tracks of the Michigan Central Railroad, but she could hear the train whistle. She walked back to the office hurriedly for fear Paul might go there early.

She left the office promptly at six, as soon as her copy was all in the wire basket on her desk. At the foot of the stairs of the Flat Iron Building she looked eagerly up and down the street and even paused a minute before she walked up to the corner to take the trolley.

At home she found flowers waiting for her and a card: *"Bachelor dinner at Chauncey Lake's. I'll call for you at eight. Can't wait to see you. I love you, Sara. Paul."*

Paul had never said it before. The words stood out starkly in blue ink on the white card. She wore the card in her dress during dinner.

The new dress, made from another of Anne's, fitted beautifully. The full gathers in back showed off to advantage the rich luster of the sky-blue taffeta. Her hair, gathered up a little higher on her head, showed the whole curve of her cheek and ear and the sweep of her neck and shoulders. Belle and Anne watched her dress as she had used to watch them so few years before. Belle brought out a velvet evening cape that Derrick had brought back to her from New York. It was lined with white fur.

"I want you to have this, Sara."

"Belle, I couldn't take it. It's one of your loveliest things," Sara protested.

"I'll never wear it again," Belle said firmly. "I meant to leave it with . . . the other gifts." Even now Belle avoided saying Derrick's name. "I couldn't bear to part with this and the intaglio."

Sara pulled it around her without more words. Belle was very beautiful and romantic but her face was sad, almost stern.

"You better not wear it until Paul comes, Puss; it's warm enough for winter," Belle cautioned.

"It's time for him now," Mama said. "I suppose he feels it isn't fashionable to be on time."

At eight-thirty Anne suggested calling Paul by telephone.

"I should say not! Not if he never comes!" Sara said

hotly. Paul's card was under her bodice. His flowers were pinned to the shoulder of her dress.

It was quarter of nine when the doorbell rang. Sara heard Papa saying good evening, and picking up the velvet cloak, she hurried down the stairs, forgetting already that she had meant to keep him waiting.

"Why, Philip! Where's Paul?"

Philip Briden seemed embarrassed. "Well, Paul was detained, Sara. He—he asked me to stop by for you."

Sara hesitated.

"How thoughtful of Paul," Belle said quickly. "Have a lovely time, Sara!"

Philip's father had a glass hack and a coachman that made the smartest turnout in Armitage City, but Sara took no pleasure in it.

"Where is Paul, Philip?"

"Well, you see, Sara, Chauncey Lake had this bachelor dinner. And his old man got mellow thinking about the old days at Harvard when he was young and ordered up champagne for us."

Sara waited.

"And, you know how Paul is. . . ."

"No, I don't," Sara said.

"Well, what I mean is . . . he's so lively and, oh, you know, Sara, he's the life of the party and I guess he drank a little too much."

"Oh," Sara said, sitting farther back in the seat.

"Oh, he'll be all right. He'll be there soon after we are, only it was so late and he didn't want to keep you waiting and I wasn't taking anyone . . . I jumped at the chance to take you, Sara." Philip took out his handkerchief and wiped his round face.

"I see," Sara said. The stiff little card that came with Paul's flowers scratched against her skin. When she got there she would take it out and tear it into bits. She unpinned the flowers on her shoulder. She would drop them on the ground as soon as they stopped. "I can't wait to see you," Paul had said.

As Sara ran up the carpeted steps to the front door Philip ran after her.

"You dropped your flowers. Here they are!"

Sara was dancing with Mr. Ingalls when she saw Paul. He laid his hand on Mr. Ingall's sleeve. Sara looked at the fingers of Paul's glove, not raising her eyes to his face.

"May I cut in, Mr. Ingalls?"

"Rescuing her, are you? Think I'm too old to have the prettiest girl in the room? All right, young man, I don't blame you!"

"But, Mr. Ingalls, you can't leave me in the middle of the dance like that!" Sara said.

Mr. Ingalls chuckled. "You know the way to keep 'em coming, don't you, Sara?"

Paul stood against the wall watching her. He looked a little more pale than usual. His eyes held hers an instant as she danced by. They had a cloudy, sullen look in them that made her remember the ride in the cutter at Christmastime.

As soon as the music stopped he came across to her.

"I guess I'll have to surrender you this time!" Mr. Ingalls said. Sara looked around for John Baxter.

"I have the next dance, Paul."

"It hasn't started yet. Let's go down to the conservatory where I can talk to you," Paul said in a low, urgent voice.

Sara's voice was clear. She showed him the little dance program hanging from her wrist. "You were a little late, you know," she said sweetly.

"Sara, you know I'm sorry. You don't have to be so vindictive."

"I'm not. What you do doesn't concern me at all. Only I wish you hadn't bothered to say things in your letter you didn't mean."

"I meant every word I wrote, Sara, and you know it. Didn't you leave a single dance for me?"

"I didn't know you wanted one. Excuse me, Paul, there's John." Sara danced away across the yellow maple floor.

"There's nothing I love so much as dancing," Sara said gaily to John Baxter. But all the time she knew where Paul was. He wasn't dancing. He was standing alone by the end window. Perhaps his head ached, he looked so white. How different he was from William! Paul was tall and slender and dark. Nobody could dance like Paul. . . .

"I thought you were one of these advanced women who want a career," Johnny said.

Sara laughed. "Oh, no, I'm just doing this . . ." she stopped herself just in time. She had been about to say "until I'm married." She had never thought of not marrying. She had always thought she would marry Paul sometime. Did she love him? How did you feel when you were in love? She must ask the girls. But she couldn't ask Belle. And Dor and George were . . . Dor was so busy with the baby and George . . . she wanted to love someone differently from the way Dor loved George. It would make Anne sad if she asked her. It was something you had to feel for yourself.

When she came down from putting on her wraps she saw Paul waiting for her in the hall.

"Good night, Paul," Sara said sweetly. "Good night, Em." She turned to speak to Mr. and Mrs. Ingalls and Beth.

Paul took her arm.

"Where's Philip?"

"Sara, Philip couldn't find his hat and coat anywhere and rather than keep you waiting he begged me to see you home," Paul explained, his face the picture of solemn concern.

"I'll wait for him," Sara said. "Everyone seems to be worried about keeping me waiting tonight." She caught the amusement in Mr. Ingalls' face and flushed.

"But, Sara, I promise you Philip wants me to take you home." His voice fell to a whisper. "He's in worse shape than I was! I've ordered a cab. I thought we should leave the hack for him."

Sara fingered the ribbons of her slipper bag. Suddenly she didn't want to be alone with Paul. The Ingalls' house seemed safe, riding back with Philip in the glass hack was safe. If she went with Paul, she would forgive him and forget how angry she was. She didn't want to just yet.

"Well, I'll look and see if he's found it, Sara." Paul bounded up the stairs to the room where the men had laid their things.

"It's a funny thing; he's left already. Johnny said he found his hat on the seat of the hack and then went right along home. Of course, he knew I was taking you home."

"Sara," Paul said as soon as they were in the cab, "you know how sorry I am that I made such an ass of myself."

Sara waited.

"There's nothing so dreadful about drinking a little too much; you don't need to get *that* idea." His voice sounded less contrite.

"I haven't that idea, but I don't like it and I should think if you 'couldn't wait to see me' that might have kept you from getting drunk."

"You don't understand how those things go, Sara."

Sara didn't answer. The wheels and the horses' hoofs sounded loudly. The cab swayed ever so slightly.

"Sara, I came home this vacation with just one idea. Now everything's spoiled because I went to Chauncey's stag party first!"

"Why didn't you come for me at the office, Paul?"

"I never thought of that. I just thought of what time you'd be through. I hate your working anyway, down in that old Flat Iron Building. I don't see why your family let you do it. I sent the flowers to tell you . . . You didn't wear them, did you?"

"No."

"And then I went right to Chauncey's so I could leave earlier. I suppose that's why I drank too much, because I was so excited about seeing you and I knew what I was going to ask you tonight. Oh, Sara, can't you forget it. I do love you."

Sara was startled now that Paul had said it. She hadn't even forgiven him yet. "Do you, Paul?" she asked stupidly.

"More than anything in the world, Sara. I think I've loved you for years. I've never even thought of marrying anybody else. Ever since Christmas vacation I've thought of the way you looked in the cutter. You leaned your head back and looked at the stars. I wanted to kiss you then, Sara."

She could feel his arm around her, pressing the fur lining of the cape closer. It was the soft fur against her shoulder that made her think of Belle. Belle had married Derrick, expecting to be gloriously loved and happy, and Derrick had turned to Flora Bailey. She sat up straighter, away from the pressure of Paul's arm.

"Oh, Paul, I . . ."

The carriage stopped abruptly. The sharp March air rushed in against her. She clung to Paul's arm up the steps of the porch. Her fingers fumbled for the key and gave it to him. He unlocked the door and stepped inside after her.

"Tell me, Sara; you said 'Oh, Paul.' "

Sara looked over his shoulder at the dim hall, at the dark panes of glass that were red and blue by daylight.

"Sara?"

The low flame in the chandelier made his face seem so pale; his eyes were dark and anxious. She couldn't remember what she had been going to say. She couldn't hurt him. Nobody else made her feel like this.

"I guess I do, Paul," Sara whispered.

"Oh, Sara." Paul's lips were on hers. She felt his arm pressing the fur-lined cape warmly around her. This was love, this trembly feeling. She turned away her face and hid it against Paul's shoulder. His arm slipped under the cape, holding her more tightly to him.

"And we won't wait, Sara; let's be married as soon as I'm through school this June. I'll come over tomorrow and speak to your father."

"But Paul," Sara whispered. "This June is so soon."

"Not too soon. We'll go to Europe for our wedding trip," Paul went on excitedly. "Father'll be so pleased about our marrying he'll give us the trip. He's said so already." Paul leaned against the door looking at her.

"Sara, do you know how beautiful you are? I couldn't see anyone else at the dance tonight. I never will be able to see anyone else."

There was no doubting him. They stood looking into each other's eyes as though they had never seen each other before. She felt suddenly sad, without knowing why.

"Tell me, now before I go . . . this June, Sara?"

She smiled up at him, nodding her head.

"Sara, you darling."

"Paul, you must go now," Sara protested gently.

"I am going. Good night, sweetheart."

She closed the door after him and leaned against it,

wanting to keep this feeling of loving and being loved. She laid down her slipper bag and evening purse on the hatrack and bolted the front door. She took the long lighter from the corner to turn out the flame in the high chandelier. When she turned the key the wrong way, she was embarrassed at the sudden bold light that flamed in the glass globe and turned it out quickly.

She was too wide-awake to go to bed so soon. Maybe she was hungry. She went out to the kitchen and lighted a light. She sat on the corner of the kitchen table, drinking milk and munching crackers. Even the simplest thing was different now that she was in love. She wasn't sad any longer.

II

SARA knew when she woke that the world had changed. But it was not until her eyes, moving around the room, came to the new dance program dangling from the bracket on one side of her mirror that she remembered. Paul was coming to talk to Papa today. Papa would be pleased; so would Mama and the girls. Sara pulled the comforter up over her shoulder and lay thinking about Paul.

She thought of Paul's eyes that were so dark and insistent, and that same little uneasy stir went through her. It was more comfortable to plan things for them to do when they were married. She thought of going over to Belle's room to tell her. But it was already after nine. Belle would have gone to breakfast. The Sunday-morning aroma of sausage and hot-cakes and coffee came faintly up the stairs.

Would Paul come over before lunch or wait until this afternoon? She wished she had asked him to go to church with her. She wanted to see him again; to hear him tell her he loved her. She wouldn't say a word even to Belle until after Paul had seen Papa. She could hardly wait to see him again.

Why, this was love; anybody could tell that, she thought as she went down to breakfast. She hesitated before the big mirror in the hall, looking at herself, wondering if they would notice anything different about her. She was surprised when Mama looked up from pouring the coffee to ask as she had on so many ordinary mornings, "Did you have a pleasant evening, Sara?"

And Papa at the other end of the table smiled at her affectionately. "I'm glad to see our business woman still enjoys parties."

Sara went to church and looked across to see Paul in his pew, but only Mr. Sevrance sat there, his gold chain gleaming across his white vest. She looked at him to see if Paul were like him. Mr. Sevrance was heavy. He had bushy gray eyebrows and his mouth made a downward line. Mr. Sevrance had been mentioned for senator, she remembered, but there were "too many round forties," Papa had said. She wondered if Paul knew that people said things about his father. He didn't look like Mr. Sevrance at all.

She could hardly hear the words of the service. She knelt and her head was bowed over the open prayerbook, but she had turned the leaves to the wedding ceremony. She read them now against the solemn cadence of the chanted responses.

Paul came just after dinner. He asked Mr. Bolster if he could talk to him in his study. How brave he was, Sara thought. She, herself, was suddenly shy. Their going left the drawing room queerly empty.

"My dear," Mama said, looking at Sara. Why, Mama's eyes were full of tears.

Sara went across the room, feeling the flower pattern of the carpet stretching endlessly between them.

Mama kissed her. "My last little daughter; but Paul is a fine young man."

Belle was playing at the piano. "That was why I gave you

the cape last night, Puss, because Paul was just home and I guessed."

Anne kissed her, crying a little. George and Dor were reminiscent. "I remember when I asked Father for your hand," he said, smiling at Dor. Of all of them, they were the only ones who seemed to stand out clearly to Sara. She watched them intently. She was suddenly uncomfortable for Anne and Belle. She couldn't look at them.

"Why didn't you tell us, Sara?" Mama asked gently.

"I don't know," Sara said. "I was going to tell you this afternoon. Paul wants to be married in June. Mr. Sevrance is going to give us a trip to Europe for our wedding trip."

"Oh, Sara, what a happy girl!" Mama said delightedly, clapping her fine small hands together soundlessly.

"You must hand in your note of resignation to Mr. Griffith at once. I never thought he should have given you a position in the first place," Mama said.

Sara thought for just a second of Anne's asking her for money to pay Mrs. Higbee.

Papa and Paul came in together. Papa's hand rested affectionately on Paul's shoulder. He came over and kissed Sara.

"You know, Paul, Sara has been almost like a son to me."

"Paul, I am so happy that you and Sara have grown up together," Mama was saying. No one talked of anything else.

"I talked to Father this morning," Paul said. He looked very manly, standing in front of the fireplace. Sara's eyes were on him. "Of course, he's delighted. He's glad to have me settle down. He said to tell you, Mrs. Bolster, that he would esteem it a great honor to have one of your daughters for his daughter."

"Your father and I have had some differences of opinion, Paul," Mr. Bolster said quietly. "We haven't always seen alike, but all that is past."

Sara stood by Paul. She could feel the pressure of his hand on her arm, but she was remembering with startling clearness standing by the window in the Land Office watching the log jam. The voices of Papa and Mr. Sevrance came out to her angrily. She remembered how Papa had said, "Thank you, Hiram; I'll make my money my own way." And they had been very distant with each other since. And Mr. Sevrance had grown more wealthy, and they seemed always embarrassed for ready money. But now it was all right. Her marriage to Paul would bring the two families close again. The pressure of Paul's hand tightened.

"We must drink to their healths, Mother," Mr. Bolster said. Sara thought of Mr. Henkel bringing in the tray with the bottle of homemade wine. She wondered if Dr. Henkel would care very much when he heard she was going to marry Paul.

"To you, my darling," Paul whispered under cover of the talk and drank the last drop of sherry in his glass. They didn't hear the doorbell. Mary came in and murmured something to Mrs. Bolster.

"Sara, that young doctor is here to call; Mary must tell him that we are having a little family celebration, that you can't see him."

Sara stood a minute like an obedient child, then she moved swiftly from Paul's side across the room. "You can't tell him that, Mama, he'd be hurt." She went out to the hall.

"How do you do, William. Won't you come in?" Her voice carried clearly back into the drawing room. Mrs. Bolster had only time to say hurriedly:

"Ever since she took that position she's met the strangest people, Paul. I'm glad she will be resigning tomorrow. You must insist upon it."

Sara brought William back into the room. Mrs. Bolster's greeting was very formal. Belle nodded to him. "How d' y' do, Henkel," George said casually. Mr. Bolster shook hands with him as always in his gravely formal way, unaffected even now by the sharp currents of feeling in the room. Dor's annoyance expressed itself by the quick impatient way in which she went out of the room to see about the baby, and Anne followed. Small spots of red deepened in Sara's cheeks. She had never taken the initiative before with Mama and the girls there, but everyone seemed waiting for her.

"You and Mr. Sevrance have met before, William, in Madame Modjeska's palace car."

"Oh, yes. How do you do, Mr. Sevrance, I'm glad to meet you again," William said.

"How d' you do. I know the name, of course. It stands out prominently on the east-side skyline." Paul laughed. He had not shaken hands, only nodded.

A quick shadow of hurt darkened to anger in Sara's eyes. She turned away from Paul. There was the crystal decanter on the tray and the little glasses.

"We've just had some sherry, William. May I pour you a glass?" She heard her voice, but it was hardly hers. It was too high.

"No, thank you, you have finished," Dr. Henkel said. They moved across the room as though to be by themselves. George was talking now to Paul. The uncomfortable, empty silence had filled in.

"This is a book I thought might interest you," Dr. Henkel said, bringing out a leather-bound volume from his pocket as though it were of no importance now.

"Oh, thank you!" Sara said. She sensed that he had bought it very specially for her, that he had intended to read it aloud. She read the title slowly: "*An Inland Voyage and Travels with a Donkey*, by Stevenson. I know I shall like it," she added, looking up at him.

"You said you'd like to travel," Dr. Henkel explained with a smile.

"Dr. Henkel is just back from studying in Germany, Paul," Mr. Bolster said when they were sitting down.

"Yes, I remember hearing that," Paul said. "You must have been at home there."

"No, not quite. But I enjoyed it greatly." His voice was pleasant, yet a hint of rebuke lay in his words. Sara flushed.

Paul's voice when he spoke again was almost over-hearty. "Now I remember where I first heard of you, Dr. Henkel. On the train coming back from Boston I met a chap from the State University. When he heard I was from Armitage City, he asked if I knew you, and said you used to be quite a wrestler there."

Dr. Henkel smiled.

"He was a farmer's son from upstate and most enthusiastic about you. He said, 'Why, Henkel's got the wind and muscles of one of his father's big brewery horses!'" Paul laughed.

He will be like this when he tries cases in court, Sara told herself. He won't care how he hurts people. But Dr. Henkel seemed only amused.

"That was a flattering description. The physique of those horses is something only the old Greek athletes could approach, I'm afraid." He rose and turned to Mrs. Bolster. "I'm sorry that I must be going."

Sara went with him to the door.

"I'm sorry I disturbed a family party, Sara."

"But you didn't. I was so glad to see you, William."

✦

"Well, the young man had the grace to leave shortly," Mrs. Bolster said.

"I imagine he would be good in the lightweight class," George said to Paul.

Anne and Dor came down with the children. Little Dorothy Elizabeth went to Sara and put up her face to kiss her. Roger in all the glory of his Sunday suit went over to Paul and put out his hand. "Congratulations," he told Paul, stumbling over the big word. Their mothers watched them from the doorway like two conspirators. Roger, exhilarated by his success, said, "Shall I call you Uncle Paul now?" Everyone laughed delightedly.

"I guess not quite yet, but I wouldn't mind," Paul said.

Sara didn't laugh. Belle put her arm around her and murmured, "Don't be foolish, Puss; men are jealous things. Paul just didn't like anyone else calling on you just then."

"I promised Mother and Father I'd bring you back to see them for a few minutes, Sara," Paul said.

"Here, Sara, let me kiss you again, and you, too, Paul," Mrs. Bolster said as they went out. Papa put one arm around Sara and one around Paul and said solemnly:

"God bless you both."

Sara was quiet as they drove away.

"I had to get you away by myself, Sara. Let's not be in any hurry about getting to our house."

Sara kept her eyes on the street ahead. Paul laid his hand on hers, but she seemed not to notice it.

"Wasn't that the biggest nuisance to have Henkel come bounding in just then," Paul said good-naturedly.

"He happens to be my friend, Paul. You were inexcusably rude."

"I suppose I was a little hard on him, Sara. I'm sorry. I'll go and invite your friend to have a drink with me tomorrow if that will make you happy."

Sara's eyes flashed. "Oh, Paul, I think you're . . ." she groped for the word and fell back on the childish one ". . . horrid."

Paul was contrite. "I said I was sorry, Sara; what more can I do?"

They were driving up the river beyond the town. Sara looked at the farms as they passed. Her eyes were troubled. Last night she had been so happy, so warm and sure; even this morning in church, she had knelt and thought of Paul, and now everything was spoiled.

"Paul, how could you be like that?"

"I won't be, Sara, ever again. Forgive me now, and don't go on being unhappy." She felt his arm around her, drawing her closer to him. "And I'll do anything you say, Sara, to make it up. There, isn't that handsome? Sara, say you love me."

"I was so sure I did last night, Paul, but now, I don't know."

He didn't protest as she expected him to. She tried to make him understand.

"It's that I feel as though I didn't know you very well when you do something like that." She was trying very hard to be clear.

"Sara, you're making a mountain out of a molehill. Dr. Henkel probably didn't even know that I was chaffing him." He flung out the words impatiently. "I s'pose we better turn around; Mother and Father'll be waiting. Kiss me, Sara, and we won't ever quarrel again."

"No, Paul." Sara shook her head. "I don't want to be engaged; not now, anyway." She spoke slowly. She was shocked at her own words. The whole late afternoon seemed shocked.

Paul didn't answer. He played with the key hanging from his watch chain. Finally he said, "Why do you care so much how this Dr. Henkel feels? I notice you called him William."

"Why, I like him; but I'd care about your being rude to anyone."

"You like him enough to break your engagement with me on account of him."

"Oh, Paul, it isn't that at all!"

"That's what it sounds like."

"Well, it isn't. It's the way I feel about us; if we were engaged I'm afraid we'd go on like this. You'd do things like last night and—and today; maybe I'd do things you didn't understand, too, and we'd keep on explaining and forgiving each other. . . ."

"That's the way people do, two people with different ideas. They're bound to. You sound as though I'd committed a crime. All that matters is that I love you and you love me, don't you see?"

Sara shook her head. "I can't help it, Paul. I don't want to be engaged now; maybe not for a long time. I want to forget all about kissing you," she ended in a low voice. She stared unhappily out over the river, pewter-colored in the late sunlight. Then the moody expression of her face changed.

"Look, Paul, the logs are coming down!"

Paul nodded. "Much smaller drive this year, though."

Sara watched the wet barked logs bobbing swiftly along in the water. Soon they would fill the river. She felt better just to see them. The logs were coming down that time in the Land Office when her father and Paul's father had disagreed. Perhaps there was something in Paul that was like his father.

"Sara, you couldn't have felt the way you did last night, and then today turn right around."

"Let's go home, Paul. It doesn't do any good to keep talking," Sara said miserably.

Mama and Belle and Papa were all in the library when she came home. Sara stood in the doorway taking off her hat and coat.

"Wouldn't Paul come in, dear?" Mama asked.

"You might as well know, right away; I'm not engaged to Paul any more," Sara said.

"Why, Sara!" Mama exclaimed. "What do you mean?"

"Just that I'm not sure that I want to marry Paul, so I told him I didn't want to be engaged."

"Oh, Sara, it seemed perfect to me; you and Paul were meant for each other," Belle said.

Papa was slower to speak. "Sara, you were always impetuous. An engagement isn't a thing to be broken off lightly."

"I'm afraid you're making a terrible mistake," Mama said sorrowfully.

"I'm sorry. I can't help it. I don't want to talk about it any more." She went up to her own room.

After a while, Belle came up to see her. "Sara, is it that you care so much for that German doctor?"

"Of course not," Sara answered hotly. "It's that . . . oh, Belle, when Paul does something like that I feel I don't really know him at all, at least, not enough to marry him."

"Why, Puss, you have nothing to worry about. You and Paul have grown up together, you have the same background; that's what counts most."

"But you see, Belle, I want to be sure. I want to love him so much if I marry him. And, Belle, you and Derrick had the same background and when you left him you must have decided you hadn't known him, after all."

Belle fingered the topaz pin at her neck. "That's different, Sara," she said sharply.

"Why is it, Belle?" Sara looked at her with troubled eyes. If Belle could tell her . . . "Did you love Derrick very much?"

Belle went swiftly out of the room.

12

PAUL came over the last night of his vacation. They sat alone in the little music room. The family had discreetly retired to other parts of the house, but their hope that this "childish quarrel" would be all straightened out stayed in the room, in the fire that someone had laid on the hearth, in the flowers, Paul's flowers, that Belle must have arranged in the tall vase on the piano.

"Well, Sara, I'm leaving tomorrow."

"I know."

"I wish we could straighten things out before I go."

"Paul, I've thought and thought and I'm just not sure in my own mind." It was so hard to explain.

"Sara, you do it all with your head. You sit there as cold as ice. You don't know what love is!"

She felt like a priggish child, sitting primly on a chair. She went over to the mantel and looked in the big mirror above it at herself, at Paul standing by the table. His face was flushed. He was angry. She saw him coming up to her. She watched him in the mirror. He put his hands on her shoulders and turned her around. Suddenly he kissed her, not as he had the other night, but violently, almost angrily, as though he would never stop, pressing her against him.

For an instant she let herself be held to him, her lips

seemed to melt under his, to lose their shape, to be mixed with his. Then in anger she pushed him off with her hands in fists against his coat, turning her face away from him. His lips were wet, hateful. His strength was hateful.

"Paul, let me go!" She beat her fists against him. She felt that Paul liked to feel her struggling. She was helpless until he dropped his arms. He laughed, an exultant, triumphant sort of laugh.

"You're waking up, Sara. You've got fire if you'd only let yourself go."

She looked at him across the small room. His hair was damp around his forehead, his collar was wrinkled. She knew he felt he had proved something. He looked pleased. How could he! Her throat felt dry.

"Sara, I love you," he said in a low voice, not like his own, almost humbly. He came over to her, pushing back his hair. He was someone else, not Paul Sevrance who had grown up with her. Someone she didn't know at all.

"You can do anything in the world with me if you'll marry me. Sara, don't you see?"

But would that do any good if she didn't really love him?

"Paul, I don't know whether I love you or not," she began again.

His face changed so quickly, even his eyes. "And you'd like to keep me dangling while you make up your mind. Or do you love the brewer's boy?"

"Paul Sevrance, you stop right now and go home!"

"All right, Sara, and I won't come back either."

She let him go out by himself.

The next afternoon, from the second floor of the Flat Iron Building, she heard the whistle of Paul's train. She glanced at the round, expressionless face of the clock as she had been doing all day. The train was on time. It was five minutes after five. Paul was gone.

She had expected to have such a glorious time when Paul was home, and she had seen him only three times. The work on the *Courier* seemed dull, the building dingy. She was tired of writing weddings, and births, and trips. Little Rollo did the deaths. When she said dispiritedly, "They're the same things over and over, Rollo," he shrugged.

"They're the props for life, though. Every time you write up a wedding you want to think, S'pose it was my wedding! S'pose I was that German girl marrying that stocky little German with the big mustaches. . . ." Rollo loved to give advice on writing. He grew expansive with his theme.

"I doubt if I'll *ever* marry," Sara said. "I'll be like Miss Alma when I'm fifty." She picked up her pad and pencil and slipped on her gloves. "And I won't have money enough to go on trips," she finished as she went out the door.

Rollo whistled. "So that's the way of it!"

She walked home in spite of the light drizzle of rain. No one had mentioned Paul at home. She never wanted to see him again. She walked faster and faster down the street that was shiny under the gas lamps and dark and wet between. Her overshoes made a thick sound on the plank walk. She put down her umbrella and let the rain sprinkle on her blue beaver hat. She bent her head to keep the rain out of her face. She passed people without looking at them. She could still feel Paul's mouth, the hardness of his teeth catching her lip suddenly. Why did she have to remember? Why hadn't it made her more angry? It was only when he had said that about Dr. Henkel that she had hated him again; when his face was sneering.

She saw the horse tied to the hitching post under the light. His coat was striped with rain. He shook his head and the bridle rattled loosely against him, almost with a jingling sound. She glanced up at him. "Hello, boy." It was Dr. Henkel's horse. She stopped to pat him. The front door of the house in front of them opened wide, letting out a broad path of light.

"I'll drop in in the morning." Sara saw Dr. Henkel clearly against the light. "I think he'll be better by then," she heard him say. He put on his hat and came down the steps.

He mustn't see her. Sara put up her umbrella, holding it well down around her. She hurried along the walk, sloshing through an unexpected puddle. She caught her breath to listen. She heard the creak of the carriage as he got in, the loose slap of the reins, the little sound he made to the horse. Now he was going. A sharp wave of disappointment swept over her. He hadn't seen her. He was driving right past. The wheels whirred heartlessly on the cedar blocks. Sara trudged home in the rain feeling abused.

At least she could write him about the book.

Dear William:

I am sorry—

It was better not to refer to that Sunday afternoon. "Dear William" looked too informal on the page.

Dear Dr. Henkel,

I want you to know how much I enjoyed the volume of Stevenson's travels. I should enjoy talking it over with you sometime.

Sincerely yours,

Sara Bolster.

But he did not come. She found herself always watching for a sight of his horse and buggy on the street.

She grew more proficient in her work. She was learning

to take the telegraphic news that began to come in at noon. Only the important words came over the wire. She had to supply the connecting links. She had to know something about world affairs.

She began to have opinions. Mr. Bolster fingered his beard and smiled with gentle amusement at this daughter of his who talked politics with him. Mrs. Bolster looked at her daughter with a puzzled frown.

Sara listened to the discussions in the office. Every now and then she put in a quiet question, until Barney said:

"Look out, little Eva, you'll be thinking the next thing you know and the Lord deliver us from thinking women!"

One day Barney came pounding up the stairs into the office.

"Boiler explosion at the Randall Boiler Works!" he announced cryptically and started writing.

"Anyone hurt?" Sara asked, looking up from her work.

"One man killed; a young fellow, twenty-six; he was walking past the works on his way downtown. A piece of steel hit him. We're lucky to get this in tonight; I just happened to see the crowd. I got there just as the boy's brother did. He's a doctor and they called him right away."

"What was his name?" Sara asked quickly.

"Henkel, Hans Henkel; his father owns the brewery. What's the matter? You look like a ghost." Barney stared at her.

"I know Dr. Henkel," Sara said.

Barney nodded. "Things get you worse when you know the people."

Sara thought of Mrs. Henkel showing her the picture of her sons, of jolly Mr. Henkel, and the sisters. William would be the only son now; they would be more dependent on him than ever. She wrote impulsively:

Dear William:

I have just heard about your brother's death. I am so sorry. Please express my sympathy to your family.

Sincerely,

Sara

Sara had bought a bicycle with her own earnings and was using it for reporting. She was on her way home from reporting a missionary meeting one afternoon, bicycling up Main Street, when she saw Dr. Henkel. He was walking toward her.

"How do you do." Sara dragged her foot quickly on the sidewalk to stop the wheel and held out her hand.

"How do you do, Sara. I haven't seen you since Hans died. You don't know how much we appreciated your note at that time."

"I was so sorry. And I've missed seeing you." She felt the color rushing into her face, but she didn't care.

"My practice is really beginning to keep me busy at last," he said, "and I have been home a good deal. My father has not been well. He and my mother take Hans's death so hard."

"Of course," Sara said.

He looked at her soberly. There was no escaping his eyes. She met them. "I wanted to come, but I wasn't sure that I . . ."

She interrupted him nervously. "I want you to come."

"Then I will. Perhaps we could go cycling some afternoon. We could ride to Frankenmuth and have dinner."

"I shall be free Saturday afternoon," Sara answered gravely, "but do you have a bicycle?"

"I shall have by then," he told her, smiling.

She pedaled swiftly back to the office. Thursday, Friday,

Saturday; Thursday, Friday, Saturday, just like that other time, only that time she had waited for Paul. Mrs. Higbee must finish the new twill bicycle suit by then.

Sara told Belle, first. She spoke casually, "I met Dr. Henkel the other day. I'm going bicycling with him Saturday."

Belle looked up quickly. She was running ribbons into the freshly laundered lingerie. "Oh, Sara, that will bother Mother so. There are so many other young men. Philip Briden wants so to do things like that with you."

"But they're so young and not nearly so interesting as Dr. Henkel," Sara said. Sara went down to dinner. She would tell Mama and Anne and have it over with, once and for all.

Mama looked grieved. "Sara, I have not said so before in so many words, because your father and I felt that it was a thing you could sense for yourself. I think it is always unwise to encourage the attentions of a young man whom it would be unfortunate to have become deeply attached to you."

"But why, Mama? You have met Dr. Henkel. You said yourself he seemed a gentleman. Papa said he was well spoken of in his profession." Sara played with her napkin ring.

"What your mother feels, Sara, is that Dr. Henkel although a well-educated, mannerly young man is of foreign parentage; his home you would find very different from yours. His father, while an honest, respectable member of society, runs a brewery."

"But Mr. Griffith runs a newspaper, and Mr. Sevrance runs a logging camp, or he used to, and anyway, William doesn't have anything to do with the brewery. He's a doctor."

Mrs. Bolster fingered the neck of her dress as though she found it tight.

That summer, bicycling seized the fancy of the town. Sara

bicycled often with William. There were parties of eight or ten. Emma and Harry Goodhue were married in June and chaperoned the parties. William Henkel became as much one of the group as though he, too, had grown up on the west side and gone to school at K.M.A. and Harvard.

Paul Sevrance did not come back to Armitage City that summer. Sara had two postcards from him: one from Paris showing the spires of Nôtre Dame and another from London picturing the lions of Trafalgar Square. Sara studied the pictures and reread the brief messages scribbled in Paul's handwriting.

On the first card he wrote very casually: "Paris is the most beautiful city in the world. I hope to stay abroad all winter."

But on the second he wrote: "I can't help thinking that we might have been here together." Sara tore the card into little bits and dropped them into the wastebasket, angry at the tears that made her eyes wet.

13

YOUNG Dr. Henkel was doing very well indeed. His name and ancestry were a professional asset. The advances in medical science made in Germany were being reported almost daily, and it was remembered that he had lately studied in Germany.

He took part in the cultural life of the community. He had sung from boyhood in the songfests at the Germania Institute, and now he sang in the glee club made up of the young blades of the city.

He was a friend of the Winthrop Bolsters on the west side. Some people said that the youngest Bolster girl was seen with him a great deal.

By October all of Sara's family were so engrossed in Mr. Bolster's campaign for Mayor that they did not realize how much Sara saw of young Dr. Henkel.

There was always someone in the library these days talking politics. Since Mr. Bolster had consented to run for Mayor, he had had no time to work on his *History of Armitage City*.

The *Courier* was backing Mr. Bolster. Posters with his picture were nailed up in the office. Sara was caught up in the political excitement. Belle and Anne were equally busy. The library at home became a workshop where they spent hours at the big table stamping and addressing envelopes.

There were receptions to attend, and Mr. Bolster liked to have the women of his family there: Mrs. Bolster looking serenely on the applause that attended her husband's speeches, the girls beaming proudly when he looked their way.

"What if he shouldn't get it?" Anne said one day, dropping her hands over her work.

"But he *will*, Anne!" Belle cried out instantly. "Why, that poor McCarthy or Mac something-or-other hasn't a chance! Did you see his pictures? He's nothing but a shanty Irishman. He owns a foundry and his supporters are all the foreign element."

"I don't think you need have the slightest fear, Anne," Mrs. Bolster assured her. "The leading men of the city are the ones who persuaded your father to take the nomination. His record is well known. Colonel Myers told me only the other day that it would be an honor to the city to have such a gentleman as your father for Mayor." Corona Bolster's eyes shone as she repeated the words.

"Oh, I know. Father is wonderful, but I picked up a handbill for McCarthy last night on my way home," Anne admitted a little shamefacedly.

"Why, Anne!"

"I know, but I saw the headlines and I wanted to read it." Anne took the sheet from her work basket and unfolded it. Letters two inches high leaped from the pink page:

VOTE FOR McCARTHY, THE POOR PEOPLE'S FRIEND

GIANT MASS MEETING TONIGHT

at

GERMANIA HALL

SPEECHES FREE BEER FREE LUNCH

Belle looked at it scornfully. "I don't see anything remarkable in that. There have been just as many handbills distributed for Father." Belle got one from the drawer of the table and laid it beside the wrinkled pink handbill Anne had brought home. "Look at them! Anybody could see who to vote for."

Mrs. Bolster looked at the two bills and shook her head. "Well, I should think so! Papa looks like a statesman."

Sara studied them. The picture of Mr. Bolster showed a fine head and face, unmistakable lines of nobility around the mouth, deep-set eyes that even on the cheap paper were arresting. The carefully trimmed beard and satin cravat gave the head an air of fastidiousness. The head on the pink handbill was that of a heavy-set Irishman with a shock of black hair, black eyes, and a wide mouth showing clearly in the beardless face. He had a kind of bullnecked vigor that leaped out from the sheet. There was no comparison between the types of men represented.

"I wonder if Papa's headquarters couldn't sponsor a free lunch," Sara suggested.

"Why, Sara, that's the same as buying votes! Here, give me the thing!" Belle crumpled the handbill into a ball and threw it back of the firescreen into the fireplace.

But on the east side of town McCarthy's free beer and free lunches were appreciated. Petty politicians talked loud and long above the clink of whiskey glasses in the saloons on lower Water Street and lower Main. Promises were made that would bear fruit at election time.

"Do you want a wealthy stuffed shirt from the west side to run the city?" McCarthy was asking the mass meetings of German and Swedish and Polish laborers. "No," he would roar back at them. "You want a man that's worked the same as you have. That's got his hands dirty and his face sweaty in honest labor, that . . ."

But Mr. Bolster heard none of this. He dressed carefully and went to the Armitage Arms to a gathering of leading citizens and spoke on the great issues of the day. This was as the breath of life to him. He felt keenly that the future of the city lay in the hands of the Republican party, and that he was called to lead that party. Except for the several hundred scholarly letters he had printed himself, his campaign cost very little. It was distasteful to him to find that Derrick VanRansom was chairman of the Republican committee. It may have been personal antagonism that led him to veto Derrick's program for making a personal bid for the vote on the east side of the city. He counted simply on his record of service in the city. After all, the west-side candidate had always been elected Mayor of Armitage City in the past.

The day of the election, Sara sat at her desk waiting for each new bulletin on the returns. The precincts on the west side turned in a large majority for Winthrop Bolster, but those on the east side began to come in one after another for McCarthy.

"Barney, you think Father will win, though, don't you?" Sara asked suddenly.

"Well," Barney drawled back. "I don't know. He's the best man, there's no doubt about that, but there's a lot of foreigners that haven't had any chance to know him."

"Clancy, you don't think he'll lose, do you?" Sara begged as Clancy came back from Mr. Griffith's office.

"It don't look so good for the home team," Clancy gloomily replied.

When the *Courier* was on the street, its headline read: "McCarthy Claims Sweeping Victory. Still two districts to be heard from."

At eight o'clock that evening Mr. Bolster had conceded the election to McCarthy. That evening old friends called to offer their condolences as though a death had occurred in the house. They were all shocked by the apostasy of the city. They looked grave and shook their heads over conditions.

"Armitage City is changing, right under our own eyes," Hiram Sevrance stormed. "It's becoming an industrial city. Every year more foreign-born flock in here to fill the positions in the factories and mills. The city's growing, yes, but on what? Slashings!" Hiram Sevrance had been standing in front of the hearth declaiming. Now he turned and paced across the room, the skirt of his Prince Albert swirling with his vehemence. "Take my lumber camps; there's hardly a name you can spell on the payroll! If we don't watch out the sons of these foreigners'll usurp the places our children should have, Bolster."

"It was the liquor interests that defeated us," Mr. Healey declared. "McCarthy had every saloon in Armitage City working for him. The drinks were on him. He as good as bought up the votes."

Winthrop Bolster was not so vehement. He had little to say. He seemed not to be listening to all that Hiram or Griffith or Healey or Carthugh said. Some fire had gone out of him. For the first time in his life, he felt bewildered by the political scene. He had consented to run because his friends had come to him and asked him. He felt betrayed.

Upstairs, the girls were gathered in Mama's room. It was chilly and a little fire burned decorously in the bedroom fireplace. Mama sat in her best poplin, which she had put on for the great occasion. She kept her hands busy with her knitting, but from time to time she shook her head. Belle and Dor and Anne and Sara were all there. The girls made no attempt to do anything.

"As we drove over," Dor burst out, "we had to wait for the parade to pass. They had torches and were singing all up and down Water Street. I suppose McCarthy was at the head of it. George said McCarthy had the solid foreign vote."

"What can you do against people who like that sort of cheap show?" Belle said. Sara sat on the end of Mama's big mahogany four-poster. The indignation she felt burned in her cheeks.

"I wish we had it to do over again. The party should have arranged meetings in all those new sections of the city. Papa could have gone down there and let them see him, told them what he would do for the city. He could have given them a free lunch."

"Sara," Mrs. Bolster remonstrated. "There are things your father wouldn't stoop to do."

"But there's no good in letting people beat you, either," Sara muttered.

Mr. Bolster's friends left early. There was only so much to say, however deeply they felt. George and Dor went home. Mr. Bolster turned out the lights and locked up the house, while down in the other end of town the celebration of McCarthy's victory was only just starting.

Mr. Bolster stood in the doorway and looked at Mama and his girls. He smiled wearily.

"You must be tired, Winthrop," Mama said.

"A little, Corona," Mr. Bolster admitted. "Well, I feel we did our duty. As Hiram said, it was the foreign element that defeated us. I feel I had the loyal support of all . . ."

"All the people who really mattered," Belle finished emphatically. Anne brought Mr. Bolster's slippers as he sat down by the fire.

Sara slid down from the bed rail. "How do you know what people really matter? You don't know anything about the people that live on the other side of town, I mean, really. I've been to see some of them for the news. They live in little houses and they have queer names, but they're just like other people. They just didn't know you, Papa. I wish you'd given them a chance to."

"I shouldn't care to know them," Mrs. Bolster said.

"That was Mr. VanRansom's idea, but I feel that it is the duty of the electorate to inform themselves as to the character of their candidates," Mr. Bolster said wearily.

"But . . ." Sara started to explain.

"Sara, be quiet. Papa's tired out, don't you see?" Belle murmured.

Sara felt suddenly her old childhood sense of separateness from the family. She was so sorry for Papa, but he was wrong, she insisted stubbornly to herself.

14

"I WISH the fall could last another month," Sara said, leaning on the handlebars of her bicycle.

"It's good to see a Michigan autumn again. In Germany that fall there were only yellow leaves that grew slowly browner and dirtier and then fell; no scarlet leaves like these," William said.

They had ridden down along the river as far as the brewery to see the ivy turned red against the gray stone.

"It's at its best now. You must see it," William had said.

"Is it very beautiful in Paris in the fall?" Sara asked suddenly.

William Henkel looked at her quickly.

"Yes, it is. What made you think of Paris?"

"I don't know," Sara said evasively. "I've always wanted to go there."

They walked their bicycles across the field toward the brewery.

"Young Sevrance is in Paris, now, isn't he?" William asked.

"He has been. I don't know whether he's still there." Sara's eyes were on the notched top of the brewery that looked like some Rhenish castle from this side.

"He means a great deal to you, Sara, doesn't he?"

Sara watched the pedals of her bicycle going around foolishly, as though someone were riding them. "I grew up with him. We used to live next door. I was engaged to him and we were to have been married last June and go to Europe on our wedding trip."

"Then Paris would have seemed many times more beautiful to you than it did to me," William said with a whimsical smile.

"But I broke my engagement."

"You're both very young. Perhaps when he comes back . . ."

"No," Sara said firmly. "It won't make any difference."

"Perhaps it's wrong to feel glad, Sara," William said after a long pause. Neither of them spoke of the ivy hanging red against the stolid wall that they had come to see. Neither of them saw it.

She was suddenly uneasy. "I'd like to go through the brewery sometime," she said, although nothing had been farther from her mind. "Couldn't we go in now?"

"Of course, if you're really interested."

From the other side, the brewery was all bustle and noise. A load of kegs clattered out to the street. Two men were pushing a giant lager barrel across the cobblestoned yard. It made a hollow rumbling on the cobbles as it rolled, its twelve iron hoops shining in the sun. Out of the manhole in the barrel head curled a thin wisp of smoke.

"They're doing that in order to get the pitch evenly distributed over the inside," William explained, nodding to the two men handling the barrel. "We'll hunt up Father first. He'll be pleased that you came. He's not well enough to be here, but we can't keep him home."

Sara felt herself in a foreign world. The two men in high rubber boots washing kegs looked up and nodded to William.

One of them called out some word in guttural German to the other. William led her carefully around the washing operations up flights of stone stairs. He spoke German to a workman on the way.

"Father's in the brewroom. He has a braumeister now but he still likes to watch the brew himself."

They went up the stairs into a room where a great copper kettle stood beneath the cross rafters, drawing to it all the light in the room.

"Da drüben, Gottfried!"

Sara and William stood still at the top of the stairs. They stared at the tall man lying on his stomach on a rafter.

"Hello, Father. What's Gottfried up there for?" William called out.

"Ach, how do you do. Ein Moment! Gottfried is chasing me that butterfly. Höher now, Gottfried! Sorgfallig!"

Slowly the man on the cross rafter lifted a net on a long stick, then swiftly but carefully lowered it.

"Ah!" John Henkel let out a long-drawn breath of satisfaction. He reached up for the net, keeping it carefully closed, leaving the tall, gray-haired man to climb down as best he could on the barrels piled on top of each other. William laughed aloud.

"Sara, this is mein Vater, as crazy about butterflies as about the manufacture of beer!"

But John Henkel paid no attention. Carefully he lifted the butterfly out of the net by the back of its wings.

"Ein Schwalbenschwanz!" he whispered in elation. "See, Wilhelm, the feelers are like a fern. That makes it a moth. Es ist sleepy from the dark. It must have been lured in last night by the candle flame when Mark was hopping the wort. See! Pale green like the Zoozer hops! Ach, I will not mount this one. This once I will let him go." He held it up on the back of his square, heavy hand while the moth moved its fragile wings slowly back and forth.

"Go along, fly away! The nights are cold now. Long you can't live," John Henkel murmured tenderly to the moth. "Make open the window, Wilhelm."

Just as Gottfried let himself down from the bottom keg and came over toward them, the moth spread its wings tentatively, lifted into the air, dropped again on the kindly hand of the brewer, then, taking new courage, rose again in the air and drifted above the brew kettle toward the window as though drawn toward the fresh air. It idled an instant on the sill, then floated out into the fall air, a pale green leaf, the color of spring, among the bright fall leaves.

Gottfried Werner stared at John Henkel. His mouth dropped open a little below his gray mustache.

"I risk my life für ein Schwalbenschwanz for the collection, and he says 'fly away.' Gott im Himmel, what for a fool!" he muttered to William.

John Henkel turned back from the open window. "Gut, Wilhelm, that you bring Miss Bolster to see the brewery." He held out his hand; his pleasure shone clear in his face. "Gottfried, you did well; that you meet Miss Bolster is your reward."

He stopped suddenly. The animation went out of his face, leaving it sad. "Miss Bolster—since I haf seen you, we haf lost our Sohn!"

"I know," Sara said. "I'm so sorry."

"Ach, well!" he sighed, shaking his head. Then with an effort he said more briskly: "Haf you ever seen how we make lager beer? Kommen Sie." He led Sara up the steps to the little platform on which was supported the great copper brew kettle. The ruddy sides of the polished kettle glowed as from some hidden fire.

"How beautiful!" Sara said genuinely.

"Ach, you see!" John Henkel turned with delight to Gottfried and Wilhelm. "You have right, Miss Bolster, the kettle is beautiful, but the beer, that ist more beautiful. Kommen Sie." His German words ran so into the English that Sara was not sure whether he said, "Come with me, or Kommen Sie."

"Would you really like to go?" William asked.

"Yes, I'd like to." Sara was drawn to old John Henkel by his obvious pride in the brewery. He was so sure she would be interested it would be like disappointing a child to say no. They climbed up stairs and went down stairs, through rooms that varied in temperature from that of the steamy brewroom to the chilly temperature of the storage cellars, past employees who looked at her out of fat, expressionless faces, but bobbed their heads or pulled at their caps in John Henkel's direction. The energetic little man talked all the time, waving his arms, looking to see if she understood. Sara smiled and nodded and said, "I see," though it was all confused in her mind.

"Now, I show you the hops; straight from Bohemia we get them." John Henkel opened a heavy door and they entered a room so cold Sara pulled the collar of her bicycle suit more closely around her neck. Great bales lined the room; some were still in their shipping boxes that were yellow with sulphur stain. John Henkel took a handful of the yellow-green clusters of hops from one of the bales.

"See, how clean they are picked!" He rubbed them between the palms of his hands. "Now, smell!" He held his palm with the crumpled hops up to her nose. An aromatic fragrance rose from the silvery-green fragments. "Das ist lupaline," he explained, pointing out the yellow powder. "Good hops makes good beer!"

Sara glanced at William. He was looking out the window of the storage room at the river, seeming completely disinterested in the hops. This must be an old story to him.

They followed John Henkel up to the malt house, where the barley lay spread out on the clean floor and a boy raked and turned it with a wooden shovel. John Henkel took a grain of barley between his fingers, breaking the kernel with his nail, studying the white starch in the kernel. He had to feel everything with his broad short fingers.

"I'd get lost if I ever tried to go around the brewery alone," Sara said with a laugh as she walked along with John Henkel.

"Ja," he shrugged. "I could find my way around in the dark." But he panted from the exertion of the stairs. "Now, we drink ein Glass Bier."

Sara hesitated, not wanting to admit that she had never tasted beer.

"Hier!" he called to one of the men, who then brought three copper mugs from a shelf and filled them at the spout of one of the big barrels.

"Not very much," Sara protested shyly.

John Henkel laughed. "Good beer ist good für you," he told her. "Wilhelm likes beer. Mütterchen, she likes her own wine besser." All the time he watched the amber stream flowing into the tankards from the tiny spigot in the huge vat. He raised his tankard.

"Hoch!" he said, beaming at Sara and William over his round cheeks.

Sara sipped gingerly. The beer was so bitter. She squinted as she sipped it and looked over to see William watching her. John Henkel was hidden behind his own tankard.

"If you could see yourself," William murmured. The way he said it made it a merry compliment.

Sara sipped valiantly but seemed to make no impression on the contents of the big, cold-feeling tankard. With her handkerchief she wiped the foam that clung to her lips. Then William took the tankard from her and gave her his empty one.

John Henkel set down his empty mug, sucking the foam from his overhanging mustache with his under lip. "Ach, you like beer!" He laughed, pleased at her empty stein, not hearing her feeble acquiescence. "It is better drawn from the wood; you come again any time."

When they stood in the cobblestoned courtyard William breathed the air deep into his lungs. "I don't know how Father stands that yeasty smell of the beer all day."

"Oh, thank you for finishing the beer for me. You saved my life! And it pleased your father to see my empty stein," Sara said.

William laughed. "I like the beer well enough, but not the making of it, but it sent me through school and to Europe; I should be grateful to it, shouldn't I?"

"Your father likes everything about the brewery, doesn't he?"

"Yes, too well. He's too sick now to be around the brewery; his legs are so swollen he can hardly get up and down the stairs, but he won't save himself. And he misses Hans badly. This is the first time he's seemed like himself in weeks. You were good for him."

At that moment, one of the heavy brewery wagons rumbled into the courtyard. Up on the seat with the load of barrels towering above his head sat a big man who looked vaguely familiar to Sara.

"There's Charlie Freehahn! He's grayer and fatter than when you took your ride with him. When I was a boy I used to spend most of my time at the stable with Charlie. He is blindly devoted to Father."

Charlie waved his whip at William. The team of horses stood, unmoved by the tasseled whip waving above their heads.

"Those are two new horses Charlie is trying out. He's named them Donner and Thor after the first ones."

Charlie gathered up the reins; the team started for the stable. Even for that short distance the horses arched their necks and lifted their legs with ponderous grace. Under the yellow leaves of the elm trees on the way to the stable they were like a painting.

"They look so strong, William."

"They are," he said.

They went back to the meadow by the river where they had left their bicycles. When they reached the sidewalk they struck an equal speed. The wire spokes of the wheels flashed in the late sun. They came to the bridge that separated the east side of town from the west.

"We've spent time out of this day going through the brewery when there were so many things I wanted to talk to you about," William said ruefully. He paid the toll. They rode across the bridge from his side of town to hers. People were walking on the pedestrians' path. A carriage passed. In the river a tug whistled for the bridge to raise. Sara was only slightly aware of these familiar things. She was waiting for William.

"Perhaps it was good that we went to the brewery today, after all," William said. "It's there in my background so strongly; along with my parents who speak only broken English. Do these things matter a lot to you, Sara? I know they must to your family."

Quick denial leaped to Sara's lips. How could these things matter? William was . . . he was himself.

"Of course not, William. You stand by yourself."

He shook his head. "No one does quite that. I wouldn't want you to care for me and feel in any way apologetic about my background."

How quietly the wheels could turn on the new asphalt walks! Her eyes looked steadily down the familiar length of avenue.

"It's easy to say that these things don't matter except to small-minded people," his voice went on evenly, "but sometimes they are not easy to ignore."

She thought of him that night he came out of the house and got into his carriage and drove away. She had hurried by under her umbrella without calling to him and then she had been sorry. She had watched for him after that. She had gone out of her way to pass the bank building where he had his office. She couldn't lose him again, even if these things made it hard for them.

"They don't matter, truly, William."

"I'm glad, Sara," he said for the second time that day. "After that Sunday, I stayed away. I told myself that I'd go some place else to practice where I wouldn't know that you were only a few blocks away. I could see then how your family felt and I thought perhaps young Sevrance meant a great deal to you."

Her bicycle jarred over a pebble in the road. He put his hand on her handlebars to steady her wheel.

"But staying away didn't keep me from loving you."

She met his eyes shyly. "Let's ride fast," she said in sudden, childish confusion, pressing down on the pedal. Her wheel shot ahead under the yellow and scarlet leaves. The beech tree in the Andrews' yard was like bronze. The maple was the color of the great copper brew-kettle. It was glorious. Sara laughed for very high spirits. Faster and faster! Her hair was coming down under the brim of her hat. She reached up to tuck it in.

"Don't," William said, just behind her. "I like it that way."

As they went up the front walk to the house, William stopped to pick up a bright red maple leaf. "To remember the day by," he said. "The day I told you I loved you. But I won't need anything to remember the day when you tell me that, Sara."

"Remember today, William," Sara said. She opened the door and went into the house before William had understood her words.

15

"OF course, he's a doctor. That makes a great difference," Mama said to the girls. "But I can't believe that mixing backgrounds is ever successful. Look at you and George, Dor. How happy you've been, and you practically grew up together."

"Yes," Dor said, trying not to remember how short she had been with George that very morning over the household expenses. George thought a house and maid and a child cost nothing at all. "Dr. Henkel is very well fixed for a young man just starting in a profession. His father is worth considerable, Papa says," Dor admitted grudgingly.

"What I can't believe," Belle remarked, "is that the quarrel with Paul Sevrance was anything serious. If he had only come back last summer Sara wouldn't have seen so much of this German."

"She's so headstrong," Anne said, pulling her thread through the taut drawn circle between her embroidery hoops. The needle made a sharp ping. "I can't see how she could be in love, really."

"I should think Papa could . . ." Dor began.

"Papa has talked to her and he expressed himself very clearly to Dr. Henkel."

"What did he say?" Dor asked eagerly.

"Papa said Dr. Henkel was very gentlemanly but quite obstinate. He said he appreciated our point of view and that he'd talked that all over with Sara. He said that Sara and he could be happy in spite of the differences in their backgrounds and he went on with some nonsense about the romance of America."

"Fiddlesticks!" Dor said indignantly. Mrs. Bolster's plump face was worried. She looked old in the bright sunlight.

"Henkel!" Anne said. "I should think Sara would hate to have a name like that. You can't think of it without thinking of the Henkels' brewing company."

"There's Sara!" Dor said warningly.

Sara called from the hall. "Oh, there you are!" She stood between the curtains of the doorway, holding her hat in her hand. The dark "business dress" only made the tints of her skin and hair and eyes warmer. For just an instant she stood there, looking at them as though she were holding some good news of her own in check.

Dor put her embroidery away in her bag self-consciously. Anne's eyes lingered on Sara's face. Her sense of missing Roger had dulled a little. Looking at Sara, it rose again, catching her like a pain in her side. Belle thought suddenly of how fond Derrick always was of Sara and then was annoyed; she tried not to let Derrick cross her mind. Mrs. Bolster looked a little helplessly at her youngest daughter. She had understood the other girls better.

"It's beautiful out! William drove me along the river before we came home."

"Did you go out past the old house, Sara? Were the leaves all gone from the maples, did you notice?"

"Oh, Mama, I'm sorry. I didn't notice." Sara was contrite.

"I suppose you were so absorbed in each other," Anne

said tartly. There was an edge to her words more often of late, that started as the selvage edge of sorrow but raveled to a rough edge of self-pity and bitterness.

Sara laughed. "I suppose maybe we were. Mama, do you mind too awfully?" Sara dropped swiftly to her knees beside Mrs. Bolster's chair. "I promised I'd marry William in June."

A quick look of hurt slanted across Mrs. Bolster's usually placid face.

"Why, Sara, your engagement hasn't even been announced," Belle said before Mrs. Bolster could speak. Belle was taking Mama's place more and more.

"I know, but we can announce it right away."

"But, Sara, you aren't sure, my dear! You're so young. Marriage is such a serious thing!"

"Oh, Mama, I *am* sure." Sara's own words swept her to her feet. "If you only knew William! He's fine and sincere and . . . and he loves books and music and . . ." Sara's young face, so lighted by her love, hurt Anne. Anne said more dryly than she had meant:

". . . and has a brewery!"

Sara turned on Anne. "He's a doctor, Anne. He doesn't have anything to do with the brewery, and I like the brewery. I've been all through it and I like Mr. and Mrs. Henkel, and the girls are very nice."

Mama and the girls looked at Sara as though she were a stranger.

"I suppose you'd rather have me marry a milk-and-watery old thing like Jethro Healey because he comes from our side of town and his family can't speak anything but English! Oh, Mama, I'm sorry, but I do love him," she burst out incoherently.

"Then I suppose you will marry him, Sara," Mama said as

one who assents to some great disaster beyond her control. Sara flung her arms around Mrs. Bolster.

"I must tell Papa. Is he in his study?"

When she was gone the girls looked at each other and Mama.

Mrs. Bolster sighed. "I suppose we must call on the Henkels, Belle."

The Sunday after Sara's engagement was announced, she went with William's family to church. Afterwards they would have dinner at the Henkels'.

"I hope, my dear, that this doesn't mean that you will feel you must attend the Lutheran Church all the time," Mrs. Bolster demurred. "Mr. Oldsworth would miss you at Christ Church." She stood in the front hall buttoning on her long black gloves, waiting for the girls. The soft flesh of her hand puffed out at the opening of the glove, making it hard to button. "Sara, see if you can . . ." Sara buttoned them.

"No, Mama, William wouldn't want me to, but this will please his mother and father so much and Mr. Henkel is ill, you know. William is worried about him."

"Mrs. Henkel mentioned his being ill that day we called, but she said he insisted on going to the brewery." Mrs. Bolster winced as she said the word "brewery." "Here they are—good-by, dear."

Sara stood on the porch watching them all get in the Healeys' carriage and drive off. How queer it was for her to be waiting for William to go to another church. She would like sitting beside William in church. But she was a little nervous about going to the Henkels' for dinner.

Sara did not sit beside William. In the strict Lutheran service, the men sat on one side, the women on the other. Sara sat between Mrs. Henkel and Marie, and Ottilie sat next. The church was ugly after Christ Church. Sara looked at the garishly bright red and green and purple stained-glass windows, at the light varnished oak furniture on the pulpit. The women sitting together on one side of the church had a more foreign look than when interspersed with men, it occurred to her now. She glanced covertly at William's mother. Her face looked almost severe. She sat watching the minister, her lips moving silently.

Even in church Sara felt that the girls resented William's marrying her. William said they were very happy, but she could tell. "Perhaps, they're a little in awe of you, beloved," William said. She had laughed at that, stopping though in her thoughts to treasure up the word, "beloved." But it wasn't any such foolish thing as that; it was that they felt no one could be good enough for William.

The congregation sang a hymn in German. The hard-sounding words surrounded her, making a wall that reared above her. Everyone sang. Sara hummed. The wall of strange syllables made her feel lost in a foreign place. She looked down at the German words on the hymnal that Marie held for her, then up at the strange faces around her. Quick, before it was too late, she must step behind Mrs. Henkel and hurry up that strip of bright red carpet out the door of this German church into the fresh air beyond it. She could slip into Christ Church where a mellowed light came softly in through windows that were beautiful. There the people were, the kind she was used to. And the singing . . . the voices of the little choir boys, of the congregation, singing words she knew, that made a river, not a wall. Some feeling akin to homesickness rose in her, catching her by the throat. She had been crazy to think she didn't mind William's German background. It was too alien.

She glanced over toward the men's side for William. Her

eyes found him at once, the second from the end of the pew. Among the thick-set, bearded faces, his was different. It was more than a surface difference; that he was clean-shaven, that his collar had a different cut, it was something about his face that made him hers. He was singing. He liked to sing. The foreign syllables would sound differently as he sang them, soft, not hard. "It is a wonderful tongue for love, meine Geliebte," he had said once. As though her eyes drew his, he looked over at her, and smiled, taking away the strangeness of the atmosphere.

"Vaterunser. . . ." The congregation knelt. They were praying. Sara knelt happily.

It was strange, too, sitting at the Henkels' table. Mr. Henkel was in bed, in the bedroom off the sitting room. He scarcely seemed like the same hearty, jovial man she had seen standing in the doorway of the brewery. His color was altered. He was very weak. But his face lighted up when he saw her. He lapsed into German talking to her. William said his mind wandered lately.

William's mother looked very quiet and sad, sitting at Marie's left hand. She was abstracted and seemed to forget that Sara was here. William was so gentle with her, making her smile in spite of herself.

Marie sat at the head of the table, William at the foot, Sara on his right, Mrs. Henkel and Ottilie on the opposite side. A maid with a broad, cheerful face and flaxen braids around her head brought in the food and changed the dishes. When she walked across the room, the little Dresden figures on the sideboard rattled faintly.

"These noodles are Marie's own, Sara. Nobody can make them the way she does, even in Germany," William told her.

"They're delicious," Sara said to Marie, wondering

whether the girls would be pleased or not if she praised the other things, the fried chicken, the spiced peaches, the biscuits. She did compliment them on the Törten. Mrs. Henkel smiled a fleeting instant, but Marie dismissed it quickly.

"Of course, it's German cooking, but we like it."

Sara was glad when dinner was over and they sat in the sitting room with Mr. Henkel's door open in the bedroom. It was close behind the lace curtains and the screen of plants. She wished that she and William could go out walking. She sat up a little straighter. She wanted them to like her.

"William says you have resigned your position on the *Courier*," Marie volunteered.

"Yes, I was sorry to leave. Everyone in the Office has been so kind to me."

"I should think they would be," Ottilie flashed out impetuously. Sara smiled her pleasure in the genuine compliment.

"I'm afraid I was very stupid at the beginning."

"But you must have liked *doing* something," Ottilie said naturally, without constraint. "I want to go to Art School in Detroit in the fall. William says I may." The face above the high-collared dress changed again from the ordinary plain-featured face to one that was alight.

"How splendid! You should go, you're so gifted," Sara said.

"You must see the chocolate pot Ottilie painted last week," Marie began proudly and then stopped, catching her breath, looking at Ottilie with real anguish in her expression.

"Oh, never mind. I don't care. Perhaps she wouldn't have liked it anyway," Ottilie answered sulkily. Some screen had fallen again, hiding the glowing eagerness that had lighted it a moment before. Sara looked at William in perplexity.

"I don't know, but I hope Ottilie is painting something

for a wedding gift for us," William said, smoothing things out by the way he looked at them.

"I do hope so," Sara said quickly. "Don't show it to us beforehand." She could see that Marie was still hurt because she had spoiled the surprise. She must say something to make her feel comfortable again.

"Did you do this, Marie?" Sara asked, touching the embroidered armrest on the couch. She knew she did. "I wish I could do as beautiful needlework as that."

"I'd be glad to show you," Marie offered.

Sara shook her head. "I've learned to mend to Mama's satisfaction, but I could never learn to embroider like that."

"I'll do some for you," Marie promised.

When Sara went in to say good-by to Mr. Henkel, he took her hand in his square short fingers.

"You und Wilhelm will be married before I . . ."

He looked so sick. Sara forgot that Mama wanted her to be engaged a long time.

"Yes, Mr. Henkel," she said softly. William stood beside her with his arm around her. Mr. Henkel's eyes rested on them both. He nodded his head wearily against the pillow.

Out in the carriage Sara sighed, unconsciously relaxing after the strain of the day.

"Was it so hard, meine Geliebte; you sighed so heavily," William asked.

"Oh, I didn't know I sighed."

"No one else could be so understanding or so sensitive, Sara. I know how it is, but I can't hurt them."

Sara flushed. "I wouldn't want you to." This was what she had wanted with Paul, this sense of sureness about him. She was so sure of William.

"There are always going to be things that will annoy you. The girls are fiercely sensitive and proud. Sometimes it makes them . . . stiff like that."

"I know, dear." Sara was chary with endearments. She said "dear" now with a little hesitation that made William smile at her. "That doesn't matter."

"I sang all the hymns to you in church this morning, Sara. I've hated that church sometimes, for the things I was taught in the wretched parochial school, things to make a little boy wake at night screaming with terror, and the bigotry and blindness, but this morning in church, with you across the aisle, I lost all that feeling. I felt it was a holy place again. You've changed everything for me, Sara."

They were almost home before Sara remembered her promise to Mr. Henkel.

"William, your father meant he wanted us to be married before . . . while he was living, didn't he?"

"Yes, it would mean a great deal to him, but I don't want you to go against your family's wishes."

"How sick is he, William, I mean . . ."

"I don't believe Father can live till spring. If he lives through Christmas, I don't hope for much more. Mother and the girls don't know that."

"Then you wish we could be married . . . at Christmastime, really, don't you?"

She read his answer in his eyes.

16 DECEMBER, 1894

SARA BOLSTER and William Otto Henkel were married on Christmas Day. It was a different wedding from the one Mrs. Bolster had dreamed of a year ago in June. Sara was not even married from her own home. There were no guests beside the two families. She was married in her dark green suit, standing at the foot of John Henkel's bed. The Reverend Mr. Oldsworth from Christ Church read the service and the Reverend Jacob Ahnfeldt of the Deutsche Evangelische Lutheran Kirche offered the prayers. Belle sat at the piano in the other room playing softly during the brief service, and the canary in the birdcage in the dining room shrilled in across the piano notes, found the key and ended with a long-held trill of piercing sweetness.

Mr. Henkel had lost his hearty look. His face against the pillows was the color of the gray sacking bags his hops came in, but during the ceremony his eyes were bright as they rested on Sara and William. The sound of his breathing ran just under the minister's words.

From the kitchen came the sweet hot smell of Christmas cookery. Through the open doorway of the sitting room, so Mr. Henkel could see it, was the Christmas tree, hung with balls and tinsel and candles and Christmas cookies, decorated with colored sugar.

When Sara gave her hand to William, Mr. Bolster stepped back beside his wife. Corona Bolster watched her daughter with a proud little smile as though this were the very wedding she had desired for her. Mrs. Henkel sat in a chair beside the bed, holding a square of lace and cambric against her trembling lips. Only Anne cried, silently, standing against the doorway.

"I pronounce thee husband and wife. What God hath joined together, let no man put asunder." The minister's voice sounded the more solemnly because of the small, tight little room.

They went to Sara's house for Christmas dinner and stayed to sing two carols around the piano afterwards. Sara could hardly sing. Her heart seemed hushed with its own happiness, but she heard William singing and Papa and the girls. William was one of them after all. The family was reconciled to her marrying him; she needn't have worried.

It had grown dark early. Papa moved across the room to get the lighter. Sara watched him, knowing beforehand each movement he would make. Now the deer and the forest on the frosted globes sprang to life at the spurt of flame in each jet. The light polished the holly leaves hanging from the chandelier.

Sara put on her new beaver toque and short coat. She saw Mama and the girls in the mirror and whirled around to face them.

"I'll be back in a month! I hardly need to say good-by. And I love my gifts. You are such darlings!" Out of the abundance of love in her own heart came the words.

"You have William send us a telegram, dear, before you leave there and we'll have the house all ready and Mary can start the girl," Mama said, trying to keep her mind on practical things.

"I feel almost as though I were going away to school again," Sara laughed. "Oh, I didn't write my address!" She rushed to her desk and scribbled with conscious pride on the paper:

Mrs. William Henkel
Waldorf Astoria
New York City

"I'll write you from Atlantic City and give you our address there."

PART TWO

Nestor's noble son . . . gathered the reins into his hands. Then he struck the horses with the whip: and these, glad to be loosed, flew out onto the plain: which all day long they steadily traversed, with the yoke nodding to and fro over their necks.

Down sank the sun. The road became blind.

THE ODYSSEY OF HOMER
BK. III
Translation by T. E. Shaw

I JANUARY, 1895

"FATHER is much worse; we are so thankful that you are coming home this week," Marie wrote. They received the letter the last morning in the hotel at Atlantic City. When they went for a turn along the boardwalk the news saddened their spirits. They walked without talking a long stretch of the way, striking the same pace, Sara's hand tucked in William's arm.

How strange and wonderful it was to come to know William so well in so short a time that this silence between them seemed full, Sara thought shyly. She looked out at the sea and a little smile curved her lips.

"Sara," Mama had whispered, just at the last, drawing her aside, "you mustn't be frightened. There are things about marriage that will seem . . . difficult to understand, but they are a part of it, daughter. After a while, you will want children . . ." and Mama had kissed her again with a worried look in her eyes.

Mama needn't have worried. But Mama didn't know William, she thought pityingly. Nothing was difficult with William.

He met her eyes. She felt his love as deeply as though he had taken her in his arms.

It was warm in the winter sunshine. The sea lay still beyond the wide beach. People wrapped like mummies sat in the chairs on the sand. On the other side of the boardwalk the booths and shops glittered with a hard brightness, but on this side, the colors of the sand, the sea, and the sky lay softly against each other.

"I like this place best of all, William," Sara said. "We must come back often. I've never seen the sea before, you know."

"Next year we must go to Europe. We'll leave in the spring."

Anticipation shone in Sara's eyes. "I hope we can."

"Of course, we can. We'll just pack up and go."

William bought a bunch of violets in a shop along the boardwalk. They took one of the little donkey carts that plied back and forth over the sand, and rode back up the beach. There was a brisk breeze so close to the sea and a sharp briny stench from the watersoaked piers. Sara peeled back her gloves and held out her hands to the warm sun. It sparkled on her diamond ring and the wide gold band of her wedding ring.

"I like to look at them," she confessed. She moved her hand so that the sparkle flashed in William's eyes. They laughed together. William lifted her hand to his lips.

When they stepped off the train at the Baker Street station in Armitage City, it was winter. A raw sleet stung their faces as they crossed the station platform to take a cab. They had not written the time of their coming, so no one was there to meet them.

"Do you mind, Sara, if we go to see Father first?"

"Of course not, William," Sara said, feeling a shade of guilt at not letting her family know when they would arrive. She was ashamed of her inner reluctance to see the Henkels, too. The month had been so completely theirs. Now that they were home, so much of their time would belong to the families.

The little white house looked smaller than ever through the sleet. There was so much snow in the path that the picket gate was blocked open. William lifted Sara bodily over the drift.

"This is like lifting you over a new threshold, Geliebte," he murmured. Sara's feeling of strangeness here at her husband's home disappeared.

They felt the worry that filled the house the minute they saw the girls. Mrs. Henkel's pale face was drawn with anxiety. She came in from the other room with her arms outstretched.

"Mein Sohn, mein Sohn." Her voice broke and William put his arms around her, patting her shoulder tenderly. Sara found her own eyes wet, watching them.

"We've wanted you so, William," Marie said.

Oh, they shouldn't have been away enjoying themselves, Sara felt guiltily.

"Yes, it was delightful!" she said to Ottilie. "We were worried, of course, after we had your letter." Ottilie looked older. It was as though they saw Mr. Henkel's condition in these faces.

Sara sat in the little parlor that she was coming to know so well. She went into the bedroom for only a moment. John Henkel did not know her, and she tiptoed back to wait for William.

"Father keeps calling 'William.' We would have sent you a telegram today if you hadn't been coming home," Marie said. Marie was calmest of all of them. There was an acceptance of the knowledge that her father was dying that seemed worse to Sara than Mrs. Henkel's whispered prayers or Ottilie's rebellious sobs.

"We shouldn't have gone," Sara said finally, closing her mind on all the joy of their month.

"No, Father wanted you to go. It was a comfort to him that William was happy," Marie said sadly.

And William was happy. Out of the richness of his love that surrounded her, Sara said very gently, touching Marie's hand on the couch beside her, "But you have been under such a strain."

"Yes," Marie said. "It is a strain. Mütterchen will go to pieces when Father goes. First Hans, and now Father."

"William will be a comfort to her," Sara said.

When they went out of the little house, William's mind was so taken up with thoughts of his father that without thinking he let Sara go through the deep snowdrift across the walk.

"You'll want to go home first, won't you, dear?"

"Yes, William, they'll want us to stay there overnight."

"I must come right back. Father won't live much longer."

They were silent in the back of the cab. Sara put her hand in William's. Just as they turned up Chestnut Street, William spoke.

"Father's worrying over the brewery. He keeps thinking about it and about Mama and the girls."

"But the brewery is all right, isn't it, William?"

"Yes," William answered slowly. "Gottfried is managing it."

"Why is he worrying, William?" William's voice sounded more serious than his words. What was the matter? A trickle of apprehension leaked through Sara's warmth.

"The brewery needs to be expanded and Father doesn't think Gottfried has enough business ability to do it. 'He's a braumeister,' he keeps saying. He counted on Hans to take over the brewery, you know."

Sara could see the lights of their own house now. She was as eager as a young girl to run in on them with William. Then her eagerness faded in the face of William's long silence.

"What, William?" she asked, not as a young girl at all.

"Father begs me to promise to run the brewery," William said. The cab was stopping in front of the house. Sara forgot that she had arrived home.

"But, William, you couldn't do that! What about your profession? All the years you've spent in study?"

William shook his head. "Father doesn't seem to consider that. He can't rest until he knows the brewery is going to be in safe hands."

They still sat in the cab. The driver had come around to open the door. "Just a minute," Sara said. Something was at stake. They must get it settled now. "William, you don't know anything about the brewing business. You don't even like the business. You said so yourself!"

"That's true, Sara, but Father wants it in the family. He'd feel safe about it then, don't you see, Sara? It means so much to him."

"No," Sara said, "I don't. I don't see how you could give up your profession."

The family had heard the carriage stopping. Someone was opening the door. It was Papa.

"Quick, William, we're here. There's Papa! Papa!"

"Is it Sara, Winthrop?" Mama's voice came out to them.

"Sara!" Papa cried out.

"Oh, Papa! We had a wonderful time. Belle! Oh, Anne! How's Dor?"

"Well, William!" Mr. Bolster shook William's hand.

"You'll stay here tonight, Sara?"

"Yes, Mama. But Mr. Henkel is so much worse; William will stay there."

Mrs. Bolster shook her head. "Papa stopped in to show them some of the letters you wrote us. He said Mr. Henkel seemed very low."

"Yes," Sara said. They didn't know what Mr. Henkel wanted William to do. Only half her mind was on what Belle was telling her about the house that the girls and Mama had settled for them. The other half was with William, worrying about him. She was relieved when he had gone back to be with his father.

"The brewery, Wilhelm? You haf not promised." John Henkel's speech came slowly, gutturally. His tired eyes searched William's face. From the other side of the bed Mrs. Henkel watched William, sometimes moving her lips silently, touching her mouth with the wisp of cambric, not speaking aloud. This was a matter between her husband and her son.

William's mouth was hidden behind his hand. His elbow rested on his knee. He was thinking of the year he had studied in Germany, of working in Orth's laboratory, of Professor Orth's nod of approval of his work, of his words when he left: "We will hear from you, Dr. Henkel, in your country." What would Orth say when he heard he had given up medicine to run a brewery?

"Wilhelm?" The old man's voice was querulous.

"Father, I will watch it closely, but I must go on with my medicine. Gottfried has been with you so long; he is the one to run it."

"Ja, but, Wilhelm," John Henkel said with unexpected

vigor, "Gottfried ist ein braumeister; he has not the brains to build it bigger." He breathed heavily. "If Hans were here, I would not trouble you."

The room was still except for his breathing and the spray of snow blown fitfully against the windowpane. A small stove had been set up in the bedroom and the red coals glowed behind the isinglass squares in its door.

After a while Mrs. Henkel consented to lie down on the couch in the sitting room, and the girls went on to bed. William sat the rest of the night in his chair. John Henkel drowsed and woke to take a swallow of water, and then drowsed again.

Once he turned his head restlessly on the pillow until his eyes found William. "John Henkel Brewing Co.," he said, as though the name itself should be enough for William.

When his father seemed asleep William closed his eyes and leaned back in his chair. He must have fallen asleep himself, because he started, to hear his father muttering.

"If Marie marries . . ." A long pause of labored breathing. ". . . A good, bright young man . . . you can take him in the brewery, too, maybe. Just the family."

"Yes, Father," William answered reassuringly. He wished Marie were married and that her husband could take over the whole thing now.

"The girls und Mama, Wilhelm. There is plenty for all of you if you run the brewery. You know how I watch it . . . only the best hops und barley. Keep always things clean, and never no workmans drunk." William's face relaxed, thinking of his father's pride in the brewery. "Such good business; an odder year und I would haf made it haf again so big. Now ist the time." John Henkel shook his head as though with sorrow at not being here to see it. "Mark Fiedler ist no good as cellar man . . ." he began again. "Too lazy."

"Never mind, Father. Try not to bother any more now, just sleep. That's what you need," William said gently, laying his hand on his father's arm.

How little, after all, had he known about his father, he thought remorsefully. Hans had been closer to him. He had been away so much, studying. When he had first talked of medicine, his father had said:

"Ja, go ahead. It will please your Mutter. A good doctor is a good thing. Hans will be in the brewery bei me."

His father had been generous, too. He had urged him to go to Germany to study. "You take your time, Wilhelm, you learn more, you'll be a better doctor! Und when you drink beer in the old country, you see how good Henkel's beer is!" he had said with his ready laugh.

All the laughter had gone out of the old man on the bed. William saw the gray eyelids raise. His father's eyes rested on him.

The business he had built up was his whole life, and he wanted a son to carry it on. He had given him everything; now he asked only that he run the business. Looked at that way, it didn't seem so much to ask; just till he expanded it. "Now ist the time to build it bigger," his father had said. Three years, five at the most. He could keep up with the medical journals, and take a year of study, and then go back into his profession. But five years out of a career was a long time. Sara wouldn't like his doing it. He must talk to Sara.

He went softly out of the room, crossing the parlor so quietly that his mother did not wake. But Marie was already downstairs. Her question was on her face.

"He's sleeping well just now," William answered.

"You must have your breakfast, a cup of coffee at least, Wilhelm," Marie said.

He thought how much she looked like his mother. Already

there was so little girlishness about her, or had he grown so used to Sara's glowing face, her grace?

"There is no hope, Wilhelm?" Marie asked once, but the inflection of her voice was hopeless.

"Nein, meine Schwester," William answered as he had when he was a little boy, as though speaking in German softened the cruel fact.

The teakettle was boiling noisily. Marie got up to push it to a cooler part of the stove.

"I'll drop over to see Sara and then look in at the office and the hospital. You can call me there, Marie. I'm going to send a nurse."

"No, Wilhelm; we can do . . ."

"There is plenty to do, Marie. Let me have a nurse here, anyway."

"No, Wilhelm! I couldn't have strangers here!" Marie's eyes were stubborn.

When he went in to look at his father again, his mother was there, sitting silently by the bed, looking as though she had not slept at all.

"Mein Sohn, what would we do without you?" she whispered.

Charlie Freehahn kept his horse for him at the brewery stables and usually sent a stableboy over with it. But this morning Charlie, himself, was standing by the horse, pretending to fuss with a buckle.

"Guten Morgen, Charlie!"

"Guten Morgen, Herr Doktor."

Usually Charlie's face crinkled into lines of secret amusement that the little boy he had taken for rides on the big wagons and taught how to harness a horse and scolded out of the stables should be "Herr Doktor." But this morning there was no line of amusement in his face.

"Herr Henkel?" Charlie asked.

"Nicht gut, Charlie," William told him.

Charlie shook his head and tramped back through the snow. William watched him. He looked beyond Charlie to the gray sandstone bulk of the brewery. Then, picking up the reins, he drove off toward the west side.

He drove Sara from the Bolsters' to the house they were renting on Sycamore Street. Going for the first time into the house together was different from the way Sara had expected. William was preoccupied. She was troubled. The things that had taken so much time to decide, so many consultations with Mama and the girls: where the white marble chime clock from the Healeys should stand, whether to have a lace spread or one of the new swiss ones . . . all these things were insignificant details. It was only a house to be alone in with William.

They walked through the rooms and came back to the sitting room. They sat down without taking off their wraps.

"I must go. I want to stop in at the office and the hospital and I don't want to leave Father too long," William said, but without moving.

"Sara, Father lies there with his eyes on me, waiting for me to say I'll go on with the business."

"Can't you humor him, William? He's sick; he doesn't know what he's asking. Let him think for his own peace of mind. . . ."

William shook his head. "His mind is hazy, but that's one thing he's clear about. It's been such a part of his life, Sara."

"But he's had his life, William. You have yours all ahead."

William shook his head. His face had an expression she

had never seen on it. His features seemed to lose their quick intelligence; their responsiveness had retired behind some inexpressive mask. His eyes were turned away from her toward the window. This was not the William who had been gay and teasing and tender and passionate. This was someone she hardly knew.

"William!" Her voice was sharp with its fear.

"He's my father, Sara. Now that Hans is gone he can't rest until he knows the business is safe and that my mother and sisters will be cared for. My father never speaks of what I owe him, but I owe him a great deal."

There it was; his filial feeling was like a wall. His acceptance of the reasonableness of his father's wishes angered her. Hadn't she married him when her family wanted her to marry Paul?

"If your father hadn't wanted you to marry me you wouldn't have done that, either, then, would you?" Her voice was quiet, but there was an unmistakable hint of anger in it.

William turned quickly back to her, incredulity in his voice.

"Why, Sara, nothing like that could have come between us. You must see how different this is."

"No," Sara said. The first hour in their own home they should not be talking like this. But it was so important, for her, for William. He must not let this feeling of duty to his father make him change his whole life.

"You wouldn't make a success of it, William. People don't make a success of work they don't like."

"If I ran the brewery I'd make a success of it," William said firmly. To Sara, watching him, he bore a sudden striking resemblance to John Henkel.

"And you'd give up all you've studied and learned." Sara's tone of voice was accusing. But William was so walled around by his own thoughts the tone seemed not to touch him.

"I could enlarge it as Father had planned; make it thoroughly modern, double its output so that it would give us all an ample income. Then I would hire a manager, take a year in Europe to brush up, and go on with my medicine."

Sara felt herself speaking coldly. "And that would take half your life."

"No," William said. "Five years at the most."

Sara's long silence broke into William's thoughts.

"But, William, I can't believe it's right for you to give up so much."

His eyes were wretched, sleepless. "Of course, Sara, if my being a doctor is the all-important . . ."

He was hurt.

"No, William, it isn't that," she said quickly. "I just don't think you should do it. I don't think you can be happy at it."

"The change won't be pleasant for me and I know how unpleasant it will be for you, but, Sara, I've got to do what I think is right." He kissed her before he left. "I do love you, Sara. I'm sorry about all this."

She watched him from the window as he drove off. It wouldn't make any difference in her life, and yet it would. Running the brewery would tie him again more closely to his family, and that part of his life that was so foreign to her; that she couldn't enter into. It was like those books of his on the floor, waiting to be put into the bookcases, with the hard-looking German titles she couldn't read. She thought of Paul saying, "You can make me anything you want." It wasn't so with William. There were things he had to do, to be, in spite of her.

2

WHEN Sara heard the gate click she dropped the freshly fluted curtains she was running on their rods and ran to look out the front bedroom window. Even from up here, looking down through the branches of the maple tree on the top of his hat, she had known him instantly. It was Paul. The paper had said last week that he had landed in New York April 10th. She had wondered where she would see him first, whether he would come to see her.

She heard the doorbell and Pearl coming through the house from the kitchen. She sat still until Pearl came up to tell her. She almost didn't want to see him. She glanced in the mirror at her hair braided around her head. Paul had never seen it that way. William liked it better than with the puffs that were so stylish. She looked plainer, hardly fashionable at all. She took off the bar pin and fastened the coral brooch William had bought her in Atlantic City. It gave color to the dark brown stuff of her dress. How silly! Her hands were cold. She laid them a second against her face.

"Why, Paul, how nice to see you!" She held out her hand to him. Did she sound too glad?

"Sara! It's good to see you!" He took her hand in both of his. She had forgotten how dark his eyes were. They held hers. She drew her hand away.

"I couldn't stay angry," Paul said.

"Come into the library, Paul. We'll have tea. William prefers this room because of its southern exposure." She talked as she led the way. Did the words sound stilted? She was perfectly at ease, she told herself. Mentioning William's name made her feel at ease.

Paul acted as though nothing had happened. How well he looked! She liked his tallness, the long sharp lines of his face, his quickness of expression. She tried to bring before her the way he had looked the last night she had seen him.

"You must have wondered at not having a wedding gift from me. I was in Vienna when your announcement came."

There was a long instant's awkward pause that held like a drop of water before you break it with your finger. She broke the silence now with a foolish speech.

"Of course, you must have been having such a gay time in Vienna you didn't have time . . ."

Paul's eyes held hers. Again a silence like the drop of water on the table's surface, standing of itself, seeming almost hard.

"I gave a party in my rooms that night for some chaps I knew there and we drank to you in champagne. Then we went out and did Vienna, really did it, and didn't come back until morning in the approved manner. No matter how much I drank I stayed dead sober. Funny, too!" Paul laughed.

Sara was glad that Pearl brought in tea then. The tea service made a safe barrier between them.

"We bought you a wedding present that night and one for Dr. Henkel. But I decided to bring them. I'll go get them." He went quickly through the rooms. She poured his tea.

"How generous you were to bring one to each of us!"

"I wanted yours to be to you alone." He took his tea.

She felt him watching her. Her fingers were clumsy with the knot.

"Here, let me cut it for you."

She opened the wrappings and lifted out a jewel box of Dresden china, beautifully shaped. She tipped back the top by the intricate china handle. A tinkling tune came from beneath the white velvet lining.

Sara laughed delightedly as a child. "It's lovely, Paul!"

"I remember that jewel box of Belle's we used to love as children. I woke up the man who owned the store to buy it. He swore it had belonged to Marie Antoinette's mother," Paul said with a laugh.

"Shall I open William's or save it for him?"

Paul shrugged. "Perhaps he won't care for it; it's the best of its kind, though."

There!—that was what she hadn't liked about Paul: his patronizing air. She picked eagerly on the fault. She unwrapped the gift but before the wrappings were off she knew what it was: a stein in some ivory pottery with a pewter handle and lid. There were raised figures on the sides and some German words beneath.

"I thought perhaps he might make a collection of steins."

Sara said nothing, making laborious business of smoothing the ribbon.

"I was surprised, Sara, when I heard Dr. Henkel had given up his practice."

"Yes," Sara said shortly; she wouldn't discuss William with Paul. "Won't you have more tea, or some fruit cake?"

"No, thank you," Paul answered, unrebuked. "Let me take those things out of your way." He picked up the music box and the stein and laid them on the table. When he came back to his chair he said, "Do you know, when I passed the salt sheds on the way over here, they didn't look as steep as they used to!"

Sara laughed. "No, but the sawdust was deep!"

"I remember how you used to look with your skirts and pigtails flying. You look too sedate now to have done anything like that!"

William had been so quiet and tired learning the business of the brewery these last few months, and they had been with Mrs. Henkel and the girls so much, that she had begun to feel old and serious herself. It was good now to laugh.

"By the way, the last of Father's peacocks died!" Paul told her. They laughed again.

"Sara, what a bounder I was! I was coming back in June to tell you so, then Mother wrote me you were going with Dr. Henkel. I should have come on the first train instead of going off to Europe like a sulky schoolboy. I can't help but think, Sara, that I lost you by such a little!"

"Why, Paul!" He took her unawares. A minute ago they had been laughing over their old pranks and now he was so serious. "It was more than that, Paul. I . . . I found I didn't love you." She felt relieved that she had gotten it into words. It was true, wasn't it?

"I still love you, Sara," Paul said abruptly. Sara stood up quickly. She set the cup and saucer down on the tray so it made a harsh clink.

"Paul, you mustn't!" She was angry that she didn't feel more angry.

"But I do. What can I do about it? What harm is there in saying it?"

"Paul, I can't have you talk like that to me," she said a little tardily.

"I'm sorry. I'll try not to mention it again. It just came out."

She sat down like a child that has become unduly excited.

"What I really came for, Sara, was to wish you happiness and to ask you to wish me luck in my law practice. I'm going in with Blanchard, you know."

"Thank you. I do wish you luck. You haven't told me anything about your trip. Was it glorious?" Why had she said that? Paul would remember that she should have been there with him. There was no safe ground between them.

"Oh, I stayed in a place in Devon that you would have liked. There was a whole forest of beech trees like the beech tree we used to play in," Paul said easily. With his tone of voice he lifted the tension. He went on casually to make her laugh about his landlady in Paris. Paul had changed a great deal, she thought, watching him. She had never liked him so well. She checked the thought guiltily. She was glad that he left before William came. She hurried upstairs and bathed and dressed in her most becoming dress. When she heard William she ran down the stairs, her taffeta skirt swishing against the spindles.

"Oh, William, I'm so glad to see you!"

"Why, Sara, Geliebte!"

William was here now, with his arms around her, blocking out any thought of Paul.

But after dinner William opened the books on brewing he was going over. Sara sat on the other side of the table with her sewing. She looked across at him, studying him. He was so different from Paul. He seemed stolid and serious. He went at the strange problems of beer as systematically as he must have gone at his languages and his medicine.

He looked up from his book as though he felt her looking at him. "Sara, on the way home today, I found the place for us to build. I don't know why I never thought of it before. We can have a garden that slopes all the way down to the river, not the tame old bayou, but the river itself. Only," he looked at her dubiously, "it adjoins the vacant land beyond the brewery. Would that bother you to be so near the brewery? The trees would hide it completely except in winter from the upstairs windows. Or would you mind too much living on the east side?"

"No, I wouldn't mind; it doesn't matter at all," Sara said. "It would be lovely to be near the river," she added quickly to make up for her lack of enthusiasm.

William went back to his books. Sara pulled the needle back and forth through the material. Paul's words came back to her; the way he had looked. She seemed to know him better than William tonight. They had grown up together. Maybe that was more important than she had thought. Perhaps she should have waited. Paul had changed. Perhaps she had been wrong to marry William. She loved him, but his world was so different. It was so hard to feel at home with his sisters. Now they would build a house by the brewery! A little fear grew in her. She put down her sewing. William was so absorbed. She must say something to bring him back to her.

"Oh, William, I forgot to show you. Paul Sevrance came to call this afternoon. He just got back. And he brought us each a wedding gift."

William put back his head and laughed. "Sevrance is a fine young man, but he can't forgive me the brewery." He turned the stein in his hands. "It's really a beautiful stein. The woman with the vine around her head represents hops and this woman with the cornucopia of grain symbolizes the barley, and out of the two comes good beer. Old Gambrinus here astride the barrel is the patron saint of beer."

"Oh," Sara said, tracing the figures with her finger. "I didn't know that beer had a patron saint."

"There are all kinds of traditions about beer. Very few people know that beer was made in Egypt in the days of the Ptolemies, for instance. To most people, like Sevrance, beer just means fat Germans. They wouldn't believe that George Washington made his own beer at Mount Vernon. After all, the Colonists drank it with their meals until the sea captains came in with their rum and slaves from the West Indies. . . . Oh, Sara! it's all so foreign to you and you try so hard to be interested in it because I'm mixed up in it. And I love you for it. Well, five years isn't a lifetime, darling."

He threw his book across the room. "Here, let me show you how a stein should be used!" He went to the piano and struck a few chords. Then he turned around to her, flourishing the stein in time to his song.

She could not understand the German words, but the rollicking tune was infectious. He ended the song by pledging her in pantomime in the empty stein. How could she have thought him stolid or too serious?

"The night Friederich and Hans and I passed our examinations you should have heard us! We celebrated to make up for all those months of grinding. We called the waiter with:

'Bier hier, bier hier, oder ich fall um.' "

William's deep voice filled the room.

"But here's my favorite; it's in Latin and it's more than a drinking song:

'Gaudeamus igitur, juvenes dum sumus.'

It means us, Geliebte, let us rejoice, therefore, while we are young." He broke off in the middle of the song. "It means let us take our youth and our love and our heart's desire." Then he began it again and sang it through in Latin.

"I love it when you sing for me, William."

William laughed. He lifted her lightly in his arms.

"I'm too heavy!" Sara protested. She could feel her heart beat in a breathless feeling, half reluctant, half eager, that rose in her from William's words and his voice. He held her under the high chandelier in the hall while she turned off the gaslight.

"Sara, I do love you," he said as he carried her easily up the stairs.

"I love you, William," she whispered. She laid her face against his hair. She had never been so sure. Her surety was a triumphant surge within her.

3 JUNE, 1896

SARA stood watching the painters at work on their new house. She came over almost every morning, wheeling little Winthrop in his carriage. Winthrop was six months old. She had been touched that William had insisted on naming him after her father.

All the workmen knew her and spoke to her. There was a new painter Sara hadn't seen before, a red-haired, freckle-faced Irishman, sitting up high on the scaffolding. He looked down at her from his perch.

Sara wheeled the baby around the house to see how it had progressed. As she passed close to the house she heard the new painter up above her say in a good-natured Irish brogue:

"Faith, the brewer's dame is pretty!"

Sara wheeled the carriage carefully past the piles of shingles out by the two spindling new elm trees William had planted, and set the brake. In front of her the new house was turning out just as she wanted. She took joy in every corner and cupboard, but for a minute she stared at it, not seeing clearly. For a minute color flamed in her cheeks. She resented being called the brewer's wife. "Dame," the man had said. Even now, after William had been running the brewery a whole year and a half, she was not used to it. In her secret mind she still separated William from it.

"Missus Henkel, we changed the hall window the way the Doctor wanted. Would you like to go up and see it?" McBain, the contractor came up to ask her. "Sweeney can mind the baby while you're gone. Sweeney's got five of his own, M'am."

Sara went, resentment fading from her mind. It was thrilling to go up the stairs to the second floor of her own house.

"Now this here window'll be leaded," McBain told her. "Your husband sure wants the best of everything, Missus Henkel."

"Yes," Sara said a little proudly.

She paused at the corner to look back at the house. They would be in it by the end of the month. It stood two full stories high with four gables on the third story; built of wood as it should be in a town that began with the lumber, William said. It was as fine as any of the new houses on the bayou, and the garden would run down to the river.

She pushed the baby carriage slowly along Pomona Avenue. The grounds of the brewery took up an entire block. Their new house stood in the next block, but no cross street had ever been cut through from the avenue to the river, so their garden was separated from the brewery grounds only by the big grove of elms that had been John Henkel's pride. By next summer Win would play in that grove, Sara thought.

Across the avenue the houses were small, but each one had its carefully tended flower garden and neat fence. For the most part, they were owned by employees of the brewery.

Mama had pointed these houses out to her when they had first talked of building here. "You don't want to live in that neighborhood, Sara. Even William's sisters have moved to the west side!" But she didn't mind the little houses. Their house stood far back from the street and she loved the river and the elm grove.

She passed the Henkels' old house. Marie and Ottilie had sold it to Gottfried Werner, the brewmaster. It seemed more than a year and a half ago that William had lifted her over the snowdrift the day they came back from their wedding trip. This was the second spring since their marriage, she thought wistfully, and still they were not going to Europe. They would wait now until William was through with the changes in the brewery.

It had been as he had said; if he took over the management of the business he would succeed. Already, the new addition was started and the brewery had been incorporated as John Henkel had wanted. William was working as hard at it as though he had never thought of anything else. That was his way. He wasn't like Paul. Paul was practicing law now and Papa said he seemed more interested in politics. He was running for the legislature in the fall. She and William met Paul occasionally, but she had not seen him alone. She watched the shadow of the leaves on the top of the baby carriage. Then her thoughts came contentedly back to William.

When she reached the river the bridge was up. She looked at it with something of the same astonishment that she had felt as a child to see a bridge that had been flat and solid with the street stand bolt upright in the air. The tugboat passed so slowly it was like a painting; the blue of the tugboat captain's shirt the same shade as the sky; the river a darker shade, still blue; the rust-stained deck a warm copper color. The smell of the watersoaked wood rose to her nostrils, making her think, suddenly, of Atlantic City.

A heavy wagon clattered up beside her with such a rumble and jingle of harness it woke the baby into frantic crying. Sara took him up from the carriage, holding him over her shoulder.

"There, Win, you're all right. It was just a wagon," she told him. Then she saw it was one of the big red drays from the brewery. The lettering stood out proudly on the side: JOHN HENKEL BREWING CO. William would never change it. "Look, Win, see the horses!" she urged, turning him around in her arms. "Those are Papa's horses." She nodded to the young German who sat high up in the driver's seat. He waved his whip at Win: he knew she was William's wife.

The baby stopped crying and smiled, watching the red tassels waving from the bridle and the silver balls on the hames. The horses stamped and pawed impatiently on the planks of the bridge. The sun caught the edges of their shoes. The near horse tossed its head and the muscles of the big neck rippled under the glossy skin.

Looking at the big horses, knowing them for pure-bred animals, she had an odd feeling of security and pride. The draw was down. The brewery wagon rumbled off across the bridge.

A few blocks from Sycamore Street Sara passed the Henkels' new house. She must stop when she was out tomorrow with Win. Grossmütterchen loved the baby so. Grossmütterchen had grown smaller and quieter since her husband's death. She loved to hold Winthrop in her arms and murmur endearments to him in soft guttural German. He was as blond and blue-eyed as Hans had been, she said.

The Henkels' new house was graystone with a wide-pillared stone porch that made the glass-curtained windows look dark. Stone lions lay on either side of the front steps. "The lions of Trafalgar," William called them, chuckling a little at the girls. William loved to tease them, especially when they questioned some of his plans and changes in the brewery. Now that the girls were stockholders and directors they felt it their duty to show an interest in these things.

As Sara turned onto her own street she met Emma Carthugh. Emma had grown very plump since the birth of her second child. She had under the wide-brimmed feathered hat the same earnest, serious face that she had had as a little girl.

"Hello, Em! I haven't seen you in ages."

"I've just been to your house. I don't know what you'll think of me." There was a shade of embarrassment in her manner.

"Why, Em, what is it?"

Emma hesitated. "Well, we women are organizing against the terrible curse of drunkenness."

Sara frowned slightly, looking down the pleasant street. The word curse was a curious word from Em's mouth.

"Everyone's joined. I mean all the old crowd and . . . we're having a tremendous mass meeting the Fourth of July and today I just had a wire saying Miss Willard can be here for it." Emma's eyes shone. "We're all so thrilled."

"I'd like to hear her," Sara said.

"Oh, Sara, if you only would! That's what I came to ask you. It would be such a victory!" Emma's face was glowing. She seized Sara's hands and kissed her suddenly.

Sara recoiled within herself, although she still stood there with Emma's hands on hers. Emma's warm, moist kiss had come between her and the fresh summer morning.

"Why would it be a victory, Emma?"

"Why, don't you see, Sara, with your husband in the business he's in, for you to join the cause of prohibition makes it twice as effective."

Sara was startled. She hadn't thought particularly about "the Cause"—only that Miss Willard was an interesting lecturer she had never heard.

"Oh, no, Emma, I might go to hear her, but I couldn't

join your society. None of my own family ever belonged either. . . ."

"Belle joined last year and she's one of our leading members," Emma interrupted eagerly.

"Belle feels strongly, of course, because of her husband's dissipation."

"Yes, woman has always been so slow to arm herself against the forces that threaten the home," Emma said as though she were repeating a lesson. "Think of little Winthrop. You don't want him growing up in a world with beer and whiskey!" Emma was a different person from the round-faced, shy little girl who had grown up with Sara. Sara hardly knew this Emma.

"With William in the business, as you say, Em, it would be pretty silly of me to join."

"But, Sara, don't you see, you more than anyone else can be an influence for good. No one blames you. We all think it was a perfect shame the way he married you as a doctor and then changed the minute you were married so he could make more money, the Devil's money!"

"Emma Carthugh, don't you ever speak like that about William. He did it for his father. He never wanted to." Sara's anger made her voice shake. She stepped elaborately around Emma and pushed the baby carriage ahead of her down the street.

"Sara . . ." Emma called after her, but Sara never turned.

That was what they were saying about William! Emma was a silly little fool. . . . Sara's eyes were blazing when she came to her own house. She was glad to get inside, to shut the door between herself and the street. Even when she sat in her cool, shaded bedroom she went back and forth over Emma's words. And afterwards, when Pearl came up for the money for the laundress, Sara took it out of her purse and thought as she counted it out that Emma had called it "Devil's money." She put her encounter with Emma Carthugh out of her mind and went over to Mama's in the afternoon.

Belle was out. This was her hospital day. Anne and Mama were there, and Mrs. Higbee was up in the sewing room. Home was always the same.

Mama had been having neuralgia, but except for the light cashmere shawl she wore she gave no sign of it.

Roger ran down the stairs and flung his arms around Sara.

"Aunt Sara, can I go down to the brewery Saturday to see Uncle William? Mother says I'll get in the way, but I won't."

"Of course, Roger, Uncle William would like to have you."

"Oh, Sara," Anne said plaintively, with the whining note that was becoming permanent in her voice, "do you think a brewery is the place for a child? I mean, he might get hurt."

Another day, Sara would not have been annoyed. Today, she fancied a slight toward the brewery. "How silly!" she answered sharply. "He plays around the stables with old Charlie. Charlie is wonderful with children."

"Well . . ." Anne consented vaguely. She turned to a simpler problem. "Oh, Sara, see what you think of this dimity for a spring dress, or do you think blue is too bright for me?"

Anne still kept the semblance of widow's weeds, choosing, if not black, at least pale shades that made her light hair and eyes seem faded. Her air of grief had changed slowly into an injured air that implied, ever so subtly, that Life had treated her badly.

"Of course, it isn't too bright. But those bow-knots make me think of temperance ribbons. I met Emma Carthugh on the way home this morning. She tried to get me to join the W.C.T.U."

Mrs. Bolster smiled and shook her head. "Did you ever! The Carthughs always were great joiners." Her quietly amused tone soothed Sara's spirit.

"It seems they're having a great mass meeting and Miss Willard is going to address them."

"From all I've heard," Mrs. Bolster said, "Miss Willard is an able woman, but it seems a pity that she must traipse around the country leading women to make such sights of themselves with their going into saloons and parading in the streets. They would do better to stay home and bring their children up to be strong in the face of temptation." She emphasized her old-fashioned ideas by tapping her thimbled finger against the arm of her rocker. "I heard your father tell Mr. Healey the other night, after Belle had been talking about the W.C.T.U., that you can't substitute a pledge for character and breeding."

"Belle's going to that meeting," Anne said. "She's heart and soul in the W.C.T.U. movement. It's her latest love. She ought to have these bows on some dress of hers." A light animosity tinged Anne's tone.

"They're all right, Anne. I was just joking," Sara said. "I was put out because Emma talked about William's connection with the brewery as though it were a sin."

"As I've said before, I think it was a great pity that William gave up medicine. That was too much for any father to ask of his son, but I can't see but what it's an honorable business if it's run honorably," Mrs. Bolster said.

If Mrs. Bolster said sadly to Mr. Bolster, in the privacy of their own room, "Winthrop, I can't make it seem right that Sara should be a brewer's wife," she said it nowhere else.

"You couldn't ask for a finer son-in-law," Mr. Bolster remarked.

A week after they moved into their new home, Sara gave her first big dinner party. She had been busy all day with the preparations. Now everything was ready. She came through the dining room into the hall. She could hear William still singing in the bathroom. Why didn't he hurry? She ran upstairs.

"William, they'll be here any minute!" she called to him from the bedroom.

William came in, draped in a towel, still singing. He stopped in the middle of a line.

"Whoa, Sara; your cheeks are too red. You're really worked up over this dinner party!"

"Well, no; but I do want it to go well. Mama always takes such pride in her dinners, and Beth Ingalls entertains beautifully and . . ."

William started dressing without making any answer. He began to whistle. The tune had an airy indifference that irritated her.

"William, you forgot to get any port! I had to telephone and have Mama send some over." Sara's tone of voice was reproachful.

"Oh, to have after dinner?"

"Of course. I told you we had to have it. I was lucky to get terrapin for soup. Mama says the soup sets the tone of the whole meal." Sara's mind was on the dinner. She stood in front of the dressing table, fingering the pattern of the lace cover abstractedly, unaware of William's eyes on her.

"Sara, you're too serious about this meal. After all, we've had other meals and other guests and all went well."

"But this is the first time we've had the Ingalls and Pettigrews and Healeys . . . It is so important, don't you see, William?"

"No, I'm afraid I don't. I like good food and wine and I like having guests in our house, but not if they come to see how we do things, and not at all if it makes you so serious. Sometime, I will invite some people to dinner; your father and mother and Belle, perhaps, and I'll cook the meal. I make wonderful hash, Sara. I'll have hard bread and a pitcher of milk; I might give them some beer if they asked for it." He was arranging his tie. His eyes twinkled, but Sara was in no state to answer his mood.

"After dinner, William, we're playing whist. You'll get the tables and cards and everything, won't you?"

"And after everybody's had enough to eat at my party, we'll leave the table instead of sitting there until ten. We'll make a little music or just talk or someone might read aloud. The men will not linger at the table for the port and stories and come away feeling stuffed in mind and body. The women won't have time to discuss styles and their neighbors' failings."

"There they are. Hurry, William! You should be downstairs with me." Her voice was sharp with exasperation.

But at dinner, looking down the shining table at William, she forgot her irritation. William was talking to Mama on his right. He was saying something that pleased Mama.

The evening went smoothly. The food was delicious. Mr. Ingalls said that the terrapin soup reminded him of soup he'd had at La Pérouse in Paris.

It was a little hard to keep her mind on the whist, after dinner, but perhaps no one noticed that. And standing at the door with William, saying good night, she had a pleasant glow of satisfaction. She stopped to set the flowers in the vestibule for the night. When she came back into the drawing room, William was standing on his head in the middle of the floor.

"William!" Sara laughed.

William came lightly back to his feet.

"I just wanted to see you laugh naturally," William said. "May I congratulate you on the success of your dinner party, Mrs. Henkel?"

"It did go well, didn't it!" Sara said complacently.

William nodded. "There was too much food, beautifully served; too much wine and too much whist. It was like a hundred dinner parties that all of these people have gone to before, and it wasn't very much fun."

"Why, William!"

"Sorry, Liebchen, but I don't like course dinners with a wine for every course and port afterwards. They leave me with a headache and there's no . . . no joy in them. We all go solemnly through our paces; there's no spontaneity. Women worry too much over their dinner parties; you can see it in their faces.

"Come on, Sara, let's walk around the grounds of our estate before we go to bed."

"Oh, William, I would, but this dress is so long and I'd have to change and it's midnight now . . . Really, I'm tired."

"I'll fix the dress." He fastened the end of her skirt in her belt in spite of her protests. "There, it gives you a very fashionable bustle!

"Look what we've been missing all evening," he said as they came out on the porch. The whole fragrant June night was around them. The air was cool on Sara's neck and face and arms. She drew a long breath. The heavy smell of the new-laid sod was freshened by the air from the river. The grove of trees at the edge of the lawn was a thick wilderness, barely touched by the starlight. From the porch they could just catch sight of the dark shine of the river braided into the black trunks of the trees.

"Come on, Sara!" William was skipping down the lawn like a child. With her arm tightly in his she had to skip with him.

"Where's the girl who used to walk on the log booms and climb trees? Don't grow too matronly."

"I haven't a chance with you," Sara answered, laughing.

They stood together on the bank of the river.

"Hear it?" William asked delightedly. In the stillness the water lapped and chuckled against the bank. "Right in our own grounds, Sara!" William gloated.

"Cold?"

"No."

"Tired now?"

"Not any more. How could I be?"

"Look up at the stars, Sara; I'll give you any one you want."

"That one, over the top of the willow tree," Sara said. Suddenly, she pulled her arm out of his. "This sedate matron can beat you back to the porch!" She ran swiftly back up the lawn, her light gown gleaming white in the dark. They reached the porch together, laughing and out of breath.

He caught her close to him. "Oh, Sara, this is our life," he whispered.

"I know it, William," Sara whispered back happily.

4 JULY 4, 1896

"SARA, the float's ready. Come and see it!" William stood at the foot of the stairs calling up to her.

"I'm coming." Sara pinned on her new sailor hat as she came, and fastened her gloves. "Pearl, be sure and keep Win in the back garden; the streets will be full of people!" she called from the hall.

"You should see old Charlie, Sara; he's wonderful! He's the living image of Gambrinus. He's just a little sheepish about his bare legs, though."

"I wonder if Paul will see the float. He'll know we've taken Charlie's costume from his stein."

"I doubt whether he'll remember what was on the stein, but it makes a perfect idea for a float."

As they came around the stables of the brewery they saw the big float that was to represent Henkel's Brewing Company in the Fourth of July parade. Every industry in town was entering a float.

"William, it is wonderful!"

"Sh-h, Sara, you'll embarrass Charlie," William cautioned, but Charlie beamed and nodded at her.

The largest dray was lined with barley. At one end was Gottfried's daughter, dressed in Grecian costume, holding a cornucopia of grain. At the front stood the wife of one of the brewery workers, a tall, fair-haired German girl, wearing around her head the wreath of hop leaves that Sara had painstakingly fashioned of crepe paper. But the crowning figure was old Charlie Freehahn, dressed like a Saxon chieftain with a flaxen wig and beard, and a horned helmet on his head. In his hand he held the stein Paul had brought back to William.

"Such foolishness!" Charlie called out, but his merry eye belied his words.

Eight horses were harnessed to the dray, each with his garland of flowers around his neck, every piece of metal on the harness shining, tassels dangling from each side of the bridles. Even their flowing tails were braided with red ribbons.

"I never thought it would be so effective," Sara exclaimed. "Lining the wagon with barley was so much better than covering it with bunting."

"I think it's all right, myself!" William said proudly. "I'm glad we still had this Bohemian-style wagon; it's higher than the new wagons."

The yard of the brewery looked more than ever like the courtyard of some old Rhenish castle. Only enough men were working to turn the barley and watch the sprouting grain in the malthouse. The others all had a holiday. But many of them had walked over to see the float. They filled their mugs with beer at the Sternewirth just through the brick archway and stood there washing down their breakfast with the ice-cold beer, admiring the float.

"Now hold your stein up again, Charlie," William directed. Charlie had no need to be told how to lift it with a flourish. Then he scowled.

"Wilhelm, für ein brewery to haf an empty stein ist nicht gut!"

"Ja, Charlie's right," the silent little weighmaster leaning against the scales agreed.

William laughed. "Otto, go get some bottles and we'll put your little boy down in the bottom of the float where he can open the bottles and fill the stein whenever the foam dies down."

"Ja!" Charlie shouted with pleasure.

"But what can you do about the beer in the stein, William?" Sara asked.

"He can throw it out at some inconspicuous place."

"Throw it out like bad beer! Nein, Ich will drink!" Charlie declared. "And wipe my mustache this way!" He wiped his great flaxen mustache with a powerful sweep of his left arm.

"All right, we'll see you as you go by," William said.

Most of the men hanging around the courtyard followed the float out to the street. They were all in their Sunday clothes. One man had his little girl on his shoulder. Another had his wife with him.

"They seem to like the brewery as much as though it belonged to them," Sara said.

William nodded. "That's the best part of running the business. The men have a real loyalty to the place; of course, some of their fathers worked for my father.

"Wait for me here, Sara. I must stop and see Gottfried a minute and then we'll go."

But he was gone so long that Sara went in to find him. She hadn't been in the brewery many times since the first visit when John Henkel took her through.

She liked the clean look of the newly whitewashed brick walls, the wide low archways, the orderly aspect of the rooms. The whole place had a faintly foreign air. The notices on the walls were printed in both English and German, and there were foreign names on the machinery. She went up the stairs to the room where she had come upon the brewmaster catching the moth for John Henkel. In spite of people like Emma Carthugh and Paul's amused attitude and the raised eyebrows of her old friends, she was coming to have a feeling for the place. It was a growing concern. It was doing well; she liked the air of efficiency about it. William had glassed off an office for Gottfried and put in a larger desk and chair. She saw William through the side window.

In the chair in front of him sat one of the workmen, his undershirt opened to the waist. William was listening to his chest with his stethoscope. Sara waited outside the office. A few minutes before William had seemed so wrapped up in getting the float off for the parade, now he had dropped off every thought of the brewery. She wondered if he often took care of the men.

"Heinrich, I want you to go down tomorrow and see your doctor. You can take the time off. You've got a trouble there that must be attended to." William was speaking sternly, trying to impress the man.

"Bitte, you take care of me, Doctor Henkel," the man begged. "My wife say . . ."

"No, Heinrich. I'm not a doctor now. I'm running the brewery. I'll write a note to Dr. Welch for you."

Sara went back down to wait for William in his office. She went down the steep stairs slowly, hardly noticing the great ruddy beauty of the brew kettle, past the charts lettered in red ink in neat figures. They made her think of medical charts, today. The way William had said, "I'm not a doctor now," hurt her. He was busy with the brewery; he liked to see it grow, but in his heart he was no more reconciled than ever.

John Henkel's office was changed, too. William had lined

one side with bookcases. There were books on the manufacture of beer, all in German. The hard-looking, incomprehensible words had a hostile look. Underneath, neatly stacked, were pamphlets: the *Western Journal*, the *Brewers' Journal.* Next to them was a stack of *Journals of the American Medical Association.* Paper markers protruded from the edges of the last number.

Sara looked at the walls. There was a picture of John Henkel talking to Gottfried Werner in the courtyard with the big iron-studded door of the brewery behind them. There was a picture of one of the great breweries on the Rhine. William had sent it home to his father from Germany. The next was a picture of . . . she bent closer to read the name: Louis Pasteur. She remembered when William bought it. He had said, "Pasteur was able to do so much for medicine and his work started in the breweries. Who knows, Sara," he laughed, "perhaps I can learn something from beer, too!"

She sat in the chair on the other side of William's desk. She could look out the window at the field by the river where William had told her about his father. That was the day she had begun to love him.

"Here you are! I'm sorry to be late. I was held up by Heinrich Schwartz. I had to explain something to him. He's a stubborn old Dutchman; you have to pound a thing into him to make him understand."

Sara waited, but he didn't say what he had to explain.

"We'll have to hurry. I'm afraid the girls will be fretting now."

Oh, yes, the girls; they were going to take them in their carriage to see the parade. "I like the office this way, William."

"So do I. I wish we could take time to see the new tanks,

Sara. We're the only brewery this size in the country to have them. I'll show them to you next time."

"Those were the things the girls objected so to your buying?" Sara asked.

William chuckled. "Yes. They can't see beyond their noses when it comes to spending money. They feel it's a sin to borrow money for these improvements. You should have been at our last directors' meeting," he told her. "I had all I could do to get them to vote for the loan at the bank. You see, with the new malthouse we're going to need more money."

"But, William!"

"Don't worry, Sara, our market's increasing all the time. With any luck we'll be able to pay it all off within five years."

"But you were going to leave the brewery next year."

William nodded. "I haven't forgotten that, but the brewery will be in a position to carry itself. Oh, I'll still keep my eye on it; you know I'll be on the board of directors. But the girls mean well," he ended affectionately. "They take great pride in being stockholders and directors."

The stableman had the carriage waiting. They drove out the curved driveway to the main avenue. The trees made a green tunnel far down the street. It was a beautiful July morning, perfect for the parade.

Marie looked annoyed when she came out. What a fussy hat she had bought. Ottilie was more attractive, but her face was stolid until she was interested. Mrs. Henkel waved to them from the front window. She looked smaller than ever in the high-necked black dress, standing there back of the row of potted plants.

"Won't your mother change her mind, William? Do ask her again. I'm sure it wouldn't hurt her," Sara urged.

"I'll ask her," William said, turning back to the house.

"No, William!" Marie spoke sharply. "Don't. Crowds

always make her nervous and she couldn't possibly go up that double flight of stairs to the paper office."

"Perhaps you're right." William stepped into the carriage. "Well, girls, see if you're not proud of Henkel's float!" His enthusiasm carried off the air of tension the girls had brought with them.

"Oh, I hope we win the prize!" Ottilie said. Sara looked back at her. When her face was alight it was more like William's. Since her father's death Marie had grown older, more spinsterish. She was the head of the family since William had married. Sometimes Sara felt she managed little Mrs. Henkel too firmly. But she put her irritation out of her mind.

The streets were crowded as they neared Grand Avenue.

"This is the biggest Fourth of July celebration in years," Sara said.

"I was surprised at the amount of the prizes the Chamber of Commerce is offering!" William said. "They've watched the decline of the lumber industries long enough. Now, they're making up for lost time and doing all they can to make the city attractive for new industries."

"I think it's a great mistake to bring in another bicycle plant and another boiler plant," Marie observed tartly. She always expressed her opinions with great firmness. Since they had moved to the west side, they were of the town's upper strata.

"But that means more consumers for Henkel's beer, Marie, don't forget! Most of the workers in the boiler factory are foreigners."

William had to walk the horse now, the street was so crowded. They were nearing the judges' stand. They would leave the horse around the corner and walk up to the Flat Iron Building.

When they went past the Ingalls Sara was aware of Mrs.

Ingalls' quick glance at Marie and Ottilie. She laid her hand on Marie's arm almost protectively as they turned into the dark stairway of the Flat Iron Building.

"Don't trip; I remember some of the treads were always loose. I think Barney used to slam down the stairs so fast he kicked them up."

"I can't see how you ever stood it to work down here in a public office," Marie said.

"That was what interested me first about her," William laughed. "You should have seen her at work, very serious, very pink-cheeked."

But even to her the office had an air of unfamiliarity now as she introduced Mr. and Mrs. Griffith and Barney and little Rollo to the girls. It was pleasant to feel little Rollo's quick glance of admiration again and Barney's warm handshake. While the band was marching down the street, her eyes stole over to her old desk. She remembered the day she had kept Paul's letter underneath her handkerchiefs.

Little Rollo caught her glance. "Homesick, I know. Once a newspaper woman always a newspaper woman!"

Sara shook her head. "Well, perhaps a little." But she wasn't. She had never thought of working always. She was very busy at home. And next year, perhaps—she didn't want her children too far apart. She broke off in her thoughts to speak to Mr. Griffith. Across the street in the window of the Bank Building she could see the Ingalls and the Healeys. Her family and the Sevrances were watching from Paul's office.

The windows were opened wide. The buildings were hung with red, white, and blue bunting. The band played patriotic music.

"Here they come!" Mr. Griffith clapped loudly as the slightly tipped Statue of Liberty was drawn along on a float representing the Chamber of Commerce. A big sign at the back read, "Equal Opportunity for All." The men's hands made a bare sharp sound; the women's hands were muted by their gloves and sounded more like book covers flopped closed again and again. Little Rollo made some humorous comment to William. They were laughing together.

The largest department store had a float depicting an early trading post, complete with log cabin, Indians, and furs. The Sevrance Lumber Company showed a young man poised a little unsteadily on logs that he was supposed to be running, while at the rear of the wagon two more lumberjacks worked at a crosscut saw. A great crossed ax and peavey made an arch above the wagon.

"He ought to have a scene in the Land Office with old Hiram explaining how he figures a hundred and sixty acres," Barney muttered, and the others laughed good-naturedly.

Float after float passed, the popularity of each being attested by the volume of the clapping. The heads on the judges' stand leaned this way and that in consultation. Pencils wrote on pads. Only Mayor McCarthy and the clergyman who was to offer a prayer at the exercises and the speaker of the day, Senator Radcliffe, and a slight woman with glasses in the front row on the stand sat still watching.

"Who is that woman on the grandstand, Sara?" Mrs. Griffith asked, looking at her through her lorgnette.

"I don't know her," Sara said, but little Rollo chuckled. "That's the visiting celebrity of the day. She's more famous than the Senator. If you were still with us, Miss Bolster, I mean Mrs. Henkel, you'd be interviewing her and reporting her speech tonight. That's Miss Willard. The Mayor asked her to sit with him."

"That's a good one for the Mayor," Mr. Griffith muttered. "He must have stuttered a little as he asked her."

"Oh, Emma Carthugh asked me to go to the meeting," Sara said.

"She's got all the silver-tongued orators like Bryan beat a mile, I can tell you," little Rollo exclaimed. He was taking notes on the parade as he talked.

"Our float must be way at the end!" Marie complained to William.

He nodded. "Just wherever it happened to land, I imagine. Look, that's a clever one, advertising the Glass Works." A float came by representing glassblowers at work. Beautiful transparent glass shapes caught the sun and the colors of the bunting. Enthusiastic clapping attended the passage of the float.

"There's ours, William!" Sara whispered excitedly when she caught sight of the float just turning the corner.

"That's a pippin!" Mr. Griffith announced. "Henkel, that's all right. Was it your idea or your wife's?"

"It was Paul Sevrance's," Sara said. "He gave us a stein with these figures on it."

"Will, it's lovely!" Ottilie said. "The grain around the wagon makes it so pretty."

"Whew, those are some horses. Where did you get the old German?" Barney asked.

"He's our stable boss and more important to the brewery than I am by a long shot," William said. He chuckled at the gusto old Charlie was putting into his quaffing. The stein foamed in appropriate fashion and even dripped a little to one side. Loud applause greeted the float's appearance as it neared the grandstand.

"That helmet was hard to make," Sara was explaining to the others. "We copied one out of an old book of German fables. It's just cardboard covered with tinfoil, but it glitters nicely in the sun, doesn't it?"

Suddenly the slight figure on the platform rose at the sight of the float and covered her eyes dramatically. From somewhere a group of women clad in white rushed across the street holding hands, singing wildly in high voices that flatted a little as they sang. The words were drowned by the band far down the block. They stopped just in front of the tossing heads of the lead team. The driver had to stand in his seat to hold the horses in. Someone shrieked. One woman stumbled and fell down only a yard from the horses' hoofs. William was on his feet.

"Those fool women!" Mr. Griffith growled.

The driver pulled so hard on the reins the horses' teeth showed. People crowded back against the buildings and into stores and doorways to be out of danger. Charlie dropped his stein and, pushing past his daughter, climbed to the high driver's seat. He set the brakes and snatched the reins from the terrified driver's hands.

"Old Charlie'll hold 'em," William muttered. He hurried out of the office.

With almost superhuman strength Charlie held the lead horses steady. They set their heels, holding back the younger horses.

"Nice work," Mr. Griffith murmured.

Still the women continued to dance and sing in front of the frenzied horses. A policeman appeared and tried to drag them out of danger, but the women beat at the officers. One woman scratched at the face of a big Irishman. There was no place to turn. People crowded on every side in a frantic struggle to get out of the way. From the window they could see the muscles standing out in Charlie's arms. He bowed the necks of the two front horses in his efforts to hold them still. He was calling them by name in his heavy German voice. But above his voice rang out a half-hysterical battle-cry from the grandstand.

"Courage, Sisters!"

A shudder ran down Sara's spine. A sick revulsion turned her stomach. Marie was crying nervously beside her and the sight angered her.

There was William on the sidewalk now. He was talking to the policeman. The officer yelled at the women:

"If you'll get out of the way for a minute and let the brewery float proceed to the corner it will drop out of the parade. They cannot be responsible for the horses unless you give way!"

"Let them kill us, let them run over us!" one of the women yelled back, her face set. "One death will do more for the cause . . ." Her voice was drowned out.

Charlie Freehahn, red in the face, a figure of wrath in his big horned helmet and flowing flaxen locks and mustache, had taken the long whip from the socket.

"He mustn't, Barney!" Sara caught her breath, clutching at Barney's arm.

William sprang up on the high wagon he had learned to climb as a child. He grabbed the whip out of Charlie's hand, saying something to him. Sara's tension eased when she saw him there. He was so calm compared with the hysterical women below and Charlie on the wagon. He motioned to the policeman, who started crowding the people back from the curb. Charlie began maneuvering the four teams that he had harnessed with such pride for the impressive spectacle they would make. He drove them up on the sidewalk, past the band of women. The wheels bumped over the curb.

There was a curious silence in the street. The women, exhausted with their efforts, had given up singing. "Hallelujah! Down with the breweries!" one thin voice shrilled out, but an uncomfortable, murmuring stillness held the crowd. The disorganized float turned the next corner out of sight.

Behind the big windows of the *Courier's* office fell an awkward constraint. Marie was still sniffing into her handkerchief. Ottilie's face was set sullenly. Sara was pale. Mr. Griffith was nearly apoplectic.

"Did you ever see a parcel of women set out more pigheadedly to get themselves and everybody else killed? I'll write an editorial on the need for common sense in crusades."

"Oscar, you mustn't. You can't have all those women down on you. You've no idea how powerful they are!" Mrs. Griffith cautioned.

Mr. Griffith snorted. "I write the editorials in my paper without . . ."

"My dear, Dr. Henkel was so brave and cool," Mrs. Griffith murmured soothingly to Sara.

"I feel disgraced and insulted before the whole town," Marie said.

"Why should you?" Ottilie answered, staring out the window. Barney was already at his typewriter writing the story for the evening edition.

Sara smiled at Mrs. Griffith. "Yes, William was brave." She wanted to get away, to get home. She was all mixed up. She didn't feel as Marie did. The women were absurd out there: hysterical fools as Mr. Griffith had said. She had looked down at Emma Carthugh and Alice Wakeley. She was thankful Belle hadn't gone out in the street. Above all she wanted to find William.

The rest of the parade dragged past. The band struck up again, but people were busy talking. They scarcely bothered to watch.

When they came out of the office building with the Griffiths several people picked out Sara as the wife of William Henkel, nudging the next person. Sara felt queerly conspicuous. All her life she had belonged to one of the leading families of Armitage, representative of all that was best in culture and tradition in the city. It was a new experience to be connected now with a business that a whole group of people felt was detrimental. She had never encountered hostility until today. She held her head under the sailor hat a little higher as she crossed the street to Mr. Griffith's carriage.

5 1900

SARA started over to the brewery with Winthrop. In four years she had grown used to living near the brewery. Even the smell of the hops and malt had come to have a not unpleasant pungency that seemed to mix naturally in the air. Mama and the girls always spoke of it, but she, herself, hardly noticed it. Few gardens in Armitage had such a view of the river, and she had come to be as fond of the grove of elm trees as old John Henkel had been.

Sara wasn't going out very much this spring, but she often took the path through the park to meet William. If she was plainly pregnant even in her cape, she didn't feel uncomfortable stopping to talk to Charlie or Gottfried Werner.

"Go see Papa?" Win asked in a small piping voice. He always asked that when they started for the brewery. He ran along the hedge-bordered path a little way and then came back to take her hand.

"Yes, we'll see Papa, Win. Look, there's Charlie. You go and see Charlie!"

The little boy ran down the path on his sturdy legs, calling, "Charlie, Charlie!" Charlie swung him up on his shoulder. "We see the horses, kleine Mann, eh?" Sara heard Charlie say.

Sara walked around back of the brewery. William would

be down in a few minutes. She had telephoned him to say she would walk over and meet him. She went past the new part that was brick instead of stone. There was the corner-stone with the date: "1900"; the other part had been built in 1867. William took pride in this new section. William had done so much to the outside of the brewery, too. He had planted new trees and started ivy against the new brick walls.

Now William was looking for a competent manager. Next spring they would go to Europe for a whole year and then he would take up his medicine again. She had felt a twinge of envy when Marie and Ottilie left in March for six months abroad, but she was having the baby in May and William couldn't leave just yet.

It was pleasant this afternoon. She walked toward the river a little way and then back up. She heard the five-o'clock whistle blow at the brewery, and the whistle on the Ledyard mill. She saw a big dray turn in from the avenue. The wheels rumbled over the cobbled yard. She didn't know the driver; he must be a new man. The horses were coming fast, anxious to get to the stable. William came out on the platform talking with Gottfried. He saw her and waved.

"I'll be right there, Sara!" He was always so glad to see her. His whole face lighted up. "See our new dray!" he called out, pointing proudly to the big shiny red wagon. JOHN HENKEL BREWING CO. was freshly painted in gold on the red side.

The dray pulled up with a flourish by the loading plat-form. The driver tied his reins around the whipstock and jumped down on the wagon to unload. The men on the platform taking the barrels called out something in German. The driver laughed and answered, making as if to throw the keg.

"Lassen sie kommen!" called back the man on the platform and caught the empty keg against his aproned front as though it were nothing. He made as if to hurl it back. The keg was wet and slipped out of his grasp, landing on the near horse's back.

Sara saw the horse rear, starting the double team. The horses started to run. The reins were dragging.

"Gott im Himmel!" She heard Charlie's angry shout. The horses galloped around the yard toward the stable. They weren't stopping. They ran past Charlie, circling back toward the loading platform. They looked the way they had the day of the parade: their ears laid back, their eyes rolling.

Win had seen William standing on the platform and was running across the yard toward his father.

"Das Kind!" She heard Charlie's cry of fear. She saw William jump down from the platform. Win heard Charlie. He stood still in the middle of the yard. She couldn't see William as the dray came past. She heard Charlie shout again. The wagon scraped against the platform. The horses were slowing up. Someone had the reins.

Where was William? The dray had gone so close to the platform she couldn't see him. It had banged against the platform—Sara caught her breath with a sob. She was running now.

They were lifting William onto the platform. Charlie had sent for a doctor. William's hands were cold as ice. She slipped off her cape and laid it over him. He opened his eyes and looked at her.

"Sara," William whispered. "I got caught . . . I . . ." It hurt him to talk. "I've cautioned the men . . ."

"Darling, Geliebte," Sara murmured his word for her. He was terribly hurt. He was dying. She knew from the hopeless certainty in her heart. William was so white; all in a minute.

He smiled faintly at her using his word.

"Geliebte Sara," he whispered. "I love you. . . ."

He died before the doctor came, lying on the wooden platform, covered by Sara's cape.

Sara followed Charlie and Gottfried as they carried William's body back into the house and up to her bedroom. She had walked from the brewery with Win, hardly knowing that she was walking, feeling only Win's warm plump little hand after William's. Just yet she didn't want to call Mama or Papa or any of them. She must call Mrs. Henkel. She must . . . she knelt beside the bed, hardly noticing that Gottfried and Charlie stood silently over by the door.

"William, oh, Wilhelm!" She called his name in German, not knowing she did it.

6

"BUT, Sara, how perfectly foolish to go off up to the lake alone with a new baby! In May, too, Sara, why, it isn't warm at the lake until the middle of June anyway!" Anne said.

Anne and Belle sat in Sara's bedroom. Sara lay in the big bed with the new baby in the crook of her arm. Little William Henkel had been born a month early, two days after his father's funeral.

"Come home for a little while, Sara," Belle urged. "There's plenty of room and you mustn't be alone."

"I remember how I felt," Anne said. "I couldn't stand it even to sleep alone. Belle slept with me for a long time." Her eyes misted over at the recollection of Roger's death; she fumbled in her bag for her handkerchief.

"Dor says Win is just as happy as can be with Dorothy," Belle added.

But when Sara didn't answer, the uncomfortable silence the girls had been fighting off swallowed up their words. The curtains moved in front of the open window. Sounds came in from the street: a dull rumbling sound and the clatter of horses' hoofs.

"There goes the brewery wagon," Sara said dully. She was still weak.

Belle rose impatiently and closed the window toward the brewery and pulled the shades.

"You've had enough of that brewery for life, Sara, and the sooner you sell this house the better! Thank goodness William's sisters were off in Europe. They'd only have made it harder."

But Sara did not hear. Underneath the sound of Belle's voice she was listening for the sound of the brewery horses, growing fainter now as they went along Pomona Avenue. She woke up in the night and heard the horses, the clink of the harness, Charlie Freehahn's cry, the sudden deathly hush. Or she remembered the day of the Fourth of July parade. She saw again the horses rearing in front of those women. She would never let Win go down to the stable again. She remembered that she had used to look at them with a feeling almost of pride, thinking they meant a kind of security, and instead they had ended by crushing William to death.

"Are they coming back, Sara? Have you heard?" Belle's question broke in on her thoughts.

"Oh, you mean the girls! I haven't heard yet. I urged them not to, but I'm sure they will because of Mother Henkel. Gottfried Werner brought her over yesterday to see the baby. She just cried and cried.

"I don't think you should see her, Sara, until you're stronger. You have yourself to think of. You won't be able to nurse the baby if you're worried all the time."

"Oh, yes," Sara said. "I'll nurse the baby. Dr. Barnes says it's important when he's so tiny."

The nurse came in and took the baby. Sara moved out of her tense position, but she missed the small blanket-wrapped body on her arm.

"Well, I'll go on back home," Anne said with a sigh. "Mother will be down this evening. She was so upset over your saying you thought you'd go to the lake as soon as you could take the baby. Sara, you look like a child yourself." Anne stooped to kiss her. Her eyes filled again as she went downstairs with Belle.

"I'm glad you said that, Belle. It would be criminal for her to go off up there alone. Of course, one of us could go," Anne added.

"She said she wanted to go alone, but I think it's just an idea," Belle said. The girls talked in hushed voices in the front hallway. The solicitous murmur came faintly up to Sara. She lay looking around the room with wide-open eyes. If she closed her eyes, too many things crowded her mind. She saw again the double line of men from the brewery standing with bowed heads along the front walk from their house. Each one had placed a flower on the coffin as it was carried by. The sight of them there had touched her more than anything else in that hard day.

Perhaps Anne was right about her leaving this house. She wouldn't be able to go down in the library for a long time without seeing William's mother sitting there, a crumpled black figure; hearing her cry, "Mein Sohn, mein Sohn!"

Sara shuddered and tears ran out from under her tightly closed eyelids.

Even this room! William had loved to go to sleep with the firelight on the ceiling. "We always had stoves that smelled of hot iron when I was a child," he had said.

And then she was back again, wondering how it could have happened. How could William be dead? It could have been somebody else just as well. If they had gone to Europe this summer! If only William had never gone into the brewery! It had meant nothing but misery to them from the time

William's father had asked him to take charge; he had never been happy running it.

Belle was coming back up. Sara turned her face away from the light so Belle wouldn't see she had been crying.

"Dear, some clothes came from Mrs. Wadsleigh's; a hat and dress and coat. You can order others when you're ready."

Sara stared at the black dress Belle held up in her arms, the black coat. The small black hat had a little band of embroidered organdie and a long black veil. They were strange; it was hard to realize they were meant for her.

"It's a cunning hat," Sara said, inappropriately. "Let me try it on." She sat up in bed. Belle brought her a brush and comb and pins.

"Won't it tire you?" she remonstrated.

"No, I'm getting up tomorrow." Sara brushed her hair and braided it the way William had liked it best. It was strange that the hair felt the same under her fingers, that it coiled so familiarly into place. She put on the hat. The black veil fell down over her shoulders, covering her gown. She could see herself in the long mirror across the room. She smiled at her own reflection. The dead black gave her brown hair a bronze light. The sheer white fold of organdie suited her pointed face.

"It's the most becoming hat I've ever had, really, isn't it, Belle?"

And Belle, stooping suddenly to pick up an imaginary thread, muttered that it was. As she said to Mama and the girls, "Wasn't that a queer thing for her to say?"

"Do you think the veil will scare Win?" Sara asked.

"Oh, I don't believe so," Belle assured her dubiously.

Sara gathered the veil up in one hand and held it on top of the small black hat.

"I'm afraid it will, Belle; rip it off and I'll just wear the hat."

With May the lilacs sprang into bloom by the porch and all the bulbs along the front walk blossomed. The hedge-bordered path across to the brewery was green and the mountain ash William had set out for her himself uncurled its pointed leaves. The days were of a sudden too warm, too fragrant.

The girls were back from Europe, in deep mourning. Sara and the girls and Grossmütterchen sat around the big table in the library while Mr. Blanchard, the attorney, explained the financial situation. Sara would never have to worry. Neither would the girls or Grossmütterchen as long as the brewery continued to do business. William had made Sara executrix of his estate. Besides the insurance, the brewery was doing very well. Of course, there was considerable indebtedness just now, due to the construction of the new malt plant and the new equipment, but nothing to worry about.

Sara's attention wandered. She had no interest in these matters. She glanced at the girls. Marie had always disapproved of the expense William had gone to. Her disapproval sat now upon her thin, pale face. Sara looked over at Grossmütterchen and met her small faded brown eyes. She herself cared no more for these matters than Sara. She cared only that William was gone.

"The brewery management, of course, will lie in the hands of the deceased's wife and sisters and Gottfried Werner and Adolf Steiner . . ." Mr. Blanchard was saying in a voice of determined cheerfulness.

Paul called. He stood a little awkwardly there in her parlor. His usual lazy grace of manner was gone.

"Sara, I never meant to like William; I couldn't believe it when you broke your engagement with me to marry him. But he was a fine fellow," Paul said with grave formality.

Sara's blue eyes softened from the pale coldness with which she looked at the world these days. She smiled faintly, looking across at William's chair with his meerschaum pipe still in the bowl on the table by it.

"If there is anything I can do . . ."

"Thank you, Paul. I'm afraid there isn't anything anyone can do. I'm going up to Lake Superior the end of the week. I've taken a cottage there for a month anyway."

Paul frowned. "Is Belle going with you?"

"No," Sara said. "Belle wants to go, or Mama, but I feel as though . . . as though I had to go away alone for a little. And I'll have the children."

Paul stood silently a minute, studying her face. "Going to put your head on the railroad track again, Sara?"

Sara shook her head, but she was smiling.

7

AFTER the anxious protests of Mama and Papa and the girls, Sara felt only relief as she sat in the dusty old coach. Even Grossmütterchen had shaken her head sadly and remonstrated about taking a six-weeks-old baby off up to such an out-of-the-way place. But the baby was healthy. There was a doctor in Braxton if she needed one.

She didn't know herself just why she must go away alone like this. She wanted to get away from the house for a little. The house reminded her at every turn of William. She wanted to get away from the kindly, well-meaning friends who came to see her. Mama wanted her to come home, but she wanted to get away alone, where she would have to keep busy.

"I can't see, Sara," Marie had said, "why you go off now when there are so many matters to be attended to." Marie had gone right to the brewery office and was going over all the business with Gottfried Werner and Mr. Blanchard.

"You and Mr. Blanchard can attend to everything," Sara insisted.

Sara was very gentle with Mama, but just as firm. "After all, a woman ought to be able to take care of herself and two children; I'll have nothing else to do." Papa had finally stopped them. He had seemed to understand.

Sara sat on the red plush seat with little William in the basket on the opposite seat. Win sat next to the window, his head in Sara's lap. There were only two other passengers on the train.

"Too early yet for summer folks," the conductor told her.

Win and the baby slept and Sara watched the cut-over land pass drearily by the window. Even the country looked lonely.

Win's head bobbed up from her lap. "Will we play in the sand, Mama?"

"Yes, Win. Of course, we will. I have a shovel and a tin pail in the trunk."

Win's head sank back against her, only to bob up again quickly. "Will we have fun?" His eyes were large with a more than three-year-old seriousness.

Sara squeezed him. "We'll have wonderful fun, Win. You wait and see."

Their cottage was the last little house on the single street that followed the curve of the lake shore. Mr. Gates led the way, carrying the baby.

"Kinda cold yet, but it'll be nice soon," he said encouragingly.

"I don't mind," Sara said.

"Things are out a lot farther down your way, ain't they?"

"Yes, it's almost summer down there," Sara said, thinking of the lilacs in bloom and the daffodils and tulips almost past and the leaves out full. It was a relief to see the bare trees with tight-curled buds and feel the chill from the lake that made even the little cottage look inviting.

"Well, you can enjoy the spring and summer all over again up here," Mr. Gates told her.

"Yes," Sara agreed, wondering how she could stand another bursting spring without William.

"I made a fire this morning. I don't know whether you can manage alone or not. I supposed your husband . . . beg your pardon, Ma'm, or someone would come with you."

"Thank you, I can manage. You aren't far away."

"That's right, and if you want anything you just step outside and call. Unless the lake's in a lather we can 'most always hear you. I got in the provisions like you said in the letter, an' my wife sent over a cake." He put some fresh wood in the airtight stove.

When he had gone, Sara looked around the main room of the cottage. Two rooms opened from it: a kitchen and a bedroom. It was very plain and bare but clean. The trunk she had bought new for her wedding trip stood in one corner, the newest object in the three rooms. Outside the window the lake was a cold gray sheet. It was growing dark fast.

Suddenly, she wanted to run down the path after Mr. Gates; to take the train back home, to do anything but stay here. She couldn't stand it here.

"Mom!" She knelt on the floor beside Win to take off his coat and hat, kissing his serious little face that reminded her so of William.

"We'll have a picnic supper, Win," she told him gaily. She pulled out the table in front of the stove and poured two glasses of milk and cut the cake. It was time to feed the baby, too. She brought the baby from the other room and nursed him by the stove while Win ate his supper. The baby let go of her breast in sleepy satiety. She laid him in his basket on a chair by the stove. Then she drank a glass of milk, herself, and ate a piece of cake; it was the first food that had had any taste at all. Win smiled across the table at her. Cake crumbs clung to his mouth; there was frosting on his fingers.

"Picnic!" he said with a full mouth.

Sara smiled at him. She poured him another glass of milk and had a second one herself.

"Now, Win, we'll open that bed and warm the sheets and blankets . . ." It didn't matter what she said, only that she kept talking. She spread out his nightgown on a chair by the stove, and her own. She put fresh wood in both stoves and fixed the dampers. After she had undressed Win and tucked him in bed she moved the baby's basket in beside the bed.

"Don't go to sleep, Win, till Mama comes. Mama's coming just as quick as she gets undressed."

"No, Mommy," Win said sleepily from the bed.

Sara undressed quickly and blew out the light. For just a moment she pulled up the shade and looked out into the dark. It must be cloudy. There were no stars. She opened the window only a crack and got in bed beside Win. He was already asleep.

"Win, Win!" She tried to wake him to hear him say something more, but he was too soundly asleep. She put her arm around him and lay with her body curled around his. The lake made a constant whispering shush. Beyond that the stillness crowded against the windowpanes. She lay tense, holding her breath to hear more. How mad she had been to come up here alone! She knew nothing about keeping fires. What if the baby were sick! She leaned out of bed and listened to his regular breathing.

"William, oh, William!" She buried her face in the pillow. She could cry here; there was no one to hear her and tell her she mustn't.

Sara lay in bed looking around the room with a kind of amazement. She must have slept. She could see out into the kitchen. The stove looked cold. She pushed back the covers;

the room was cold. The baby was fussing in his basket, sucking at his finger. She reached over and lifted him in bed with her. Win was still asleep. After she had fed the baby she tickled Win's feet to hear him laugh.

"Come on, Win, it's time to get up!" Her own words sounded forced in the still house.

"Can we have another picnic?" Win asked, clambering out of bed.

"No, Win, we must eat regular meals today, but it will all be like a picnic!"

She laid her hand on the stove; it was as cold as stone. She must have done something wrong with the damper; the stove was full of wood that was only charred on the underside. She opened the door of the kitchen and the bright sunlight rushing in across the sill onto the bare boards of the kitchen floor warmed the house. It took away all the fear and loneliness of the night before, touching every object with naturalness.

Win ran out the door across the stoop toward the lake, pointing and shouting at the water that was bright blue in the sun. Sara dropped the charred wood she was taking out of the firebox and ran after him. Morning coolness, edged with warmth, came against her face and arms and ankles. She caught up with Win and the two of them ran along the shore in sight of the open kitchen door. Sara lifted her face to the sky as she ran.

"There's so much to do, Win; you and Mama are going to have to work hard this morning. First, we're going to . . . " And then she forgot to finish her sentence, thinking that if she hadn't telephoned William he might not have come down to the loading platform just then.

"What, Mama? What are we going to do?"

Resolutely, she went on. "Well, first, we're going to bathe

our baby just the way people used to before they had shiny white bathrooms."

The three rooms took on a feeling of home by the time she had washed the dishes and made the bed and scrubbed two potatoes for baking. She gave Win a big kitchen spoon to dig with in the sand by the door.

Mr. Gates brought over a fresh fish for their dinner. "You know how to fix it, don't you? You have to scale it, like this."

"Oh, yes," Sara said readily. "Thank you so much."

She had never scaled a fish. She took it out back of the cottage and attacked it with a sharp knife. But she held it the wrong way; the tiny shining scales flew over the knife blade against her wet arms, clinging there like sequins. The sun shone on them, making them glitter. Win was excited.

"Mom, Mom!" he cried out, pointing to her arms.

Sara laughed, and holding her arms out in front of her, palms upraised, she did a dance for him, her black skirt whirling out from her ankles.

"I'm a mermaid, Win, and my jewels are the silver scales of the deep-sea fish!" But suddenly the impulse died in her. She stood still on the sand with her arms covered with fish scales. She was only a lonely woman in widow's weeds trying to play with a little boy. Tears came to her eyes and a sob of self-pity choked in her throat. She went soberly back to the job of preparing the fish.

Mr. Gates brought over the mail every day. This friend and that one expressing their sympathy, the heavy spot of ink here and there showing the hesitation, the attempt to find the best word. A letter from Belle or Dor or Anne telling what they were all doing; if she wanted them to come up just to write. One letter came signed "Marie Sophia Henkel, secretary of the Board of Directors," a very formal missive that read: "By unanimous action of the Directors of the John

Henkel Brewing Co. you were made director to fill the existing vacancy." She tore the letter across and dropped it in the stove.

She had brought nothing to read for herself, because at home when she picked up a book nothing had held her interest. She read Mother Goose rhymes and the tale of Peter Rabbit to Win. She knew them by heart now, so it didn't matter when her eyes were too misty to see clearly. One day, she took the old newspapers that had been used for shelf paper from under the dishes in the cupboard and read them, even to the slightest item. But when she looked at the date she remembered that William was alive then. She had been happy then, with nothing in the world to worry about. She wrote Mama to send some of William's German books and a German dictionary and grammar. She would, at least, see the word "Geliebte" on the page.

The shy spring came slowly, holding its chilly reticence morning and evening, warming up only in the middle of the day. Its very restraint helped Sara. Every day was a battle against the cold, trying to keep the house warm. When she woke, the cold and her grief were there alike to be fought off again. Out in the sun, with the baby on a blanket and Win filling his pail beside her on the sand, it was not so hard. The sun warmed her through. The trunks of the fir trees had a red beauty, the needles of the pines were a fresh slippery green. Dandelions for Win to pick grew between the planks that led up to their cottage. There was no lush flowering to remind her of the flower-filled house. The beauty was tempered, the day endurable. They were out of the house whenever it was warm enough. And each day the warmth lasted longer.

"I couldn't have stood it in the fall," Sara whispered to herself. What would she ever do in the fall? She made no plans. One day followed another. She didn't realize she had been there a month until Mama wrote asking if she weren't ready to come home now. She wrote back, "No, why don't you and the girls come up the first?" She was almost ashamed that she didn't want them before that. She didn't want anyone to help her. She must find a way of living by herself, with only the children.

One night she woke in the dark to hear the wind banging the door of the woodshed and lashing the lake up against the shore. Sheet lightning glared in through the drawn shades at fitful intervals, searching out her loneliness and fear. It was followed by hopeless rolls of thunder. The rain pelted down so hard that it came through the roof in one place. She slid out of bed, trembling, and set a pan under the leak.

She couldn't sleep. She sat up in bed, listening, her throat dry with unreasoning fear. Even the children sleeping serenely through it were no comfort. Where was William? Did he know how frightened and lonely she was?

Now the thunder was like the sound of the kegs the men rolled over the cobbles of the brewery yard to distribute the pitch evenly on the inside . . . like the rumble of a dray, drawn past the loading platform, crushing a man against the platform. She hid her face against Win's warm little form.

"Hello, Mrs. Henkel, are you all right? There's a gentleman come up from Armitage to see you. He got held up by the storm." Mr. Gates called to her from the porch.

Sara leaped out of bed thankfully and wrapped herself in William's woolen dressing gown.

It was Paul! The rain dripped from his hat brim. His collar was turned up around his neck.

"Paul! Come in. How did you get here at this hour; it must be five o'clock!"

Paul laughed. "I guess it is. The train was held up by a washout. I slept in that little station house until I could see the sky growing lighter; then I walked over here and woke up your neighbor."

"But, Paul, how did you happen . . ."

"Oh, I got to thinking of you up here alone. I don't know, I thought the fishing might be good up here."

"I'm so glad you came!" Sara said. She had never been more glad to see anyone. "Go into the bedroom and change your wet clothes and I'll make you some breakfast."

The whole atmosphere of the place was changed. It was so good to have another grown person in the house after she had been so long with the children. The rain seemed to thump on the roof and woodshed with a kind of gaiety. She fried bacon and made coffee. When she dropped the pot-lifter the clatter had no fearsome sound.

When Paul came out in his fishing clothes, she gave him the toasting fork.

"You make the toast, Paul, and I'll dress." She fed the baby but she let Win sleep. All the time she could hear Paul whistling in the kitchen.

"You shouldn't have come way up here, Paul," Sara said a little later.

"It's hot in Armitage. Business is slow."

"Did you tell Mama you were coming?"

"No, I decided yesterday afternoon. I just caught the train."

"More coffee?" Sara said quickly. "I haven't eaten such a big breakfast since I came." But for the most part, it seemed natural enough to have Paul there.

After breakfast, Paul hired a boat and took Win fishing with him. Sara could see him out there on the lake while she was busy with the baby. And when she went to sit outside in the sun that seemed all the more brilliant after the rain, the sight of the boat there and the two figures, the man's and the little boy's, comforted her.

They ate their lunch outdoors by the lake. Paul told her all the news of people at home. But when Win had gone to take his nap and Sara and Paul sat just outside the cottage on the sandy bank, a long silence grew between them that made the buzzing of a fly and the lap of the lake sound loud.

"Thank you for coming, Paul," Sara said finally.

"I just came for myself, to make sure you were all right. What are you going to do, Sara?"

"I don't know; live with the family for a while. I can't go on there in our house right next to the brewery. I feel as though the brewery killed William; the brewery horses did, anyway. I can't seem to make plans; everything's stopped for me, except, of course, for the children."

Paul looked as though he would speak and then he was silent, filling his pipe, studying the empty lake shore.

"I hear you're running for the legislature this fall," Sara said abruptly.

Paul laughed. "I like politics. You know Dad almost ran for Senator, once. I suppose I have his liking for it. Funny thing, I see Derrick VanRansom quite a bit. He runs the party. People say he's hard, but he has his soft spots. He asked me about you."

Sara did not seem to be listening.

"Well, if I'm taking that four-thirty train . . ." Paul stood up.

Sara watched Paul's train until it was out of sight. Paul stood on the back platform and waved. Then she and Win stopped at Mrs. Gates' for the baby and walked back to the cottage.

After the children were asleep, she took out her German book and the new German grammar. But suddenly she dropped her head on the open page and cried. It wasn't any easier, even after the whole month of keeping busy. She had run away from grief and hurt, up here where William had never been. What good was it? She would go back to the city at the end of the week.

8

WHEN Sara came back from the lake she went to stay with her family as a matter of course. At dinner that night Mr. Bolster looked around the table at his family with his gentle smile. Dor and George were there, too, in honor of Sara's homecoming.

"It seems good to have our girls all together again, Corona."

Mrs. Bolster nodded behind the tall silver coffee urn. "We have a nursery, too, with Winthrop and William and Roger. Sara, Win is old enough to have some meals downstairs with the family now. No child ever learns manners in the nursery." Mama was very gently, very definitely taking over her family's guidance.

It was all so familiar: Mary serving the food, calling her "Miss Sara," looking only a little more lean and wrinkled.

"I can't see that the girls have grown so much older, Corona," Papa said, looking at each of them in turn, and the girls looked at each other appraisingly, recognizing the same narrow bridge of nose and high arched eyebrows, and laughed. There was a close family resemblance in them all. Belle was forty-five, but who would know it? Anne was forty-one, Dor was thirty-five, Sara twenty-five, but in her black dress she looked older than that.

But while they laughed, they must all feel how they had changed, Sara thought. Anne had never used to talk with a whine. Belle had never been so emphatic in her ideas, and she, herself—why, she had been a child when she lived here before. Sitting here, eating Mary's méringues again, it seemed odd that she had two little boys of her own upstairs.

"If you'd like, I'll stop in and see Wentworth and Higgins about advertising your house for sale, Sara," Mr. Bolster remarked. "I thought of doing it this summer while you were away and then I decided there was plenty of time."

Sara dipped her fingers in the fingerbowl. "It seems almost a pity for you not to move over there. You wouldn't have to rent this house then."

A slight hesitancy hung in the air. Mrs. Bolster disliked business matters discussed at the table. Mr. Bolster had never had any idea but that he should maintain his family under his own roof, never that he should live under his daughter's permanently. That they had rented this house rather than buying or building again was never mentioned among them and scarcely acknowledged in their thoughts. Sara had grown too used to William's forthrightness. She had learned to be forthright, herself.

"I'm afraid our friends, Sara, are mostly on this side of town," Mrs. Bolster answered.

"It's a lovely house; I hope being so close to the brewery won't interfere with its sale," Anne said.

"You'll have no trouble in selling the house; a family with a Polish name and lots of money bought the Nugents'," Dor told her. "Besides, they will probably sell the brewery now, and whoever buys it will want your house, George thinks."

"Oh, they'll never sell," Sara said quickly.

"I shall be glad when you are through with the whole business," Mrs. Bolster said, pushing back her chair. "Sara, you blow out the candles; you remember how you used to beg to as a little girl?"

Anne had Sara's old room. Sara moved into a smaller room across from the children. It seemed cramped after the big bedroom with the fireplace in it. The way of living was cramping, too; Mama and the girls tried to forget that she had ever been away, they took for granted that she was just the same. And the children did not seem so close to her here as at the lake. But she was fortunate to be able to come home like this, she told herself repeatedly.

Sara took Win with her when she went to see the Henkels. She felt a little shy about seeing them at first. Without William the close tie was gone. When she was there, conversation with the girls seemed stilted. Each seemed a little jealous of the other's grief. Only Mother Henkel, murmuring endearments to Win and taking him out to the pantry for cookies, seemed entirely natural.

"Ottilie is going to New York this fall to study art; unless," Marie added, "conditions at the brewery should restrict our income."

"Why, what do you mean, Marie? William was pleased with the way things were going, and Mr. Blanchard seemed to think we need never worry," Sara said.

"If William had lived everything would be all right, but Gottfried is running the brewery now. He has no idea of how to push the sales. When I mentioned to Gottfried that I noticed the Armitage Arms was advertising Old Mill beer on their beverage list instead of ours, he snorted and muttered, 'Dem hat's ans Malz gefählt,' as though the public could tell!"

Sara frowned. "I don't understand."

"Oh, he meant that their brewmaster pinches on the malt!" Marie explained impatiently.

Sara was silent a moment. She had felt almost lighthearted this afternoon. The day was warm and sunny; Charlie Freehahn had brought William's horse and buggy way over to the west side for her. "The horse knows he to you belongs now, Missus Henkel," Charlie had told her, giving her the reins. And she had driven down here with Win. Now the atmosphere of this house fell heavily on her spirit. It seemed anxious, full of forebodings.

"But you must go to art school, anyway, Ottilie," she said. "After all, it could be no more costly than your trip to Europe." Did that sound as though she envied them their trip? Sara wondered uncomfortably.

"There's nothing that I want to do here. There's no interest in art in this town." Ottilie's eyes flashed suddenly. She dressed her hair in an unusual pompadour now and wore silver earrings she had bought in Europe that were heavier than the little jeweled flowers Mother Henkel wore. Already she looked different from the young girls in Armitage City.

"You received the notice of being made a director, I suppose?" Marie asked.

"Yes, Marie; I should have answered it. I supposed it was just a formality."

"There will be a meeting of the directors, Friday. I'm sending out notices today."

"I'll come, of course," Sara said, feeling a revulsion to Marie's brisk tone of voice.

Sara kissed Mother Henkel when she left. She was so quiet, so sad. She left everything to the girls except certain dishes she liked to make. "I make no wine this year," she told Sara sadly. "The girls care not to drink. John and the boys liked my wine."

"I liked it, too. William always kept some of the wine you gave us last year in the cut-glass decanter."

"Wilhelm was a gut boy," Mrs. Henkel murmured, laying her small veined hands on Sara's arm. "He did not want to do the brewery. Es war schrecklich!"

"Mama, that's foolish. He was heart and soul in it. It wasn't as though he had practiced long," Marie rebuked her quickly, almost sharply. Mrs. Henkel's face seemed to grow more quiet. All expression retreated from it. It was a relief to Sara to leave.

Sara had waited until the last minute before going over to the brewery for the directors' meeting. Marie had called to remind her. She left Mama and the girls sewing on the veranda. Belle was indignant at her going at all.

"I suppose there's a *little* difference between the evil effects of beer and whiskey, but very little. The man who drinks beer will always be an easy victim of the hard-liquor habit. And now that it isn't William's business, Sara, why do you have anything to do with it? It's such a . . . a disreputable business!"

Mrs. Bolster shook her head slightly over her hemming. She could never become entirely accustomed to Belle's spirited harangues.

"After all, the money on which the boys and I live happens to come from there, Belle; and William worked so hard over it. It meant more to him than just a brewery," Sara said. Belle's attitude irritated her. Except the day of the Fourth of July parade she hadn't worried about what people thought of brewing. She had accepted William's evaluation of it. It was a business like any other.

"But you can sell your interest, Sara!" Belle insisted.

"Well, I'll see," Sara answered evasively.

All the way across to the east side of town Sara felt Mama's and the girls' disapproval. And yet Marie expected her to come to the meeting. The Henkel Brewing Company was such a family affair that they preferred even her to someone else.

When she turned into the yard of the brewery she tried to keep her eyes on her driving, avoiding the sight of the loading platform; hardly looking at the stone wall of the brewery. It wasn't easy to come here again.

She knocked timidly on the door of William's old office. Gottfried Werner opened the door and pulled out a chair for her at the table across from Marie and Ottilie. Adolf Steiner sat at one end and Gottfried took his place again at the head of the table. They were all silent as she came in.

"How do you do. I'm sorry I was late."

Marie nodded without smiling. Ottilie smiled quickly. Adolf Steiner bowed solemnly.

"Excuse." Steiner went over to close the door Sara had left open, shutting out the indistinct sounds from the brewery.

Marie sat with the minute book open before her, smoothing down her shirtwaist that was starched so stiff it protruded over the page. Both she and Ottilie wore hats and veils. Sara was aware that her own hair was blown around her face. She tucked it under her hat a little self-consciously.

Gottfried Werner's face was solemn. He tugged at his drooping mustache. His hair lay on his head in separate lines as though he had just wet it and combed it with a coarse comb. But there was dignity about him. William had said he held degrees from the brewing schools in both Munich and Hamburg.

Sara had seen Steiner only at the tall desk in the office of the brewery the few times she had waited there for William. She remembered now that he had been one of the men to carry William's body over to the brewery. He was a little man with dark bushy hair and thick glasses. He might have been one of the silent, thick-set workers she glimpsed around the brewery, except that he wore a white shirt and collar and a neat pepper-and-salt-mixture suit.

Gottfried cleared his throat and began sorrowfully: "The John Henkel Brewery has had a so great loss." He spoke precisely with a marked accent. "But the brewery must go on. Mr. John Henkel and Mr. William Henkel would both want it so. . . ." He blew his nose loudly on a colored handkerchief. "We shall haf the reading of the minutes."

"Shall I go back and read the minutes of the meeting when the loan was recorded?" Marie asked.

Gottfried Werner nodded. "If you will please, Miss Henkel."

Marie read in a high thin voice:

"April 4, 1900. Upon the above date at two p.m. the directors of the John Henkel Brewing Company assembled in special meeting at the principal place of business of the corporation. President William Henkel called the meeting to order. It was regularly moved by Gottfried Werner, seconded by Adolf Steiner, that the action of the president in borrowing $50,000 at the First National Bank of Armitage City be ratified and confirmed and the signatures of the officers upon the notes evidencing such a loan be approved.

"The motion was carried.

"There being no further business, the meeting was adjourned."

Sara thought of William sitting at the head of the table in Gottfried's place. His easy humor came back to her sharply now in this room where everyone was so serious. How different these meetings must have been when he was here.

"April 17, 1900. At a special meeting of the Board of

Directors, called by Gottfried Werner, vice-president, on account of the sudden death of William Henkel, formerly president of the John Henkel Brewing Company, it was moved by Adolf Steiner and seconded by Ottilie Henkel and unanimously carried that Gottfried Werner be made chairman of the Board of Directors and acting manager of the corporation."

Sara stared at Marie, reading with such seeming calmness of William's death. Then she saw how pale Marie was; that she bit her lip to steady it twice during her reading. Sara looked at Gottfried sitting at the head of the table. His mouth was puckered so that the drooping ends of his mustache were brought closer together on his chin. His forehead was furrowed in a frown. Under their bushy eyebrows his eyes stared unseeingly at some point halfway down the long table. She remembered uneasily that William had said, "I can see what Father meant about Gottfried; he has no executive ability; he's a brewmaster, an artist, pure and simple." She was startled to hear her own name.

"It was moved and seconded that Sara Henkel, wife of the deceased, executrix of his estate, and owner of 500 shares of the John Henkel Brewing Company, be chosen to fill the existing vacancy. The motion was unanimously passed and the secretary instructed to send official notice of same to Mrs. Henkel."

Sara glanced around at the serious little group; they were the John Henkel Brewing Company. How amused Mama and the girls would be when she described this meeting to them!

Marie turned a page. The sharp edge made a crackling noise. The edge seemed to have no color of its own at all, but when it fell against the other pages the edge of the ledger was red. She had lost track of what Marie was saying. Words fell on her ears without distinct meaning. Some of the formality of a meeting seemed to have relaxed.

"Wilhelm was a great one to have his plans all worked out in his head before he say much about them, like the old man," Gottfried was saying.

"It was a sore thing that he had to be killed just then," Adolf muttered.

"Well, business is good. We're doing a bigger business this month over a year ago October," Gottfried reminded them.

When Sara came into the house and found Mama and Anne and Belle there drinking tea it was difficult to fit in at once. Mama had the baby on her knees. Belle was pouring the tea. The room was cool after the hot, stuffy room she had just left.

"How was your directors' meeting? Did you tell them the next time Roger goes over there with Win to see Charlie we don't want them playing in the cellar with the brewery cats?" Anne asked lightly.

Sara didn't answer Anne. "Oh, I didn't understand it very well." She had no urge to make them laugh at Marie or Gottfried. She was tired and took the tea Belle handed her, gratefully.

"I hope you told them you wouldn't go again," Belle said.

"I'm going to see Mr. Blanchard about it."

"Or Paul? I understand that Mr. Blanchard entrusts his younger clients to his new partner, particularly if they are feminine and charming!" Belle teased.

Sara colored, absurd as it was. When the girls were together like this it was hard for any of them to remember that Anne's or Sara's husband had died, or that Belle had left Derrick, or that any change at all had entered into their lives.

"I shall insist on seeing Mr. Blanchard," Sara said so firmly that they all laughed.

"Oh, well, since Paul was elected to the legislature he won't be in town much," Anne remarked.

"Sara, there's no reason why you can't start to do a few things with us," Dor said. "After all, it's been six months since William's death."

"Is that all? It seems years ago since he was here," Sara said, staring around the room.

Obediently she went out a little; as Belle's guest to the meetings of the Winter Club, to the concerts at the Academy, to small dinners, but none of these things interested her. Life stretched ahead as empty as William's closet. What did women do with their lives when they were left at twenty-five? Surely more than this, she thought, reading aloud to Win about Peter Rabbit for the hundredth time.

She thought about her house that still stood empty and wondered if she really wanted to sell. It was hers from William. There were so many things to decide. But she couldn't seem to make decisions. She seemed to sit in the center of an empty calm. Nothing was important. There was no hurry. "Wait a bit," everyone said when she tried to plan. "You have plenty of time." The calm was monotonous, heavy. It shut out all sound of life. Sometimes she couldn't remember what her days were like when William was living. William used to laugh, to sing, to call her "Geliebte."

9 1901

MARIE HENKEL telephoned to ask if Sara would be home.

"Then I'll come over to see you; it's important." Marie had only called at the Bolsters' once before. Sometimes a month went by between Sara's visits at the Henkels'! Mrs. Henkel had not been well in the winter and Marie had felt that the children would tire her. She would take them down more often now that it was spring, Sara thought as she arranged a tea tray.

But Marie waved the tea aside. "No thank you, Sara; I want your help. It's about the brewery. Things aren't going well; you know we had to pass the last quarterly dividend."

Sara nodded.

"Gottfried thinks that all there is to running a brewery is making good beer. But the Old Mill is outselling us, whether they slight on their malt or not." In her excitement Marie's face took on a faint color. She sat forward in her chair.

"Now there's a possible solution. A Mr. Schrader and a Mr. Siegel are here from Detroit for the Hess Company. They are interested in buying the brewery! They are coming to see you. They saw Gottfried first and, without even consulting the rest of us, he told them there was no possibility of buying the brewery!" Marie's eyes flashed their indignation.

"I suppose he felt William would never have sold it," Sara said.

"If we can get our price we'd better do it," Marie went on as though she had not heard Sara's remark. "Gottfried and Adolf will not like it but we have the controlling shares!"

Marie's eagerness to sell angered Sara. It had been so important for William to carry on the brewery for his family. Now his sister could consider selling out so easily.

"I'll have to think about it," Sara said slowly. "I'll have to talk to Mr. Blanchard."

"I know you would be glad to get rid of your interest in the brewery, especially with a sister active in the W.C.T.U.," Marie said.

Sara did not answer. An awkward moment lay between them.

"Well." Marie rose. "They're coming to see you and I thought I should explain the situation."

That evening Gottfried Werner and Adolf Steiner sat in the library.

"The thing is, Missus Henkel, we were afraid this concern from Detroit would persuade you we ought to sell. And Adolf, here, said why not go and see you about it." Gottfried's face was solemn. He smoothed down his drooping mustache. He was freshly shaven and a faint aroma of hair pomade came from him. Adolf Steiner stared owl-like out of his thick glasses.

"You see, Missus Henkel, the brewery's the best in this part of the state. You couldn't have money in a thing that would bring in better profit," Adolf put in.

"An' you haf to think of the little boys," Gottfried urged. "It'll be a business ready for them to go into."

Sara shook her head. "I'd never have them go into it."

Gottfried brushed her remark aside as the foolish remark of a child who knows nothing about business.

"It's their father's business and his father's before him. Look at your own husband; he give up his medicine to carry it on. I know how hard that was for him, but he was good at the business. He had some of the old man in him for all his book learning. Missus Henkel, he would never haf sold the Henkel brewery!" The impossibility of such a step was in his voice.

"No, Dr. Henkel didn't mean to sell it. But it . . . it was the cause of his death," Sara said, looking past the two anxious old men.

Gottfried shook his head. Adolf took off his thick glasses and polished them on his colored handkerchief.

"I know now that he never should have done it!" Sara said bitterly.

With one hand Adolf rubbed his knee that was already shiny. He looked helplessly at Gottfried. Gottfried swallowed loudly.

"Missus Henkel, it's wrong to look at it that way. His death was accident; a terrible thing, Gott knows, but if Wilhelm had it to do again I believe he'd take over the brewery."

Sara started to speak but Gottfried held up his hand. "Missus Henkel, it was more than a business to Wilhelm."

"I know all that and it was wrong for William to feel that way about it; the brewery was a terrible burden to him. I . . . I hate it!" Tears were running down her face.

Gottfried patted her shoulder heavily. Adolf stared at the oil painting in front of him without seeing it.

Sara wiped her eyes. "I'm sorry," she said quietly.

"Missus Henkel, it is to remember this: if the business meant so much to Wilhelm that he'd run it when his heart was in his medicine, shouldn't it mean too much to us to sell it?" Gottfried stood up. "We haf taken enough of your time," he said with quaint courtesy, "but could you please be at the meeting Thursday?"

"I . . . Yes, I'll be there," Sara promised.

"Who on earth were your callers, Sara?" Belle asked when she had closed the door behind them.

"Men from the brewery," Sara said slowly.

"Really, Sara, you must put a stop to their calling on you. It's nothing for a woman to have anything to do with. And you haven't given Mr. Blanchard definite word yet about selling your house." Belle opened two windows in the library as though to dispose of any air breathed by the recent callers, then she moved across the room and lighted the lamp above the big rosewood piano. Sara sat down on the chair by the door, feeling for the moment like a younger sister.

"They came to beg me not to sell the brewery."

"Don't be foolish. A brewery doubtless means a great deal to two sentimental old Germans who have worked in it all their lives but it isn't anything to you as long as you get your money out of it."

Belle struck a few chords lovingly, stopping to turn over the music on the rack. She opened Brahms' "Academic Festival Overture." It was difficult to read, and she fumbled along until she came to the robust chords toward the end.

"What are you playing?" Sara asked sharply.

"Something of Brahms'," Belle said carelessly. She could play this part. The ease of it pleased her.

"But that's a student song; William used to play it."

Belle nodded. "I think Brahms wrote it for some student

friends, using their own songs in it. We studied Brahms at the Winter Club last year."

"And this one, Sara, this is for us . . . 'Gaudeamus Igitur' . . . let us rejoice, therefore, while we are young," William had said.

Belle swung around from the piano. "You don't want the children to grow up half in a brewery."

"An' you haf to think of the little boys," Gottfried had urged.

She was between two separate worlds.

Monday morning Sara was bathing the baby in the nursery when Belle told her two men were downstairs to see her.

"Oh, Sara, they're rare. One of them looks as though he'd pop right out of his suit. More of your brewery friends, no doubt."

Sara dried her hands and took off her apron and went down to see them as she was, in her morning dimity.

"My name's Schrader and this is Mr. Siegel, Ma'm," the taller of the two explained, disposing of his cigar in the potted plant on the taboret near him. "We're from Detroit, Mrs. Henkel, interested in the brewing business. We've known of the Henkel Brewing Company for a number of years; fact is, there's no better beer brewed in Detroit than what you folks make." He paused impressively, as one paying an extravagant compliment.

"When we heard of the demise of your late husband we was shocked and grieved. I didn't have the honor to know him personally, but Siegel had met your husband's father a good many times."

Sara waited.

"We understood that you'd want to dispose of your share

of the brewery. Now, as it happens, our company wants a plant in this part of the state. We're not interested in driving a bargain, Mrs. Henkel. We wouldn't think of it. We stand ready to make you a top price for your interests. If you'll give us the name of your lawyer we'll work out the details."

Sara held their cards with the tips of her fingers. She looked from Mr. Schrader's fat red face, his straw-colored mustache and thick neck that rose tightly from his collar, to Mr. Siegel. Mr. Siegel was also fat. His bald head shone an unhealthy pink in the morning sun. The gilt parlor chair creaked ominously under him.

She spoke a little nervously. "I shall have to think this matter over and discuss it with the others."

Mr. Siegel cleared his throat loudly. "You're likely to meet some opposition from that brewmaster and the bookkeeper. I understand they own a few shares."

"Negligible number of shares, Siegel," Schrader put in. "They want to keep the brewery because they don't want to lose their jobs. What's his name, Werner, likes running it pretty well."

Sara rose so quickly her two callers were taken by surprise. Schrader rose. Siegel lifted himself by means of the piano.

"I would not understand the particulars. My lawyer is Mr. Blanchard of Blanchard and Peabody. You can present the proposition to him. And in the meantime, I shall talk it over with the others."

When they had gone Sara removed the cigar stub gingerly from the base of the rubber plant. She thought of men like these running the brewery that John Henkel had built, that William had worked so hard over. These men would make it into something else, something . . . "disreputable," Belle had said.

✦

That afternoon Sara walked all the way across the city to the brewery. The ivy was leafing out. It had been red against the gray stone that day so long ago when William had brought her down to see it. But they had scarcely looked at the brewery that day. Now she looked carefully at it.

Men were loading one of the big drays at the platform. Perhaps it was the same dray, the same horses. They stood quietly enough today. The silver balls sparkled heartlessly on the hames, the horses' sides shone. She watched the kegs rolled across the platform and swung up on the dray. The big German with the leather apron called out. The dray rumbled off. Who could have believed the drays they were so proud of could be the cause of William's death? The horses trotted smartly up the slope to the avenue.

Sara stepped inside the brewery. A workman glanced up at the slim, black-garbed woman with surprise. There were no women around the brewery. Then he recognized her and pulled hesitatingly at his cap.

"Guten Morgen, Frau Henkel."

"Which way—where do I go to find Mr. Werner?" Sara asked.

"Im Ruhkeller."

"Ruh . . ." That meant rest, she thought, as she followed her guide. Then she remembered: "Ruh-platz," Mrs. Henkel had called the grave. Sara shivered a little as she stepped into the freezing temperature of the storage cellar after the warm spring air outside. The great ninety-barrel wooden tanks standing in rows partially obscured the light, but in places the light struck out amber color in the oak graining of the wood.

They found Gottfried watching the cleaning of one of the great tanks. A man was inside with a light. He peered out of the manhole like a gnome from a hollow tree.

"Ach! Missus Henkel, how do you do? Come, it ist too cold here." He was so careful of her, trying to let her go ahead, getting in the way, opening the heavy doors, muttering his excuses. "Take a chair," he said at the entrance to William's office. Sara's eyes slipped quickly over the "Pathologie . . . Orth" that had seemed to mean so much to William.

"No, Mr. Werner, I came over to see the brewery. I want to go through it again."

Gottfried's pleasure showed in his slow smile.

She thought of that other tour, with John Henkel beaming at her, panting up the stairs ahead of them, showing each object so proudly, of William beside her. She had been so remote from it, yet taking pains to show some interest. This time she tried to look at everything intelligently, to remember that part of this was hers.

Gottfried explained each operation, yet assumed that so much was clear to her that wasn't. When they came back to the office her mind held only a confused set of pictures and scents: the smell of rosin in the cooperage, the warm, dry air of the malthouse as they stood in front of the big furnace; the fruitlike odor of the barley, the dusty sunshine streaming in on the pale yellow grain.

Gottfried had pointed out the chart and indicators near the big furnace in the malthouse. "At every hour I can tell here just what the temperature is. Now the heat goes down." But she remembered only the great iron doors of the furnace with the figure of a goddess holding a big torch and over the picture the name of the German manufacturer.

In the brewhouse there was the kettle glowing just as it had that other time, and there, too, was the view of the river from the window. She remembered how William had looked out the window as though the brewery didn't interest him very greatly.

In the room where the beer ran over the series of pipes, "ein Kühlschiff," Gottfried called it, she saw the swallows swooping outside the window. She watched them, not hearing Gottfried's explanation of the wort.

Gottfried made her touch the inside of an empty tank. "Wilhelm!" he said significantly, indicating by the jerk of his head, his expression, the appraising way his finger touched the glassy surface, how far-seeing William had been. "The little boys will one day be proud their father bought these new tanks." He put the remark in with a kind of transparent cunning that made Sara smile.

She liked the engine room where a gigantic red wheel turned constantly, and the steel and brass parts gleamed like the parts of a fire engine. A man stepped up to speak to Gottfried. Sara walked away from them and stood watching the slow-driven wheel. She became aware of the rhythmic click and hiss of a pump behind her.

Here was the driving power of the brewery: John Henkel's energy, William's. The machinery was so clean and shining and tireless. There was nothing cluttered or useless or stagnant about it. There was more power here than in the rush of the logs in the old drives. She liked it.

She hadn't thought the brewery was so big. Before she had felt so little connection with it. William would be through with it in a few years she had always thought. She had only half heard him when he talked about the little laboratory he was putting in, the new equipment, the malthouse. Now a sense of pride of ownership stirred in her. She watched the ceaseless rotation of the wheels without seeing it.

"Ein glass Bier?" Gottfried asked as they came to the final stage of the beer.

"No, thank you," Sara said apologetically. "I don't really like it." But Gottfried poured one and held it up to the light proudly. "Liquid bread!" he said. It seemed a small thing to be the result of so many processes, so much equipment and energy, but Gottfried acted as though it were sufficient, something to be proud of.

She went back to the office. Steiner was there, at his desk. "Mr. Schrader and Mr. Siegel came to see me this morning," Sara said. Gottfried waited. "I told them they could present the proposition to Mr. Blanchard." Steiner dropped his pen. It rolled off the slanting desk and he fumbled for it on the floor. "But I don't believe we want to sell. Tell me, Gottfried, has a woman ever run a brewery?"

10

ON Thursday Sara went to the special meeting of the directors of the John Henkel Brewing Company. She was there before Marie. Marie smiled her approval as she sat down and arranged her minute books. Adolf had his treasurer's books. He fussed with them nervously and wished he could smoke in here. Inwardly he cursed having women mixed up in directors' meetings. A curious air of tension prompted each of them to painstaking politeness.

"Would you like more air, Miss Henkel? Missus Henkel?" Gottfried asked.

"It's all right," Marie answered impatiently.

"The meeting of the stockholders of the John Henkel Brewing Company will come to order," Gottfried announced, rising. Usually he sat down to preside. It seemed like a kind of game to Sara that without shifting their seats or their manners they could be at one time stockholders, at another, directors. Now it seemed they were stockholders.

Marie read Ottilie's name and after it the number of shares she held and her signed proxy. The minutes of the last meeting contained only Gottfried's report of the condition of the corporation and the auditor's report.

Sara smiled inwardly at Mr. Blanchard's face yesterday when she had gone to him with her plan. He had adjusted his glasses and stared at her as though he were seeing her for the first time.

"Impossible, Mrs. Henkel! You have no background of knowledge. . . ."

"No," she had said, "but I can learn."

Gottfried was discussing the present situation. Sara had gone all over that with him yesterday and last evening until late at night. The brewery was holding its own, managing to pay the interest on the loans, paying off a small sum every three months; the bank was more than satisfied. Marie's pen scratched across the page. Adolf stared at the neat figures he read from his book, frowning at the red figures.

Gottfried cleared his throat. His manner was suddenly informal. "As you know, two representatives of a larger brewing company haf come about buying the John Henkel Brewing Company." The silence in the office was heavy with personal reactions. Gottfried waited as though expecting the very walls to cry out. He glanced significantly at the picture of John Henkel hanging opposite him above the door of the little room. It was a flat picture showing a short, rotund little man, giving no idea of his exuberance or gusto or merry humor, but Gottfried saw all these things in it.

"Their offer is fair," Gottfried went on, "but I am frank to say that I discouraged them in the idea that the business was for sale." Marie compressed her lips. Adolf nodded slightly. Sara sat placidly watching Gottfried.

"Their interest shows that they know our brewery is a solid business," Gottfried said impressively.

"With new capital and new management," Marie put in acidly, "we haven't bettered our situation in the last six months."

Gottfried paused and then without comment went on.

"These men have been to see each of the directors." His disapproval of this backstairs method was apparent. "We should now talk about the proposition together."

Marie laid her blotter between the pages and closed her book. She looked directly at Gottfried.

"I feel that we are fortunate to have this opportunity to sell at a good figure. It is plain from the financial report that the brewery has run behind this year. I am not blaming the present management. Perhaps my brother was too ambitious in his program. Without his leadership and management it is hard to see where we will come out. Mr. Werner has done the best he could; we appreciate his stepping in, but the work of management is new to him."

Gottfried stared at the papers before him. When Marie had finished Gottfried looked at Sara. Sara could feel the hot color in her face as though she were a little girl about to speak a piece.

"I have not interested myself in the situation of the brewery as deeply as I should have. But when the question of selling the brewery was brought up I could not help but remember . . ." her voice shook suddenly with her feeling ". . . how much my husband gave up because his father could not die in peace unless he promised to carry on the business. That was wrong. . . ." She said it boldly, not looking at Marie or Gottfried, staring past them out the window that gave on the cobbled courtyard where the big drays were loaded. ". . . But my husband promised and he put all his energy into the business of this brewery. It represented his father's dream of success, and of independence and security for his family. He was killed just as he had completed the plans his father wished carried out. It seems like . . . like not keeping faith with him to sell out now, to let the John

Henkel Brewing Company be taken over by strangers. If he had done that . . . sold out his father's business, he would be alive today, doing the thing he wanted, enjoying his sons."

Sara was through. She looked down in her lap. Her clasped hands were cold. One hand pressed the prongs of her engagement ring too hard against the soft flesh of her fingers.

Adolf spoke quickly. "I agree with Missus Henkel. John Henkel would never haf sold his brewery, neither would Wilhelm Henkel."

Marie's voice was harsh. Her face was pinched. "If you are trying to suggest that the business my father and brother built up means less to me than it does to any of you, you are very, very unjust. My father could not foresee the present situation, nor could my brother. I am facing things as they are. I repeat that, in spite of Mrs. Henkel's speech, the sensible thing for us to do is to sell now."

Sara had regained control of her feelings and was looking at Marie. For the moment, the two anxious old employees were set aside. The duel was between Marie and herself. Why was it not better to be rid of the brewery? She had meant to be. It had brought her nothing but unhappiness. Perhaps Marie was right, perhaps the brewery would only get in worse circumstances; she might end by losing everything of hers and of the boys.

Out the window back of Marie, she saw a dray returning from its round. The empty kegs rumbled hollowly. The harness jingled. The big horses held their heads high. Once she had thought of them as meaning security, then they had crushed William and she had dreaded the sound of them. They shook their heads as the last keg was rolled off, and now they trotted toward the stables. Sara's eyes came back to Marie. Very gently, as though she were speaking to Win, she said:

"I know you care, Marie, but I don't agree that we should give up the brewery."

And then they were voting on the motion to sell. Marie read the name of each stockholder, beginning with Sara:

Sara Henkel, voting 500 shares . . . . No
Marie Henkel, voting 250 shares . . . . Yes
Ottilie Henkel, voting 250 shares . . . . Yes
Gottfried Werner, voting 25 shares . . . . No
Adolf Steiner, voting 25 shares . . . . No

The motion to sell to the Hess Brewing Company of Detroit was defeated.

"At this meeting," Gottfried said, "I am resigning as manager of the Henkel Brewing Company. I feel that I have all I can do as brewmaster."

Marie was plainly startled.

"I move that we accept Mr. Werner's resignation and tender him our great appreciation of his work," Sara said, feeling for the sonorous phrase. Adolf seconded the motion. Marie agreed in a low voice.

"I thank you," Gottfried said, looking suddenly like a German statesman standing at the head of the table instead of only a studious old brewmaster. He cleared his throat.

"The question then of a new manager comes up before the stockholders." With only a slight pause Gottfried continued: "I nominate Missus William Henkel as manager of the John Henkel Brewing Company."

"This is absurd!" Marie said angrily. "You decided this whole thing before the meeting!"

But they voted again by the number of their shares.

"If there is no further business, the meeting stands adjourned," Gottfried announced.

✦

Adolf Steiner shook Sara's hand. Marie was buttoning on her long gray duster. Sara went over to her.

"Marie, I may be wrong, but I can't see why it shouldn't be possible for a woman to run the brewery. It's simply an enormous bakery and women have made a success of running bakeries."

Marie put her minute books under her arm. "You are taking advantage of those two sentimental old fools," she said bitterly, "and you will ruin everything!"

"But William . . ." Sara began.

"What do you know about beer or business? You've grown up on the west side and felt superior all your life. I believe you did love William, but you hated to have him connected with the brewery. You hated to have him have a German family. Now that he's gone you never really want to come to see us!"

"Oh, Marie. . . ." Then Sara was silent. It was useless to protest. Some of it was true. She turned away and found Gottfried waiting beside her, looking more than ever like a member of Bismarck's cabinet.

"Missus Henkel, you must notify Hess and Company right away."

"Yes," Sara said. "I'll tend to it. I'll be at the brewery the first thing in the morning."

Sara went back home. Her confidence had run out. What did she know about business? What if she should fail? Anyway, William wouldn't have given up so much for nothing now that they were keeping the brewery. At least she had something to do; something for her children and herself and for William.

She went upstairs and took off her mourning dress and bathed. She put on a blue dress that William had always liked. Tonight she would tell the family. She would tell them, too, that she was going to move back into her own house that was just across the park from the brewery. The aching idleness of the last year was behind her.

PART THREE

Forth they drove through the court-yard gate past the echoing porch. Again the driver swung his whip: again the willing horses flew forward. Presently they entered the wheat-lands; with such speed had the horses pressed on. Again the sun grew low and the roads were darkened.

THE ODYSSEY OF HOMER
BK. III
Translation by T. E. Shaw

I 1901

PAUL SEVRANCE drove his new automobile back from the lake at a furious rate. Even going at twenty-five miles an hour he felt the heat of the valley. As he drove into Armitage along lower Water Street, men in shirtsleeves sat out in front of the wholesale houses. No one seemed given to any undue exertion. In front of Jerry's Place he saw on the window a crude painting of a glass mug of beer with white foam above the amber contents. On the muggy heat the sour smell of the saloon came out to him from above and below the swinging half-door. His thin lips twitched slightly with disgust. How could Sara Bolster be concerned with beer?

He had gone to see her after Blanchard had told him that she intended to manage the brewery. "Are you going to call it Sara's beer?" he had asked, half laughing. At first he had thought the whole idea was a pose to annoy Belle. Sara's eyes had a suspicious gleam in them.

"You're fooling, Sara!" Belle had said. "Paul, don't you believe a word of it."

"I'm not fooling, Belle. Wait until you see the new letterheads. But I think I'll put 'S. B. Henkel, Manager,' when I write our hop merchant in Bohemia. The 'Sara' might upset him as much as it would you. You see, Paul, I already have some business sense." She wouldn't be serious all evening.

"Do you think I should put on weight for the good of the business? It would be easy to gain on beer, but I don't like the taste of it."

"Sara, will you stop it!" Belle had begged. "No lady has ever run a brewery!"

"But I shall and I'll be the first Bolster to make a fortune!"

"Now you're being vulgar," Belle had said. "Paul, I leave her to you; she's beyond me."

"You can't possibly make a go of it, Sara," he had said when Belle had left. "Conditions aren't the same as they were in old John Henkel's time. There's unsavory competition and likely to be more."

Sara had sat smiling at him, unperturbed. "I don't know why I can't make a go of it!"

"Well, it's not the kind of business you want to be mixed up with. There are things about it you won't like." He couldn't seem to make Sara understand that politics and saloons were mixed up with brewing.

"They won't be mixed up with my brewing," Sara had said stubbornly. And she had gone ahead with her plans. Belle had moved over to live with her in the house by the brewery, as Belle said, "to keep those poor children from contamination."

Paul stopped at the house, but he might have known she would be at the brewery. He drove over to the brewery for the first time in his life. He drove slowly, wondering if the red car with its brass trimmings would scare the big draft horses in the yard. But the driver held the reins tight, talking to the horses. Paul drove the auto to the far side of the cobbled yard and got out, throwing off his duster and cap. It was quite a place, but the penetrating smell of the beer offended his nostrils.

He went into the office and was told to have a chair and

wait. "I'm an old friend; I'd like to look around a bit. Is Mrs. Henkel somewhere in the brewery?"

The stocky little fellow at the desk stared at him sternly through his thick-lensed glasses and told him she was probably in the fermenting cellar.

"This way?" Paul asked.

Doubtfully the little man left his desk and led the way through a room where the base of a big mash-tub stood. "Through that door," he told him.

Paul pushed open the heavy door, and a chilly atmosphere met him. The light was dim in the big cellar. A guttering candle burned in an iron bracket, throwing a faintly colored shadow against the whitewashed brick wall. Great wooden tubs towered above him. They ran in two lines the length of the room. Ladders lay against the tubs. Paul was grateful for the coolness. At the bang of the door a big blond German in overalls and boots looked around a huge barrel.

"Ja?" he asked.

"I'm looking for Mrs. Henkel."

"She ist oop here," the man with the blond mustache told him without the least flicker of amusement crossing his heavy face.

Paul made his way between the big vats, buttoning his light coat together so it wouldn't brush the sweating sides. Then he saw Sara. She stood at the top of a ladder that leaned against the last vat. The slightness of her figure was more marked against the wide rotundity of the vat.

"Sara! I came down from the lake to see how you were standing the heat and I find you as cool as a cucumber in an icebox!"

She laughed down at him. "I haven't had time to think about the heat. Have you ever seen beer fermenting? Climb up there."

He felt awkward, climbing up the ladder that lay against the next tub. He looked across the thick, brownish foam floating on top.

"Taste it!" Sara said. "It'll make you think of the spruce gum we used to get."

He touched the soapy-looking stuff with one finger and put it to his mouth. He felt that the big German standing below was laughing at him behind his stolid face. The stuff was so acrid it choked him.

Sara was laughing. "That's hop rosin." She was down the ladder as swiftly as she had climbed up and down from the salt sheds when they were children. "Come on back to the office. I was through anyway. Danke," she said to the cellar man standing there in the aisle, his amusement now obvious in his small eyes. Paul followed behind Sara. She seemed perfectly at home.

"Have you ever been in a brewery, Paul?"

"No, I must confess I haven't. Sara, why on earth are you doing this? Your husband wouldn't have wanted you to. You know how I feel and your family. People in town . . ."

". . . think I've lost my mind. I haven't. I'm entirely sane. I like it."

Paul looked at her, an expression half of amusement, half of exasperation on his face. There was no use talking about it now.

"Will you have dinner with me, Sara, and then we'll drive out in the country and try to find a breeze."

"I promised Win he could have dinner with me, Paul. Come and eat with us."

Sara led the way out of the office into the main hall. They passed a workman filling his mug at the "Sternewirth" that stood against the wall.

"Good night, Heinrich," Sara said. The workman nodded, pulling off his cotton cap.

"Do you know every worker by name, Sara?" Paul asked mockingly.

"Not quite yet. Gottfried knows all about them; what town they came from in the old country . . . they're nearly all Germans, you know . . . how many children they have and all their troubles. Gottfried says John Henkel and William did too." She touched the iron studding of the door as she went out. "We could have gone out the other way, but I like this way. John Henkel was always so proud of this door."

In the cobbled yard a man was hosing off the barrels to keep them from drying. Paul watched her stepping around the towering kegs as unconcernedly as though they were garden furniture. She held her thin black skirt up a little as she went across the wet cobbles. She was bareheaded. Tendrils of hair escaped from the twist high on her head and curled in her neck. She was thinner.

"I suppose you understand everything about running the brewery now!"

Sara's lips set; her eyes were indignant. It was so like the way she used to look at him, when they were children and he had said something to bait her, that he smiled.

"Gottfried tends to the real working part. I just decide the . . . oh, the policy of the brewery and dictate letters. It's not so hard as it sounds."

Paul's mouth twisted to one side in gentle derision.

"Mom, Mom!" Win had been watching for her from the porch. Now he came running so fast along the path that Sara called out to him not to stumble. He was dressed in a clean white sailor suit and his black buttoned shoes were polished to shining. Sara caught him in her arms. "I should have let the children go to the lake with Belle and I will later on, but they are so much company. You remember Mr. Sevrance, Win? Can you say good evening?"

"Good ev'n'n," Win mumbled and put out his fat little hand.

"Good evening," Paul said. "Would you consider riding on my shoulder back to the house? Or are you too big for me; let's see, how old are you?"

"I'm five and I'm heavier'n a beer keg, Charlie says," Win told him gravely.

"Well, up with you and let's try."

"Charlie lets me hold his hair when he carries me!" Win suggested. "But I don't guess your hair is long enough." Sara and Paul laughed. Paul wondered if Sara was aware of how large Charlie and the brewery bulked in Win's world already.

"I like to ride the real horses best. Charlie lets me climb on all their backs when they're in their stalls."

Paul galloped ahead toward the porch with Win on his shoulders.

"You see, Paul, it is cool here facing the river in the evening," Sara said as she came out on the porch to join Paul after the children were in bed.

"Cooler than the middle of the day, but it's close. At the lake there's a fine breeze. I have a new sailboat you'd like."

"It couldn't be any better than your first sailboat."

That was the trouble, Sara thought, rocking gently. Everything with Paul went back to the time when they were children and joined that time with the present, making even casual remarks more important than they were. Paul made no move to go for the drive he had suggested. The smell of his cigar thrust across the sultry sweetness of the syringa and honeysuckle. When he puffed at it the end burned red. The trees were a dark mass walling in the garden. From the porch you couldn't see even a light in the second story of the brewery, Sara noticed.

"I'm going over at four Monday morning to watch Gottfried start brewing. I haven't done that before. When I get there around seven it's already started."

"At seven every morning, Sara?"

"Yes, why not? I have so much to learn the days aren't long enough. Some day I'll go over in a leisurely fashion at eight or nine. But I often wake up anyway at six when the wagons start out."

"Sara, don't you see how foolish and impossible the whole thing is?"

"Don't be like the family, Paul. Maybe I won't make a success of it. Marie is sure I won't, so is Papa; but maybe I will. Mother Henkel and Gottfried and Charlie are the only ones who give me any encouragement. Mother Henkel says, 'Du kannst if du willst.'" Sara laughed.

Paul was silent. He went over to the porch railing and threw his cigar off into the bushes, standing there a moment, breathing in the air.

"By God, Sara, it even flavors the honeysuckle."

"What?"

"The beer. Don't you smell it?"

"No, I don't. I'm so used to it. In the brewery I've come to like it. It isn't unlike the smell of bread rising."

"Sara, come out in the auto with me away from here. We'll drive up along the river the way we went the day of the fire, remember?"

"You were showing off your new horse that time; now it's your new auto, Paul," Sara said when they were driving. "It has a gasoliney smell that flavors the night air worse than the smell from the brewery! It makes too much noise, too."

"It's a great improvement over the steamer I had, though."

Sara watched the yellow streak of light from the acetylene lamps coloring the leaves and trees at the edge of the road.

"Stirs up a good breeze," Paul said.

"I like it with the top down like this." She had brought a scarf to wind around her head but she held it in her lap and let the wind blow through her hair. She leaned her head back and looked up at the sky. "I guess I was tired," she admitted.

"I should think you'd be worn out every day, climbing up those ladders and running around that place!"

"I don't do that every day. Mostly I'm in William's office."

"You look thin, too," Paul grumbled. The auto chugged a little on the hill, and then they were up on the brow looking down over the city. When Paul turned off the engine, the chugs ceased reluctantly, making the night seem hushed. They could pick out the river by the lights from the toll-bridges.

"I haven't been up here in years," Sara said. "The Bigelow's mill is gone."

"There aren't as many mills as there used to be. There's an automobile factory coming in here; I've bought stock in it. If you want to invest a little money, Sara, I think it's a good thing."

"No, thank you, Paul, any extra money I have I need to put back into the brewery these days."

Paul half turned in his seat. "You're tying yourself up body and soul with that brewery, Sara. It hasn't been out of your conversation more than a few minutes all evening. You mustn't do it!"

Sara said nothing. This afternoon in the brewery she had been almost happy; she had been so busy she had had no time to think of anything else, even of William's being gone.

Paul's slender gloved hands moved nervously on the wheel. She thought irrelevantly of John Henkel's broad, short hands letting the barley run through his fingers, pinching out the starch between his thumb and finger.

"There's nothing wrong with making good beer!"

"Just the same, Sara, there are things a woman like you doesn't understand. I was talking to your father the other day at the lake and he said, 'Explain to Sara, if you can, what she's getting into.' "

"I know. Father doesn't think a woman should work."

"Not this kind of work, anyway. I'm going to show you what I mean, Sara. I'm going to take you for another ride down Water Street and over on Second." Paul had to get out to crank the engine. Sara was glad of the noisy chugging breaking into the stillness of the hill. Paul got in and released the brake.

It was so hot the lower end of Armitage City had no thought of going to bed. The men sat out on the sidewalk in front of Maloney's Wholesale Grocery. Women leaned out of the upper windows of the rickety tenement houses that squeezed between the warehouses. Children played and screamed over the walks, stopping now to stare at Paul's red car as it passed.

"There're your professionals." Paul nodded at an open window where a slatternly looking woman leaned out, resting her scantily covered breasts on the sill.

Sara stared, feeling herself scarcely more experienced in the world than she had been as a child. They were conspicuous driving down Water Street in the red, brass-trimmed automobile. Chairs tipped down straight so that their occupants could see the red car better. Instinctively Sara tied the scarf over her head so as not to be seen so clearly. Paul drove the car very slowly.

"How do you like that, Sara?"

Sara looked across the street at a show window with THE TAVERN in bright gold letters on the glass. Between two whiskey bottles a moth-eaten pheasant stood stiffly poised.

"But that's whiskey, Paul," Sara objected, frowning a little at the men leaning against the window and the smell that issued from the open door.

"They sell whiskey, but it's one of your places. See the card there in the corner?"

Sara read the square, fly-specked card. "We sell Henkels' Beer!" Beneath the swinging doors she glimpsed men's trousers, the flash of a brass rail, men's feet. Above the swinging doors she could see the chandelier hanging from a dark ceiling. The smell of whiskey and beer floated out to them.

"Paul, they'll wonder why we're stopping here. Let's go."

Paul released the brake on the outside of his door. They drove on down the street. In the same block three more half-doors announced the presence of saloons. Sara averted her eyes like any lady of Armitage City, but Paul pointed each one out to her.

"I've been at pains to find out the ones you back. William had dropped off some of the more disreputable. Now Heine's, there, is a credit to you."

Sara looked at the neat front window and the card advertising

SATURDAY NIGHT	FREE LUNCH	HENKELS' BEER
5¢ a Glass	*10¢ a Seidel*	*15¢ a Bottle*

"No hard liquor sold there at all," Paul said. "It really is a poor man's club. The men eat their lunch and have a mug of beer and play billiards; rather nice." Paul's voice was patronizing. "I'd keep them on, but some of these others!" He shook his head.

"Paul, what do you mean we back them? We sell them beer, of course, but we don't run these—these places."

"Oh, yes, you do, Mrs. Henkel. You see there are things about this business that no one has ever explained to you. You own the furniture and the polished bar and that handsome brass rail under all those boots, perhaps even the roof. It gives an outlet for the sale of your beer; all the breweries do that."

"But . . ."

"Listen, Sara, there's another thing. You can't keep beer and hard liquor separate. They're all mixed up with each other. It may be your saloon and your beer, brewed in the brewery of honest John Henkel, but the saloonkeeper is going to sell hard liquor there, too. People think of you as a saloonkeeper. When their husbands get drunk and spend all their money and the children go hungry the women are going to curse you. And all these W.C.T.U. workers, like your own sister, are fighting you. Some day they'll make a political issue of it. I don't think they can ever get prohibition across but they think so. If they should, where would you be? Where would your business be? I'm not trying to scare you, Sara; I'm just trying to show you that you're into something that's bigger than you know. You can't be in the brewery business and keep your skirts clean. It isn't the way it was when John Henkel decided to make some beer for other Germans over here who liked it."

Sara sat very straight in the red leather seat. Paul's words spun in her brain: "Women are going to curse you . . . you can't keep your skirts clean . . . hard liquor, too." She saw the swinging door of Jerry's Place across from the window where the woman leaned on the sill. She thought of the spotless cleanliness of the brewery, of the shining brew-kettle, of the grain spread to dry in the malthouse, of the quiet Germans moving about the brewery. There could be no connection. John Henkel and William wouldn't have been mixed up with places like these.

She was tired. She had been up since seven. Paul was exaggerating. He would like to have her give up her work and marry him. That was the reason he talked this way.

2

MONDAY morning Sara went over to the brewery at four. It was still cool. Before the heat clapped down over the city the air was fresh. Sara felt rested. Her doubts of Saturday night were gone. The cleanness of the brewery, the neat flower plot in front, the ivy on the gray stone, the many-paned windows glowing pink in the morning sun, were proof that everything was right.

Gottfried was surprised to see her. His solemn face broke into a pleased smile. "Guten Morgen, Missus Henkel. You make it early!"

"Of course, Gottfried. I said I would. I want to see the very beginning."

Sara stood watching the ground grains and boiling water pouring into the cavernous depths of the mash-tub. The only light in the tub entered through a sliding door on the opposite side like the one through which she was looking. The light caught the flat surfaces of the slowly revolving blades that stirred the contents. Finally the blades were covered over by the deep-moving mash. Gottfried closed the slide door. Sara laid her hands on the mash-tub; it was hot to the touch.

She liked watching Gottfried. He made a motion with his

hand or muttered a word in German and the kettle man seemed to understand what he meant.

"See here, Missus Henkel!" Gottfried called. "Here are the recording thermometers that show the exact temperature at every moment. Wilhelm heard about them from somebody who had studied in the old country. He had them come from Germany. Here are some recordings he, himself, made. I keep them as example to the foreman." Gottfried handed her a circular sheet on which the mechanical pen had dragged a steady line.

"See here, this climbing line! That is the heat where we get the right malt sugars; they are for the tongue! And here we fix the albumins for making that creamy Henkel foam, that is for the eye. There it must be held to keep your yeast healthy . . . you got to think of everyting."

Sara held the paper in her hand. She was no longer listening. It was suddenly as though Gottfried had handed her a note from William.

She was sitting in the office that was hers now, dictating a letter, when she saw Win's towhead emerging from the open door of the barn loft. She stopped in the middle of a sentence and pushed back her chair.

"Adolf, you finish it. I want to see what on earth the children are doing up above the stable. It worries me when Charlie isn't with them." She was out of the room before Adolf could offer to go, a sudden fear at her throat. Win played around the big stable often, but she didn't want him there alone. She ran across the yard, her skirts kicking out above her flying heels.

Win saw her and shouted. He had Billy beside him in the open door.

"Stay there, Win; don't move. Keep hold of Billy's hand."

They mustn't come near the brewery any more. It scared her so.

"The children . . ." she was panting. The stableboy looked up in surprise.

He smiled. "Ja, they play Haus!"

"Mama, look! We have lots of furniture." Win ran over to the head of the stairs excitedly. Sara stared around the big loft room over the stable. Chairs and tables were piled on top of each other. Against one wall leaned a big mirror. There was a long counter, a bar! Sara turned back to Win. He had made a house with the chairs laid on their sides, their iron legs covered by horse blankets.

"Do you want to go in, Mama? You have to crawl down," Win explained. "Maybe you wouldn't like it very much."

"No, darling. Win, you mustn't play up here any more. You mustn't bring Billy over here; he might fall down the stairs. Come now, dear. You run back over to Pearl and tell her you want some cookies."

"But, Mama, it's almost the best place in the whole brewery and Charlie said we could play here." Win looked at her with aggrieved eyes.

"Next week, dear, Pearl is going to take you up to the lake. Remember what fun we had that other time?"

"Are you coming too?" Win asked dubiously.

"No, not right away. Mama has things to do."

Belle had wanted to take the children before and she hadn't wanted them so far away. As Belle said, the brewery was no place for children. What if Belle knew they were playing with old barroom furniture, furniture from some saloon!

Sara carried Billy down the steep stairs and saw him and Win on their way down the hedge-bordered path. She watched them go: Win's light head and stocky little figure, Billy's brown curly hair and slender body. Win turned and waved and Sara waved back. She would send Pearl up to the lake with them tomorrow. Their lives mustn't be any different from other boys' because their mother ran a brewery.

Sara walked swiftly back. She was by now a familiar figure around the brewery. " 'ne hübsche Frau" the men told their wives who asked curiously about Missus Henkel. Sometimes they shrugged a little, but loyalty to old John Henkel and William made them all respectful. Sara's eyes were angry as she came into the office.

"Adolf, get Gottfried for me."

"Gottfried," Sara said as soon as he was sitting in the chair by her desk. "What connection has the brewery with those filthy, disreputable saloons on Water Street?"

"Why, they sell our beer!" Gottfried's shoulders raised ever so slightly by way of disclaiming any sense of responsibility.

"Why?" Sara shot out the question sharply.

"Why? Because Henkel's beer ist the best they can get; better than Milwaukee beer even."

Sara shook her head. "We own their furniture, don't we?"

"Well, in certain cases. John Henkel was alwus kind. If some honest saloonkeeper needed a little help . . . but all breweries do that. In the old country, the government . . ."

"I saw the furniture up in the barn loft. There's enough to furnish two or three saloons right now. Do we own their places, too?"

"Well, you see, Missus Henkel, it's this way . . ."

"Jerry's Place and the Tavern and McGinnis' and Heine's?"

"Heine Gratz ist a fine man. There's no more respectable barkeeper in town."

"But what about Jerry's or McGinnis'? It's a disgrace even to have Henkel's beer sold down there."

Gottfried frowned. "If you make bread to sell, are you going to say some poor bum along the docks can't buy your bread? Just good people can buy?"

"Oh, that isn't the point, Gottfried. I don't want us to be part owners of places like those. It's true that we hold their mortgages or own their buildings, isn't it?"

"Well, I tell you the truth, Missus Henkel, it ist a bad system. It wasn't so when John Henkel started. But now all the breweries do that way. Wilhelm didn't like it. Just before he died he took back all the furniture from a saloon out on Diamond Street; it's a no-good place."

"In the future we're going to sell beer—that's all," Sara said quietly. "We're not going to be tied up with any of those places."

"But, Missus Henkel, it would ruin us. They would go to the Old Mill Brewery or get in their beer from Milwaukee or Detroit. In business you haf to do what your competitors do."

"I don't think we do, Gottfried. Henkel's has always stood for the best beer and we ought to be able to sell it without bribing those places to buy it. How shall I go about it?" Sara picked up a pencil.

Gottfried shook his head. "Missus Henkel, you don't want to do a thing like that too sudden. You haven't been in the brewing business so long; maybe we ought to talk it over at the directors' meeting."

"A directors' meeting just means Marie and Ottilie and the three of us here now. If you and Gottfried back me . . ." Sara's eyes were on Gottfried's troubled face. She looked at Adolf, who sat at his desk scowling.

"Of course, Missus Henkel, we'll back you, but I don't want to see you do anything you'll be sorry for," Gottfried said.

"Missus Henkel, it ain't so bad as it seems. Take Jerry's Place: that's bad. But there's plenty of saloons, 'specially in the German part of town where I live, that are a credit to Henkel's. Wimmin go in or send their kids for a pail of beer to drink at home and their men drop in maybe for the evening and have one or two glasses of beer the whole time. Some of those places are more respectable as the Gentlemen's Club from what I hear." It was a long speech for Adolf.

Sara smiled. Her father was a charter member of the Gentlemen's Club and Paul's father and Paul and George all belonged.

But she was firm. She went steadily ahead to separate Henkel's from the saloons. No one, she told herself, would be able to say that the Henkel Brewing Company owned or ran disreputable places in order to sell their beer.

During the next week Sara met a varied assortment of saloonkeepers in her office. She depended on Gottfried or Adolf for an estimate of the different men.

"You see, Missus Henkel, you don't know very many saloonkeepers," Gottfried told her hesitatingly. "In the first place, you got to remember that most of 'em are . . . are proud of their places. They just think Henkel's helping them is the natural thing for us to do." He was worried.

"I know, Gottfried. I don't want to hurt their pride or work any hardship on them."

The owner of the saloon was almost invariably bewildered and incredulous when she told him that the brewery could no longer hold his mortgage or own even the fixtures in his saloon.

But before he had recovered enough to become indignant she went on to offer him the furnishings for some nominal sum; sometimes for as little as a dollar, and to tell him that she could arrange for the transfer of his mortgage.

"And, by golly!" Gottfried said to Adolf, "you know what she did? She got some of her west-side banker friends to carry the mortgages on the good fellows!"

A few were unreconciled to her changes. One saloonkeeper was belligerent. He leaned over Sara's desk and pounded with his fist to emphasize his words.

"I ain't buyin' no furniture!" he shouted at her.

With heightened color but keeping her voice steady Sara said, "Very well, if you prefer we will send a dray to collect the furniture, Mr. McGinnis."

Mr. McGinnis was a man who did not back down easily.

"And you can get your barrels, too. The Old Mill people treat their saloonkeepers right."

"Certainly, Mr. McGinnis, if you don't feel that Henkel's beer is the best we don't want you to buy it."

"You'd have thought she was the old man, himself, the way she handled him," Adolf told Gottfried afterwards.

"McGinnis bought heavy from us," Gottfried said mournfully.

Thirty saloons had been tied to the Henkel Brewing Company by their obligations. In the end, Sara's change of policy cost the brewery the active antagonism of only four of them. The furnishings of these four were brought back and dumped for the time being at one side of the cobbled yard, a dejected pile of iron-legged tables and chairs and several birchwood bars, stained to look like mahogany.

The morning the last load was returned Gottfried and Sara stood in the yard watching the furniture added to the pile.

"Only four places is not so bad," Gottfried said, "if it was sure that was all! One driver told me today when he come back from his route that one of his regular customers told him, 'No more Henkel's beer; we get from Milwaukee or

Old Mill!'" Gottfried did not tell Sara that the drivers said they were taking plenty of joshing about that widow of Henkel's.

"We'll just have to make it up some other way, Gottfried," Sara said. Her eyes rested on the pyramid of tables and chairs in the corner of the yard. "We must make people feel that Henkel's beer is best."

"We could maybe put a sign up where you turn into the brewery and haf it read in big letters: HENKEL'S IS BEST!" Gottfried suggested.

"Oh, no, Gottfried, we've got to do it more subtly than that!" Sara waved her lace-edged handkerchief at him, laughing.

"Subtly is it! Hmpf!" Gottfried snorted as he went back up the stairs to the brewhouse.

Sara was glad that the children were with Belle at the lake. She did not mind going home to the empty house, she had so much to think about. Tonight it was too hot to get supper. The only thing in the icebox that looked cool was a bottle of beer that Gottfried had given her to taste; it was a lighter beer, Gottfried said, than the beer they had been making; more like the beers they sold in the East.

She poured it into one of her best glass goblets and sliced cheese wafer-thin on bread. She set it all on a tray and carried it through the empty house to the porch. Even as she started to sip it she saw the picture it made: the clear, golden beer, in fine glassware instead of a mug. And it tasted differently out here on the porch. The tartness of the beer was refreshing this hot night. If people could drink it like this . . . she looked out across the lawn and the garden to the park that lay between the brewery and their own land.

This was the way people drank beer in Europe. She remembered the beer gardens in Vienna and Germany that William used to tell about. They had the finest orchestras and people took their whole families. They sat under the trees, William said.

The idea of having a beer garden over in the park beside the river came naturally: they could have music, a good orchestra, and tables out under the trees. There was plenty of room. She could see how it would be: lanterns in the trees and waitresses running back and forth, waitresses in German or Austrian costume with bunches of radishes and scallions in their belts. They handed them out as they served the beer, William said. They could serve German lunches; Mother Henkel knew how to make those special German foods. The orchestra would play the Strauss waltzes Mama loved. It would be beautiful. She could make it the fashionable thing to do. People who had never heard of Henkel's beer would come there and drink it.

She was still sitting on the porch when Paul came up the walk.

"Paul!" She met him at the steps. "Paul, I've separated from the saloons."

"Oh, Sara!" Paul sat down on the step and laughed. "I thought you were really eager to see me and it was just to tell me that!"

"No, there's something else, Paul. I'm going to have a beer garden; a lovely one, the kind they have in Europe. I'm going to call it 'Der Sommer Garten.' "

3

EVERYONE discouraged her starting the garden so late in the summer, but Sara could not wait a whole year. "We have August and September and October," she had insisted. And once started, the idea flourished. Many of the older employees in the brewery had known such gardens in the old country. Whether it was getting old Fritz who swept and cleaned in the brewery to make flowerboxes for the lower windows of the brewery, or the cooper, Chris Schmidt, to make tables, she had only to explain her idea and her workers were quick to say, "Jawohl, Missus Henkel, ja." Everyone seemed to know someone else that might be useful. "Mein Brüder, he wait table"; or "Mein wife . . ." A German orchestra was gathered from members in the Arbeiter Verein, to which Adolf belonged. "I play the horn," Adolf admitted proudly.

And by the middle of September Der Sommer Garten was established. The colored lanterns glowed from the trees. Carriages were parked all the way down the avenue and in around the stables of the brewery. Along the curb usually stood two or three shining automobiles in all their splendor of paint and brass.

"Gerade wie die alt country," one German told another, and they came. But there were women in large hats and long white silk gloves from the west side, too, and gentlemen with gold-headed canes who ordered lavishly.

And the music! The orchestra sat in the cobbled courtyard of the brewery and played Strauss waltzes that floated out to the avenue. Every evening except Sunday the beer garden was open, and each night, except for rainy nights, there was a larger crowd. The élite of Armitage City were returning from the summer resorts and they flocked to Der Sommer Garten.

One idea led to another. Sara could think of things to do faster than she could carry them out. On one point she was firm: the waiters must handle the beer not as though it were a cheap drink, but as though it were the finest. It was served in thin glasses that were polished to sparkling. Except for coffee no other beverage was served. Charlie's son and two of the lads from the bottling works policed the grounds. No one could enter who did not pass their keen young eyes. When Sara tried to tell them what the standards should be, young Otto Freehahn nodded his close-cropped blond head vigorously.

"I know, Missus Henkel."

Sara, herself, was always there in a long black dress that ruffled softly against the grass as she walked, and a big black hat and long gloves. She had her own table where she sat all evening with her one glass of beer, smiling and nodding at the people who had known her as Sara Bolster. Some of them she knew came only out of shocked curiosity. She smiled more warmly at the foreign-looking women who came with their whole families. Sometimes the babies cried, but the crying was lost under the swing and melody of the music. Sometimes Gottfried Werner sat beside her at the table, looking more than ever like a statesman in a stiff white collar and big satin tie, with his black broadcloth suit well brushed. The brewery workers often stopped to introduce their wives, shyly, not knowing how to leave until Sara suggested a table for them.

Tonight she sat alone at her table. She had no need to count the crowd. Even Gottfried, who had been sure the idea was impossible, admitted that it was a success. Few things had ever caught on in Armitage City like Der Sommer Garten.

"And it isn't the money for their glass of beer, so much," Sara kept reminding Gottfried, her cheeks pink with excitement, her eyes shining. "It's that they will come to associate the music and the food and the pleasant evening with Henkel's good beer, Gottfried!"

Gottfried smoothed his mustaches and muttered something about "Time will tell" and bethought himself of an errand in the brewery. At night when he was over here he could not keep from going into the brewhouse to look at the day's temperature charts. Or into the fermenting cellar to arouse a sluggish yeast in one vat or check an overactive one in another by a hair's-breadth turn of its brine-coil valve.

Sara pulled off the hand of her long glove and tucked it in at the wrist. She picked up the glass of cold beer and sipped it slowly. Even yet she was not fond of the taste, but it was pleasant sipping it under the trees. She took out of her beaded bag the letter she had had yesterday from Belle. She turned to the paragraph at the end.

You know how difficult a position you have put me in by insisting on running the brewery. But now to hear that you are running a common beer garden! Everyone at the lake is talking about it. I do think you might think of your family.

And the letter from Papa, written in his clear handwriting: she could read it easily even in the softly colored light from the hanging lantern above her table.

Your Mother and I have always expected that our girls would engage only in enterprises that were becoming to gentlewomen.

You have always been the most headstrong of our girls. . . . I do not say because of that that you have not been the most lovable . . . but perhaps I have not restrained you sufficiently. Your Mother and I regret your taking that position on the paper, your marriage, but, most of all, your going into a business that must, of necessity, lower you in all eyes.

And now this latest venture! Mr. Healey and Mr. Ingalls have already spoken to me of it, censuring me, I know, in their minds. My dear Sara, a lady cannot run a brewery nor operate a "beer garden" without sacrificing her dignity and self-respect.

We were going to stay the month, but we are returning from the lake at the end of the week because we are too disturbed over all this to enjoy vacationing farther. The boys are both well. . . .

"Well, Sara!" Sara glanced up quickly. Sudden color rushed into her face, but she did not put out her hand.

"Good evening." Derrick VanRansom had grown heavier; he was still a pattern of fashion, with a flower in his buttonhole. His hair was beginning to gray.

"Sara, I want you to meet Mrs. VanRansom."

Sara bowed coolly, glancing only for an instant at the woman on Derrick's arm.

"You've made a great thing out of this. Mr. VanRansom's told me about you; he said you always were the smartest of the Bolster girls," Mrs. VanRansom said.

"And the prettiest, barring not even my former wife," Derrick added.

Sara could think of nothing to say. Unconsciously she crumpled the letter she held in her hand. Derrick had treated Belle so badly and now he dared to introduce this Flora Bailey whom everyone knew . . .

Derrick understood. She saw the pressure of his hand on Flora's arm. "Well, I didn't think you had it in you, Sara, but I congratulate you on your nerve," he said.

At that moment, a chunky man in shirtsleeves appeared at the table so suddenly he seemed to have burst out from between the elm trees. Otto Freehahn had him by the arm, but the man was strong enough to drag Otto along with him.

"I see her. I talked to her once before; lemme go!"

"Missus Henkel, he got in back of the stable when I wouldn't let him in by the gate," Otto explained.

"Hello, McGinnis," Derrick said in an off-handed manner before Sara could speak.

The man hesitated. "Hello, VanRansom, I got something to say to Missus Henkel."

"And she'll listen to you, I'm sure, if you can say it decently. Mrs. Henkel, I want you to meet Mr. McGinnis."

Sara was standing now, the letter crumpled in her hand, all the color gone from her face. She was thankful that her table was so far to the side, that the music went on above their conversation.

"What did you want, Mr. McGinnis?" Sara's voice trembled a little. An unreasoning panic made her heart beat faster. She did not know that she stepped closer to Derrick.

The waiter spoke to Ernest Hoffmyer, who led the orchestra. He nodded and raised his baton a little higher, and the music swelled to cover over any angry words at the third table along the edge; incredibly gay music, incredibly sweet, lifting, swaying; heads moved with it.

"Lady, you says you ain't going to own no more saloons. You say it's better for us saloonkeepers that we ain't tied up to a brewery and dish out a lot of damned stuff about good-will. Then, by God, you go and open up a saloon of your own and steal our business. You ain't foolin' me!"

"That's enough, McGinnis; get moving," Derrick growled at him.

"No, wait." Sara's hand moved up to her throat nervously. Then her mind cleared. "Mr. McGinnis . . ." Sara, who could never remember names, called his easily. "I'm not stealing your business. What I'm offering here is something different from anything the saloons can offer. Walk around and count the number of people you recognize as your regular customers. Most of the people here never drank beer in a public place before I made it fashionable. They come here because of the music; and because they want to see how I look running a beer garden," she ended a little bitterly.

McGinnis jerked at his trousers and straightened his suspenders over his shoulders. He looked around at the crowd for a moment. "Well, maybe you're right, Missus Henkel. It got me so damned . . . so mad, your throwing us over. I've bought from John Henkel ever since I been in business." He looked at the others a little sheepishly.

"Naturally," Sara said. "But you understand now; I'm not really hurting your business here.—John, give Mr. McGinnis a glass of beer before he goes," Sara said to the waiter who hovered near. "Good night, Mr. McGinnis." She inclined her head briefly toward Derrick and Flora.

"Good night, Mrs. VanRansom; Derrick. I'm going home early so I'll say good night." She made her way between the tables. At one table a woman sat holding a sleeping baby in her arms. Her husband sat beside her, his glass of beer in his hand, listening to the orchestra. A young girl at another table was holding hands with a young German boy. She recognized Jane Tilden and the younger Ingalls boy in a group at a table. Sara smiled, seeing how well the waiters were doing, though they were so new at it.

She saw Martha Hathaway, who had gone to Madame LaVerne's with her. There were the Pettingills and the Stouts. Sara's smile froze a little going by them, nodding to them, feeling they had come out of curiosity.

"It's beautiful, Mrs. Henkel. Upon my word, I wouldn't have believed it possible," old Judge Healey called out, waving his gold-headed cane.

Sara usually stayed until the orchestra stopped playing, but tonight she hurried along the path toward her own house. The house seemed dark and lonely. She could never become quite used to going in alone and locking the front door and turning out the light. If only William were living! Without warning, the sense of missing William came at her so sharply she clung to the newel post an instant. Then she went on upstairs.

She sat on the bed without lighting the light. It was close and hot in the house after sitting all evening under the trees. The music came clearly through the window; too clearly. It made her loneliness more bitter. It made the beer garden seem too near.

Tonight she would like to go home, over to the west side where no one ever talked of beer. She laid her head on the pillow and relived the whole evening. Mr. McGinnis had frightened her. And what if all the other saloonkeepers felt the same way? What if Der Sommer Garten had only gone well because it was new? Her expenses for running it were high and there were only six weeks more before cold weather set in.

People were talking about her. "The Brewer's Dame," someone had called her. . . . It was the carpenter, way back when they were building the house. . . . The dark bedroom oppressed her. "A lady cannot run a brewery nor operate a 'beer garden,'" Papa had written. What had she gotten herself into?

They were clapping loudly across in the garden. The music had stopped. She waited, wondering why they didn't begin again. She heard the sound of horses on the avenue; were people leaving so early? What if some other saloonkeeper had come to break up the beer garden! She should be there. She sat up, ready to go back over. Then the music began again.

She had danced to that music at the Ingalls' dance, years ago when she was a young girl; the night that Paul had kissed her. If she had married Paul, how different her life would have been!

There was nothing wrong in what she was doing. People went to Europe and raved about the charming beer gardens. It was charming here under the trees. If her old friends on the west side found it unladylike, shocking, they could stay home. There were enough of the "foreign element" who would come. She thought of the woman with her baby and the young couple holding hands and the thought comforted her.

And the brewery sales were increasing. People were talking about Henkel's beer who had never heard of it before. She was looking forward to the directors' meeting at the end of the month. Adolf Steiner's report would convince Marie. She must remember to tell Marie that Henkel's beer was on the beverage list at the Armitage Arms again.

4

SUNDAY-NIGHT supper at the Bolsters was always the same: the table laden with things to eat, chicken and jellied tongue for Papa, deviled eggs for George, ginger pear for Belle, Mama's favorite orange bread, potato salad in the green water-lily bowl for Anne, sugar cookies for the children, coffee.

"If you stay awake Sunday night, I always think it's rather nice; you have the service to think of and Mr. Oldsworth's sermon and whom you saw at church," Mrs. Bolster was fond of saying as she poured herself another cup of fragrant black coffee.

But tonight it was not the same Sara felt. Mama had kissed her with a certain sadness and held her off at arms' length as she had used to do when Sara came home from boarding school. She didn't ask, "And what did Madame LaVerne say of my girl?" as she used to, but the same questioning look was in her eyes.

Sara had not been in the house ten minutes before Belle said, "Sara, you must give up this absurd business and sell the brewery. I can't tell you how embarrassed I was when I saw Mrs. Jolan at the lake."

"Mrs. Jolan?"

"Yes, she's the head of the W.C.T.U. movement here, you know."

"Oh," Sara said. She lifted Billy up again on her lap, kissing him in his fat neck where the brown hair made deep curls. "It's been the longest month, Belle, and I've missed you all so." But now that they were back Sara felt the criticism in their minds that held her off at arm's distance. No one mentioned the brewery again until George brought it up at the table.

"I heard about your cutting loose from the saloons, Sara. Good work—if it doesn't mean too great a loss for you."

Sara was aware of Mama's pained expression and Dor's murmured, "George, at the table I do think . . ."

Sara smiled. "It seems the only thing to do. Making good beer is one thing, but being part owner of saloons like those at the lower end of Water Street is another."

"That's right. If the brewers were smart they'd all do what you've done. It's the saloon more than the stuff itself that Belle and her friends are fighting, isn't it?" George turned to Belle.

The mention of her business, of beer and saloons, at the table was a grave breach of taste in Mama's eyes. Papa pushed back his chair and left the room. Sara flushed hotly. She had worn a new dress tonight; the first new dress since her mourning things. It was black, too, but it was trimmed with pink ribbon and a row of pink buttons ran from the neck to the hem. She had put it on especially for tonight, with a little velvet bow in her hair. The girls should see that she cared how she looked, even if she was running a brewery.

"Paul spoke at the Fourth of July celebration, Sara, and he was wonderful," Dor said quickly to get George away from the subject of the brewery.

"What did he talk about?" Sara asked, wondering that Paul hadn't mentioned his speaking.

"Oh, loyalty to the country and the need for the same spirit of service that the early patriots had."

"How original!" Sara said teasingly.

"All right, but wasn't he fine, Mama, when he spoke about stamping out corruption and evil that are the cankerworms at the roots of our culture?" Dor exclaimed.

Mrs. Bolster nodded. "Fine, dear. Your father says he wouldn't be surprised to see him Governor, some day."

"Cankerworms! What did he mean by cankerworms?" Sara went for the dictionary. This was like old times again. Mama used always to send them for the dictionary to settle disputes. Sara came back reading aloud: " 'a cankerworm, figuratively, anything that corrodes, corrupts, consumes slowly.' "

"You know, political corruption, liquor . . ." Belle stopped in confusion.

"Well? Go on," Sara said. "Beer isn't hard liquor, if that's what you're thinking. People don't sit down to get drunk on beer. You should see the people who come to our Sommer Garten."

"I shouldn't care to," Belle said. "Martha Hathaway said she was there one evening and saw Derrick with *Mrs.* Van-Ransom!"

In an instant the whole atmosphere had changed. Mama made a little sniffing grimace as though Derrick and Flora Bailey and, indeed, Martha Hathaway, were beneath interest.

"Let's go in the other room and have some music, Belle," Mrs. Bolster said. "I've missed that all summer.

Belle's fingers followed each other across the keys in a succession of chords. George tuned his violin. Papa laid his cigar on the ashstand and came over to the piano.

The King of Love my Shepherd is, whose Goodness faileth never;
I nothing lack if I am His, and He is mine forever.

The music made everything seem natural again. Sara forgot to sing, remembering that they were singing this same hymn that time when William came to call. She could almost see him coming in the doorway. She remembered how she had looked at him against the background of her family. And she had gone with him out of here into such a different world. She was not sorry, even after all that had happened.

Belle sang "Drink to Me Only with Thine Eyes" for them while George played the accompaniment on his violin. Then they went out to sit on the long, narrow, front porch.

"Do you remember how the wistaria vine climbed the porch of our old house?" Mama asked wistfully.

"Dorothy Elizabeth is going to start dancing school in the fall. Are you going to start the boys, Sara?" Dor asked irrelevantly, so that Mama wouldn't go on about the house.

"Oh, I hadn't thought about it. Win is so young," Sara answered.

"Did Mrs. Rader send you an announcement of the opening of her class?"

"No," Sara said, "but I'd send him there if any place."

"She probably just overlooked it," Dor said, but something in her tone of voice caught Sara's attention.

"You tell her, Dor, that Sara's little boy is old enough for dancing school," Mama suggested.

"Don't bother. I shan't send him for another year or so," Sara put in quickly.

The phone ringing inside the house broke in on their talk. It was for Sara.

"Wouldn't you think she'd feel foolish going over to the brewery every day?" Anne asked as Sara left the porch.

"George says she's the only woman in the whole place!" Dor said.

Sara came back with her coat on. "Gottfried called me. He wants me to come over to the brewery. George, will you drive me over and leave me? Then you'll have the carriage to bring Belle and the boys home."

"Sara, you can't go over there at night!" Mama said. "Why, it's almost nine o'clock!"

"Of course, I can. I told Gottfried I'd be right over."

"Papa, Sara mustn't!" Mama stood up quickly, her handkerchief sliding down over the silk folds of her skirt to the floor.

"Sara, this business has got to stop," Mr. Bolster said firmly. "I can't have a daughter of mine running a brewery and a beer garden, traipsing around at night like this; you're making yourself a common laughingstock."

Sara stood facing him on the top step of the porch. "I'm sorry, Papa, but I've started; I'm going to keep on with it," she said quietly.

Mr. Bolster went on into the house. The door made a little bang behind him. The girls didn't speak. Mama sighed.

"Good night, dears," Sara said sweetly. George went with her silently. "Hurry, George, please. Gottfried sounded worried. I can't imagine . . ."

George drove the horse at a smart trot across the bridge and over to the east side.

"Sara, in a business like this something can happen any time. It's no kind of a thing for a woman to be in. You are getting yourself talked about. Naturally your father was upset. He's worried about his business affairs. I'm afraid he's going to lose his property down on the river."

"Oh, he mustn't do that. He thinks the city will build out that way some day. I can help him," Sara said happily.

When they drove into the brewery yard, Sara was out as soon as the carriage stopped. The brewery towered up like a great stone fortress. It was dark except for two of the high windows and a warm glow of light from the engine room.

The night watchman appeared out of the dark. "Good evening, Missus Henkel. Mr. Werner is waitin' for you in the fermenting cellar."

"Thank you, George. I'll be all right."

"But, Sara, hadn't I better stay and see . . ."

"Oh, no," Sara said firmly. "There's no need of that."

Inside, the brewery was redolent of a heavy grainy smell. Sara glanced up the stairs to the brewhouse. The light from the brewhouse threw the shadow of the stairs on the white-washed wall. It picked out the copper mugs hanging on their hooks or standing along the shelf by the deserted Sternewirth. She had never been here before when it was so still. She pushed open the heavy door and made her way down steps, across a passageway, down again to the fermenting cellar. She opened the door and felt the clammy cold around her. The flame from the candle in its iron bracket guttered in the draft. It was eerie. Sara shivered. Then she saw Gottfried up on the ladder.

"Gottfried!"

"Missus Henkel," Gottfried's voice boomed out of the half-lighted room. She picked up the skirt of her new dress and went around the great oak rounds. Gottfried had climbed down from the ladder standing against the last barrel. He brought another ladder and laid it against the barrel's side. "Missus Henkel, I want you to see . . ."

Sara climbed up the rude ladder, holding her skirt in one hand, holding on with the other. Gottfried climbed up the other ladder beside her. They were both standing where they could look over the open contents of the vats. She had never seen Gottfried's face so troubled.

"Missus Henkel, I come in here late tonight to check temperatures an' I didn't like the looks. See, it is fifteen days here an' it don't clear. The fermentation's off. Look here!" He pointed to the vat whose surface was piled with bubbles, like soap bubbles.

Sara stared at the discolored froth over the surface of the vat.

"See, es ist muddy, what you call foxy; it won't settle." Only from Gottfried's tone of voice could Sara tell how serious the calamity was. "Wild yeast . . . mycoderma," he pronounced solemnly. "I have had it under Wilhelm's microscope."

Sara listened without speaking. The fermenting cellar was ominously still, only half lighted. The stone floor was wet, the dampness increased the penetrating cold. The great oak vats topped with froth, that moved perceptibly as though by breathing, crowded the big cellar.

"Is that very bad, Gottfried?" Sara asked finally.

Gottfried balanced his heavy body against the vat. He lifted his hands hopelessly in the air. His mustaches drew down forlornly. "Wild yeast ruins the beer!"

"What can you do?" Sara asked, feeling herself stupid.

"Nothing is to do but drain the beer all out in the sewer."

"But, Gottfried, how much would we lose?"

Gottfried's face took on its sagacious look. "All the beer in the cellar; about three thousand dollar worth." He climbed down the ladder. "I can't see where it got infection." He looked around the cellar again in perplexity. Sara climbed down stiffly and stood waiting.

Three thousand dollars! That would swallow up the

profits from the beer garden! Just as they were making progress. How could anything like this happen? How could Gottfried let it? She walked between the vats to the end of the aisle, feeling the water through the thin soles of her slippers. She waited there for Gottfried. Beneath the window it was a little warmer. She could just catch a breath of air from the outside that cut freshly across the suffocating dampness of the cellar.

After his tour of inspection, Gottfried walked over to her, shaking his head. "Ach, was ist los? Our cellar man will say, 'The devil has crept in!' Always it is the devil when something goes wrong!"

Gottfried jerked his head up. "Gott im Himmel! The window! That's how the devil got in. The wind blew in dust and wild yeast off the roof here. Dumheit! Only the other window with cloth screens is to be opened. That's it, Missus Henkel!" He looked at Sara as though she had made a great discovery. "See, the vat nearest the window is the worst!"

All the way back to his office in the brewhouse, he explained to her the way it had happened. His sorrow over the loss was lightened somewhat by finding out its cause.

Sara looked in William's microscope at the queer-shaped cells. Gottfried, himself, holding up the flask he had filled with the yeast, seemed like some medieval necromancer. The little office with its window looking down on the huge brewkettle and the mash tub was a magician's tower.

"But isn't there something you can do to save all that beer, Gottfried? I can't believe . . ."

Gottfried shook his head. "It ist all ruined, Missus Henkel. Wild yeast spoils cheese, spoils rice, spoils beer! That ist what that Pasteur, Wilhelm has the picture of, found out."

"But, Gottfried, three thousand dollars! That more than wipes out the profit from the beer garden!"

Gottfried shrugged mournfully. "That ist the way in a brewery! It happened so once before, when I first come to work for John Henkel. He was just starting out big; it was hard. Wait, I'll turn on more lights till you get down."

The big copper kettle that had been half hidden in the dark seemed to burst into rosy luster with the light. Sara laid her hand against its smooth surface as she did nearly every time she went by it.

"It's beautiful. It seems like the heart of the brewery," Sara said impulsively, glancing at the old man to see if he thought her foolish.

But Gottfried only nodded. "Sometimes I think brewing ist like a symphony in music. First, the largo, the heavy movement, grinding the malt, pouring in the rice, adding the water, lighting the fire; then the second movement, light . . ." Gottfried's pudgy hands became light. He held them out, his fingers spread, slightly curved. "That would be the beer fermenting, the little bubbles rising." He made the light music with his hands. His fingers danced to it. "Then the slow simple movement when the beer ist still in the cold cellar, and it comes out clear and sparkling like starlight." He broke off in embarrassment. "No fool like an old fool, Missus Henkel." He pulled at his mustache, and his eyes, which had been lighted by his own idea, seemed to become smaller and retire between the wrinkled folds of his eyelids.

"Why, Gottfried, I never thought of it like that," Sara said. "That's lovely."

She went ahead down the stairs from the brewhouse into the main hall and waited for Gottfried, clumping after her in the dark. He knew his way about the brewery as well as John Henkel.

Gottfried walked with her over to the house.

"It ist too bad. We was just going so good with the beer garden," he said heavily.

Sara was silent until they came to the porch steps. "We'll have to think of some way to make it up, that's all," she said stoutly.

"It's not so easy, Missus Henkel. We lost some sales when you . . ." he paused before he concluded generously ". . . when *we* cut off from the saloons." He shrugged. "Well, our report to the directors' meeting won't look so good as we thought, now. But it could be worse. Good night, Missus Henkel."

Sara tiptoed into the nursery to see the children. Belle heard her and called out: "The brewery didn't blow up?"

"No, it's still there."

"It's a pity," Belle said.

5 1906

"I AM leaving early this afternoon, Adolf. We'll let those letters wait," Sara said. "The directors' meeting isn't until Friday." She laid the crystal paperweight she had had on her desk at the *Courier* office on the unanswered letters and notes that were to be incorporated in her report for the directors' meeting.

It seemed a long time ago since the thought of the little meeting in the next room had made her nervous; since she had worried about Marie's attitude. If Marie still felt they should have sold the brewery she never said so; she was proud of the brewery's progress. And Ottilie was using the room over the stables, where the bar fixtures had been stored, for a studio; Sara could see from her desk the big glass window she had put in on the north side of the barn. Ottilie was up there today working away with her clay. If Belle and the girls could see her when she was working, they wouldn't think her odd or stolid. She was working on a horse's head. It pleased Charlie to have her using his newest horse for a model.

Above Sara's desk where the calendar advertising porcelain stoppers used to hang was a calendar bearing the caption: "Junge Crown Cork and Seal Co." The wire stoppers were no longer used at Henkel's. The little tin caps with cork lining had taken their place. On the calendar pad today's date was marked with a red ring: December 20, 1906 . . . Win's birthday.

Sara laid other papers in her desk drawer and closed it. She had promised the boys she would be home in time to play with them before dinner. She was going to take them to see *The Mikado* to celebrate.

"I'm going now, Adolf. It's Winthrop's birthday, today." Sara stood in front of the little mirror by the clothestree to put on her hat, but she hardly looked in it.

Adolf smiled. Even his eyes seemed to smile behind their thick lenses. "The little boy ist growing big. How old is he, Missus Henkel?"

"Win is ten, today, Adolf. And Billy will be six in April."

Adolf sucked in his breath in a way he had of expressing any emotion. "Oh, Missus Henkel, two wimmens telephoned and wanted to know why they didn't get souvenir sets of glasses from Henkel's, like somebody they know."

Sara pulled on her gloves. "Did you tell them we were only giving glasses where the order was at least five dollars for the month of November?"

"Yes. They say it was; but sometimes they buy from a saloon near them."

Sara frowned. "Well, I suppose you might as well give them a set. I like to see families have beer delivered to their homes. There's no reason why they have to buy from the saloons. I hope a lot of other women won't discover how much they love beer just so they can get a set of glasses free!" Sara said dryly.

"It was a good idea of yours, Missus Henkel. I bet the Old Mill and Weiss' ist red in the face they don't think of it!"

It was starting to snow as Sara came out of the brewery.

She could hardly make out the ship weathervane on top of the red stables, and the avenue beyond the gate to the brewery was completely veiled in the snow. She felt like a child let out of school early, leaving the brewery at this hour. More often than not she was at the brewery after the whistle had blown and the men had gone. At first, there had been so much to learn; it was all strange to her. Even Mother Henkel the last time she was down had patted her hand and said anxiously:

"Don't work too hard, mein Kind. You are too young." Absurdly her eyes had filled. Sometimes she, herself, forgot that she was still young at thirty-two.

Her family left her alone with her work. They tried to avoid any mention of the brewery, but always a faint air of reproach colored Mama's manner. Since Sara had offered to give Papa money to pay his taxes and he had refused, she had never spoken of her business to him. She often gave the girls little gifts of money and bought things for Mama. When the property Papa had owned was sold for taxes she read of it in the paper. Papa could be hard when he felt he was right.

She hurried along the path that had been paved now, between the brewery and the house. They would never train the hedge to grow across the entrance. The house was part of the brewery; the brewery was part of her life.

Gottfried was a good brewmaster, but he couldn't see beyond the brewhouse. Adolf was a good clerk. They were both slow to agree to anything new. They had objected bitterly to most of her changes, but only yesterday Gottfried had said contemptuously of the Weiss Brewery:

"They don't do enough business to tend to making beer; they gotta go out and set up saloons."

And Der Sommer Garten! This year they were going to

have an orchestra leader from Munich. It had been a good idea to start serving lunch and beer to people in their carriages along the curving driveway; the notion had caught on.

Sara turned the front doorknob quietly and tiptoed in to surprise the children. She stood behind the portières watching them. Winthrop and Billy were playing with the new blocks and soldiers on the rug.

"Here, Billy, we'll build a fort over here by the hearth and one by the bookcase and then we won't have to go way back to the big fort every time!" Win's voice was shrill with his own excitement. She wondered if he bossed Billy too much.

Billy's curly head was bent over two lines of soldiers he had drawn up by the table leg. "No, I want to make a tower on the fort, Win."

"But Billy! They send ammunitions out to the small forts and people can take refuge in them!" There was an echo of Winthrop Bolster's careful diction in Win's use of big words. His voice was tried but determined. William was absorbed in balancing a soldier on the block drawbridge.

"Uh-huh. I have to build a tower with the blocks, Win."

The library was warm with the coal fire and the big red rug. The light from the fire touched Win's light hair to gold and cast a ruddy glow over his sober little face. At ten, he had lost his chubby look and grown slender. He sat back on his heels, undecided. He hated so to have his ideas squelched. His lips pouted a little. Billy was as different as his brown curly hair was from Win's fair, straight hair. He was more handsome but he was never so carried away with the beauty of his own ideas. Win faced Billy triumphantly now.

"Anyway, Billy, it's my birthday and I can do what I want on my birthday! We'll build the little forts."

Sara stepped from behind the curtains quickly. Win saw her first.

"Mom!"

She threw out her arms to him. Then it was Billy's turn. "Bless you, darlings. I came home early as I promised. What time is it, Win?"

Win took out his father's watch from the tight pocket of his sailor suit. With infinite care and gravity he snapped open the fancy gold cover. Billy stood beside him, awed by the flashing beauty of the watch.

"Seven minutes after four," he announced proudly after careful study.

"Is it, Mom? Is that right?" Billy preferred adult confirmation.

Sara nodded. "Exactly right. Have you had fun? How did the new blocks go?"

"They're fine. Look, Mama, isn't this a good idea?" Win dropped the watch back in his pocket and was kneeling on the floor by the bookcase. "See, Mama, we can have littler forts in different places and then the soldiers won't have to carry food and ammunitions every time they march out."

Sara knelt down on the rug beside him, but her mind was not on the block forts. Why couldn't they establish storage houses in small towns in the state, and send their beer up there in the spring? There must be icehouses for ice storage. Perhaps she could rent storage space for her beer. Then the people in each town would get their beer right there . . . it would cut down on freight costs. . . .

"Isn't it, Mama? Isn't it a good idea?"

"Yes, Win, I think it is. I should think it would work," Sara said slowly, but she was not thinking of forts.

"Sara! I didn't hear you come in. The boys have been as good as gold all day."

Belle stood in the doorway. She was all dressed for the opera. She had gained, but she was very handsome with her hair brushed into a pompadour and her new green velvet gown that came to the floor.

"William," she said, "run and ask Pearl to bring the tea, and you and Win can have some with us. Sara, for pity's sake, take off your wraps and stay a while."

Sara laughed. She sat on the floor beside Win, her coat and hat still on. She took off her hat. Belle made her feel shabby. She glanced quickly at her hands. She had neglected them. The nails were cut down close, one was broken. Her forefinger was inky. "I must go and dress," Sara said.

They had grown into a family in these years. The boys were used to having Mama and Belle at either end of the table. Belle managed the house and looked after the boys when Sara was busy. She ignored Sara's business as much as she could and went her own way with her music and literary club and charities. In the spring and summer she made a great point of keeping the windows on the side toward the brewery closed and she objected strenuously to the boys' going near the brewery grounds when Der Sommer Garten was open.

If Win and Billy sometimes crawled through the hedge and went over there by way of the big red stable they understood that Aunt Belle should know nothing of it, and that if she did hear about it, Mama would back her up. For four years, now, on summer nights they had gone to sleep with the music from Der Sommer Garten. Belle wore the little white ribbon of the W.C.T.U. even on her evening dress as a tacit protest against the brewery.

"This is more grown-up than having a children's party," Win commented with satisfaction as he sat at the head of the table and served the roast that had been already carved in the kitchen. Now that he was ten Aunt Belle was to sit at his right and he at the end of the table across from Mama, and pretty soon he was going to carve by himself. The boys were resplendent in white serge suits and long white stockings and black pumps, and Sara wore her long black lace.

"Marie and Ottilie were here this afternoon and I sent the boys down to see their grandmother this morning," Belle said, virtuously.

"Oh, Mama, their house smells all spicy, and Grossmütterchen let me have every kind of cookie. I liked the Lebküchen best."

"I didn't. I liked the ones with all colored sugar on top," Billy said.

"Marie said they tried to keep Mrs. Henkel from baking Christmas cookies this year because she gets so tired out with it, but she wouldn't hear of it; so foolish of her!" Belle said.

"It wouldn't be Christmas to her without baking Christmas cookies," Sara answered. There was something about Mother Henkel that always made her think of William.

They drove to the academy in the cutter with a brave jingling of bells. Old Charlie drove them and his fur cap was salted with snow to match his beard. The sleighbells made Sara think of the night she had driven down to see Modjeska; that was the first time she had met William. Paul had been home from school for Christmas vacation. He had held her hand inside her muff.

She wondered if Paul would be there tonight. She had grown used to having him drop in every week or ten days when he was in town. She missed him when he didn't come. But she hadn't seen Paul for over a month now; not since the last night of the Sommer Garten in October, when he had asked her to marry him.

She liked knowing he was there; she counted on it, but she didn't love him, she thought a little wistfully. Her life was full . . . full enough; she was so busy at the brewery every day and so tired at night she often went to bed when the boys did. It wasn't the sort of life she had thought of for herself but it seemed to take all her energy.

What was the idea she had had this afternoon? The boys had been playing with their blocks . . . "See, Mom, we can have littler forts in different places," Win had said. Oh, yes, she had thought of renting storage space in icehouses for her beer. If she located them in the right towns, towns where there were plenty of Dutch and German people, the idea should work; it might expand their market.

Things were going more smoothly at the brewery, she thought with satisfaction. They had reduced the debt. But their market wasn't large enough to use the full capacity of the brewery. When William had made it so much bigger, he must have had plans to enlarge the market, too.

Win snuggled closer to her and slipped his hand into her muff. "Isn't it a nice birthday, Mama?" he whispered.

"Yes, it is, Win," Sara whispered back, ashamed that she had been so far away in her own thoughts.

6 1910

ON the calendar pad in Sara's office the date was marked with a red ring: December 20, 1910 . . . Win's fourteenth birthday.

Sara was leaving early. "Good-by, Adolf," she said, smiling. "Don't forget to bring the note!"

Adolf beamed. Even his glasses seemed to smile. He shook his head. "I could not forget that. It ist all tied with red ribbon like you said. What time, Missus Henkel?"

"Quarter of seven, Adolf!" she told him as though he didn't know it perfectly.

Sara hurried across the cobbled yard, through the grove of Der Sommer Garten. It should be called "Der Winter Garten" today with the snow on the ground. Some year they must put up a small building and use it for a Winter Garden. They could make it pay; there was nothing like it in the city. That would mean more work . . . she felt equal to work today. She came to the hedge-bordered walk that led to her own home.

Maybe it had been absurd, as Belle said, to celebrate the burning of the note on Win's birthday and have the directors to his birthday party, but she had worked so hard partly for the boys. She wanted the boys to share in the good feeling of achievement.

"H'lo, Mom!" Win came running down the steps to meet her. He was growing tall. Billy was after him in a minute.

"Hi, Mom!" Billy called out. She loved to have them meet her when she came home from the brewery.

The guests arrived promptly at quarter of seven. Ottilie and Marie brought a basket of German Christmas cookies from Mother Henkel, all the boys' favorite kinds, and two bottles of wine she had saved since the year before William's death.

Gottfried had lightened his usual black Prince Albert with a green vest, embroidered in tiny nosegays. Adolf's usually serious face never ceased to beam. They shook hands solemnly with the boys, calling them "Wintrop and Wilhelm."

"Congratulations, Wintrop," Adolf said. "And congratulations you, too, Wilhelm. It is a proud day for us all!"

"Oh, Sara, how clever of you!" Ottilie exclaimed as they went into the dining room. In the center of the white cloth surrounded by holly were two little forts built of children's play blocks, flanked by tall red candles. Between them was the canceled note for the debt on the Henkel Brewery, tied as Adolf had promised with red ribbon.

Sara saw the puzzled look in Gottfried's eyes. "It's a queer centerpiece, but it seems appropriate," she explained. "You see, it was on Win's birthday four years ago that I came home and found the boys building forts with their blocks, a main fort and several outlying forts. It gave me the idea of storage depots and renting space in the icehouses through the state to store our beer. That helped us so much in paying off the debt I thought we'd use them for decorations today."

"Missus Henkel, that ist good. The start of Henkel's shipping business, it was building blocks! They started us to be the biggest shipping brewery in the state." Gottfried's big laugh filled the dining room.

"Did I play with blocks four years ago, Mom?" Win asked, disbelief in his frown.

Gottfried offered grace solemnly with long pauses between his sentences.

"For the memory of those who have borne the name of Henkel before these boys, John Henkel and Wilhelm Henkel, we give Thee thanks, O Lord . . . and for this memorable occasion . . . and all it means . . . Gott sei dank."

"Amen," Adolf echoed after Gottfried.

Sara looked down the table at Win, who was standing to carve the turkey. He had taken lessons from his Grandfather Bolster and executed the task with some skill. His face in the candlelight was grave with responsibility.

She met Marie's eyes in mutual affection and pride in Win. How comfortable she felt with Marie now. Marie sat at Win's right hand; Gottfried at hers.

"Well, Missus Henkel, I propose a toast to Wintrop and wish him many happy birthdays more," Gottfried said. They drank it in Mother Henkel's grape wine. The boys had tiny liqueur glasses of wine too. Sara remembered that Mother Henkel thought wine was good for them. Sara saw Ottilie whisper something to Billy. Then he was standing, holding his little glass with its drop of red wine.

"To Mama!" he proposed, flushing.

It was as William would have loved it, Sara thought: gaiety touched with sentiment; old people and young together; a celebration!

"Remember the time, Missus Henkel, we started der Garten and peoples were slow coming that night!" Adolf said. They reminisced happily about the worries and successes they had been through.

"There are people who come from Detroit, now, to hear the orchestra in the Sommer Garten," Marie said proudly.

"Ja, it has sold us as much beer out of the city as we could sell if we owned all the saloons in town." Adolf nodded.

"Remember how that wild yeast set us back!" Gottfried said, shaking his head.

Sara glanced at the boys. Gottfried went on to explain to Billy how wild yeast worked. "You must read about Pasteur, Billy. Your father had great admiration for Pasteur!"

"Aunt Otti, I like my ship book-ends so much," Win said, remembering now that he hadn't thanked her.

"I used the weathervane on the brewery stable for a model, Win. Your father always liked it when he was a boy," Ottilie told him.

They couldn't have sold the brewery, Sara thought. It was so wrapped up with the family. It was to the Henkels what . . . What did take its place in the Bolster family? Not the Land Office. That lived only in Papa's mind. The house on the bayou, then, that had burned to the ground—that was it; that stood for more than anything else to Mama and the girls. It seemed an empty substitute beside a robust, growing business.

"When you run the brewery, young man," Gottfried was saying to Win. Sara met Win's eyes and smiled. Win would never run the brewery; neither would Billy. They would be free to go into medicine, engineering, whatever they wanted; the brewery would be there to back them. Tonight it was easy to forget how the brewery had changed her life.

"I gave the order for thirty-five turkeys," Marie said. "We're packing bigger baskets than ever this year." Marie had charge of the Christmas baskets for the employees of the brewery. She took great pride in them.

"Now, Wintrop, it is your birthday, so it is to you to burn the note!" Adolf said when they stood in front of the fire in the library after dinner. It looked like a small diploma, rolled and tied with ribbon. Adolf looked at Gottfried. Gottfried could always be relied upon for the proper oratory, but today he spoke almost with difficulty:

"So it would please John Henkel and Wilhelm."

Win threw the paper in on the fire. Billy stood beside him. The stiff paper burst into flame.

"Gott sei dank," Gottfried muttered under his breath. There were tears in his eyes. He shook Sara's hand.

"Sara, you've done well." It was lavish praise from Marie.

"We've all done well," Sara said, smiling happily at the little group. "It's taken us a long time but we've done it."

7

WINTHROP came around the corner of the porch after dinner whistling. At the corner the leisurely whistle gave way to a short, sharp whistle followed by two shorter blasts. Winthrop waited.

"Where you going?" Billy thrust himself halfway out of the front doorway, propping the screen door open by a wide straddle of his legs.

"Just over to see Chris. Wanna come?"

Billy hesitated. He liked going where Win went. Win was fourteen and had long trousers, at least for best. Win wasn't always willing for him to go along. But Billy didn't like it at Chris's; lately he had developed definite preferences as to companions.

Win continued down the walk toward the avenue. He had resumed his airy whistling. The airiness had a kind of taunt in it. Billy scuffed one sneakered foot. Then the screen door banged sharply after him.

"William!" Aunt Belle appeared behind the screen door. He looked back and saw her there, her face and arms looking queerly dark behind the black mesh of the screen.

"Yes, Aunt Belle."

"Where are you going, dear?"

"With Win; just around." They were polite to Aunt

Belle; that was one of the first laws of life, but they were not expansive. They avoided being specific out of principle.

"All right, dear. Don't sit on the ground, it's too cold yet; and come home by 8:30, we're going to the train to meet Mother."

Chris's was the second house in the string of little places across the street from the brewery. It was a good thing, Billy reflected sagely to himself, that their own house was set so far back from the street and that the trees and shrubs hid the little houses from view. Aunt Belle didn't like the little houses being there much; and Billy sensed that she didn't like Win's being so thick with Chris Schmidt, either.

Mr. Schmidt sat on the side porch smoking his pipe. Mr. Schmidt was a cooper and Win was always hanging around his shop, when he wasn't hanging around with Charlie.

"Wie geht's?" Mr. Schmidt raised his pipe in greeting.

Billy answered with a dignified "good evening." He noticed that Mr. Schmidt sat there in his stocking feet.

The kitchen was filled with bright colors and warm smells and people.

"Hi, Bill!" Chris called out. Chris was as short as Billy although he was a year older than Win. He had his hair cut off, German style. Secretly Billy looked at his head with loathing. The sight of it always moved him to run his hand through his own thick curly hair.

"Hello, Billy," Mrs. Schmidt said. Once he had come into the kitchen and found Mrs. Schmidt nursing the baby and she didn't even try to cover up her breast or anything. He had tried not to see it, but the sucking sound the baby made disgusted him.

Tonight, Mrs. Schmidt was filling a pail with cold water. "Here, Chris, pour out the water when you get there, like always, and mind you ask for Henkel's bock beer. Win, you can carry the beer chip. That's gut!" She laughed and gave him a little slap on the shoulder. "You carry it. Part goes into your Mama's pocket anyhow! You don't have to go buy bock beer, do you, Billy?"

"No," Billy said. They were just going to go for beer for Mrs. Schmidt, then. There was no fun in that. Chris was always doing some job and Win always helped him.

The three boys went down the plank walk to the back alley. "They give away pretzels as long as the bock beer lasts," Chris was saying. "And there'll be a German band; it goes from saloon to saloon an' we kids follow an' get more pretzels an' see the funniest things. One time, Pop Wienzel got feeling good and he got out an' danced in the street and then everybody danced."

"Hope they have pretzels this time," Win said, forgetting that he had had to refuse his dessert at dinner.

"Sure, they will! The bock beer only started two days ago; you oughta know."

But they didn't know. Mama never talked about the brewery at home. And she didn't like to have them go over to the brewery as much as they used to. They could go to the stable and talk with Charlie, or they could climb the stable stairs to Aunt Otti's studio and sit quietly watching her work.

Billy loved going up there. Aunt Otti had made a head of him that was in a museum in Detroit. Sometimes she let him play with the clay. She said he would do better than she did some day. They went to the office sometimes for Mama, but even yet they had only tasted beer on the sly with Chris. Win pretended to like it, just as he pretended to like smoking the time it made him sick, but Billy didn't even pretend to like it; it came up in his nose.

When they came to Voss's saloon, Chris pushed the swinging door open with his shoulder. William admired his sureness. It was brightly lighted even though it was early for customers. Billy shivered with pleasure at the warmth. The place smelled a little like the brewery, only a little sour. He looked small in the big mirror, so he squared his shoulders and walked up to the bar after Chris and Win with a consciously mannish swagger. The bar was high. He wondered why there weren't stools like there were at the soda fountain in the drugstore. He stood with both feet on the brass rail. Chris was right; there were baskets of pretzels, and pretzels hung across the face of the mirror.

"Bock beer for Papa, Mr. Voss," Chris said. "Watch out, there's water in the pail. I forgot to dump it out."

"Ja," Mr. Voss nodded. He rested the tin lard pail on the top edge of the white apron that enveloped him and pulled off the tight cover. "I was wondering where your papa was. Tell him we haf big times tonight; pinochle."

Billy tried turning around on the brass rail; leaning against the bar he surveyed the rest of the saloon. Everything shone: the glass globes of the electric lights, the white-topped tables over by the wall even the pretzels looked varnished. There was fresh sawdust on the floor. Two men sat at the table playing checkers. While one man made his move, the other drank from his mug.

Mr. Voss was so broad he was barely able to get through the door from the back room. The pail was full. The foam rode above the top.

"Tell your papa to come. After while we haf a band, maybe," Mr. Voss said, his eyes peeping merrily above the fat bulges of his cheeks. "Music, just like Henkel's Beer Garden we haf it!"

"Mrs. Henkel is our mother," Win said proudly. Billy's face turned a deep scarlet.

"Sure; these are the Henkel kids," Chris said.

"Well, well! Mama!" Mr. Voss called through a curtained doorway. "Come here, Mama!"

Mrs. Voss beamed. "Pleased to know you," she said. "Haf some pretzels? Here, take all you want."

"Sure, help yourself. I'd give you some bock beer only it's against the law," Mr. Voss encouraged them.

"I guess they get all the beer they want, eh?" Mrs. Voss chuckled.

Mr. Voss leaned comfortably on the bar. Billy stared in admiration at the size of his arms.

"Well, I sure thought it was hard when your Ma told me I gotta buy these fixings off'n her; but now, I guess . . ."

"We do better as is. Missus Henkel's a smart woman," Mrs. Voss announced firmly.

"When is the band goin' to start?" Win asked.

Chris pulled Win's arm. "Come on, I gotta get this home to Pa."

"Pretty soon now. Here, haf anodder pretzel." Mr. Voss came out from behind the bar and held the door ceremoniously for them.

They delivered the pail to Mrs. Schmidt and hurried back. The band was in front of the Heidelberg.

"Z'Lauterbach hab i mein'n Strumpf verlorn," Someone back of the swinging doors was singing the words to the band's music. Win climbed up on the fence next to the saloon. He waved his arms like a windmill to keep his balance as he walked the fence. Billy followed, but Chris knew the limits of his agility and walked on the sidewalk. Win reached a point from which he could look down into the dazzling brassy throat of the big horn. The music came out of it in a splendid deafening blast. On the front window of the Heidelberg was a crudely printed sign:

Win looked at it with respect. That was the cause of all the celebration: bock beer. And he had never heard of it before!

"Hi, you, sauerkrauts! Have you had your bock beer to-day?"

"Shut up!" Chris Schmidt yelled back.

Four boys, two of them bigger than Win, swaggered over, yelling above the blare of the band and the singing.

"You wanna fight?" The biggest boy was rolling up his sleeves.

Win scowled. He stood now, balanced on the fence, watching Chris. Billy sat as he was. Chris Schmidt stuck out his chin. "Not with the four of you."

"Scared, aintcha?" A second boy in the group danced up to Chris just out of reach of his fists. One of the boys whispered to the biggest boy.

"Aw, yer out playin' nurse to Mama Henkel's little boys! Don't let 'em play around saloons. Mama Henkel don't have nothin' to do with saloons!" The boy's voice took on a shrill falsetto tone. He picked up the corners of his coat and walked with mincing steps past Chris on the side nearest the fence.

Chris swung around him, but Win had jumped from the top of the fence. The boy fell under him to the ground. Win dug his knees into his ribs and bumped his head on the sidewalk.

Chris took on the nearest of the other three. Billy, with a hopeless look at the brass horn of the German band moving now up the street, slid down from the fence and faced another dutifully. But the boy gave him a blow in the stomach that knocked him down against the fence, out of the fight.

Win rolled onto the pavement with two of the boys on top

of him. He shook them off long enough to get to his feet. He tried to remember what old Charlie had taught him over at the stable with the boxing gloves, but one of the boys had slipped around behind him.

"Wait a minute, wait a minute! If we're going to have a fight, let's have a fight!" A big man had come out of the saloon. He grabbed two of the boys by their collars. "Three against one ain't no fight. You, with the rolled-up sleeves, see what you can do alone. Five rounds; all right, go to it!"

More men had come out of the Heidelberg's swinging doors. Chris and William climbed up on the fence to watch.

"Who's the referee?" one man asked.

"Jack Brady, nearly took Kid McCoy a few years back."

"That's the stuff! Boy, you ain't got the muscle but you know what it's about!" Brady seemed impressed by what Win showed of Charlie's teaching. Win's nose was bleeding hard, but the other boy had one eye closed and the sight of it gave Win courage.

"There now, time out!" Brady separated the boys and held them at arm's length easily.

The news spread that Win was the oldest Henkel kid.

"Got the old lady's spunk!" one man told the man next to him. "Get Heine Erdman to tell you about the time she fired him for gettin' drunk! Heine says she's hard as nails."

Some of the spectators brought their mugs with them and drank bock beer while they watched the last round of the fight.

"That's enough! That was five rounds. Did ye hear me?" Brady laid iron hands again on Win and his antagonist. "You wanta kill each other before you quit?"

"I'm not going to stop until he apologizes for talking about my mother!" Win said in a low voice.

The black-haired youngster glared sullenly at Win. "I didn't mean your mother," he muttered.

"There, now, shake hands!" Brady ordered. The boys touched hands gingerly.

"That's the way!" Brady turned to Win. "You might make a good lightweight, young fellow, with a little training. Come around and I'll show you a trick or two."

"Thank you, . . . sir," Win said, not quite sure about the "sir," but adding it out of admiration. Billy came over from the fence. "Are you all right, Bill?"

"Guess so," Billy said. His face still looked peaked in the street light.

"Oh, boy, that was Jack Brady, d'you know that?" Chris spluttered.

Win thrust his hands down to the bottom of his pockets, knotting them into fists in sheer pleasure. One fist encountered his watch. He brought it out anxiously, for fear that it had been broken in the fight. He stopped under the street light and pressed the spring of the lid. Its quick noiseless opening never failed to please him. Chris and William stopped with him to watch the golden miracle.

"Look at the time!" Win's voice sank to a horrified whisper. "It's quarter after nine."

Sara and Belle arrived while the boys were still trying frantically to repair the damages of the fight. Billy dropped his towel and ran to the stairs.

"Mama, here we are!"

Win struggled with his clean shirt. "H'llo, Mom!" he called from the stairs, affecting great nonchalance. "I'm awful sorry we missed the train. You see . . ."

"There is no excuse, Winthrop," Belle said. "I am very

much disappointed in you; you can't be trusted out of my sight."

"Win, what happened to you?" Sara pulled his fresh starched collar away to look more closely at a smear of blood behind his ear. "And what a bump on your head, dear!"

"Oh, we just got into a little fight with some boys, Mom."

"I hope you see, Sara, what comes of living on this side of town, next door to a brewery," Belle said.

Sara unpinned her hat and took off her veil without answering. "Tell me all about it, Win. I'm thankful you're not worse off."

Next morning Sara heard more about the fight from Charlie. She stopped at the stable to say good morning to him and found him in the big boxstall at the rear of the barn, working over a sick horse.

Charlie was obviously proud of his pupil, and the fight lost nothing in his telling of it.

"Jack Brady said it was on account some big boy said somethin' against you," Charlie told her after he had given the full details. "I told Brady his father was a champion wrestler at the University and the boy oughta be a good scrapper! He's a chip off the old block, eh, Missus Henkel?"

Sara smiled. "It sounds like it, Charlie, but where was the fight?"

"Over by the Heidelberg saloon."

"Why should the boys be hanging around there?"

"They was followin' the band. They got to know their town. Don't you worry, Missus Henkel, they're as fine boys as they come. They've got character same as good beer."

Sara looked out through the open stable door at the south wall of the brewery. Even from here she could see the light gray square that was the cornerstone. She had come back from the meeting in Chicago in a troubled frame of mind. The sight of the stone fastness of the brewery reassured her.

"What did the boy say about me, Charlie?"

"Ach, somethin' about your not havin' nothin' to do mit saloons. He was the son, maybe, of some feller what couldn't keep up even after you give him the furniture 'n the bar 'n the whole works. That don't matter. I would myself have left this horse to see the fight mit mine own eyes!"

Sara walked over to the brewery slowly. The big drays had left long since. The courtyard was empty. The high brewery wall shaded one end of the cobbled yard. The bright sunlight fitted into the sharp-cut notches of the shadow. Sara's slender figure was darkly outlined on the sun-washed cobbles.

A warm resinous smell came from the open doorway of the cooper's shop, where the iron kettle of pitch heated over the fire. There was a buzzing sound of bees drawn by the sweet smell of the beeswax and rosin.

Sara nodded. "Vulcan" had been William's name for Herman Klaus, who tended the fire under the black sheet-iron hood.

"A man told me in Chicago that we'd be using steel kegs some day, Herman!" She had to raise her voice above the noise of the men rolling the kegs.

"Ja, Frau Henkel?" he muttered suspiciously. "Beers belong in wood!"

"Ja," Sara nodded, laughing. They were all alike, from Gottfried down to Herman: suspicious of new things. She had gone over to the stables really to tell Charlie she had stopped in Detroit on her way back and bought a new automobile truck. But she had found him working over the sick horse and she hadn't dared tell him then. Charlie wouldn't like having an automobile instead of a new team of horses.

But the big breweries in the large cities were using trucks. William would have tried them out.

The office looked good to her: Adolf bowing and smiling at her through his thick-lensed glasses. Walter, the new clerk, rising quickly and sliding back into his chair. Even the picture of Pasteur looked down amiably on her.

"A gut trip, Missus Henkel?" Adolf asked.

Sara hesitated. "I suppose it was, Adolf. But, of course, I have never been to one of these meetings before. I had no idea what to expect."

She busied herself with the letters and orders. Gottfried would be down as soon as he could leave the brewhouse. She sat back in the old desk chair, but was careful to catch her foot around the leg so it wouldn't tip. The chair had been John Henkel's. It was too big for her. She jerked forward to bring it up to the desk. It was a heavy old thing to try to move. Suddenly, alarmingly, it seemed a symbol of the whole business. The tired, confused feeling that she had had in the smoky air of the room where the Brewers' Association had met came back to her.

Perhaps this was all too much for her. The brewing business was nothing for a woman to be mixed up with; Paul had told her that over and over again, so had Belle and Papa. Only Gottfried and Adolf were back of her, and now, Marie and Ottilie.

Win's fight bothered her. He had said, "Oh, we just got into a fight"; and Billy had hugged her so tight without saying anything. But Win had fought because some boy had said something about her. "Something about your not havin' nothin' to do with saloons," Charlie said.

The boys were fighting in front of the Heidelberg saloon. That was no place for her boys to be! She tidied the papers in front of her. Was she hurting the boys by running the brewery?

She glanced up at the picture of John Henkel. He had been proud of his brewery. It had meant to him security for his children and his grandchildren. People had respected John Henkel. Sara jerked the big chair closer to the desk.

8

"WELL, I'm sorry you can't go, Sara. It seems absurd to stay home and watch Charlie doctor his sick horse." Belle stood in the doorway of Sara's bedroom that evening.

Sara's head and shoulders emerged above the full gathers of the old gray skirt she had slipped over her head.

"Oh, but not to Charlie! This is the horse he named Donner after John Henkel's first pure-bred horse. You look lovely, Belle."

Belle glanced across the room into the mirror and then back at Sara. "I wish I could say the same for you."

Sara was pinning up the hem of the gray skirt with safety pins so it came above her shoe-tops. She rolled the sleeves of her shirtwaist above her elbows.

"It'll make a charming dinner story," Belle laughed. "Paul will certainly enjoy it."

"Is Paul going to be there?"

"Of course. Cynthia Pettigrew always takes care to invite the personages of the town to her dinners. Paul is a more important figure than you realize, Puss. Senator Sevrance!" Belle struck an attitude. "There's the carriage. I'll stop and see how Mama is on the way."

Sara took an old hat from the closet shelf and put it on her head. "You certainly are the most beautiful of the Bolster girls, Sara Henkel," she told herself, looking in the mirror. Then she picked up a sweater and went out of the house.

"Where you going, Mom?" Win asked. He and Billy were playing croquet at the side of the house.

"Over to see if I can help Charlie. Donner's sick."

"Can we go, Mom?"

Sara hesitated. "Yes, come along." She liked having them with her, but she mustn't keep them too close. Always she kept warning herself of that. She mustn't lean on them as Anne did on Roger. "He's all I have," Anne had a tremulous way of saying.

They walked over to the stables together, past the lilac bush that was in full bloom again, just as it had been that spring.

"When does the beer garden start?" William asked.

"Next week," Sara said. "Why?"

"I don't know; I like it. Can we go this year?"

Sara laughed. "Not to drink beer, but you can go over and hear the orchestra and eat supper."

Already the iron tables and chairs were set up. There were all new lanterns this year, electrically wired. Der Sommer Garten was a gay place. She was anxious to have it start, herself.

A wide swath of light came from the open stable door.

"The barn has a good smell," Sara said. She wanted the boys to like these things as she did.

"Look, Mom, those two horses over there are lying down!" Billy exclaimed excitedly.

"Of course, how'd you think they slept?" Win demanded scornfully.

"I knew they lied down, but . . ."

"Lay, Billy."

"Lay, but I've never seen them, really. Charlie says they don't mostly like people to see them."

There was a certain reticence, Sara thought, about the big horses in their stalls. One of them turned so he could watch them with his dark eyes shining softly in the bright light. Some of them had gone to eating again, pulling at the hay. The sound of their munching was a contented sound.

"Mama, don't we own all these horses?" Win asked abruptly.

"And Aunt Otti and Aunt Marie and Gottfried and Adolf with us."

"Oh, well, but they're mostly ours. I like knowing they're ours."

"Listen," Sara said. They could hear the labored breathing of the sick horse above the munching sound of the other horses.

Charlie looked up and shook his head when he saw Sara. "I don't know, Missus Henkel. The vet, he say no good to come any more. He is as good as dead. Look at his legs!"

The big Clydesdale was a sorry-looking beast. Each leg was swollen to half the size of the oak posts in the stables. He had been fat and sleek like the barrels he carried, but now his hairy coat had a matted, dispirited look. The gray eyelids fell over his eyes as though he couldn't keep them open any more.

"Look, his neck's too swelled for a halter," Charlie said mournfully. He got up from the stool he had been sitting on and stood staring at the horse. The boys were awed into silence.

"Twenty-two hunderd pound he weighed. He weighs more than that wid the dropsy," Charlie muttered almost to himself. It was as though he were reading the horse's obituary. "I 'member the time we had that, what was his name, de feller you caught selling the barrels off the wagon?"

"Oh, Steinbocker," Sara said. It was easy to remember. He had been the first man she had ever fired.

"Ja, Steinbocker. He drove Donner a while. But he didn't match." Charlie shrugged. It was Charlie's feeling that drivers and the horses they drove must be matched up. "Donner knew he was no good. One time Steinbocker vas unhitching him and Donner give a jerk." Charlie jerked his own head by way of illustration. "And Steinbocker caught his fingers in the bit and Donner jerked off the tips of his three fingers, just like that! He couldn't do that now," Charlie finished sadly.

"Charlie! What did you do?" Billy asked, shuddering at the grimness of the incident Charlie told so casually.

Charlie shrugged again. "Die man yelled so hard you could hear him way to the bridge. I come out running and picked up his fingers."

"Yes. I remember," Sara said quickly. "That was why I hated to fire him. He drove for us almost five years after that, didn't he?"

"Ja, but he thought he could get away with anything 'cause of those fingers. But it was his fault, not Donner's."

"Why, Charlie?" Win asked. "Why was it his fault?"

"He hadn't learned to make Donner like him. He never did the same thing twicet the same way. You gotta be steady around a horse."

"Oh," Win said, thinking Charlie's words over solemnly.

"Dere ist one ting we might try. I don't say it do any good. . . ."

"What, Charlie?"

"Make a big pot of black coffee . . . oh, half a gallon of coffee, so strong it stand alone . . . we try."

Win helped Sara carry the big pail of coffee back to the stable. Halfway down the path they set it down to rest their arms. The coffee sloshed a little, slopping over on the path. Its rich aroma drowned the spring scents of lilac and wisteria.

Sara forgot to talk. She was busy with her own thoughts. She was thinking that Donner had been the name of the horse Charlie drove for the first time that day he had taken her for a ride; she must have been . . . she had been seven then. Twenty-eight years ago. That was right; she was thirty-five years old. She was so busy she didn't stop often to think of her age, to think of herself at all, but tonight, it seemed incredible that she could be thirty-five.

They went back into the stable. Charlie smelled the coffee. "Ach, that's good!" He took a tin cup from the ledge in the stable and dipped out a little. Blowing on it, he drank it.

"Besser als bier . . . almost! Missus Henkel," he chuckled. "Look at Wilhelm."

Billy had waited with Charlie and had fallen asleep on some sacks of oats near the stall where Donner was. Charlie had covered him over with a horse blanket. "Leave him be; I'll carry him back to bed for you.

"Now." Charlie had a book opened on the ledge of the stall. He glanced at it again and then poured some spirits of niter from a bottle into the coffee, stirring it with a long stick.

"Dere you are, gent-ly, boy," Charlie talked to him as he fastened Donner's head up by a pulley that ran from the ceiling of the stall. Win helped him. The horse opened his eyes and looked at Charlie, hopelessly.

Getting the mixture into the horse's mouth was a long process. Win poured the coffee into his mouth from a long-necked bottle while Charlie held his head steady.

"Dere, we got every bit into him." Charlie turned out the

bright bulb in the stall and left the patient beast in the dark. It was a relief, Sara felt, not to see the distorted limbs and swollen head.

"I don't know. I never see the dropsy so bad in any horse," Charlie muttered. They walked over to Charlie's office at the front of the stable.

"Charlie, do you remember the first Donner? The one you were driving that day you took me for a ride when I was a little girl?"

Charlie laughed. "By Gott, that's right. He was a beauty, gray like this one. You never think you'd be running the Henkel Brewery, eh?" Charlie shook his shaggy, gray head that had the same massive air of dignity that old Donner's had. Sara thought abruptly of the contrast with the red-faced bullet-headed man in the meeting at Chicago who had talked about the dangers of woman's suffrage as though Sara had not been there, or the brewer from Milwaukee who had seemed like a caricature, he was so flashily dressed, and had pounded the table so hard with his fist, talking about getting money to fight prohibition.

Sara leaned against the open counter where the drivers stopped for their order sheets.

"Charlie, do you think it's bad for a woman to run a brewery?"

"What! bad is it? Missus Henkel, I think it is a fine thing. John Henkel, Wilhelm Henkel, would be proud. The boys are going to be proud."

"But will they, Charlie?" Sara looked at Win still lingering by Donner's stall, watching him in the dim light from the front of the stable.

"Of course, they will! Isn't it a fine business? Isn't it growing bigger all the time! And the men are treated right.

Der isn't a man in the brewery wouldn't jump to do what you say. Didn't you cut free from saloons when everybody thought it would wreck the brewery? I did, myself, Missus Henkel. But you were right. I've told plenty people, 'See, we make out better without owning dose saloons.' "

Sara pushed the old felt back on her head and rubbed her forehead wearily.

"Missus Henkel, don't you worry a minute. You're a brave woman." He laid his big hand, stained with coffee and smelling of horse sweat, on her shoulder a minute and then he plunged it into his pocket as though embarrassed.

Sara smiled. "Thank you, Charlie." She looked around the stable. The sleeping animals, the deep brown shadows of the dark end of the stable, the smell of hay and liniment, the spring night lying just beyond the wide-open door, made the meeting of the Brewers' Association that had troubled her so seem unimportant.

"Charlie, what do you think about prohibition? You can't say the word without the brewers going into a rage, yet they feel we must give more and more money to protect ourselves. Do you think it will come?"

Charlie shook his head. "Missus Henkel, I think this way: maybe some day they get the law to do what you haf already done—separate the saloons from the breweries. Maybe they do away with the saloons altogether; maybe they set government control of sales . . . all right. The saloons are not good. But to get entire prohibition they would haf to change the whole United States Constitution. Is the President or Congress going to do that just because some poor peoples don't know when they haf had enough to drink?" Charlie shrugged. "I don't tink so . . . Nein!"

"Sara!"

Sara turned quickly toward the door of the stable. There were Belle and Paul.

"We're home from the Pettigrews' and you missed a lovely dinner party. What on earth are you doing?" Belle looked regal in her evening cape. Paul was . . . He did look like a "personage" as Belle said. Sara's hand reached up instinctively to straighten her hat and then dropped to her belt.

"We've been working on the horse. Paul, did you ever meet Charlie?"

"Hello, Senator! Ja, I vote for him!" Charlie said.

"Belle, you know Charlie."

"Yes," Belle said briefly. "Win! Sara, what are you doing with the boys here at this hour?"

"Oh, but William's been asleep. Win's been helping." It annoyed her that Belle and Paul made her feel a little ridiculous.

"I carry Wilhelm home," Charlie said, picking up the sleeping boy as though he were a small child.

"Oh, no, Charlie; he's too big. He can wake up."

"Excuse me." Charlie went ahead carrying the boy. They all followed. Belle was telling about the evening.

"You should have been there, Sara. The Pettigrews have a house guest from Boston, a delightful person, didn't you think, Paul?"

"Yes, I enjoyed her and the champagne was especially good. Poor Belle wouldn't touch it," Paul said, smiling.

"But I've had a more exciting time by far, thank you," Sara said, and felt the remark was childish.

"Won't you come in, Paul?" Sara asked at the door.

"You must be tired," Paul said.

"I'm not." And suddenly she wasn't. "I'm hungry." She was a hoyden again, glorying in being a hoyden. "I'll fry you bacon and eggs and make you coffee. The coffee I made for

Donner gave me an appetite. It was excellent." Sara tossed her hat on the hatrack.

"I hear you've been in Chicago, Sara," Paul said when they came back in the library.

"Yes, to the Brewers' Association," Sara answered coolly. "Very interesting."

"Paul, she grows worse and worse," Belle complained. "Imagine her going to such a thing! She said there was just one other woman there."

"I was surprised to see even one. I had flattered myself that I was the only lady brewer. But there was a woman from Philadelphia who has run a brewery longer than I have."

"What was it like?" Paul asked curiously, watching Sara with amusement.

"Oh, black cigars, fat German brewers, speeches, discussion, a banquet. I even spoke a piece."

"Sara, you didn't!" Belle was clearly shocked.

"Of course I did. You would have been proud of me. The consensus of opinion among brewers is against woman's suffrage. I rose to my full height and objected. I told them woman's suffrage was inevitable and that it was a mistake to link it up with prohibition in their minds."

"It is linked up, though. When the women get the vote they'll put an end to the liquor traffic, once and for all," Belle said.

"They'll try to," Paul agreed. "Sara, I'd have given a lot to have heard you!"

Sara looked at him, laughing. "I was very good but I know I couldn't have equaled Paul Sevrance, the boy orator."

9 1914

THE Ingalls always held an eggnog party Christmas Eve. Going to it had been part of growing up when they were young. And even now that old Mr. Ingalls had to sit in the big leather chair in the library and couldn't move alone, they still held their party.

The first Christmas Eve after she had taken over the management of the brewery Sara hadn't intended going to the Ingalls'.

"Why should I if you all feel I've done something so out of the way, Belle?" she had asked.

But Paul had come for her. She remembered so well. He had stood in the hall holding his hat and coat, looking at her quizzically.

"That's admitting you're wrong if you don't go."

"Then I'll go," she had said quickly, "but I haven't a new thing to wear, Paul. I haven't had time to think of clothes this fall. We lost so much with wild yeast at the brewery."

"You know no other woman there can hold a candle to you, Sara," Paul had said. How pathetic that she had remembered it all this time!

She had gone, wearing an old evening gown, with a piece of holly pinned in her hair. Some of the women had looked at her curiously. Emma Carthugh bowed coldly, but Mr.

Ingalls had congratulated her on her success as a business woman and Paul had stayed beside her all evening.

She thought of that other Christmas Eve tonight as she and Belle drove over in the taxi, by themselves, like two old ladies. She wouldn't say that; she herself wasn't forty yet and Belle hated to be reminded of her age any more.

"I wonder that Paul didn't come over for us," Belle said. "I suppose, though, he's terribly busy and so much in demand these days. I wish you had heard him speak, Sara."

"I read his speech in the paper. No wonder you like it; he certainly came out strongly for prohibition."

"He's come to see that it's the only way. With Europe at war the Allies need all the grain we can export. That's Paul's point. If it weren't for the brewery you'd see it, too."

"Paul couldn't very well come tonight, then, could he? Unless, of course, the Ingalls feel the way you and Paul do and have no whiskey in the eggnog," Sara said.

The Ingalls' house hadn't changed greatly since they had used to come to dances, Sara thought. The stair rail was twined with green and mistletoe hung under the chandelier. Once she had written an account of the Ingalls' open house for the *Courier*. She could remember some of her phrases that still seemed to fit: "Over a hundred guests called last evening to partake of Christmas cheer before they went on to celebrate by their own hearths. Always a gala affair, the Ingalls' open house last evening was an occasion to be remembered by all who attended. . . ."

She was drinking her eggnog when she saw Paul through the doorway. He came across the room toward her, holding his cup in his hand.

"Merry Christmas, Sara! I was out of town and didn't

get here till eight o'clock, or I would have come by for you."

"Have you been away making more speeches, Paul?" Sara asked without smiling.

"No, not this week; why?"

"I read your speech in the paper. Belle was delighted with it."

Paul frowned slightly. "Oh, you mean the speech before the Republican Club?" he said as though just remembering.

"I hardly expected to find you here drinking eggnogs after such a powerful dissertation on the evils of drink." Sara turned to speak to someone else. She avoided Paul the rest of the evening, and she and Belle left early in order to trim their own tree.

"Why didn't we trim the tree this afternoon?" Belle exclaimed, taking off her coat and rolling up her sleeves.

"Because I wouldn't have them see it beforehand for anything. Even if they are almost grown, I want it to burst on them in all its glory," Sara said.

She climbed up the ladder and fastened the big silver star on the top point of the spruce. "Give me that tinsel and I'll start it up here, Belle." She roped the tinsel around the highest branch and twined it down through the green tree. There had been so many Christmases, the tinsel was tarnished a little on the edge, but it wouldn't show in the candlelight. She and William had bought most of the trimmings for their first Christmas tree. The blown-glass toys were on Win's first tree.

"Do you know, I was married twenty years ago tomorrow, Belle!" Sara said suddenly.

"That's right. It seems longer ago than that," Belle answered. "I remember I hoped right up to the last minute that something would make you change your mind and that you'd marry Paul. What did happen, Sara? I always wondered."

"Oh, I just wasn't sure of him, I guess." Sara sat on the top of the ladder with her hands in her lap. "There's something about Paul, even now, that you can't be sure of. William was . . ." Her voice that had been warm and confident thinned into uncertainty. It had been so long ago. She couldn't remember. William seemed shadowy, remote. William was . . . She looked down on this room. Nothing had been changed since William had lived here; even the brass bowl where his pipe used to be was there by the leather chair. There was the piano. He had played by ear, fumbling a little for the right chord, but these were only fragmentary things. William was . . .

"Was what, Sara?" Belle asked more gently, seeing the bleak expression of Sara's face.

Sara felt a wave of shame that she could not bring William's whole presence to her as she used to be able to.

". . . so honest," she finished weakly.

Belle started to speak and then was silent. Sara climbed down from the ladder and began hanging round colored balls on the tree. William had used to be in her thought continually, but thinking of him and not having him had hurt so she had tried not to let herself think of him so much. And she had been busy. She had worked so hard; she had scarcely gone anywhere but Mama's or Dor's or the Henkels' since fall . . . the service at Christ Church, a concert now and then, and tonight the Ingalls' party—that was all. No one invited her any more. She held a ball too tightly in her fingers, and it broke in sharp bright-colored fragments in her hands.

"Geliebte," William had used to call her, she remembered

suddenly. She hadn't thought of that for so long. "Geliebte." Sara walked over to drop the colored pieces in the fireplace. Oh, yes, William was here. He would want a beautiful tree for the boys. She stood a second in front of the fire, feeling the warmth through her dress, through her very flesh, in her soul.

"I always remember how Derrick loved Christmas. Do you remember the Christmas we went to New York and Mama felt so bad to have us away?" Belle said. "We had a wonderful time."

Sara glanced at Belle quickly. How separate they were, each with her own thoughts. And Anne would be thinking of Roger tonight. Sara was picking up the boxes and papers while Belle laid the boys' presents around the tree, when the doorbell rang.

"I'll go," Belle said, untying her apron.

"Why, Paul, how nice to have you stop. Come in!" Sara heard Belle in the hall.

"It's after midnight, Belle. Merry Christmas," she heard Paul say.

She picked up a left-over ornament and was busy fastening it to a twig of spruce when they came into the room.

"Merry Christmas, Sara! I was afraid you'd all be in bed."

"Merry Christmas, Paul," Sara said smoothly.

"Look at the roses Paul brought us, Sara, and the candy for the boys," Belle said. "I'll go put the flowers in water."

Sara stood off and squinted one eye at the tree. "It needs something else on the left, don't you think?"

Paul ignored her question. "I couldn't let you go away like that, Sara; not on Christmas Eve. You were so angry. Was it all because of that speech of mine?"

Sara met Paul's eyes. "Isn't that enough? You make a speech for prohibition that makes anyone who has anything to do with beer or whiskey seem like a criminal and then you go to the Ingalls' and drink like everyone else.

"I wouldn't like politics if you have to be so . . . so hypocritical! If prohibition were a principle with you, but it isn't; it's just a way of getting votes!"

"Sara . . ."

Sara was too angry to listen. "Someday you'll ruin my business if you can. For what? Just so you can be Governor, probably; that's what you've always wanted to be. You care more about being Governor than anything else in the world." She could see Paul was hurt. She didn't care. "I think I'd rather run a brewery and be my own boss and be honest in my own eyes." Her voice trembled over the words.

Paul stood silently watching her. "It seems a little flat to wish you a Merry Christmas now, but at least I can take myself out of the way," he said.

When Belle came back, she looked around in amazement. "Did Paul go so soon?"

"Yes," Sara said, bending down to fasten a ball more securely to the branch of the tree. "He was in a hurry." Sara struck a match and lighted the first candle.

"Are you going to light the tree tonight? It's one o'clock now!" Belle asked.

"Just for a minute," Sara said shortly.

The light from the myriad of candles touched the tarnished tinsel and the flimsy ornaments with magic beauty.

"Magic; so gaudy and yet so spiritual," William used to say, Sara remembered suddenly. She stood watching the tree. She thought about Paul. She had been right about him years ago.

"It's beautiful, but I'm so afraid of fire!" Belle said fearfully.

"I'm not; there's no danger if you stay right by it," Sara said, but she cupped her hand around each flame and blew it out. Wistful spirals of white smoke climbed up from the black wicks. The room was pungent with the sharp sweet smell of the wax.

10 1915

THE family had moved from the Higgins' house to an apartment.

Sara went back for the last load of small things that were too fragile or valuable for the movers.

"Let me go. It's just a few blocks and I love driving the auto," she had said.

"Well . . ." The girls and Mama were always saying, "Well, if you really want to, Sara"; letting Sara do this or that or make the decisions. Since Mr. Bolster's death Sara had managed everything, consulting Dor's husband, of course, but George seldom had any counter-proposal. George had become, at fifty, one of "the older men" in Bradford and Lang's law firm. He no longer tried cases in court. Dor often said, "George is so wonderful at settling estates and that sort of thing; Mrs. Healey said she wouldn't think of having anyone else . . ." or Mrs. Ingalls or Mrs. Carthugh, as the case might be. Many of the families that used to bulwark Sara's world, in the days when that world was bounded by the bayou and Sycamore Street, were having estates settled. The widows or daughters were apt to take what was left from the estate and move to California or New York. Now with "this terrible war" there was no more going to Europe to live as the Higgins had done. Others, like Mama or Anne, moved into the fashionable Sherbrooke.

And the old houses were fast passing into new hands. The Novaks, who were said to be making money hand over fist in rubber, had the Healey place, and the Timothy Greens were building "a regular estate" on the site of the old Kirsted salt sheds that Sara had slid down years and years ago. The whole town was changing. There was no longer such a difference between the east and west side.

Armitage had become an industrial city almost overnight. The fortunes that built the large houses on the new West Boulevard were no longer made in the forests up north, discreetly out of sight. These fortunes were made six blocks south or only across the river on the east side, in factories that their owners neither could nor wished to ignore.

"Sometimes I'm contented that Papa isn't here," Mrs. Bolster said sadly to the girls. "There are so many changes." But Sara didn't feel that way. She was part of the growth of the city. She was even part of the foreign element!

The top of Sara's new car was down. Belle sat beside her. The long tonneau was filled with a basket of silver that had been saved once, long ago, from the fire. Even the painting of Great-Grandmother Bolster was there, covered now by the plaid car robe.

"It's so sad breaking up this house; even though it was rented it's always seemed as though it belonged to the family," Belle said.

Sara nodded. "I'd have been glad to go on renting it as long as the Higgins were willing, but it is too big for just Mama and Anne with Roger away at college. I do wish Mama and Anne would come over with us. Win will only be home in the summer now and Roger can share his room."

"I'm sure that Mama and Anne wouldn't be happy there,"

Belle said. "You can't understand that, Sara, because you're so wrapped up in the brewery." Sara parked the car in front of the Sherbrooke. She had long since given up defending the brewery to Belle.

The apartment in the Sherbrooke was small but convenient. Its rent was high, but then, Mama and Anne would be comfortable and happy there. Mrs. Healey and Jethro had an apartment on the floor above.

"Grace Healey and I are still neighbors," Mama said with a smile.

"Isn't Mama the bravest person!" Anne said when she and Sara were alone.

Sara nodded, looking about the small living room that seemed amazingly like a corner of the old sitting room in the house on the bayou, with Grandmother Bolster's portrait looking down on it, still smiling, still undisturbed by the vicissitudes of the years.

She fingered the familiar silver card tray on the table. She was back for an instant on the stairway overhearing Papa talk about raising money to go into the new bicycle factory: the bicycle factory that had given way to the automobile works and was now the second industry in Armitage.

"It will be necessary to make a drastic cut in our living expenses . . . we could live in that house on the east side . . ." Papa had said.

"But it would mean changing our whole way of living," Mama had objected.

And even now Sara could remember the weariness of Papa's voice saying, "No, Corona, I wouldn't think of it. You're right, my dear, some things are a good deal more important than money."

It would be so much less expensive if only Mama and Anne could come to live with her, but, of course, they couldn't think of that. She was thankful the brewery was doing so well. They had never had a better year.

"Sara," Anne said, looking up from the khaki sweater she was knitting, "you know how much I wish I could help with the rent. I hate to have you do it all, but I feel that just now I should put all I have into Roger's education. I know Roger would want me to."

"Of course, Anne; why, I'm so glad to. Whatever made you think . . ."

"You looked around the apartment in a funny way and were so quiet as though you felt it was too expensive."

"Don't be silly, Anne," Sara said impatiently. Anne was always doing that. But at the same time, Sara was thinking that Roger was taking his fourth year at Harvard. The State University where Win was—Anne had felt it inferior.

"I must go. Good-by, dear. I hope you'll be so happy here." Sara kissed Mrs. Bolster. Mrs. Bolster sat as complacently as though she had never moved from her own home, the very picture of serenity, with her daughters around her. It was worth the expense to have Mama look so contented, Sara thought.

When Sara and Belle reached home, Ottilie and Marie were waiting in the library.

"Why, Marie and Ottilie, how nice!" Sara greeted them gaily, but inwardly she braced herself. The atmosphere was always heavy when Marie and Belle were together. Belle took a certain pride in Ottilie's success, but when she was with her she had little to say. Ottilie sat on the window seat, looking moodily off into space. Marie had something on her mind; Sara could tell by the way she sat so straight in her chair.

"We saw Mother and Anne nicely settled . . ." Sara

made easy talk. They were too different; Belle was always so well turned out, even to the champagne button kid shoe fitting like a glove around her ankle. She glanced at Marie's black laced shoe that was the embodiment of firmness and sense. They did not often come together; when they did, each managed to convey her criticism of the other.

Belle sat gracefully in the little gilt chair by the door, her feather boa falling in a soft loop of white over the chair arm, and began with an air of sociability that was too determined. Sara wished Belle wouldn't.

"It was so lovely along the drive this afternoon, it didn't seem as though that terrible war could be going on over there."

Ottilie swung around from the window. Usually she worked all afternoon up over the stable in her old brown smock. Today she wore her best black dress. The high-necked, long-sleeved wool added distinction to her pale, almost colorless face. Her finely modeled hands that were so like William's were knotted together in her lap.

"The war is going on over here, too!" Her voice had a curious, half-hysterical note. Suddenly she got up and left the room: they heard the screen door bang after her.

"Why, what did I say that . . ." Belle began.

"Nothing," Marie said. "Mrs. Bickmore asked her to meet with the committee of the Women's Century Club. . . ."

"Oh, about her woman's suffrage figure?"

"Yes." The small word exploded like a bomb from Marie's thin lips. "It seems that there had been a good deal of criticism about Ottilie's being commissioned to do that work because . . . as near as Ottilie could make out . . . because her name happened to be Ottilie Henkel!"

"But, Marie, they asked her to do it because she is a competent sculptor. What has her name to do with it?" Sara burst out. Ottilie had been working on the statue for months. She hadn't wanted anyone to see it until it was all finished, but she had been so happy over it.

"My dear Sara, the name is too German. The committee seem to feel it would be unwise to have it made by 'a Hun.' " Marie's voice was like a sharp draft cutting into the warm October afternoon.

"I never heard anything so stupid!" Sara's eyes blazed. "I'll go and see Mrs. Bickmore, myself."

"I was in the Century Club Thursday, and when I went in the dressing room for my hat I thought Mrs. Bickmore and Stella Gray seemed embarrassed. They must have been talking about it then," Belle said.

"I shall see Mrs. Bickmore," Sara said. "Something can be done about it. That's completely idiotic."

"Don't bother," Marie objected. "Ottilie wouldn't let them have the statue now if they came to her on bended knees. It's a pity, though. Father came to this country as a boy. He was proud of his citizenship. Uncle Hans fought in the Civil War. Now we must be insulted because our name happens to be German! But this is really incidental, Sara. What I came to tell you was that we've decided to sell our home here and move to New York."

"Oh, Marie, you don't want to do that. Why, this is your home. Mother Henkel would be so homesick any place else."

"We've made up our minds. This is no place for Ottilie. It will be better for her in the city. No one here knows as much as she does about sculpturing. She needs teachers. She needs to know other artists."

"Marie, don't make up your mind so quickly," Sara begged. But Marie was like William when her mind was made up.

"Mütterchen feels badly now, but she is willing to go for Ottilie's sake. I haven't told her about this . . . this insult, of course. We'll take an apartment there. At least, we'll be able to breathe there without feeling that our German breath is polluting the air!"

Belle rose, pulling her feather boa about her. "I'll go straight to Jane Bickmore and Alice Stevens and tell them what I think of such a bigoted performance. They can't do a thing like that. Why, Ottilie has genius. The city ought to be proud of her." The Bolster family had reached out to take in Marie and Ottilie. Sara saw Marie's expression soften.

"Thank you, Belle, I can't let you do that. We have talked of moving to New York for a long time; this merely decided us. I'll go and find Ottilie and then I want to talk to you about some business matters, Sara."

"Let me go, Marie." Sara rose. "You must both stay and have dinner with us."

"H'lo, Aunt Marie; hello, Aunt Belle, Mom." Bill came through the hall. The eyes of the three women brightened, looking at him. He was in tennis clothes, his shirt hung damply on his broad shoulders, his hip pocket bulged with tennis balls.

He's a regular Bolster, Belle thought to herself, and Marie and Sara both saw a striking resemblance to William.

"You look all fussed up; where you been?" Bill asked. Sara laughed out of sheer relief.

"There's a letter from Win, Bill. Hurry along and change for dinner." Sara went out to find Ottilie, deliberately leaving Belle and Marie together.

Sara knew she would find Ottilie in her workshop above the stable. Ottilie was not working. She had taken off the cloth that usually covered the statue and was sitting idly studying the figure and smoking a cigarette. She smoked only in the studio. Smoking shocked Marie.

Sara came in without speaking and stood looking at Ottilie's work. It was very simple; there were no symbols of suffrage or freedom or talents. It was the figure of a woman, a little larger than life, her head lifted, her hands hanging by her sides. Her plain dress had a curiously real look for plaster. It was no new woman, it was simply a woman, but the expression on the face was serene, the mouth and throat and shoulders had strength.

Sara walked around it again. She sensed an eager, forward motion in the profile as though she were moving, but when Sara faced the figure she felt only the calm intelligence of the face.

"Ottilie, it's the best thing you've done," Sara said.

Ottilie's lips smiled slightly. She was no longer angry. "I think it is," she said. "Of course, it isn't the way they suggested it. They wanted a ballot box at her feet and books in her arm, but some day woman's suffrage will be a dead issue. People won't remember when women didn't have the vote. A woman like this will . . . will mean more." Ottilie was never good at explaining her ideas. When she had met with the committee she had been so quiet they had wondered if she took in all they said.

"I think you're right." Sara sat down opposite the big window.

"Does the woman look familiar to you, Sara?"

Sara looked at it. "How do you mean, Ottilie?"

Ottilie leaned down to tie her shoelace tighter. "I thought of you, Sara, when I was doing it. I've looked down from the window, sometimes, in the morning and watched you cross the yard down there and you've looked like that."

"Why, Ottilie!" Sara looked at her incredulously and then back to the figure.

"Oh, I changed her a little; I gave her a heavier frame,

but see her hair, braided around her head, and her mouth and chin. They're yours, Sara, and that energy you have. You're not like your sisters or Marie or any of the women I know. You're stronger."

Sara laughed, but she was touched. She had never known how Ottilie felt about her. She glanced almost shyly at the figure on the worktable.

"You're different from the way you were when William brought you to call on us. Do you remember? I thought you were the prettiest thing I'd ever seen, in that blue dress and hat. You praised my paintings and then I thought you were just doing it to please William and I tried not to like you."

"Ottilie, I wasn't like that," Sara protested.

"No, I guess you weren't, but Marie and I didn't like you. After you were married you had all your fashionable friends and we felt you were taking William away from us."

Sara started to speak, but Ottilie went right on as though all this had been pent up inside her and had to come out. "And when he was killed and you went to live with your family and only came down once in a while so Mütterchen could see the boys, we . . . I don't know why, but we almost hated you. It seemed as though you were taking what was left of William away from us too.

"When you wouldn't sell the brewery we couldn't understand it. We wanted to be rid of it. We'd have gone to New York then if we'd sold out. And then you set out to run the brewery. 'I wonder what her family think of that!' Marie wrote me. You've made a success of it, Sara, but that isn't it; it's you that's changed. I guess the brewery's changed you."

If Ottilie had been Dor or Anne or Belle, Sara would have gone over and put her arm around her, but Ottilie was different.

"Thank you, Ottilie," Sara said simply.

"I don't really care about the Women's Century Club." Ottilie threw the wrapper over her figure. "If I'm going to New York I need it to show Bartholomew. I want to do more work with him, you know; but Marie will never get over this."

They sat quiet for a moment, each busied with her own thoughts. Sara looked around the big studio. There was the head Ottilie had made of Donner, and "The Child Beside the Pool," her first ambitious piece, which Billy had been the model for. There was a head of old Charlie as Gambrinus; Ottilie had persuaded him to pose as he had looked when he drove the brewery float.

"I'll miss this place," Ottilie said abruptly, as though their thoughts converged.

"I'll miss your being up here working, too," Sara said.

"Why don't you call up Paul and see what he can do about Ottilie's statue?" Belle suggested to Sara that evening.

"I can manage nicely without Paul's help," Sara said. "I'm going to call Mr. Griffith: he might know someone."

Mr. Griffith's response was immediate. It did Sara good to hear his indignation and made her feel as though she were back in the *Courier* office.

"You know I happened to be on the committee that helped gather the statues for the Detroit Museum and I had the very great privilege, at that time, of meeting Mr. Lorado Taft. . . ." Sara smiled to herself. She had heard Mr. Griffith tell this many times. "Let him see it," Mr. Griffith went on, "and if it's good he'll help her to place it where it'll put those small-brained fanatics to shame! I'll write him a letter tomorrow!"

Three months later Sara came back into the house after seeing Marie and Ottilie and Mütterchen off on the train.

"Mrs. Henkel does look frail, but they only have to make one change, and in a drawing room she'll be able to rest," Belle said.

Sara thought of Mütterchen's small, tired face, looking at her through the car window, her eyes streaming with tears. For her this moving was an uprooting, an exile. She would never come back here where she had lived all her life. She had clung to her and Billy as though she couldn't let them go.

"Wasn't it wonderful to have Ottilie's statue exhibited in Detroit before they left, with that splendid article in the paper about it?"

"Yes, it was," Sara answered slowly. "Marie felt better, but I think Ottilie has dropped the whole business out of her mind."

"I imagine it won't drop out of Mrs. Bickmore's mind very soon," Belle gloated.

"Isn't it strange, Belle, that William's family have all gone away and the brewery is left for me to run?"

"You're a fool, Sara, to go on with it. It's a millstone around your neck!" Belle flashed out.

"No," Sara said. "I don't feel that way about it any more."

II

WEDNESDAY night, Sara met Gottfried and Adolf at the office of the brewery to go over the books. They were used to these conferences. Sara always sat at John Henkel's old desk in the big swivel chair. Gottfried held his pencil sternly on a figure.

"That's for those new filters; Herman ordered those when I was away!"

They had an assistant brewmaster now, a young German named Herman Anspach. He had come from the Wahl-Hennius Institute in Chicago instead of a school in the old country. Gottfried was inclined to be critical of American schools. The only thing that mollified him was that Anspach's father and grandfather had both been brewmasters in the old country.

"If America goes into the war," Adolf said abruptly, "what good will Herman do us?"

Sara tried to close her mind to such remarks. If the United States went to war Win would join up. He was eager to go. He had already talked about it. She heard echoes of war talk going around the brewery. There were some whose families were all in the old country. They listened with serious faces. Mark Voss in the malthouse had lost three brothers in the German army.

They went over the unpaid bills owed them.

"Those two saloons on lower Water Street are the worst. I telephoned them no more beer could they have till they paid us. McGinnis owes us two hunderd an' eighteen dollars," Adolf said. "I wrote him too, and now I will go see him!"

This last year was the best year the brewery had had. If this coming season were as good she could build the Winter Garten this fall . . . unless prohibition came. She did not put her thought into words. Gottfried grew almost apoplectic at the mention of prohibition. Adolf shook his head morosely as though it were some serious mental derangement very hard to imagine.

Belle had taken pains to tell her that Paul thought prohibition was bound to come because it had become a major political question.

Sara thought of the long faces of the men at the Brewers' Association meeting last month. Not one of them really believed it would come, but they were worried. They had voted large amounts of money to fight it.

"We must fight the dry machine with a machine as well organized and with just as great resources . . ." one speaker had declared.

A fine-looking old brewer from Milwaukee had spoken earnestly: "Beer is the great temperance drink, but people must be taught. We need beautiful beer gardens like on the continent, in Vienna, in Denmark."

"They don't pay," someone interrupted the speaker.

Sara had sprung to her feet. "I have a beer garden with a good orchestra. It pays besides being very good advertising!" When she sat down, they clapped.

Then the speaker went on: "We should separate beer and hard liquor. Too long have they appeared to the people as bedfellows."

Dor's husband, George, didn't think prohibition would come. He said "the upper classes" wouldn't stand to have their personal liberties interfered with.

"Lissen, how it rains!" Adolf said.

They were still a moment to listen. The rain sounded noisily on the cobbled yard and the tin roof above the loading platform.

"It's gut I got my garden in a-ready," Adolf said. Sara smiled. They might not have been the executives of a sizable business, at all, she thought; just two old men and a woman talking about the rain, about their gardens.

Then Sara brought up the subject they had come to discuss. In all these years she had learned the circuitous reasoning of Gottfried and Adolf as though it were her own. They talked around things, coming to the point gradually.

"We'll go ahead, then, with our plans for building the Winter Garten?" Sara asked. "The architect is sending his plans."

"How ist the music this year?" Gottfried parried.

"Splendid, Gottfried. We're going to have three orchestras, one from Cincinnati, one from Buffalo, and one from Chicago, three weeks each."

"Good, good!" Gottfried murmured, patting the desk with his fingers. "It was beautiful last year!"

"The building alone will cost ten thousand dollars," Sara said tentatively.

Gottfried was nodding his head in approval.

"Easy that much," Adolf nodded.

"I'll tell the contractor to go ahead then?" Sara repeated. There was a long pause.

"Maybe we better wait just a little," Gottfried admitted grudgingly.

So they were apprehensive, too. The word prohibition was there as loudly as though it had been spoken.

When Sara reached home she found Belle was out.

"I didn't know Miss Belle was going out, Pearl. Do you know where she went? It's pouring."

"To that revival meeting, Mrs. Henkel; the Billy Sunday one. It's the biggest revival meeting that's ever been to this town!"

Sara drove down for Belle in the car. There was no mistaking the place. The long, unpainted building covered half a block. Bright lights streamed out from every window. Cars and busses were crowded along the curb. Such a volume of song came from the open doors that it drowned out the sound of the rain. Such singing must draw the people just as the music of the beer garden on summer nights drew the crowds. Sara had to leave the car a block away.

The music had stopped. A man's voice came out to her, vibrant with emotion. He was praying.

"You know how things are with us, Lord. We got our own troubles, same as you have. We're worried about the mortgage and how to pay for Joe's tonsil operation and whether our wife loves us any more . . . you know all that, God." The voice was warm and familiar. Sara edged into the crowd that stood packed way to the doors. On this rainy night the sawdust was pungent. The new lumber of the tabernacle made her think of the booms along the river when she and Paul used to slide down the river bank on Park Avenue.

Sara was inside now. The man up front, across the multiplaid of faces and hats, was an ordinary-looking individual, but his voice held every human being within range of it, silent.

"Help us not to fall down on our word to you, God. When

we promised you not to go down to the corner and get that drink of beer, or into Al's for a little snifter. Help us to stick to it. We know it's the Devil's own game an' we don't want to play ball with the Devil. You know that. Help us to stand up on our hind legs like men, not crawl in the gutters like dogs. Here's our hand on it, God; squeeze it tight. Amen!"

Above the opposite door Sara noticed a sheet with the words printed in large letters on it: "Billy Sunday talks tonight on Vice, Booze, and the Devil."

Sara's face burned. The familiarity of his way of praying embarrassed her. She looked at the man next to her. His mouth hung slack. He was caught up by the words, hypnotized by the voice. As far as she could see, every face was intent, empty of its own content, drinking in what was said.

The song leader came down to the edge of the platform. "We've got a request we'll have to fill first. 'The Brewers' Big Horses.'" There was an avalanche of applause. The music began.

The leader held out his arms. The words, enunciated by fifteen thousand voices, took on a swing that moved heads and shoulders in time to it all across the tabernacle:

Oh, the Brewers' Big Horses coming down the road
Toting all around old Lucifer's load,
They step so high, and they step so free,
But the Brewers' Big Horses can't run over me.

Oh, no, boys; oh, no.
The turnpike's free wherever I go;
I'm a temp'rance engine, don't you see?
And the Brewers' Big Horses can't run over me!

Oh, the liquor men are acting like they own this place
Living on the sweat of the poor man's face,

They're fat and sassy as they can be,
But the Brewers' Big Horses can't run over me.

They were crude words that might have been chanted by some pert schoolboy, but the volume of voices lifted them into a marching song, flung them out triumphantly at her, Sara Bolster, packed in against the back wall of a jerry-built tabernacle. She was playing ball with the devil! Her cheeks were scarlet now. She could feel them.

The stanzas went on as though they would never stop:

I'll harness them horses to the Temp'rance Cart,
Hit 'em with a gad for to give 'em a start.
I'll teach 'em how for to haw and gee,
For them big horses can't run over me!

Oh, no, boys; oh, no.
The turnpike's free wherever I go;
I'm a temp'rance engine, don't you see?
And the Brewers' Big Horses can't run over me!

"Excuse me, please. Pardon me!" Sara tried to work her way out through the crowd. They were singing too hard to hear her. Their voices seemed to bellow straight into her ears. She pushed rudely against a fat woman who was deaf to her request to pass. The woman swayed good-naturedly with the song and beamed at Sara. She couldn't wait for Belle; she wouldn't be able to find her, anyway. She pushed her way at last past the policeman who stood at one of the red-lighted exits.

"Whatcha hurry, lady? He's in fine feather tonight, ain't he? It's a shame some of these boozers ain't here to listen to him!"

Sara escaped without answering. It was still raining. She stepped off the curb into a running river of water and plowed through it without feeling the cold water around her ankles. Still the voices followed her. She slammed the car door and fastened the side curtains into place. She started the car with a loud roaring of the motor.

"The Brewers' Big Horses can't run over me!" came from the lighted tabernacle, piercing even through the curtains of the car, following her as she drove off down the street.

That man, Billy Sunday, had no right to talk that way. The brewing business was an honest business. He didn't know anything about it. It was a more honest thing than his revival meeting. What did he make but a heady drink of emotionalism that people drank down like whiskey until it made them drunk? And the drink he gave them, all those empty, listening faces, was not clear and sparkling. It was muddy. It had too much yeast in it. Those who drank it lost all dignity and restraint, stumbling down the sawdust trail to wallow in their own abasement of self; most of them, anyway. Only a few were sincere.

She had worked hard. She had kept her business free from anything that was shoddy or disreputable. She had freed herself from the saloons. There was no drunkenness around the brewery. There was no graft mixed up in the business as there had been in the lumber business. No one condemned the lumber business that had brought plenty of evil in its wake; it had built the dives and saloons on lower Water Street, and brought the easy money that had changed the old standards. . . . John Henkel's Brewing Company had never done that. Why should he say such things?

Of course they would get prohibition; all those people yelling at the top of their voices. She had not really been afraid it would come until now. But now she was sure.

What good would all her work be then? What would become of the girls and Mama and Marie and Mütterchen, and the boys? She would lose everything. The Brewers' Big Horses were going to run over her in the end, crushing her down into worry and want, just as they had crushed William. There was nothing she could do about it. The horses were symbols of some terrible fate; they were fate.

After William's death, she had dreaded the sound of the horses passing the house. She had used to wake early in the morning and hear them and then she had steeled herself against the sound. She had come to be proud of owning them, as proud as Charlie was. Hadn't she even worked over one as though it had been a sick child? And now . . .

She was so angry and hurt that she kept on driving; out past the city hall and the Baker Street bridge. She was closed in by the car curtains; all she could see was a blurred vision of a wet street, punctuated by street lamps. The words that had seemed directed at her kept ringing in her ears:

Oh, the Brewers' Big Horses, coming down the road,
. . . umta-um, something she couldn't remember;
They step so high and they step so free,
But the Brewers' Big Horses can't run over me.

But that was what she had loved about them; they held their heads so high and they did step so free. They couldn't run over her! She owned them. She could drive them if she had to; the way Charlie did, holding their heads up. They were beauties. Most people had never looked straight at them when their necks were arched, but she had.

Running the brewery had changed her, Ottilie had said. Ottilie had said it had made her strong. Perhaps it had; nothing could beat her, nothing could run over her.

If prohibition were coming, let it come. She could find a way to support them all. She had learned to run the brewery; she could learn something else. The Brewers' Big Horses couldn't run over her. Those people back there thought they knew what they were singing about, but they didn't.

Oh, the Brewers' Big Horses can't run over me!

She sang the line aloud, careening down Water Street in the rain. She felt elated. She forgot her worries about prohibition; that Billy Sunday said she was playing ball with the devil. She turned the car around and drove back home, humming the refrain all the way.

12 1916-1917

NOVEMBER was late to have Der Sommer Garten open, but Indian summer lasted from day to day even after half the leaves in the park had fallen. They would not close now until after election night. Sara advertised in the papers that election returns would be announced all through the evening and arranged with little Rollo at the *Courier* office to phone each new bulletin of news.

Sara had persuaded Gottfried and Adolf to agree to her building Der Winter Garten. They had objected until she had said firmly:

"If prohibition comes we can run it as a restaurant. It won't be much but it will bring in some income."

And once the whitewashed brick building was finished, it seemed the natural complement of Der Sommer Garten. They had only to open the wide windows above the river to use it all summer. Now people had their choice of the tables under the trees or the tables at a higher price in the enclosed dining room. And there were such crowds people had to make their reservations early in the day to be sure of a table.

"Anyway, the weather has been with us!" Gottfried had said to Sara as one hot day followed another.

But Sara had felt that very little else was with them. There had been constant warnings and appeals from the Brewers' Association. One communication had urged her to do all that she could locally to defeat Paul W. Sevrance for United States Senator. But what could she do? She found his picture staring at her from billboards all over town. She saw in the paper a picture of him taken on Derrick's yacht on Lake Huron and beneath it a speech that he had made:

We must put aside the selfish pleasures of the individual and think only of the common good. The liquor traffic cripples our industries, takes grains needed in Europe, keeps alive that festering place of iniquity, the corner saloon. Now is the time to blot it out once and for all in this state by voting at the November election for State Prohibition. And I pledge myself, if elected as your Senator, to fight for a national amendment to the Constitution.

She laid down the paper without reading any farther. Of course such a speech would be impressive because the public did not know what she knew; what Adolf had told her when he came back from his collection trip the first of the month! And she could not tell them; they wouldn't believe her if she did.

She had asked Adolf particularly about the McGinnis bill.

"Ja, he paid me!" Adolf had laughed. "The bartender know when I come in what I want. He said McGinnis was busy, would I step into the room at the side and wait. You know how those rooms have walls part way up? I hear McGinnis in the next room. He was talkin' to Mr. VanRansom. VanRansom, he offer McGinnis a place in the Gentlemen's Club if prohibition went through . . . I had to lissen close they talked so low . . . but only if he, McGinnis, line up the neighborhood solid for Sevrance for Senator, see?"

"Adolf, are you sure?" she had asked, not quite believing it, but there was no doubting Adolf.

"Sure, I hear it with my own ears. He told him the drinks was on him. Well, when McGinnis came out I told him I hear him havin' a little visit." Adolf had smiled at his own shrewdness. "He paid me all right."

That was the way Paul would get his election. That was the way they would put prohibition over, buying up votes with the very drinks they were going to ban. That was the way they had defeated her father. She understood her father's contempt for campaigning now.

Paul had called twice during the summer. Both times she had sent word that she did not care to see him. Once she had answered the phone when he telephoned.

"Sara, this is just a political issue, after all. We mustn't let it take away everything between us!" There was a desperate note in his voice that made her hold the receiver of the phone a moment, but she didn't answer.

"Sara!" Paul called. The receiver made a cold click as she hung it up. She was right, she told herself again, thinking of it. Paul had shown himself to be nothing but a self-seeking, dishonest politician.

The morning of election day Belle came down to breakfast in street clothes. Sara was already at the table reading the morning paper while she drank her coffee. Headlines screamed from the page:

WILL MICHIGAN VOTE DRY? LARGE MAJORITY ANTICIPATED.

"Where are you going?" Sara asked.

Belle slipped her napkin out of its ring. "Well, you might as well know. I'm going down to W.C.T.U. headquarters to help with the phoning."

"Phoning?"

"Yes, reminding people to vote for prohibition."

"Oh, yes, of course." Sara finished her breakfast quickly and went over to the brewery. Adolf had a self-conscious air as he said good morning. Gottfried seemed more gruff than usual. No one mentioned the impending election.

Once during the morning she heard Herman Anspach talking to one of the men outside the brewery. Herman's voice was distinct because he spoke without a German accent.

"It won't be long now!" Herman called out. "I was thinking I better write and get my money back from Wahl-Hennius. What good will a brewing-school certificate do me after today?"

"I will mine own beer make, aber ach! It is a funny ting when peoples don't drink beer no more," a thick German voice answered.

Sara walked over to look out the window toward the beer garden where the men were busy setting up the orchestra's chairs. Why had she kept the beer garden open tonight? She would have to be there. She would have to listen to the announcement that the state had gone dry; that Paul Sevrance was elected! It seemed more than she could face.

She could not settle down to the work on her desk. She left the brewery early and went up to her room to write the boys. They were both at the University this year. She wondered how the boys felt about the brewery.

It was ten o'clock that evening before Sara went over to Der Sommer Garten. She no longer wore dresses whose hems ruffled the grass, nor long white silk gloves. She wore a dark suit and a plain dark hat, but the waitress still saved the third table on the left for her. The orchestra was playing "Tipperary." War songs were more popular than the waltzes now. The tables were filling, but there were still some empty places. She would never keep the garden open again after October.

"Good evening, Missus Henkel." It was close to twelve when Gottfried came by. He leaned on the table and let himself down in his chair wearily.

"Good evening, Gottfried. We'll soon have the news."

Gottfried nodded. The orchestra finished with a flourish. A waiter handed a slip of paper to the leader. The undercurrent of conversation died down. Waiters and waitresses stood still to listen.

"This is the latest report," the orchestra leader announced. "Returns from all the eastern seaboard states are in. Hughes leading by a strong majority. New York papers acclaim Hughes President."

There was wild clapping. Sara had almost forgotten that it was the Presidential year. She was waiting.

"The election of Paul W. Sevrance to the United States Senate has been conceded." There was more clapping. Paul must be at the Republican headquarters. He would have himself well in hand, very cool, very self-contained, inwardly so jubilant. She understood him so well. Derrick had done well by him! Perhaps, she thought for a moment, Paul didn't know how Derrick had bought votes for him. Of course he knew, she told herself.

"State prohibition returns. . . ." The silence was oppressive to Sara. No one knew how the big cities with the large foreign populations would go; how Armitage City would go.

"Nearly all the counties in the state have been heard from, with an overwhelming majority for prohibition!"

From the tables on the covered porches came a small burst of spirited clapping that tapered into a thin, scattered applause, tentative, unsure of its enthusiasm. The occupants of the tables around Sara were quiet. Then the murmur of voices began, low at first, like the buzzing of the bees around the hot pitch. The orchestra was playing again. The waiters and waitresses hurried back and forth. A waiter paused by Sara's table, holding his tray high. For an instant, she looked through a tall glass of amber beer, pale, sparkling, Henkel's good beer, outlawed now.

"Well. . . ." Gottfried puckered his lips so that the thin mustaches grew nearer together. "This ist badder than losing that beer with wild yeast, Missus Henkel. We will haf a few months only. It is a good thing that John Henkel is not here!"

13

THE morning papers confirmed in black and white all that had been announced the night before, with one exception. California's vote had changed the Presidential victory. Wilson was President instead of Hughes.

Paul's picture was on the front page.

"He is fine-looking, isn't he?" Belle glanced across the table at the sheet in Sara's hand.

"In a way. Of course, he looks pleased," Sara answered without enthusiasm.

"George telephoned him as soon as we knew. We all spoke to him. He said he hoped this victory for prohibition wouldn't mean too much to you, Sara."

Sara lifted her coffee cup. "I should say that was one of those politic remarks that are pleasant but mean nothing."

Belle compressed her lips as though to refrain from speaking, then she said, "Mama said she couldn't help but feel glad that now you would have to give up that terrible business. Don't you see, you did what you felt was your duty and now you're free. That's the way to look at it, Sara. It's all for the good, dear!"

Sara had no desire to discuss either the brewery or prohibition with Belle. How impractical they were, Mama and the girls! The business had been their chief support since Papa's death. And she needed money now more than ever with both the boys away at college.

She dreaded seeing Gottfried or Adolf or Charlie this morning. She had been awake when the brewery wagons and two trucks went past the house. She had sat up in bed to listen. She had been almost surprised to hear them. It seemed as though overnight everything must have stopped dead as it had in the castle in the fairy tale when the spell was laid over it. But nothing had stopped yet. Eighteen months from now that would happen. It seemed so futile going on for such a little while.

Sara slipped out of the side door and walked over to the brewery. Even the massive stone fortress looked altered this morning.

"Guten Morgen, Missus Henkel." Charlie was in the doorway of the stable. It was silly of her to remember at that moment how he had looked as Gambrinus on the float. How hilarious they had been here in the courtyard, looking at the float. And then the W.C.T.U. women had stopped the float, just as they had stopped the whole brewery now.

"Good morning, Charlie." Sara stopped to talk with him.

"I was thinkin', Missus Henkel, that night you made the coffee and helped me fix up that horse, Donner, you know?"

"Yes," Sara said.

"Remember, we talked about prohibition. You asked me did I think it would come."

"Yes."

"Well, I told you wrong."

Sara smiled faintly at Charlie's understatement.

"But," Charlie emphasized his words with his finger, "what I didn't count on was the war!"

"That's right, Charlie, no one could." She went on into the office.

"The whole trouble was, Missus Henkel, the brewers didn't wake up soon enough to the fact that the people that want prohibition think of them in the same boat with the whiskey distillers." Adolf laid his pen behind his ear while he talked.

"Perhaps, Adolf," Sara said.

"While, if they only knew it, beer helps the temperance. John Henkel used to get so mad when people call beer liquor!"

Sara closed her mind; Adolf's words were only an echo of those futile Brewers' Association meetings she had attended.

"But the American peoples haf got to try everyting once. They will soon be sick of it!" Adolf looked owlishly through his thick lenses. "The orator people change them easy!"

About the middle of the morning, Sara went up to the brewhouse. She wondered why Gottfried hadn't come down.

Everything was going on as usual. The men went ahead with their work as though nothing had happened. It was hard to believe that eighteen months from now the whole brewery would stand empty. It had never been closed since the year John Henkel started it.

Gottfried stood by the brew-kettle. The door on the side was pushed open and the boiling brew bubbled and swirled past the opening. Gottfried was tossing in the hops from a tin measure. The brew swirled away with the tiny green leaves, churning them down out of sight. He was watching for the brake.

"Well, we're still hopping the wort!" he said with heavy humor.

Sara smiled. Once she had thought the names for various processes so queer; now they were as familiar as embroidery terms were to Mama and the girls. She stood beside him watching. He took longer about everything than he needed to, putting the measure back in its place, closing the copper door, looking at the thermometer. She felt as she had those first weeks when she stood around the brewery and tried to learn how things were done. Now again she felt out of place.

Herman Anspach came by, looked into the brew-kettle, not deliberately as Gottfried had, but efficiently, swiftly. He spoke briskly with a ready grin. He stood by Gottfried a minute and his very vigor made Gottfried seem old and shrunken. Sara resented him. Closing the brewery wouldn't matter so much to him. He was too young.

"I've been thinking over the situation, Missus Henkel," Gottfried said ponderously when they were both in his tiny office in the brewhouse. Today he didn't look like an astrologer wielding secret powers in his magician's tower, but only like an old man who would soon be out of a job. "There are certain steps we might take. Herman was talking to a brewer in Detroit an' he was telling how they was looking into a process for de-alcoholizing beer to make a kind of soft drink." Gottfried's voice carried no conviction.

"No," Sara said. "I wouldn't like that. That seems somehow cheapening to the brewery."

"It is expensive too," Gottfried muttered.

"And it admits that making beer was wrong, Gottfried," Sara said slowly, out of her own thinking. "It isn't."

But Gottfried paid no attention. He didn't always quite follow Sara's thinking. There had never been any question of wrong about it. What did she mean?

"No, Gottfried, we'll run the brewery all year, right up to the day that prohibition goes into effect. And then we'll stop on the dot. We'll close up tight. Whatever is left in the vats we'll let the prohibition agent come and empty out, and let him padlock the place. We'll obey the law to the very letter."

Sara's mouth had a tight look to it. As Gottfried went back to his work, her eyes watched him coldly, almost as though he were not there. She hardly asked for Gottfried's opinion or Adolf's any more than she listened to Belle's continuous philosophizing that this was all for the best, or bothered to read the seven or eight closely written pages that later came from Marie denouncing the injustice of legislation that destroyed an industry without compensation.

When Hugh Ashford, the wounded British soldier, came to Armitage to speak at a great mass meeting held in the Academy, Sara went. She bought box tickets, since the meeting was held as a benefit for the Allies.

The young soldier limped out on the stage and smiled wanly with such engaging sadness that the whole audience was brought to its feet. In a hesitating voice, enhanced by an English accent, he told of the suffering in the trenches, of atrocities perpetrated by the Germans. He spoke of the need of the Allies for foodstuffs and cargoes of grain. The word "Hun" dotted his sentences.

Sara leaned on the velvet railing to listen, as she had once listened to Modjeska. Her cheeks were pink with feeling. If the Allies needed the grains used in making beer, if they needed the barley that lay in the drying rooms, pale and silvery in the light through the heavy glass of the windows, of course, breweries should be closed. "Beer is liquid bread," Gottfried liked to say, but hungry people wanted solid bread to break off in their hands and eat. It was all right; she could understand. She could sacrifice, too. Why didn't people say, "You're closing the brewery so the grain can go to the starving millions in Europe—how wonderful!" For the first time since November the feeling of injustice and bitterness eased.

"I'm glad we took the box, Sara," Belle said on the way home. "It certainly answered anyone who questioned your sympathies!"

"My sympathies, Belle?"

"Well, of course, with a name like Henkel and being in the brewing business. You didn't see that article in the paper about their discovering the connection between one of the big breweries and the Huns?"

"No," Sara said. "No, I didn't." She drove home the rest of the way in silence.

She had been trying to look on the closing of the brewery as a noble sacrifice that she was glad to make for the starving people of Europe. But that was mock heroics. The French weren't turning all their grapes into raisins. The Tommies still had their small beer. She was no voluntary martyr; she was a helpless victim of unreasonable legislation, she thought in her bitterness. Belle's idealism made use of by politicians like Derrick and Paul.

In January Sara went down to consult Mr. Blanchard. She called and made an appointment, but she had little concern lest she meet Paul. He had scant time now for the practice of law. Yet Sara thought about Paul as she drove downtown. She would hate to meet him. Without herself being aware of it, she had drawn into a new habit of reserve. She was careful not to speak first nor too cordially to people she had known since childhood, leaving them to make any overture of friendliness. The new reserve left its trace on her face, giving it more resemblance to that of Winthrop Bolster.

She was aware that the secretary in the outer office looked at her with more than ordinary interest. Everyone seemed to, since prohibition had become a certainty, looking to see how she "took it."

She sat across the desk from Mr. Blanchard as she had sat

that day she had told him of her intention of carrying on the brewery. She thought of that now. There was something in his kindly, pitying look as he glanced at her over his half-glasses that stung her into quick, childish defiance.

"Well, Mr. Blanchard, you were right and I was wrong," Sara said.

"How do you mean, Mrs. Henkel?"

"About the brewery. I shouldn't have tried to run it. I should have been better off if I'd never tackled it." She was shocked at her own words. She didn't believe them for a minute, but it was better to say them than to have him say them or think them.

"I'm not sure of that, Mrs. Henkel," Mr. Blanchard said slowly. "Not sure of that at all.—You've made a great success of the brewery. You've supported three families on it over a considerable number of years."

The slow statement sent a stream of warmth through her.

"I've been amazed, my dear, at your success. I wouldn't have believed it possible. I know your father was very proud of your ability."

"Oh, no, you're wrong about that; Father wouldn't take any money from me he disapproved so strongly."

"Your father told me, himself, Sara, that you had been the son of the family. And at the end, when his holdings were . . . er, considerably lessened . . ." It was difficult for Mr. Blanchard to discuss a client's securities even with his daughter. ". . . he told me that he didn't worry, that you would look after Mrs. Bolster and the girls."

Sara sat quietly in her chair.

"On beer, Mr. Blanchard? He didn't mind that?"

Mr. Blanchard coughed. He was not used to women clients who spoke of beer. As a matter of fact, he and Mr. Bolster had never mentioned the word beer.

"He never said he did, my dear," Mr. Blanchard replied with evasive honesty.

As Sara went down in the elevator from the conference with Mr. Blanchard all that he had said about the hopelessness of the situation, or the futility of expecting anything from the state to make up for the complete loss of business—all this faded from her mind. She was remembering that Papa had been proud of her, even though he had never admitted it to her.

There was nothing to feel ashamed of, just because the law had been passed. The thing that mattered was that she was right in her own eyes. And she would never let anyone know how hurt she was at peoples' attitude. The Bolsters could always keep their own counsel. There was the time the doctor had let little Winthrop die. No one had ever known. Even in the family it had never been mentioned. Sara's feeling of separateness, almost of isolation from her own family, left her. She was a Bolster, after all.

14 1918

APRIL 30, 1918, might have been any other spring day. It was so warm Sara had the tables set up under the trees.

"For one day, Missus Henkel?" Gottfried asked in amazement.

"Of course, Gottfried, why not; we'll use them for the restaurant later. Tonight, the garden should be packed. We'll close out in a blaze of glory!"

She advertised in all the papers and on placards around the city:

CELEBRATE THE END OF AN ERA
AT
HENKEL'S SOMMER GARTEN!

And by ten o'clock that night the garden was filled. The tables in Der Winter Garten were filled. There were special menus tonight with the words END OF AN ERA engraved at the top. Adolf frowned over the bill for engraving, but Sara was determined. The difference between engraving and printing was more than a matter of dollars and cents. Tonight there was a cover charge of two dollars in Der Winter Garten and a dollar in the garden . . . "to guard against too boisterous an element," Sara explained.

There were special German dishes that Sara had gone right on serving in spite of the unpopularity of all things

German, but they were designated on the menu as "old foreign dishes": wiener schnitzel and sauerbraten and chicken paprika. There were all manner of torten and kuchen with steaming black coffee that was the best in town. The beer was as sparkling and clear as the tall glasses that held it. There was bock beer, by request.

"No war songs tonight," Sara had told the orchestra, and so they played Strauss waltzes that floated tranquilly out on the night air as though there were no such thing as an end of an era, nor of youth, nor the life of foreign cities. The first violinist had lost his position with a Detroit dance orchestra because he was German; the cellist had just moved from the boardinghouse he had lived in for twenty-five years because of the hostility of the other boarders. The elderly woman who played the harp had lost a nephew in the German army, but she would never dream of mentioning it. Tonight, there was no bitterness in their faces as they made music. In the intermissions waitresses brought them beer with the compliments of Mrs. Henkel.

There were young people who had never drunk beer before at the tables under the trees, seeing what it was like before it was too late; just as there were young people in the hotels and private homes of the city having their first taste of whiskey and champagne since it was so soon to be forbidden. There were tables of people middle-aged and older, who spoke with a slightly foreign accent and shook their heads over the coming prohibition. "How life would be without a glass of beer in the evening after supper?—for the old man, anyway. And what about weddings?"

Gretchen, one of the little waitresses, overheard many bits of conversation:

"I never was drunk in my life, nor one of my sons," Heinrich Apfel, who was president of the coal company, said.

"Next week we are sailing for France," Henry Schulz, home for leave in his new khaki uniform, murmured to his fiancée under the cover of the music. "They say their beer is terrible."

The beer was pretty in the tall glasses, Gretchen thought. Mrs. Henkel was keeping her on for the restaurant. But the nice old men who came to the garden almost every evening in the summer and sat over a glass of beer, and listened to the music, and tipped as much as the beer cost every time—they wouldn't come to the restaurant; she was sure of that.

Mrs. Henkel looked handsome tonight. If she was worried about the brewery closing, nobody would know it. She was the kind . . . she had helped all of them that she could to find work.

Gretchen looked across at the third table on the left. Gottfried and Steiner and Charlie Freehahn, of all people, were with Mrs. Henkel. Charlie's daughter worked in the kitchens and told how pleased Charlie was. He was spruced up to within an inch of his life. They didn't match her; little dumpy men they were, except Charlie. He was big as a barrel. Mrs. Henkel looked younger than she was, considering she had two grown-up sons. There wasn't a bit of gray in her hair. Charlie's daughter said Mrs. Henkel came from society people on Park Avenue before she married the Henkels. She looked it, too.

The orchestra leader tapped on his music rack and held up his hand. "Mr. Werner has an announcement."

Gottfried Werner made his way slowly to the platform. People craned their necks to see who he was. Very few knew the dignified old gentleman with the wonderful and sad looking mustaches. He cleared his voice before he began.

"Ladies and Gentlemen, tonight marks the end of an era." He paused. "And tonight marks the end of Henkel's Brewery, that has never been closed since the day it began in 1867. It has been a landmark in this city, certainly to the people in the city who come from the old country. What is more, it has been an honorable landmark. . . ." He was interrupted by clapping. Everyone was clapping. The applause was too much for the old man. His eyes filled with tears. He took a large white handkerchief from the pocket in the skirt of his Prince Albert coat and blew his nose loudly.

"It was never John Henkel's wish or thought to foster the evil in the city. He meant only to manufacture the best beer honestly for those who liked it. The business has been carried on by his son, Wilhelm Henkel, and at his untimely death by Mrs. Wilhelm Henkel."

Sara stirred uneasily. Gottfried was only to make an announcement. She hadn't intended to have him make a speech. People would grow restive. Their food would be cold.

"At twelve tonight—" Gottfried consulted his watch "—the manufacture or sale of beer is declared illegal by law. Henkel's will obey that law. At midnight, tonight, whatever is left in the cellars will be emptied." Gottfried's face showed his bewilderment.

"It is Missus Henkel's wish that from now on the beer is served free of charge. Drink as much as you wish, only this!" He held up one shaking finger. "Don't forget to drink to Henkel's!"

Gottfried finished with a flourish. As he turned and went back to Sara's table, his eyes filled again.

Sara touched his hand an instant on the table. She and Adolf and Charlie and Gottfried said very little. Only Charlie had had any appetite. It was queer, Sara thought, to look at the beer garden so well filled and take so little pleasure in it. It didn't mean an auspicious start for the season; it meant the end.

"It is this," Gottfried said, leaning over the table, "it is not because folks drink too much, that they is no good. The ones which is no good in the first place, they drink too much. It makes nothing to try to cure their trouble at the wrong end with this prohibition!"

Sara watched the people at the tables without answering. She knew many who came often to the beer garden, but there were many strange faces tonight. Mr. Griffith was there, and the Waverleys, but very few from her own world.

The demand for beer tonight was tremendous. The trays went by continuously. Some people were drinking too much. Well, let them. She no longer cared. There was a man slipping bottles of beer into his coat pocket to carry out. Someone else asked for a case to carry away in his auto. Charlie's son, Otto, came back to tell her.

"Let him have it; there's beer to throw away. But no drunkenness on the grounds, Otto, even on this last night."

Gottfried made a sound of disgust in his throat. "What we should do is to store all the bottled beer there is left in the cellar of der Winter Garten, Missus Henkel. We could get ten times the price after prohibition comes in," he grumbled.

"It would be nice," Sara laughed, "but we can't do it. It all goes down the sewer. Henkel's won't bootleg." She used the unfamiliar word cautiously.

Gottfried shrugged and looked gloomily at the beer in his glass. Young Otto went back to the gate. Charlie signaled the waiter for more beer.

The orchestra played. The music was a help. She would still have the orchestra for the restaurant, but it would have to be much smaller; nothing would be the same. Sara leaned back in her chair.

"Tonight, Missus Henkel, does the prohibition officer come?" Adolf asked out of his long silence.

Sara nodded. "Yes, we might as well get it over with. He wasn't anxious to come tonight, but I told him I wanted him here at twelve."

The orchestra played. The people stayed. Some of them were humming or singing with the music. In an hour more prohibition would be a fact. Sara looked across the garden. She was tired of thinking or hearing about prohibition, tired of the sound and sight and smell of beer. She was tired of life itself; it was too hard; there were too many things to worry about.

She saw a young man making his way along the aisle. People were still coming as late as this. The young man wore a khaki tunic. His hair was very smooth and light, almost white, as he passed under the lantern.

Sara put her hand over her lips, pressing them tight. Her face drained of any color. Adolf and Gottfried and Charlie pushed back their chairs and stood up. He was shaking hands with them.

"Win!" Sara whispered behind her fingers. She held out her hands to him. He sat down beside her. He was so strong and clear-featured and smiling. He was so proud of his uniform.

"Mom, I nearly broke my neck to get here. I joined up."

"How fine, Win!" Sara said, the words sticking in her throat.

"My, what a crowd. It's a whopper for this time of year, isn't it?" Win took in Gottfried and Adolf and Charlie.

Gottfried looked at him sadly. "Because of prohibition."

He took out his watch. "In fifteen minutes, the Henkel Brewery closes."

"That's right! I'd forgotten for a minute!" Win glanced at Sara with a contrite face. "It means the whole works, doesn't it, Mom?"

Sara smiled. "Oh, we'll have our restaurant." She spoke lightly. There was no sense in worrying Win. It hurt and pleased her that Win looked so much like his father. Now she was going to lose him, too.

At midnight, the orchestra came to a grand finale. People were singing with the music at the close. They didn't want to go. They clapped and shouted for more, and pounded with their glasses on the tables. The orchestra bowed; the orchestra leader bowed. Gottfried stood up.

"Ladies und Gentlemen, that ist all!" His voice drooped with dreary finality. The crowds applauded Gottfried. The waitresses were hurrying glasses off the tables. There was to be no sign of beer after midnight, Sara had ordered. Reluctantly the crowds moved toward the gate.

Sara saw the two policemen come into the garden, just dropping in to see that there was no disorder; standing civilly by, looking on. Yet their being there brought something sinister into the evening.

The agent who was required by law to be present when the vats were emptied and the padlock put on the door of the brewery was there on time. He was a meek-looking man in a gray suit.

"Mrs. Henkel, I presume," he said, coming up to her. "My name is Wilkins."

"How do you do," Sara said. "I'll change my dress and then I'll be with you, if you will wait here with Mr. Werner, our brewmaster."

"Mom, I'll tend to him. You don't have to be here," Win objected.

"No, Win, I want to be there. You come along and watch."

Sara wore her short gray skirt and blouse when she came back, and her old gray sweater. Gottfried had put on his rubber boots. He brought a pair for Mr. Wilkins.

"Will we need these?" Mr. Wilkins asked.

"We will need them. There must be four hundred barrels left in the cellar," Gottfried answered morosely.

Mr. Wilkins spread his official papers and their duplicates out upon the top of one of the empty barrels in the room outside the ruh cellar. Gottfried held open the door for them. He handed a pair of pliers to Mr. Wilkins.

"You go along and open the spigot on each barrel," he directed with as much gravity as though he were an undertaker giving directions.

Mr. Wilkins coughed. "I—I've never been in a brewery before," he said apologetically. "I—I've always been a teetotaler myself." He glanced at the faces around him for understanding, but they were unsympathetic. Gottfried looked at him as though he were some peculiar insect; Win with obvious scorn. Sara was looking at that moment at Win.

The cellar was damp and cold. It was dimly lighted by the thick candle in its bracket against the whitewashed brick wall.

Mr. Wilkins slipped out of his pointed-toed shoes and pulled on the rubber boots over his trousers. He took off his coat; he looked cold in his striped silk shirt. Gottfried led the way. Win and Sara and Adolf stood by the door.

Mr. Wilkins glanced up at the great oak barrels that towered above him on either side of the aisle. No one spoke. The chill of the cellar was oppressive. Mr. Wilkins pointed to the printing on one of the barrels: "White oak. Capacity 90 Bbls."

"These tanks must've cost a pretty penny!" he commented, but Gottfried made no answer to a remark so obvious. There was something cheap about the little man clumping cautiously after Gottfried, Sara thought. He had laid off his official importance with his papers.

"Begin there," Gottfried told him sternly.

Mr. Wilkins looked uncertain as to how to begin. He adjusted the pliers. The handle did not turn. He tried it again.

"Here." Gottfried gave the handle a practiced twist. He handed the pliers back to Wilkins. The beer ran out of the spigot, spattering on the cement floor. Wilkins looked hesitatingly at Gottfried. Gottfried had already moved down the aisle to the next vat. Mr. Wilkins tried each spigot in turn. Each time he handed the pliers over to Gottfried. A stream of beer, colorless in the dimly lighted cellar, ran down onto the floor. The last row of tanks was empty, but Gottfried led the agent of the law to each one and turned the spigot on full.

The beer pouring out of three rows of barrels covered over the whole floor, coming up on Mr. Wilkins' boots. The streams no longer made a spattering sound, but poured out into the lake of beer with only a small liquid noise, pleasant as a small brook or a garden fountain. There were streaks of foam on top of the clear brown lake. The beer covered Mr. Wilkins' ankles.

"Gosh, what a crime, Mom!" Win burst out.

Adolf muttered incomprehensible syllables. Sara stood quietly, remembering, of all foolish things, the time that William had taken her through the brewery. The cellars had seemed cold, queer places. She watched the beer on the cement floor deepen. The flame of the candle sparkled on its surface.

"I like people who get their dreams into concrete form," William had said, "bricks and good beer." And this was the end of John Henkel's dream, spilled out on the floor and run into the drain; made wrong and disreputable. All he had built up and improved was lost; nothing could be saved out of it.

"Never mind, Mom," Win said, taking her arm. She hadn't known that she was trembling. "Look at Gottfried; he's going to keep that little fellow there till it's all gone," Win grinned.

The beer came within an inch of the top of their knee boots. Mr. Wilkins looked at it anxiously.

"It does seem a great pity!" he exclaimed. "Of course, you know, this isn't my doing. I'm just an officer of the law. I'm just doing my duty." His voice came out weakly above the running sound of the beer. Gottfried grunted. "Perhaps we better move over to the step," Mr. Wilkins suggested, moving cautiously in the beer.

"No, I want you right here on the ground, so's you can see for yourself that it's all been let out," Gottfried declared. Mr. Wilkins' discomfort satisfied the heavy humor in Gottfried's nature. Once he glanced over at the big drains at the end that he had partly stopped so the beer would back up. He wanted the prohibition officer to wade in it.

"I'm a teetotaler; been one all my life, but I'd like to see what this stuff tastes like," Mr. Wilkins said apologetically. "Our orders allow for that, in the line of duty, of course."

Gottfried made no answer, but sloshed slowly through the beer to the wall where a copper tankard hung.

The three in the door and Gottfried watched in silence while Mr. Wilkins drank. His face was hidden behind the tankard. He took one swallow and then drank steadily. Silently, he handed the empty mug to Gottfried.

"Bottoms up," Gottfried approved, as though Mr. Wilkins were a child that had finished a big glass of milk.

Mr. Wilkins smiled sheepishly. "It's not unlike pop; rather bitter though," he said.

Gottfried scowled darkly. Win disappeared into the other room, laughing.

It was quarter of one before they left the brewery. Even the engine room was dark and the great red wheels stood still.

"Do you mean, Mom, that you haven't a single bottle of beer stored away in the house, even?"

Sara shook her head. "I mean to keep the law, Win."

Win whistled. "You're a great girl, Mom. And thanks for being . . . the way you were about my enlisting. It seems kind of tough on you with the brewery closing down and everything. . . ."

"That's all right, Win," Sara said. "I know you felt you had to." She added after a pause, "I'm a little tired, tonight, I think I'll go right to bed." She hurried along the path from the brewery without glancing back at the dark towered building by the river.

15

THE brewery had been closed five months. Beyond the grove of trees that separated the house and the brewery there were no sounds of activity; no smoke rose from the tall brick chimney. The early fall air held no deeper scent than that of molding leaves. There was no smell of hops or malt or beer to give it body. Sara walked up the steps of the porch slowly, feeling the day empty in its quietness, the air thin. She looked at the house.

"A big old place," Mr. Jeffreys had called it, "really a burden to you."

She had never felt it a burden. It had been a refuge in those first days when she had worked at the brewery until she was so tired she could no longer keep her mind on the rows of neat little figures Adolf was forever showing her.

The house held all she remembered of William. He had built it for her. It held the boys' childhood. Heaven knew she had had little enough of that. She had been so busy that Belle had been with the boys more than she had. Oh, no, the house was more than just a house.

"Sara, what on earth are you staring at?" Belle came to the screen door with her knitting in her hands. "I heard the gate click and then you didn't come in."

Sara looked around the wide familiar hall. She went

through the doorway into the living room. Belle followed her. She glanced at the books on the shelves. Those on the right of the fireplace had the hard-looking German titles that once were as incomprehensible to her as William's taking over the brewery. They had grown familiar enough now; it was almost as though she could read them. What apartment would ever have room for all her books, and the big carved table, and the piano?

"Sara!" Belle spoke sharply; she had turned from the door to watch Sara.

"Oh," Sara gave a little apologetic laugh. "I was looking at my house. I've just seen Mr. Jeffreys."

"Mr. Jeffreys?"

"The real-estate agent. He has a customer for the place, the new manager of the munitions plant, if we can be out by the first of the month."

Belle sat down on the chair by the door. "But you're not going to do it! Where would we go? We couldn't begin to be out in a month, anyway."

"Why, Belle, I thought you always hated living so near the brewery. I thought you only did it for my sake and the boys'?"

"I did at first, of course, but the brewery's closed now. And we've lived here half our lives. Of course, you've been busy at the brewery; it didn't mean so much to you. Because of . . . of the way things turned out for me, I've had to make it my life." Belle's tone had grown dramatic. Unconsciously she lifted her head. Her face wore a shallow air of nobility. "Sara, you can't mean you're really thinking of selling it!"

"I don't know. I need the money if I can get it."

"I thought you said the restaurant was picking up!"

"It is, but the most we can hope for will be less than

half the earnings of the brewery, and that won't be clear. Some of the expenses of the brewery keep on, too."

"Why do they?"

Sara shrugged. "Taxes, insurance—they go on all the time. We have to keep a night watchman on the place." Let Belle feel the pinch a little. She had helped to cause it. "I can't cut down any more on Ottilie's or Marie's income. You know I told Anne I'd pay for the nurse for Mama. Then there are Bill's college expenses. Win has a year of college yet—if he comes back alive. No, I've been all over it; I can't see any other way." Sara's voice faded into worried indecision.

"But your home, Sara! People are always sorry when they sell their homes. You were too young to feel it, but Mama and I suffered terribly when the old house burned."

"I know; it would mean changing our way of living if we sold and moved into an apartment," Sara said slowly.

"Changing our way of living. . . ." Sara was a child again, standing in the hall, hearing Mama say with sweet finality, "It would mean changing our whole way of living." Hearing Papa say, "No, no, Corona, I wouldn't think of it." She had run upstairs then, wondering why they couldn't change their way of living; scorning Mama and the girls.

"Sara!" Belle looked at her impatiently.

"I was just thinking," Sara said.

Belle went on talking. "This side of town is improving. Beth Ingalls was saying the other day that in a few years there'd be a restricted residence section on the east side, too. I don't mind it particularly now that the brewery's closed."

What was she thinking of? Had she changed; grown more like Mama? Selling the house was the only thing to do. The boys were going to need money more than this house. The house had served its purpose. She could find some place, a small apartment. What did it matter?

"No, Belle, it would be foolish to keep the place just for the two of us when I need the money so badly."

"I don't know why you consult me at all, Sara. You run everything as though you were running the brewery," Belle said petulantly.

Sara didn't answer. She was right in deciding to sell; Belle was entirely selfish about the house. For an instant Sara's face set, her lips closing in a line so firm it held little trace of youthfulness. Belle sighed audibly. Sara pretended not to hear it. She sat looking out the front window.

"Besides, Sara, you may be able to sell the brewery for . . . oh, for a storage plant. Mr. Jamieson said the other day that he wouldn't be surprised if you could. That's what they're doing with old breweries in some cities. Then you wouldn't need to sell the house."

So Belle discussed it with strangers! Anger rose in her. "Belle!"—Sara began and stopped. A Western Union boy was leaning his bicycle against the fence. "Look, Belle," Sara said in a different tone of voice. She had no power to move. It was a wire, about Win. She hadn't heard from Win for so long; she knew he had sailed. He had been wounded, killed maybe. Everything else had happened to her; there was only this left. Panic—no, certainty—caught in her throat. She watched Belle sign for the wire.

"Shall I open it, Sara?" Belle held it out. The warm September sun edged its sharp corners.

"No, I'll open it," Sara said, taking the envelope in her hand, not looking at Belle. She turned it over. There was no star. Someone had told her there was always a star on death messages. He was wounded then; crippled, maybe, for life.

"Sara, hurry, for heaven's sake!" Belle said sharply. Sara tore the envelope carefully across.

IN TROUBLE STOP BACCHUS GOT THE BEST OF US STOP ARRIVING HOME THREE P. M. TRAIN WITH DETAILS STOP SORRY, LOVE. BILL.

Sara handed it over to Belle. She laughed nervously.

"Oh, Belle!" Relief made her weak. "It's not Win."

Belle handed the wire back to her. "He ought to be ashamed of himself, wiring a thing like that. He might know it would scare us to death. People might hear of it through the telegraph office."

Sara wasn't listening. She had never had any trouble with the boys about drinking before. She had expected them to have enough judgment.

"You see, Sara, what living next to a brewery all their lives and seeing beer . . ."

"They've never seen drunkenness here, Belle, nor at the brewery!" Sara flashed back. She was quick to resent any remarks about the brewery these days.

"I'd die of shame if there were a drunkard in my family!"

"Oh, there won't be. One prank doesn't mean he's a drunkard."

"This is the beginning, though." Belle's voice trembled. It had a sharp, hysterical note. "He's always had enough money. He's never had any rules laid down; you've just expected him to do right because he's your son. If you excuse this, Sara, as a prank you'll excuse the next step. I know what I'm talking about. Derrick VanRansom was handsome, full of spirit. People said he was just sowing his wild oats; that when he married he'd settle down. The first time he drank a little too much after we were married I forgave him, too." Belle's face had lost the fresh coloring that made her so youthful in spite of her white hair. It was as white as the bow of ribbon pinned into her shirtwaist. "I love Bill as much as though he were my own son, but I'd rather see him dead than see him become like . . . like Derrick!"

Sara sat holding the wire in her hands, looking at Belle. She had never seen Belle like this.

"Go ahead, sell this house so the boys can have everything. I'll move into some dingy, dark little rooms with you and cook over a gas plate and all the rest of it, but mark my words! Sara! you'll be doing a kinder thing for William if you take him out of school right now and let him go to work. Let him know why you're doing it. Tell him he's had his chance and he's thrown it away. Now he can help to keep this house. He'll think more of you for it and it may make a man out of him."

Belle rushed out of the room and Sara heard her running up the stairs to her room.

Sara read the wire again. Belle was right. She would tell Bill he could go to work and help with the expenses instead of adding to them. Why should she sell the house if that was all Bill thought of school—or of her? She had made life too easy for him, been too indulgent. She should have kept the boys here in the summers and let them work in the brewery or around the yard. They would have learned then that she would stand for no drunkenness.

Sara's eyes were light when they were scornful or angry. "She can be cold like a fish," Adolf used to tell Gottfried, "when she give someone the sack or when she find something done wrong." She was cold now and angry.

Bill should have thought of her. He knew how careful she had been to abide by the law, and then he went ahead and got himself in trouble!

She moved around the room restlessly. She was glad now

that she hadn't called Mr. Jeffreys. Mr. Blanchard had advised her to take the boys out of school and let them go to work. She would teach Bill to take responsibility. His wire was too gay, cocksure. She would show him she could be as hard as any man.

On the bookshelf by her chair the German-titled books stared firmly back at her. They hadn't been touched since William's death, except to be dusted. She touched them now with her fingers, still thinking of what she would say to Bill. She came to a volume much smaller than the rest.

"Kommers Buch," she read on the back. Silver nail heads studded its wide covers, giving it a heavy look, curiously like the big front doors of the brewery. Sara opened it. The short lines surrounded by wide margins must be poetry. She leafed a few pages, half-reading the first line. Some of the words were like English.

"Bier hier, Bier hier. . . ."

This must be the book of German student songs William used to play and sing. She remembered suddenly how William used to sing them, putting his head back and filling the whole room with his voice. One time he had grabbed up a stein and flourished it as he sang.

"This is the way we used to sing them in the drinking clubs in Göttingen, Sara. The night Friederich and Hans and I passed our examinations—oh, you should have heard us! We celebrated to make up for all those months of grinding."

William had told her that the night after Paul had come to call. She had felt so lonely and strange. She had wondered secretly if she hadn't made a terrible mistake in marrying him. She had sat across the room with her sewing and her thoughts and William had been reading. Then he had thrown down his book and gone over to the piano. He was so hilarious, like a child, for no reason at all. William was always surprising her: the way he talked about the brewery and wasn't ashamed of it, and the next breath was reading poetry to her; the way he could make her feel his love without even touching her. She hadn't thought of these things for years. They came back now, warming her, making her eyes wet and her throat ache. He had sung her that song in Latin about rejoicing while we are young almost as though he had known he wasn't to live long; and lifted her in his arms and carried her upstairs. And he had lain with her almost as though he had known how far away she had been that day.

She must tell Bill more about his father. He didn't like the course dinners at her mother's house, she remembered, that had wine with every course and a liqueur with the coffee. Where the ladies left and the men lingered at the table. "There's no joy in it, Sara. It's all so solemn and ponderous and formal and I have a headache the next day," he used to protest.

That was it; if there was no joy in it, it became a kind of sin. William used to make the word joy into something simple and childlike; something Winthrop Bolster would never have understood.

William would never have been hard with his son as she had made up her mind to be. He would never have thought of taking his son's chance at education away as a punishment. "My father never speaks of what I owe him; that's why I feel it so much, Sara." She was shocked now at what she had been about to do. She thought of Belle. Belle had never helped Derrick. Instead she had driven him away and lost him. Sara put the fat little book back in the bookcase.

She was at the station a little before three. She walked up and down the platform that seemed to have shrunk since the days when the Red Sash Brigade rode into town. She tried to think how to begin. Bill had wanted to get it all out before he saw her, that was why he had wired. She understood. The Bolsters didn't talk things over easily. In all these years Belle had never talked about Derrick until today.

There was the train.

"Hello, Bill," Sara said, smiling.

"Hello, Mom!" Bill hugged her. It was good to see him. He didn't look like the prodigal son returning. He looked as confident that the world was his as though he had won all the honors at college—but that was to cover embarrassment.

"Nice of you to have the station decently empty, Mom. I imagine there'll be a pretty piece in the paper! 'Local Boy Goes Wrong!' "

"There's the car over there. You drive, will you, Bill?" Sara said.

"Mom, I might as well tell you about it right now. Maybe I shouldn't have wired first." He kept his eyes on the street as he talked. "You see there's a new place down on Raymond Street, a speakeasy; all the boys go there; lot safer than the stuff they bring around to the houses to sell. They have real whiskey brought in from Canada. We had a little too much; I guess we were pretty drunk." He waited for her to interrupt him, then he went on. "When we came home we got into a fight. I turned the firehose on the boys downstairs and Whitey Clark broke a window. Anyway, the police were called and took us down to the station."

It was nothing so very bad; nothing criminal. Sara smiled at the street.

"The Dean's a good egg; he was mad though. He sent us all home to tell our families about it. Whitey's scared sick. He says his Dad'll make him stay home. The Dean wants us back this time. He said to think it over for the rest of the month." Bill waited. "I'm sorry, Mom."

"I'm sorry, too," Sara said. "We'll talk about it later. I've been meaning to go out to see Charlie Freehahn for a long time and it's quite a trip alone. Will you drive me out there now, Bill?"

She could feel his surprise. "Sure, where's he live now?"

"He has a little farm out about five miles. I gave him Donner and Thor. All the rest were sold." Sara stole a glance at Bill. He was still ill at ease, braced, waiting for her to begin.

"Do you remember the night Donner was so sick with dropsy, Bill? Or were you too small?"

"No, I remember. I went to sleep in the barn."

"Yes, Charlie carried you home and put you to bed."

Bill smiled. "Win used to hang around the stable more than I did, though."

"Yes," Sara said. She looked at the river. There was nothing left where the old Cogley mill used to be. How the automobile factory stood out from here. She was feeling her way.

Bill sat back in the seat, driving with careful nonchalance, his left hand lying along the car door. "Nance Ingalls home?"

"Yes, I think she is. She's busy doing Red Cross work."

"Nice kid; a little young," Bill remarked, lighting a cigarette.

"Say, Mom, you're old friend Paul Sevrance talked at the Law School. Everybody says he's the sure bet for Governor."

"Yes," Sara said, "I guess he is." Paul was getting where he wanted to fast enough, Sara thought. She came back to Bill. The subject of the drinking lay between them. She could feel him trying to get to it. Talking was easier than silence.

"I bet Aunt Belle's given me up as lost," Bill said, flicking off his ash.

Careful, now. Now they were coming to it. "Aunt Belle blames this on your living next to a brewery all your life. She'll be glad to see you. You were always her favorite. Turn in there, Bill, by the mailbox. It's that little place over there." There was no time to say anything more. There was Charlie.

"Hello, Charlie!"

"Missus Henkel! Und Wilhelm!" Charlie's pleasure was clear. He was so glad to see them.

"Hello, Charlie." Bill shook hands. Sara, watching him carefully, thought there was an air of superiority in Bill's manner; something of the young gentleman to the old servitor.

"Come in, come in," Charlie urged. "Wait, you will want to see Donner und Thor first."

"Of course we do," Sara said, all the more heartily because Bill wasn't really interested. He was only being gracefully charming. It was too easy for Bill to charm people.

"They're getting too fat!" Charlie said, leading the way out to his little barn. "Wait there." He went inside and pushed open the button on the stall door. When he came back, Donner followed him, then Thor. The big gray horse seemed all the bigger, emerging from the small barn. His sides shone, his mane was combed. Even the long hair of his fetlock was clean. He whinnied. Sara put out her hand and the horse came up to her. Sara rubbed the soft skin of his nose.

"Donner, do you miss the brewery? Here, Thor." It was absurd that she felt so glad to see them. Bill came over to pat them.

"They're beauties, Charlie. Did you ever show them?"

"Wait!" Charlie hurried back to his neat cottage, leaving Sara and Bill alone with the horses. Sara went on patting Donner's head. Bill stood by Thor. It was still out here in the country with a good smell of fall in the air. Now was the time to say something to Bill. If she could tell him about the horses, about the time at the revival meeting, how they had come to stand for . . . for something special in her mind. They were strength and sorrow and disappointment . . . life, itself, but you couldn't let them run over you. You had to harness them and drive them. She tried to find the words. Bill hated anything "sappy."

Charlie came back. She was too late. She went on idiotically straightening Donner's mane, looking into his great, patient brown eyes, afraid to speak out.

Charlie had a candy box in his hand. "Look here!" The big horses cropped the grass, as tame as two Shetland ponies. Sara and Charlie and Bill sat down on the old benches in front of the house. Charlie took out medals with faded ribbons hanging to them.

"First Blue Ribbon in the Detroit Workhorse Parade," Charlie announced. He handed the medals over to them. "Seven years running the Henkel Brewing Company won first prize for draft horses!"

"Then the auto trucks came in, I suppose," Bill suggested amiably.

Charlie threw back his shaggy white head. His eyes glared. He lifted his fist. "I tell you, that was the beginning of everything. You remember, Missus Henkel, the time you went to that brewers' convention you bought that first truck on the way home?" He let his hands fall hopelessly onto his knees. "You came back from there worried about prohibition. The writing was on the wall then!" Charlie looked like some ancient patriarch. His voice had grown dramatic. "Now we haf prohibition and what have we got? Now my Otto is gone late in the night; when he comes home I smell whiskey on him."

Sara could feel Bill's interest grow. She nodded sympathetically.

"They haf closed us up, Henkel's Brewery, that made the finest beer, as if there was something wrong about making beer!" Charlie missed having people to talk to. "I remember the old man used to say, 'Good beer must haf two things: stability und brilliancy.' "

"Stability—that means holds its foam, eh, Charlie?" Bill asked, still politely, humoring the old man's garrulousness.

Charlie waved the remark away. "Stability is when a beer can hold on to the character—" he made the word with a rounded gesture of his hand and repeated it for the pleasure of its sound "—the character it is given to start out with." Charlie let his eyes travel out across the bronze and yellow countryside to the bright blue sky. On the way he lost his train of thought and came back angrily to the injustice of closing the brewery.

"Prohibition! There never was no drunkenness around Henkel's Brewery, was there, Missus Henkel?"

Sara shook her head, not wanting to speak, wondering if Bill were taking in Charlie's words.

"When a man come to work for John Henkel Company, in the brewery or drivin' for me . . . same ting . . . we tell him if you get drunk once, you get fired, like that! There is no second chances. A man who gets drunk is no good!" Charlie shrugged his powerful shoulders. Sara looked into Charlie's bright blue eyes, but they were clear and guileless as a child's.

"Missus Henkel," Charlie leaned close to her. "Would

you und Wilhelm haf ein Glas Bier? I got some of Henkel's. Otto, he bring it out before the brewery close."

Sara smiled but she shook her head. "No, thanks, Charlie." Sara stopped to pat the horses again before they left. She had worried so about what to say, how to begin, and now there was no need. They drove home quietly.

"Charlie's a swell guy, isn't he!" Bill said. There was no hint of condescension in his voice.

"Yes, he is," Sara said. "Your father used to say that Charlie helped to bring him up."

16

"PRETTY good, Missus Henkel." Gottfried stood beside her on the steps of the balcony looking down on the restaurant.

"Eight tables empty," Sara answered.

"That is so, but look at the other restaurants in the city. What do you find? Already we haf a good catering business started. That's going to be the backbone of our business one of these days, Missus Henkel. Did you see the orders we had last week for fancy cakes?"

Sara smiled. She never saw the small iced cakes, decorated with icing flowers, without remembering a certain small cake ornamented with a perfect daisy, that she had hidden behind a palm tree at Dor's wedding.

While Gottfried talked to her his eyes kept watch on the restaurant and the waitresses just as they once kept watch on the wort in the brew-kettle or the mash, when they stood talking in the brewhouse.

When she and Gottfried and Adolf had talked over the restaurant after the brewery was closed, she had suggested hiring a manager. They had carried on the beer garden with Emil, the headwaiter, to direct things, but a restaurant was a business in itself. Gottfried had pursed his lips, looked down at the table in front of him, and said gruffly:

"I was thinking; I could be the new manager."

"You!" Adolf had taken off his spectacles and leaned over to look more closely at Gottfried. "You would walk around and pull out chairs for ladies and wear a black coat with tails and a shirt boiled stiff! Missus Henkel, did you ever see a man gone out of his wits?"

Gottfreid had turned to Sara as though he had not heard Adolf. "Over here, Missus Henkel, waiters do not have the . . ." he hesitated, weighing the right word in his big hands, ". . . the style. I know how those things should be done. I would not take a salary at first. We will wait and see how it goes."

"I will be in the office to keep the books," Adolf had said as though it were a foregone conclusion.

She had thought that they might want to look for other positions and was touched to find they meant to stay to run the restaurant.

"This is like the brewery," Sara had said the first day when they were together in the office of the restaurant.

"It is as like as is old beer to fresh beer!" Gottfried had muttered.

"Ach, there is someone; excuse me, Missus Henkel," Gottfried said now. She watched him swinging open the door for four newcomers, bowing as he ushered them in, saying something that made them smile. He was not an undistinguished figure as he crossed the room ahead of them. His white hair and mustache were brushed as they had never been in the days of the brewery. He wore a boiled shirt and swallowtail coat, but with it a dark green vest embroidered in bright flowers. Sara liked it. It was reminiscent of the gay uniforms the waitresses used to wear in the beer garden.

Two more people; this was like the days of Der Sommer

Garten when she had sat at her table, watching the people and the carriages passing on the street, hoping every carriage that passed would stop.

Over There, Over There, send the word, send the word,
Over There!

The music came from the four-piece orchestra under the balcony. She wished they wouldn't play war songs. War songs chilled her. She hadn't heard from Win this month. "We'll be going up soon, now," he had written.

Gottfried came back up the stairs. He was beaming. He carried a menu in his hand.

"Gottfried, tell them not to play war music," Sara said petulantly.

"But that is what people like. They forgive us for having a German name if they know we feel that way about the war. Do you know, tonight we have had more orders from here than anything else!" Gottfried pointed to the new section on the menu entitled "Famous American Dishes." "That was a good idea of yours, Missus Henkel." The recipes Sara had taken from Corona Bolster's cookbook. "It used to be foreign dishes made people feel 'cosmopolitan.' " He raised his eyebrows. "Now they feel America is best, so American foods is best."

Sara could not always be sure when Gottfried was poking fun, when he was serious.

"Where will you have your company tonight, inside or outside?"

"Out on the terrace, I think; it's still warm enough, and it's lovely there. I want my sisters to see that you can't get even a whiff of beer."

"Your family haf never been to eat here before?"

"My brother-in-law and his wife, but not my other sisters. I want them to be a little impressed, Gottfried."

Gottfried nodded knowingly. "Outdoors is best, by candlelight. Your sister will not know the candleholders used to be in the cellars of the brewery!" He drew up his lips as though to cover over his smile. He leaned over the railing, watching the waitresses, who dressed in black and white instead of the bright costumes of the beer garden.

"I miss some of our old friends, Missus Henkel."

"Yes, the street-car conductors that always used to stop here on their way home. . . ."

"And the German music teachers? I wonder if they get students to teach now," Gottfried said sadly. "One of them has a son in the American army." He shrugged again.

"I liked best the two old men who used to play chess while they drank their beer."

Gottfried sighed. "It was better than running a restaurant any day. People had time to talk, to enjoy, to think with their beer. Now they must have pie à la mode and get their bill quick."

"There they are, Gottfried. Tell them I'll be right down."

Sara went as far as the stairs and stood in the shadow, looking down on them. In all these years Belle had never set foot beyond the hedge gate. She was looking around the room with her grand-duchess manner. George's Home Guard uniform made him look more portly; that, or prosperity. Prosperity was becoming to Dor, too. Let them wait a moment and look at the restaurant. She was proud of it, of the number of people there. It was a proof that prohibition hadn't downed her.

What did Anne think? Anne looked elderly tonight. From up here her face seemed so lined. She was wearing a black velvet ribbon around her neck the way Mama did. Anne was only . . . after all, fifty-nine. Belle was four years older than Anne; but she looked younger. Even Dor was fifty-three, ten years older than she, herself. Sara went down the stairs to greet them, feeling a sudden protective tenderness for them, feeling herself young. What was age, after all, but measuring it against someone else's? Since she and Belle had moved out of the house into Miss Stevens' front-room apartment she had not felt so rich.

"Sara, this really is nice. I like the restaurant," Belle said, a faint kind of surprise in her voice.

"You should have come before," George told her. "Belle had to wait four or five months, Sara, to let all the brewery atmosphere get out of the place." George liked to twit his sisters. "The four graces are charming tonight!" he added, looking around the table at his wife and her sisters.

"George, I look like a fright," Anne complained. "I ought to get away more, but even with the nurse Sara got for Mama I feel I must be there."

The waitress took the soup plates and brought the squabs.

"Squabs, Sara! What a treat!" Dor exclaimed.

"We use Mama's recipe," Sara said. She had ordered the dinner carefully. The giblet paste was just right; the way it used to taste from the silver chafing dish at home.

"A bottle of 1914 sauterne would go well with this," George commented, winking at Sara. Sara seemed not to see him. George irritated her with his allusions to wines and liquor.

"What a connoisseur Papa was of wines and food," Anne said. "Sara, this is delicious; you can't find such food anywhere else in town." Sara's irritation melted in the warmth of Anne's praise. She had gone ahead so long knowing the girls disapproved of her, feeling that disapproval, that it was pleasant to have them actually praising the restaurant.

"Well, girls, by next month your old neighbor, Paul, will be Governor of the state!" George said.

"It's thrilling, isn't it?" Belle said.

Sara said nothing. So much had happened to them both in this last year, she thought. She had followed the progress of his campaign in spite of herself.

"Do Senators in Washington often resign to run for the office of Governor?" Anne asked George.

"Oh, yes," George explained. "And Paul was the logical man for the party. You saw what a victory he won in the primaries." As the man of the family George liked to set the girls straight on things.

Sara looked out across the park where Der Sommer Garten used to be. The lantern at the gable end of the restaurant, the candles in the brackets against the walls, threw light against the tree trunks. A faint dank smell came up from the river that had always been lost before under the sweetish heavy smell of the beer.

"I do think you're wonderful to do all this, Sara," Dor said. "It's beautiful."

"I tell you it's an achievement to weather prohibition the way you've done, Sara. You had this place open and going the very week the brewery stopped. Take Jerry Blake; he was in the office the other day. You remember Jerry, Dor; used to be bartender at the Gentlemen's Club. He's got a chance to do a discreet little bootleg business but that's the only thing he can find. Well, I told him. . . ." Sara wondered, sometimes, if George didn't enjoy mentioning fields that were foreign and even a little shocking to the girls.

Sara smiled happily at Gretchen coming through the door with the coffee tray. It had been a good idea to use the tall copper coffeepots and trays. They were so decorative. Gretchen barely smiled. She looked almost frightened, poor child. She poured a cup of coffee for Sara first.

"Mrs. Henkel, Mr. Werner wants to know if you will come to the office a minute, right away, please," she murmured in a very low voice.

Sara excused herself. What an odd request, in the middle of dinner! The music was gay. Four pieces were not much like the big orchestras they used to have, but they did very well in the restaurant. The room was well filled even as late as this. The people at the second table were leaving. A man was holding a woman's coat for her.

"Looks like a raid to me; we better go while the going's good!"

"Oh, no, Jack, let's stay and see the fun!"

What were they saying? The people two tables over were leaving, too. There was a buzz of conversation under the music. Sara flushed angrily. Then she saw Gottfried over by the office door talking to Mr. Wilkins. Behind him stood a policeman.

"What is it, Gottfried?"

"Missus Henkel, Mr. Wilkins here's got a warrant to search the restaurant; says there's been a report that we're hiding beer on the premises!" Gottfried's voice was indignant. He was red in the face. Sara was aware of the people looking curiously at them as they went by.

"Will you step in here and explain just what . . ." She led the way into her office. The sight of the policeman, Gottfried's red face, must have told everyone that something was wrong. She closed the door of the office. "Now what is it? There is absolutely nothing in the report that we have beer hidden here. Mr. Wilkins, you, yourself, saw the last drop of beer emptied out of the vats."

"Yes, I did, Mrs. Henkel. I told the chief that I was sure there was nothing in it, but this report come through to the office pretty straight. We've gotta search the place."

"I'm perfectly willing to have you search anywhere you want," Sara said scornfully. "I should have appreciated it if you had come another time instead of right now in the midst of the evening when people would get the idea that there is something wrong!"

"But, Missus Henkel," Gottfried began.

"That's all right, Gottfried, let them search all night if they want to. Let me know when they're entirely satisfied."

As she went back into the restaurant it was obvious that the rumor had spread. Everyone was leaving. The orchestra went on playing, but no one was listening. Thank heaven, the family were out on the terrace.

She saw Mr. Wilkins and the policeman follow Gottfried into the kitchen; then she took pains to walk slowly around the restaurant, smiling and nodding to people she had seen here before, seeming not to notice their hasty departures. She paused at one table.

"This is just a formality of the prohibition department. I am afraid some people were frightened at the sight of the policeman's uniform." She smiled merrily as though it were an excellent joke, but she saw the incredulity in the woman's eyes. She noticed the plain outline of a flask in the man's pocket as he put on his coat.

"Keep playing; play 'Tipperary,'" she murmured to the violinist. This was the way a restaurant's reputation was ruined. Her anger mounted. Through the open window she could see the family. She must keep them there until Mr. Wilkins and his policeman had left. She went toward the end of the room where the Dutch doors opened out on the flagged terrace.

She heard the doors to the kitchen swing back. Gottfried came hurriedly over to her as though there were nobody in the restaurant watching. His face was so red the white mustache that was really streaked with yellow looked snow-white.

"Missus Henkel, they found beer; over hunderd cases hid in the cellar. How can it be?" His words came out with a hissing sound. He was breathing hard. The hand that he laid on her arm was trembling. "Who could have put it there?"

"I'll have to see it myself to believe it," Sara said quickly. Her legs felt suddenly weak.

She opened the kitchen door. A half dozen cases of beer confronted her. The policeman was bringing up another. The whole kitchen force looked frightened. Sara glanced at Oscar, the chef, and Otto, Charlie Freehahn's boy, at Mrs. Kahn and the waitresses standing together by the door. They had all worked for her before; she would trust any one of them.

"Mrs. Henkel, I'm awful sorry," Mr. Wilkins began.

"But I don't know anything about it!" Sara heard herself saying like a character in a play. "Do any of you have any idea how the beer could have been hidden there?" She turned on the kitchen force sternly. They all shook their heads and protested. "Did anyone not hear me give orders to dispose of every bottle of beer after midnight the day prohibition came in?" Each person nodded. But she sounded silly to herself. What did this questioning and answering prove? She could see that Mr. Wilkins was impatient to be gone.

"There's a hunderd and fifty cases down there at least, Mrs. Henkel, hidden away pretty carefully, back of the coal. We almost come away without finding them."

Sara's mind did not seem to function. She glanced hopelessly at Gottfried. He looked as bewildered as she felt. She stared stupidly at the beer. The cases, the capped bottles, rising above the sides of the cases, HENKEL's painted plainly on the outside, were so familiar they had an odd power to reassure her for an instant. But the next minute their very familiarity seemed to accuse her.

"Mrs. Henkel, our orders are to confiscate any beer or liquor we find. The state's having trouble enforcing the laws, so they're tightening the screws, so to speak."

"Of course, take it. How it ever got there is a mystery to me." Sara saw the disbelief in Mr. Wilkins' face, in the policeman's expression. "What do I do; I mean, would you like me to go down and explain to the . . . to someone that I don't know anything about it?" She felt childish asking questions.

"You see, Mrs. Henkel, this is a pretty serious thing." Mr. Wilkins looked to the policeman for confirmation. The policeman's face was noncommittal. "I'll have to make complaint, you see, and . . ."

"What is the penalty for having beer; you can see that none of this has been touched," Sara asked, cutting through his deliberate tone. "Anyone can tell you that there hasn't been a drop of beer sold here. You can ask anyone!"

Mr. Wilkins shook his head. "I know. I know how you emptied all that beer out of the brewery, Mrs. Henkel. I've told plenty of people about that."

"Then . . ." Sara interrupted.

"But the point in relation to it is just here, Mrs. Henkel: the presence of liquor except in private residences is prima facie evidence of breach of act 9181 . . ." His voice had taken on the sonorous tone of one reading.

"But I know nothing at all about this beer, how it got there, where it came from." Sara moved her hands hopelessly.

"All right, Mrs. Henkel, but the way the law reads . . ." The policeman shifted his weight to the other foot.

"But this is all a mistake, I tell you. If you'll just give me time I'm sure it can all be explained."

"You'll have a pretty hard time explaining away two hunderd or so cases of beer hidden in the cellar!" The policeman laughed.

"But Mr. Wilkins was here, himself. He saw the last drop of beer in the place emptied out!"

"Sure he did. That made a swell impression on him, too. He didn't want to come up here tonight."

Sara turned away from him to Mr. Wilkins. "What can I do? If you'll give me time, I'm sure we can find out some way." She must keep calm, reasonable.

Mr. Wilkins shook his head. "I'm sorry, Mrs. Henkel. I hate to do it, but I'll have to tell the people to go. We'll have to close the place until you can get the court to open it up again."

Sara left Gottfried to make the announcement to the few people left in the restaurant. They were standing around waiting to see the excitement. He would just say that they were closing a little earlier tonight, but he wouldn't fool them. Tomorrow, it would all be in the papers, blazoned across the front page.

The family were waiting for her; George smoking his cigar, leaning back comfortably in his chair. Belle, Dor, Anne; they looked like gentle people. They held their heads proudly. What would they think when she told them? They would feel she had disgraced them again. She crossed the flagstone floor of the terrace. She was thankful they were the only ones on the terrace tonight.

"Oh, Sara, there you are! You were gone so long George wanted to go and find you," Dor said.

"It is so lovely out here, dear," Belle said. "It's almost

like a fall night at the old house, down along the bayou, remember?"

For a moment Sara couldn't bring herself to tell them. She sat down at the table without speaking. Then she said stupidly:

"I'm glad you like it."

"I think we ought to take our dinners here every evening, Sara, that we don't go over to Mama's," Belle said.

"We can't any more. It's going to be closed," Sara said quietly. It wasn't the way she had meant to tell them at all. "Mr. Wilkins, the prohibition agent, and a policeman came here tonight with a search warrant. They found beer hidden in the basement." She felt George sitting up straight in his chair. She heard Anne catch her breath.

"Oh, Sara, how could you!" Belle said.

"Sara, you shouldn't have run such a risk. An offense like that is a serious thing!" George said.

"I didn't run any risk. I knew nothing at all about it!"

"Of course you didn't, Sara. You come on home with us and George will go down to the police or prohibition place and explain the whole thing to them." Dor spoke soothingly as though to a child. Dor, like Mama, couldn't stand anything unpleasant.

Sara pushed her chair in to the table. "I haven't done anything at all to be ashamed of." She was so angry her voice trembled. Without knowing anything about it they believed she was guilty of a sneaking, underhanded piece of bootlegging. After all she had done for them!

"Sara." Dor touched her arm.

"Sara, you must get in touch with Blanchard right away. Suppose I call him for you. And I'll see what I can do about keeping it out of the paper." George was embarrassed. Whatever he thought, he meant to help her.

Sara looked at them: Anne stood pulling on her gloves, smoothing each kid finger down over her own. Dor was squeezing her arm, Belle's face was worried. They all wanted to help, to be kind; but they didn't believe her.

"I have to see Gottfried. We must find out how the beer got there," she said vaguely.

"If there's anything I can do, Sara . . ." George said as they all went through the restaurant. It was empty now; only the musicians were there, packing up their music.

"No, there isn't just now, thank you, George."

The kitchen door opened. The policeman had Otto Freehahn helping him. They went through the dining room, each carrying a case of beer. They stepped aside at the door to let the girls and George go through.

"Good night," Sara said.

"Can't you come now, Sara?" Belle begged.

"No, I'll come as soon as I can." She wanted them to be gone now. The evening that had started out as such a success was ruined. She couldn't think clearly. She couldn't believe that they were closing the restaurant. She went by Adolf, fussing over his desk. He shook his head sadly.

In the kitchen she found Gottfried. He stood stroking at his mustache, watching them carry out the cases of beer.

"Gottfried, this can ruin the restaurant, can't it?" Sara asked it in a low voice.

"Every day it's closed we lose money." He lifted his hands helplessly. "We get a bad name; we can't make it go again, maybe."

How silly Gottfried's green embroidered vest looked with his black coat, she thought suddenly.

17

BELLE knocked softly at Sara's door and brought in her breakfast on a tray.

"There's no reason why you shouldn't have breakfast in bed for a change, Sara. You looked tired out last night." Belle's voice was kind. She leveled the shades and closed the windows as though she had to do something for her. "Everything can wait. You ought to do this for a change. There's nothing to take you out early."

And there it was, as though she had said it in so many words. The brewery was closed and now the restaurant was closed. There was nothing to take her out early. Sara bit into the thin strip of toast without tasting it.

"Where's the paper, Belle?"

Belle's face was innocent. "Oh, I must have left it in the kitchen! Eat your breakfast first, Sara." They could go on living here together as they had lived in the house by the brewery, politely ignoring anything that was unpleasant to Belle.

"That's all I want to eat, really. Was the account in the paper very bad, Belle?"

Belle closed the door of the wardrobe before she answered. "I just glanced at it. These apartment bedrooms certainly have the poorest closet space. Have another cup of coffee, Sara. I'll go get the paper."

Sara poured herself another cup, but she sat back against the pillows waiting for Belle. Belle was trying to be long. Sara pushed back her hair from her forehead and pressed her fingers hard against her head. She was tired.

Belle came back and tossed the paper on the bed as though it were of no account. "The Germans are retreating all along the line. There's a picture of Paul, of course. Wouldn't old Hiram Sevrance have been proud to see him Governor?"

Sara opened the page. The caption stared back at her just above the middle crease.

SEVERAL HUNDRED CASES
OF BEER FOUND IN CELLAR
OF HENKEL'S RESTAURANT

Mrs. Henkel claims no knowledge of hidden beer. Of prominent family socially before her marriage, Mrs. Henkel, who was Miss Sara Bolster, married into brewery family . . . after prohibition. . . . Sara's eyes traveled quickly down the columns. The last twenty years of her life were there in skeleton. *"But I know nothing about it, I tell you," pretty Mrs. Henkel declared emphatically. Prohibition Agent Wilkins closed the restaurant.*

"Pretty, isn't it, Belle? Amusing to have me arrested and Paul running for Governor in the same paper, don't you think?"

Belle stood up impatiently. "You weren't arrested, Sara; don't talk that way."

"It amounts to the same thing. Remember the time I told you and Paul that I'd be the first Bolster to make a fortune? Instead I'm the first Bolster to disgrace the name!"

"Sara, what's gotten into you!" Belle stood irresolutely by

the door. Sara, lying with her face hidden in the pillow, her slender body a firm ridge under the covers, might have been Sara in her 'teens, Belle thought.

"Sara, I'm so sorry."

Sara sat up in bed. Her eyes were dry, but her face had a curious, strained look, almost of fear.

"Dear, the whole trouble was in mixing up with something that's caused so much misery and wickedness in the world. Don't you see?"

Sara threw back the covers and slid out of bed. "Oh, Belle, for heaven's sake, don't make a temperance speech. I can't stand it this morning. Of course, you're right. The brewers' horses will run over me in the end and all the women in your society will be glad. They'll say it serves me right!"

"Sara, I didn't mean . . ."

"Oh, I know," Sara cut in on her words. "You love me, but you do feel that I've been wrong all along. And you really believe I must have known about the beer hidden in the cellar." The small room seemed to contract, crowding them too close.

Belle took the breakfast tray and went out, leaving the paper on the bed. In a few minutes she came back and closed the door behind her.

"Sara, there's a man here who insists on seeing you, himself. What do you suppose he wants?" Belle was alarmed.

"I don't know." Sara finished dressing hastily.

The man sitting in the chair by the door held a paper in his hand. "You wanted to see me," Sara began.

"Yes, if you're Mrs. Henkel. Here's a summons for you. You've got to be in court this afternoon." Sara took the paper, feeling frightened, forcing herself to appear calm.

After the deputy had gone she turned it over and read it slowly. The coldly urgent phrases brought the night before her again; the policeman's remark: "You'll have a pretty hard time explaining away two hunderd cases of beer."

She must see Mr. Blanchard. But the thought of Mr. Blanchard was not reassuring. He probably wouldn't believe her any more than Belle or George had. She picked up her coat and hat. It was better to be doing something than to sit here under Belle's sorrowful look.

Someone else was coming up the stairs. She waited, listening. Maybe it was someone from the prohibition department. He was stopping in front of their door. She opened the door quickly. Paul Sevrance stood in the hall. She looked at him without speaking.

"Sara, I just saw the paper," Paul said. "I came to see what I could do. . . ."

"There's nothing you can do. I seem to have broken one of those laws you helped to make. Now I'm on my way down to see Mr. Blanchard." She spoke hurriedly. Her voice sounded stilted.

"Tell me about it first, Sara," Paul said, ignoring the resentment in her voice.

"It was all in the paper; everything about me, my whole life for the last twenty years," Sara said.

"You don't know anything about the beer, Sara? I just want your word for it."

"No, I don't. I ordered every bit of beer dumped the night prohibition came in." Her eyes were defiant, daring him to question her.

"It sounds to me like a frame-up then. Do you know anyone who was out to hurt your business?"

"No. I made some enemies when I separated from the

saloons, of course." His complete and matter-of-fact acceptance of her statement surprised her. "Why do you believe me, Paul? Nobody else seems to, not even Belle."

"I'd believe you if everybody in the world swore you were lying," Paul said soberly, but there was no warmth in his voice. "You couldn't lie; you couldn't do anything you thought was breaking a law even to save a friend." Bitterness crept into his voice. "Once I tried to keep you out of the brewing business because I thought your ideas of what was right and honest would be too great a handicap for you. They kept your father from being the business success that mine was.

"But I needn't have worried. You made a go of it, anyway. You've kept your skirts clean; that's fine. But, Sara, it's made you hard and intolerant and even a little self-righteous. It hurts you now when someone doesn't believe you. I know what that feels like."

She was startled by his intensity. His face had none of that urbane, smiling expression that had stared at her these last few months from his campaign pictures.

"Do you remember that Christmas Eve, Sara? You said I cared more about being elected than anything else in the world. It wasn't true, but I didn't try to argue it with you. I knew what you thought of me." He stopped abruptly.

"Excuse me, Sara. I didn't mean to go on like this. I came to hear about the beer." His voice was easy again. His face had changed too. It was more like the campaign pictures again. "I'm going to find out where Wilkins got the information for the warrant. You go ahead, and see Blanchard. I'll call you if I learn anything. You don't need to tell Blanchard that you've seen me."

"But, Paul . . ." Sara began.

"Don't worry, Sara. Forget about my outburst." He seemed in a hurry to get away before she could say anything.

All the way to Blanchard's office, things Paul had said kept coming back to her. Why had she let him talk like that to her? "It's made you hard and intolerant and a little self-righteous." She had had to be sure she was right or she couldn't have gone ahead alone. That wasn't being self-righteous. She hadn't been hard; she had learned to be firm. You couldn't run a business and be soft. But she thought uncomfortably of how close she had come to turning on William when he was sent home from school.

She came out of Mr. Blanchard's office more disheartened than when she had gone in.

"You see, Mrs. Henkel, there is only your unsupported word," he had explained ponderously. His voice was dry and lifeless.

"Mr. Blanchard, I wouldn't have deliberately broken the law," she insisted hopelessly, but she knew that he didn't believe her.

What was it Paul had said? "It hurts you when somebody doesn't believe you; I know what that feels like."

She stood on the corner waiting to cross the street. "Allies Win New Victory!" a newsboy was shouting. Sara turned toward the newsboy before she realized the news was from the morning paper she had already read.

"Henkel's Restaurant Closed!" the newsboy bawled out, holding a paper toward her. His words came at her so suddenly they seemed like physical blows. She bent her head a little as though to ward them off and hurried across the street, not quite looking at people she passed. She got into her car as though it were a refuge. She stepped on the accelerator, caring only to be out of sound of the newsboy's voice.

It seemed to her that the old man at the tollgate looked at her with bright, knowing eyes. Instinctively, she drove out toward the brewery. It was quiet there and empty. The tall windows were dirty. The rain had spattered dust against them all summer. There was a broken pane of glass in the last window. She must tell Gottfried about it. Most of the leaves had fallen from the trees in the park where Der Sommer Garten used to be. With the trees so bare her house stood out clearly, the red chimney rising warmly against the clapboards on this side. She turned away from it to the restaurant.

On the door was tacked the piece of printed paper that closed it more securely than its lock. Out back stood the empty ice-cream cans waiting to be picked up. The windows were still shining and clean. The iron tables and chairs on the terrace were littered with leaves from only one night's fall. It was all so still. Just last night there had been life here: talk and food and music. She had been so proud of it.

The light at the corner of the terrace still burned. Sara got out of the car and, climbing on a chair, unscrewed the bulb. The chair made a scraping sound as she dragged it across the flags. What if someone saw her here! Would he think she was sneaking in to dispose of more hidden beer? She felt nervous and guilty here on her own property.

But she had a right to be here! She had done nothing wrong. She stopped herself. She had been shouting that at the world for too many years. "You have to be right in your own eyes," Paul had said. "That's fine, but it's made you hard and intolerant and self-righteous."

Had she been intolerant of Belle, of William, the other day? Was she growing like Papa? She had despised Paul. Had she been hard? She sat down at one of the tables where the warm sun fell on her. She picked up the dry leaves on the table top and crumpled them in her fingers.

When she reached the apartment at one, an hour before she was to appear in court, she found Charlie Freehahn waiting.

He sat in the largest chair, his hands on his knees, his head bent as though he were studying the pattern of the rug in front of him.

"Why, Charlie!" Sara was touched to have the old stable boss come to sympathize with her.

"Missus Henkel!" Charlie stood up. He was so big the small room seemed to shrink in size. He looked older. She had not noticed before how stiffly he moved.

"Missus Henkel, I work for the John Henkel Brewing Company forty years. Now everything is spoilt for John Henkel's grandsons by . . . by me!"

"Why, Charlie," Sara started to protest.

"Excuse me, Missus Henkel." He held up his big hand. "I tell you." He sat down, letting his weight slowly into the big chair. "Today Mr. Sevrance come to my place. He wants advice of me about horses. He knows horses; that makes sure he'll be a good Governor." Charlie nodded approvingly, his gloomy mood lightening for an instant. "We talk and then he says did I know my Otto was getting drinks at McGinnis' back room. Well, I know he got it ever since prohibition, and not beer no more, whiskey. Such a katzenjammer every Sunday!

"So, last Saturday night Mr. Sevrance says Otto is drunk and boasts he can get Henkel's beer where he works at Henkel's restaurant if he wants it."

Sara caught her breath. Charlie went heavily on. "McGinnis I know. He is no-good. Also, he is mad at you, Missus

Henkel, ever since you stop business with him. So McGinnis tells a prohibition man what he hears my Otto say. So . . ." Charlie spread his hands.

"Oh, Charlie! But does Otto know who hid the beer there?" Sara's mind raced ahead of Charlie's slow recital.

Charlie's eyes were wretched. He groaned.

"Ja, Missus Henkel, Otto done it himself. He got to help him that Johnny Miller that went to war. Otto says he hears Gottfried tell you how you should save the bottle beer for the restaurant so you can get ten times so much for a bottle after this prohibition is on."

"Yes, I do remember," Sara said, nodding. "Gottfried was joking with me and poor Otto . . ."

"Ja, poor Otto!" Charlie interrupted bitterly. "Poor Dummkopf! Last night when the police is come he is afraid to tell he done it. So my Otto this trouble brought you, Missus Henkel."

Charlie's grief and humiliation held Sara silent. The whine of the street car two blocks away came back clearly. Charlie covered his face with his hands. "He never was no good with horses, Otto wasn't!

"Vell, I go to take a horsewhip to Otto right there. Mr. Sevrance stop me. He says I should come and tell you so you can stop the worry. He took Otto to the courthouse." Tears stood in the old man's eyes.

"Never mind, Charlie. A little while ago my boy, William, was foolish, too. Everything will be all right. Mr. Sevrance will explain. . . ." Sara stopped, amazed at herself.

The doorbell rang loudly. Sara crossed the room like a girl and opened the door.

Derrick VanRansom stood in the doorway, panting from the exertion of the stairs. He looked past Sara into the room.

"Where's Paul?" he demanded.

"I don't know, Derrick," Sara said, wondering at his coming here. He had grown heavier in the last year or two. Thick rolls of fat hung from his cheekbones and jaw, altering comically what had once been a handsome face. Only his eyes held their look of quick intelligence. "This is Mr. Freehahn," Sara explained.

Derrick dismissed the introduction with an impatient wave of his fat hand. "Never mind, never mind. I can see he's one of your confounded brewery crew. Do you know that Paul Sevrance is going to be voted on for Governor less than a month from today?" he shouted at her.

"Why, yes."

"And do you know what he's done because of you?" He paused significantly. "He's deliberately and pig-headedly thrown away the Governorship; after all the time and money the party's spent on his campaign!" Derrick took a fine linen handkerchief out of his pocket and mopped his face.

"What do you mean?" Sara asked, frowning. She glanced up quickly to see that Belle had come into the room. Derrick did not notice her. He was glaring at Sara.

"What do I mean? Paul Sevrance, nominee for Governor on a prohibition-enforcement platform, interests himself in a prohibition-law violation and gets the John Henkel Brewing Company off scot-free. Wilkins saw where he was heading and tried to stop him. When he couldn't he called me." Derrick was red in the face. He turned his head from side to side, swaying as he talked, like some great bull.

"But . . ."

"But nothing!" he interrupted. "It'll be headlined in the paper tonight: 'Dry Candidate for Governor Saves Henkel's Restaurant.' " He went on bitingly, " 'Henkel's Widow . . . lifelong friend of Nominee Sevrance' . . . and so on."

"But, Derrick, Charlie Freehahn has just told me what Paul found out. Paul can prove I knew nothing about the beer."

Derrick groaned. "Jesus Christ! That won't help Paul."

"Derrick VanRansom, kindly refrain from using such obscene language in this house?" Belle spoke quietly.

Derrick turned. "Well, Belle! I thought of you . . . this must have hurt your damned Bolster pride."

"I told you once before never to come into my house again. Now get out of here quickly!" Belle looked coldly at him. Derrick stared back without any change of expression.

Charlie Freehahn stood up uneasily. "Missus Henkel, I better be going." He moved toward the door, but Sara did not hear him.

"Wait, Derrick," she said as he started to follow Charlie. "Do you mean that Paul will lose his election because of helping me?"

"Of course I do. He's through politically . . . all on account of you. The next time we undertake to back a man for Governor we won't pick some Sir Launcelot from Park Avenue." Derrick put on his hat. He looked at Belle. "Well, Sara's skin's saved, anyway." Belle looked at him without speaking. He turned to Sara. "If Paul comes here, tell him I want him. No, I guess I don't want him. He can't help himself now."

In the apartment they could hear him going slowly down the stairs. Belle went to the window to see him go.

"Belle, telephone Paul's office and see if they know where he is." Sara was putting on her hat and coat.

"They think he went home," Belle said, turning from the phone. "Where are you going?"

"To find Paul. Oh, Belle, he mustn't lose his election. He

cares more about the Goevrnorship than . . ." That was what she had said that other time.

Belle sat watching Sara. "This ought to show you how much he cares about you," she said dryly.

18

SARA came to the tollgate for the second time that day. The old man's eyes had not changed. He looked at her as he had this morning, with the same sharp curiosity because he had seen her name in the papers, but now she didn't mind his interest. He would know. He would read in the paper that she hadn't been guilty of any wrong. She could hold up her head again. Everyone would know. She smiled at him out of relief.

"It's growing cold, isn't it?" she said to be speaking to him.

"Yes, Missus Henkel," the man answered, a shade of reserve in his tone.

Sara remembered the first time she had felt this hard curiosity in people's eyes: at the Fourth of July parade when the women had stopped the float. She should have known then how her whole life would be. It was as though they had turned the Brewers' Big Horses against her with the criticism and suspicion and gossip they had turned on her. But they hadn't run over her! They hadn't run over her this time, either. Then her face sobered. The Brewers' Big Horses had run over William. Always the sight of them running for the stable with their ears laid back, and their eyes rolling, pulling on their bits, and William lying against the loading platform was there in her mind if she let her thoughts go back to it.

And now they were running over Paul. They would make him lose his election. They would ruin his career. William and now Paul. What did it matter that they had missed her?

She saw herself as Paul must see her. He must think that she cared only for herself and her precious pride in being in the right. How small and arrogant that pride seemed now! She had looked at herself this afternoon alone at the restaurant and seen the truth of the words Paul had flung at her. She had grown as intolerant and hard as her father. She had been so proud of her success, as though she had made it alone. She hadn't. There had been William first, and Gottfried and Adolf and even Charlie. And now there was Paul.

If Paul lost his election because of her, how could she ever make up for that? "It ought to show you how much he cares about you," Belle had said. How could he care?

Sara stopped the car along the avenue this side of the entrance to Paul's driveway. How could she go up there? If he were home what would she say? Her words that Christmas Eve came back to her. "You care more for being elected than anything else in the world!"

She would walk up to the house. If someone else were there she could go quietly away.

She drove ahead a little because of the old Bolster horse-block. It was higher than the running board of the car. The black iron hitching-post with the head of a horse holding a ring between his teeth stood beside it. She had stood here that day ages and ages ago when Charlie had come past driving the brewery wagon. He had seemed like a giant then with his black hair and his black mustache. He had nothing in common with the broken old man she had seen this afternoon.

She remembered how the horses had looked, their harness shining, red and blue tassels hanging from their bridles, and their tails braided with ribbons. There were no more brewery horses, only Donner and Thor, turned out to grow fat on Charlie's little farm. She laid her hand on the hitching-post. She remembered how her fingers used to smell of iron after she had hung on the ring and swung around the post.

No car stood in front of Paul's house. The house, itself, looked closed. She stepped lightly on the porch. She lifted the knocker and let it fall, remembering when she had had to reach for it; remembering how old Mr. Sevrance used to come out and compliment her and say, "Aren't you going to give me a kiss, little lady?" And Mrs. Sevrance used always to smile at her in her pale, meek way. She wondered if Bailey would still be there. Bailey must be over seventy now. She looked at the impassive oak panel of the door and waited. It must be very lonely for Paul here. She could hear footsteps inside the house.

Paul opened the door, himself, almost impatiently. His face was tired. Then its weariness gave way to amazement.

"Sara!"

"Oh, Paul, Charlie Freehahn told me what you had done. I came to thank you. . . ." She was a little breathless.

"I sent Charlie over to tell you. He was almost beside himself to think that his son had caused you so much trouble. It all came out so easily. I think Otto was so badly scared he would have told himself in the end," Paul said lightly.

"Unless he'd gone away to the war first; then we'd never have known," Sara said.

"That wouldn't have been so good." There was an awkward pause between them. "Won't you come in. It's so queer to have you standing on my doorstep I forgot to ask you,"

Paul laughed. All the quick, decisive manner that had been in his voice this morning was gone.

"Thank you," Sara said, stepping inside. "You haven't changed anything, Paul."

"No, I guess not."

The hall was cool, a little gloomy. The bust of Napoleon still stood in the niche on the stairs. Sara went into the familiar parlor.

"I've been away so much, I'm afraid the place doesn't look very cheerful."

"I like it for being the same," Sara said.

Paul sat down across from her. "Well, the evening paper will have you cleared up. You won't have to worry about people not believing you any more." He smiled as he said it. She had the feeling that he had been sitting here alone, waiting for the paper.

"But what will that do to you when it's known that you helped me?"

"What do you mean?"

"Derrick told me. You'll lose your election."

"Oh, you saw Derrick too. He doesn't know what he's talking about. He was just upset because I didn't tell him first what I was going to do. I left him about a half an hour ago talking to the District Attorney and some of the boys from the paper. He looked as though he'd have apoplexy any moment."

Sara shook her head. "The papers will make the most of your helping a brewer. Didn't you think of that?"

"Yes," Paul said slowly. "I thought of that, but I knew old Blanchard didn't believe you were innocent and wouldn't move fast enough if he did. You see, it just happened that I knew you were telling the truth."

"But, Paul, Derrick is sure it will ruin you!" It came to

her that she didn't know Paul. She had judged him once and never changed her mind. She didn't even know this expression of his face.

"Once, Sara, you said I cared more about political success than . . ."

"Don't, Paul!" Sara couldn't look at him. She hid her face in her hands.

"Oh, I care. I'm not Hiram Sevrance's son for nothing. I've been a good practical politician until today. But I've never stood by and let an innocent person be ruined. And when I found you were in trouble I forgot all about my campaign for once, believe it or not."

"But, Paul . . ."

"Don't worry, Sara. It's the sort of thing your father would have done without a second thought. Remember the night of Dor's wedding, Sara? When you held your head on the railroad track until the train reached the signal light? I couldn't do it then. I was afraid of getting hurt. I went back afterwards, alone, and tried to screw up my courage." He smiled oddly. "I think, maybe, I could manage it now."

"You did it today, but you got hurt." She laughed shakily. "And I never got hurt."

"You've been hurt enough in these last twenty years, Sara."

The phone rang far back in the house.

"Let it go," Paul said. "It's probably a reporter."

Its continued ringing deepened the quiet of the long, old-fashioned parlor. The sun had moved to the west window, leaving the room more shrouded. Only the dust covers on the chairs stood out of the shadows, and Sara's face, moved by the unexpected tenderness in Paul's voice.

Paul's voice changed. It sounded tired. "I wish you hadn't come here to thank me, Sara, just out of gratitude."

The doorbell rang. "Don't answer; they'll go away," Paul said impatiently. But it was hard to go on.

"People who care most for each other often don't do anything for each other; sometimes they hurt each other," he said almost irritably.

Someone pounded on the door, rattling the doorknob too loudly to be denied.

"Wait, Sara, don't go. I'll be right back."

Sara sat where Paul had left her in the half-shadowed parlor that seemed a part of their childhood.

He had cared, all these years, even after the things she had said to him that had kept them so far apart. She must have cared, too, or why had it hurt her so when she had thought him hypocritical?

"People who care the most for each other often don't do anything for each other; sometimes they hurt each other," Paul had said.

Why had she come here? She hadn't thought of going to him when Charlie told her what Paul had done for her. It was only when she knew what he had done to himself. It wasn't gratitude at all. She had come as instinctively and uselessly as he had gone to her at the lake after William's death. It seemed so clear now why she had come! She must tell him quickly. They must not let anything come between them, ever again.

"I couldn't raise you by phone." A loud voice broke in on her thoughts. "I came out to see what you thought of the old man!"

That was Derrick's voice! It sounded almost triumphant. She went quickly out to the hall.

"I don't get you, Derrick," Paul was saying.

"For God's sake! Haven't you seen the paper? Here, here's your own, not even opened." Derrick picked up the twisted roll of newspaper from the porch and handed it to him. "You're a queer fish, Paul. You're no son of the old man."

Sara came to the door.

"Well, Sara! That explains it. I might have known you'd be here," Derrick muttered.

Black headlines jumped at them from the front page.

HENKEL CASE DROPPED

Sara leaned closer to read.

Blanchard Uncovers Evidence
Exonerating Mrs. Henkel

"Blanchard!" Paul whistled. "I thought you were stumped when I left you, Derrick."

Derrick shook to his own laughter. "Not the old man! It took some quick work, though, I'll tell you. I bet old Blanchard is still dizzy."

"You kept Paul's name out of it!" Sara said incredulously, her eyes still on the paper.

"Yes, I did, Sara, but the doctor tells me I must avoid excitement!" Derrick laughed. "I'm too old to move that fast! Don't let Paul make a fool of himself again . . . not before election, anyway!"

They watched him lumber down the walk to his car. Then they went back into the house together.